THE THERAPIST

J.A. BELFIELD

D1522607

The Therapist

Published by J.A. Belfield
www.jabelfield.com

Copyright © 2017 Julie Anne Belfield

First Published: 2017
10 9 8 7 6 5 4 3 2 1

To those who tell me yay when my head's telling me nay ...
You're top of that list, Sweet Cheeks.

Author Note

Thank you so much for picking up a copy of The Therapist. When I first opened my laptop to write this tale, I envisioned a collection of small bursts of fun that, when gathered together, would create the pieces of a larger story.

And fun is the focus of that last sentence. Because I never intended The Therapist to be serious. I never intended it to be non-fiction. I wrote the story as it came to me and am totally, one-hundred percent unapologetic about that.

I guess my point is this:

If you've purchased The Therapist in the hopes of finding the key to, or a step-by-step guide for certain sexual practices, then maybe this isn't the book for you.

However, if you read with an open mind and love relaxing into a fictional world, with fictional folks, and simply switching off for a bit while getting a little hot and bothered in a good way, then you should totally read on.

See you on the far side ...

J.A. Belfield

EPISODE ONE

L etting his body sink back in his chair, Chase Walker took a moment's rest. When he'd first set himself up as a therapist almost three years earlier, he'd no idea how quickly the idea would take off. No fucking idea how many would flock to him for *his kind of advice and assistance*. He could've suggested splurging on a penthouse office on the outskirts of the busiest city in the UK had helped boost his numbers, but his clients travelled however far they needed to for his services, and he knew damned well that his practice's top-level discretion took the trophy for that.

He slid out a drawer on his walnut desk and withdrew a bottle of water. While he'd have loved a stiff drink before his next clients arrived, he doubted they'd appreciate the smell of whisky on his breath. The liquid glugged when he tipped the bottle back and took a swallow before recapping the drink. Tapping the plastic against his knee, he let his head sink back, closed his eyes, took deep breaths. His usual routine for preparing for an appointment such as the one he suspected was on its way.

Each inhalation sucked in rich woody perfumes and expensive polish—scents that spoke of money. And so they should. Behind him, the room-wide windows graced the eyes with an almost bird's-eye view of the Thames, and around him, teak panelled the entire bottom third of the walls and boarded the floor. Even the elegant chaise that passed as a visitor seat had cost a pretty penny from a dealer he'd once been hired by.

The intercom buzzed on his desk, and he lifted his lids, revealing all of his well-earned belongings. After tucking the water back inside his desk, he pressed a small camouflaged button and answered, "Yes?"

"Your four o'clock is ready for you, Mr Walker."

"Thank you, Samantha."

Clicking off the connection, he pushed up from his chair, brushing his hands over the front of his crisp trousers as he straightened his legs. Those had cost a bomb, too, but at least the fabric caressed his thighs and hugged him everywhere it should. After checking his shirt front for blotches and straightening his tie, he strode for the door.

Opening it exposed the reception area. The highly-polished desk on the left looked like a piece of art, with the way it curled around the two women sat behind it. They both glanced up as he stepped out, their lips curved into smiles that spoke of contentment in their work, while their perfectly-plucked eyebrows arched in a knowing expression. They may have reacted the same at his appearance, but in looks, Samantha was day to Raelyn's night. The innocent persona of blonde hair and blues beside the wickedness of raven darkness surrounding hazelnut eyes that Raelyn often lowlighted with smoky grey kohl.

At the slight lift of Sam's chin, he followed her gaze to the seating on the opposite side of the room, where a middle-aged couple sat side by side in nothing but the clinic-provided robes and terry-cloth slippers.

"Mr and Mrs Miller—would you like to come through?"

The duo looked at each other, like they needed permission to move. Or maybe they were both hoping the other would be the initiator. Almost reluctantly, the man and woman climbed ungracefully to their feet and shuffled their way toward the door Chase held open.

"How are you both today?" he asked, as they filed past him.

The couple of jerky nods he got in response were to be expected, he supposed. When it came to a first 'practical session', nerves often arrived with the clients. It was Chase's job to ensure they'd left those behind—at least in part—by the time they walked back out the door.

"Good." Closing them in, he watched as they slid their slippers across the floor. As they came to a stop in front of the chaise, he headed for his desk, but didn't round it when he realised that neither of them had sat. Instead, he perched his butt on the wood's edge and faced them. "Would you like to sit a moment, or did you prefer to stand?"

The lines surrounding Mrs Miller's eyes spoke more of fatigue than laughter, but Chase couldn't fault the immaculate chestnut-toned dye job covering what must have been equally tired hair. She frowned as she asked, "Are we doing it in here?"

With a soft smile, he shook his head. "Only verbal consults are carried out in my office. The clinic offers a choice of rooms that have been specially designed for the practical sessions." He waved their attention toward the far wall that supported a drop-down screen and reached for the clicker on his desk. One press of its button brought the screen to life, and a second flicked their first option into full colour.

"The bedroom," he said with a smile. "Comfortable queen-sized bed, seating ... fully stocked bedside drawers ..."

"Fully stocked with *what*?" Mr Miller asked gruffly.

"Hopefully, with anything you feel you may need," Chase answered, pressing the button for the next option.

Caramel-toned tiles covered the walls and floor of the on-screen room, soft candlelight providing a distorted glow. And in the centre of those, a sunken tub equipped to house up to four people. "The bathroom," he said. "There is, of course, also a generous shower cubicle."

"Looks like a bloody hotel room," Mr Miller muttered beneath his breath.

Pretending he hadn't heard, Chase nodded toward the next image. "The office."

Somewhat bigger than the one from which he carried out his regular consults, the client office represented the wet dream of anyone who'd ever fantasised about banging a PA on their work desk.

"And we also have the dark—"

"The office." Averting her eyes, Mrs Miller nodded. "I want the office."

Chase glanced to her husband. "Mr Miller?"

He gave what almost passed as a nod. "If that's what she wants."

"Good, okay. If you'll follow me."

Leaving through a discreet exit in the far corner of his office took them into a narrow corridor lined with closed doors, each fronted by a gold-coloured nameplate. The room they needed stood two doors to the right, and as Chase led the couple inside, he gave them a moment to take the space in.

Floor-to-ceiling glass lined the room along two of its walls, giving the space a sense of openness. Of being openly explicit, too, despite being six storeys high—and despite the outer-reflective glass that assured even those eager enough to scale the climb would never be privy to what went on within.

In almost the same position as in his own office, a broad

Cherrywood desk sat diagonally across the glassed-in corner, its topside set up with papers and pens, even a hole puncher—mundane items found on almost every office desk in the land. For some reason, his clients often got a kick out of sweeping everything to the floor before carrying out their role play. To support the scene further, filing cabinets and bookshelves had been positioned around the room, as well as an array of seating that ranged from deep and cosy, small and unassuming, to hard as fuck.

"Do you remember what we discussed at our last meeting?" Chase asked them.

They slowly turned from ogling the room and looked his way. "That we need to talk more?" Mrs Miller asked.

"Yes. That you need to *communicate* more." From their previous consults, Chase had garnered that they both knew exactly what they wanted, they just couldn't get past the barrier of making the other party aware of it. Hell, they'd taken a whole lot of prompting just to discuss their needs in a regular setting. "So, today, you'll be putting that into practice. Did you decide who would take their turn first?"

The previous week, they'd agreed it would be too much if they both started spouting demands and wants left, right and centre, so they'd strategized a plan. One week, one of them would be in full control of the situation, and the following week, the other would get to try.

Mrs Miller half raised her hand. "I am, but Christopher isn't comfortable with taking part just yet."

Chase glanced toward her husband. "You're comfortable with observing?"

The man had a stern face, his expression measured as if he didn't like showing any hint of his feelings. His kind often took a little more encouragement. The slight peppering at the temples of his dark hair told of his age, and the rigid stance of his body spoke of a man set in his ways and uneasy with change. If he didn't let go of that control, though, the physical side of their marriage would likely be unsalvageable in time.

Though it was a stiff movement, he nodded, and Chase looked back to the woman.

"And have you had time to think about what you want to do today, as I suggested? Do you know how you want to proceed?"

She jerked her chin, her eyes flickering all over the place. "I'd like to use a prop."

By prop, she meant Chase. Just one part of the service of CW Consult. A service that came with rules:

The clients couldn't ask him to touch them

He never initiated contact with the clients

He never pleasured the clients in any way

He never fucked the clients

And they never fucked him

"And you're comfortable with this arrangement?" he asked Mr Miller.

Again, the man nodded.

"And are you both aware that this session will be observed in its entirety, for both my benefit and your own—are you comfortable with that?"

The two of them mumbled consent.

"And that, if at any point I believe it to be beneficial to the session, I may call upon other parties, singular or plural, to join us in this room?"

"Yes, we understand," Mrs Miller answered, briefly brushing her fingers over her husband's arm.

"Okay, Mr Miller, if you would like to take a seat and make yourself comfortable."

"Which one?" he asked, glancing at the different chairs.

"Whichever one you feel you'll enjoy the session from the most," Chase answered, though he could've easily predicted the man's decision, even before he shuffled across to a large buck-eted armchair, padded by scatter cushions along its back.

Waiting until Mr Miller had quit fidgeting, which included tucking his robe neatly over his groin, Chase turned to the wife. "Mrs Miller, you're free to begin as soon as you feel comfortable. The idea is to specify everything you want to do as, or before, you do it, because communication is the key here. And remember, nobody outside of this practice, other than you and your husband, will see what happens in this room. Everything is completely private, so you are free to be yourself. There is no judgement here, but if at any point you wish for the session to end, you have only to say. You're in complete control of what happens here today. Understand?"

"Yes," she said quietly.

"This session in now in progress, and I won't speak again unless I feel it necessary. The room is yours."

Ducking his head, Chase pretended not to be watching as he waited to see how Mrs Miller would proceed. *If* she'd proceed— because he'd had clients before who'd completely baulked when they'd reached the practical sessions. He couldn't help but wonder if she'd be one of those.

A moment later, though, he just caught the fumbling of her fingers over the belt of her robe. She seemed about to tug it free, but paused and cleared her throat. Exactly three seconds later, her attempt at communicating began.

"I want you to undress me."

Chase skimmed his gaze up to Mrs Miller. "You know I can't do that, but it's a good start."

Another rule:

He never undressed, or removed any clothing from, the clients

"Please, keep going," he prompted, giving a gentle nod of encouragement.

"Just to be clear, you're Christopher in this scenario, yes?"

"Correct." He'd gotten used to the women in his clinic pretending they stood before someone else, and had years before stopped taking offense at the fantasies of the female mind.

"Then, can I pretend you're undressing me?" she asked.

He smiled at the question. "Of course."

A few breaths later, she'd shrugged the robe to the floor and flicked off the slippers, leaving herself naked, exactly as he'd requested the couple come prepared for the session.

While not exactly slender, Mrs Miller still had enough of her shape left that she should have been proud. According to her records, she'd been around for almost forty-seven years, and her breasts still sat plump and full, her hips rounded out from her thighs before the flesh dipped back in for her waist. Though, it wouldn't have mattered to Chase if she'd been ten stone heavier and painted in a road map of stretchmarks. He'd long ago learned to appreciate the beauty of the human body. Whatever its size and form. And he definitely appreciated that she'd waxed her pussy. Enough so that his cock stirred within his pants.

Off to the side, Mr Miller shifted in his seat a little, and Chase spared a glance at the way he stared toward his naked wife and nothing else.

So, the man still noticed the woman. It was always a good start.

Mrs Miller took a step forward. "I want you by the desk," she said, a little more assertive, though Chase noticed she didn't make eye contact each time she spoke.

He crossed the room toward the desk, as instructed. A couple of steps away came the instruction to, "Stop," and he did.

Head tilted, he tracked the padding of Mrs Millers footsteps as she approached him from behind. A hand pressed against the small of his back, another wrapped around his arm, and at gentle nudging from the woman, he turned until he faced her.

Folding the fingers of each hand over his hips, she guided him backward until his butt met the desk and she'd propped him against it. "I want you here." She took a step back, her gaze dipped. "I want your trousers undone."

Chase didn't move. Yet another rule:

If the client wanted any part of *his* body exposed, they had to do it themselves

She reached out for his waistband. Her movements were gentle, but efficient, as she worked her fingers beneath the fabric and popped the hook, and Chase wondered for a moment why her husband didn't want them on himself more often. Her skin was soft, evidently tended for, and he already knew those hands would feel pretty fucking good wrapped around his cock.

She drew down the zip of his trousers, the bulge of his forming erection instantly clear in the created gap. Skimming her knuckles over the soft fabric of his boxers made his cock twitch. "I want to remove your penis," she said.

"Audrey!" her husband hissed from his seat.

Mrs Miller's hand stilled, but she didn't move it away, while Chase glanced across to the armchair. "What offends you about this, Mr Miller?" Noting that the man looked far from offended by his wife's actions, he smiled. "There are many names for the male sexual organ, and none of them are wrong. Shaft, prick, phallus, tool, dick, cock, *penis*. A person should never feel the need to apologise for saying whichever one feels right in the moment." Supporting himself with his hands atop the desk, he gave a small nod to Mrs Miller. "Please, continue when you're comfortable."

She seemed a little hesitant after the interruption, but it didn't last long before she gripped the waistband of his trousers. She worked them down, past his hips to hug the tops of his thighs, leaving his hard length pushing against the underside of his shorts. Cupping her fingers over his cock, she brushed her palm upward, finishing with a flick of her thumb across its swelling head through the fabric. "Does that feel nice?"

His left eye twitched, but only briefly before he caught himself. How often did the clients care if he enjoyed his part played in their therapy? How many of them had bothered to ask? He found his jaw had tightened when he answered, "Yes." Because it did. Any woman's hands on his cock felt good. Always had.

The answer seemed to bolster her courage, because no hesitancy accompanied her grip of his shorts, or the way she slid them down to join his trousers. As soon as she had, his cock bounced up, harder than fucking ever and ready to play.

"God, you're big." She whispered the words, as if she only meant for him to hear, as if she didn't want her husband to be privy to the opinion.

He had to agree with her. Women often considered him larger than average, and praised him on it. They also praised him on his ability to be hard and ready and able to perform at a moment's notice. His cock deserved a fucking medal for that, because Chase could screw all day long, if he chose to, and the damned beast would still be up for another round, and then another. Which was probably a good thing, considering it'd been his cock that'd made him his money in the first place.

With her eyes wholly fixed on his phallus, she said quietly, "I want your penis in my mouth."

Chase sliced his gaze toward Mr Miller. He'd straightened a little in his chair, but no objection came from his lips.

At her fingers sliding around his thickened length, Chase sucked in a shallow breath. Finally. The first contact had been made.

Mrs Miller squeezed slightly, and Chase swallowed. She

rolled the opening of his foreskin back a little, and he had to clench his jaw to stifle a groan.

He'd had years of experience in storing his emotions, and he knew all the tricks for retaining his composure.

She dipped her head. The tips of her hair brushed his crotch a moment before her breaths washed over his cock. Warm breaths that caressed and teased and promised of more to come, and he slid his hands to the edge of the desk, almost unconsciously, his fingers hooking over the lip as if in preparation.

Tongue. Glorious fucking tongue swiped over the head of his cock.

God, how he loved his job.

Mrs Miller licked lower, curling her tongue around the solidity of his length, slurping it back upward, and yes, fucking yes, those lips of hers slipped over his head and drew him straight into her mouth—and straight back out again.

Straightening, she glanced around the room, and releasing his dick, she padded over to a low square-shaped pouffe. On her return with the rest, she dropped her gaze toward her husband with a smile of reassurance. When he gave a small nod, she seemed to let out a breath of relief.

Turning away, she set the pouffe down in front of Chase and settled atop it on her knees. Bringing her face level with his crotch. The next time she reached for him, she didn't lean in, but wrapped her fingers around his cock and drew him toward her lips. A command. Control. Taking what she wanted rather than giving to please.

"I want to ..." The breath from her words floated over his flesh, and she sent a quick glance toward Mr Miller before turning back. "I want to suck your cock."

Chase could have sworn a low groan came from his right, but he could only focus on the parting of Mrs Millers lips, on the heat escaping her mouth, on the way she rounded its opening and pressed against the soft head of his cock. The way her lips parted even farther as she slipped over the crown, and then closed in some as they reached the rock-hard shaft. He half expected that to be her limit, for her to glide right back off again, but she dipped those lips lower over his cock, taking him in deeper. And as she withdrew, a tiny moan of pleasure vibrated over his shaft. A tiny moan of pleasure that told him she'd found the place in her head where whatever she did to him had become acceptable.

Her next plunge was faster, her cheeks contracting as she sucked, and he inhaled. As her tongue stroked the underside of his cock, he exhaled. With the next upward glide of her lips, her fist followed, closing his cock within the foreskin before her downward tug released it again, and as her hot mouth sucked straight back over him, the office space narrowed to nothing more than that moment. Her husband disappeared from Chase's mind. All he gave a fuck about was the wet hotness engulfing him and the promise of ejaculation. Because he would come. His years of experience told him she'd finish the job.

Tightening her grip, she worked his cock with her hand, her mouth sucking and slurping with every yank, until her fist smacked against her lips, and Chase's fingers gripped the wood of the desktop hard enough to make his knuckles ache. Relaxing into the movement of her hand, the fucking of her lips, the steady sounds of connecting flesh, he let his lids lower and his head fall back until only his arms supported him.

The muscles twitched through his thighs at the scrape of her teeth, but settled again as the softness of her tongue chased the sting. And he forgave her alto-fucking-gether when she drove her mouth so far over his cock, her lips caressed the base, and her grunt of discomfort sent a blast of heat pulsing through him.

She slipped her lips off him with a pop, her head tipped

back as she drew in a sharp breath. "I need ..." She closed her eyes slowly. Opened them. "I need to come. I need something ..."

Chase knew what she needed. He had no doubt her cunt dripped its juice down her thighs. It was probably already pulsating and desperate for a cock.

And Chase had no intention of offering his own.

Over in his armchair, Mr Miller stared at his wife like she'd grown a fucking tail, but the tenting of his robe gave away how he really felt about the session. When he didn't so much as stir in Mrs Miller's direction, though, Chase lifted his gaze toward the disguised camera in the corner of the ceiling and gave a discreet nod—the entire evaluation and order completed in less than three seconds.

When he peered back down, he found Mrs Miller's eyes one hundred percent on him. "Relief will be here momentarily."

He really wanted to tell her to continue. His cock throbbed like a mo-fo, and his balls ached to offload. Luckily, the almost silent opening of the door came only a minute later, and Samantha entered the room.

Her bare feet made little sound against the floor, and in her hand, she carried just one of the accessories available at CW Consult. She sent Mr Miller a smile as she passed him, which he surprisingly returned. Reaching the pouffe Mrs Miller occupied, she hiked the skirt of her form-fitting dress until halfway up her thighs and sank gracefully to her knees.

"Mrs Miller, my assistant is behind you."

The woman nodded.

"I want you to reach beneath you, to between your thighs."

She delicately placed his cock against his groin, before reaching the hand she'd held him with down below her body, her gaze never once leaving his.

Giving Samantha a beat to guide the tool to the woman's waiting hand, he asked, "Do you feel that?"

She gave a small nod.

"Do you know what it is?"

"It feels like a penis, but it isn't."

"It's a dildo."

"I know what one of those are," she said simply.

"And what do you want to do with it?"

"I want it inside my pussy." She swallowed, the lines around her eyes deepening. "I want them to put it inside my pussy, because I want to suck your penis and I can't do both."

He glanced toward Samantha, and she twitched her head enough that he recognised her consent. Whereas he had his set of rules, Raelyn and Sam had their own—ones he'd allowed them to construct themselves. They only went as far as they were willing, and they always, *always*, made that choice for themselves.

"Tell *them* what you want them to do," Chase encouraged. Not just because it was part of the therapy, but one rule he did insist on was that the girls couldn't play without it being a direct request from the client.

She glanced to the side, her throat bobbing with another swallow. "I want you to put that thing inside me."

"Do you want me to fuck you with it?" Sam asked—because there could be no room for error.

"Yes," she replied, and the next sound she made was a long, low groan as Sam slid the makeshift cock into her cunt. Her back arched her ass toward what she wanted, and her eyes closed. With an expelled breath parting her lips, Mrs Miller brought her hand from between her thighs, and Chase had to stifle his rumble of relief when those fingers wrapped back around his cock. Folding her mouth back around his head, too, she sucked and licked, her moan a choked sound that hummed against his shaft.

Chase cut his gaze to Sam, who paid study to only the task

assigned her. The muscles of her arm clenched with each thrust of the dildo into Mrs Miller's cunt, while the slight slackness of her jaw, the roll of her tongue over her lips, told Chase that his client wasn't the only one enjoying the extra service. Judging by the tense concentration around her eyes, the steady pace of her thrusts, Sam held nothing back, and in response, the other woman jerked her ass back and forth almost manically, the wet sounds of her pleasure fast filling the air.

At any other time, in any other setting, Chase would have taken control already. His hands wouldn't be gripping tight to the desk, but tangled in her hair, and he wouldn't be showing restraint, but ramming her head closer, cramming his cock into her mouth as fast and hard as he could while fucking her face until she begged for breath.

Hell, even Mr Miller had given up with composure. His hand had crept beneath his robe, and the steady taps against the underside of the fabric exposed just how much he enjoyed watching his wife fuck and be fucked. Just how much he enjoyed watching her on her knees with her lips wrapped around a cock and a cock in her cunt. How much of the scenario, Chase wondered, had he slid himself into inside his head? How much of it would replay in his dreams with himself as the leading role?

A quiet buzzing filled the air, one Chase recognised as the dildo being switched to vibrate. A hitched cry escaped Mrs Miller, until his cock shut the sound off, and as saliva trickled down his hard length, he held tighter to the desk. Ordering his hips to remain tamed, he let the mouth fucking take its course. With the muffled sounds of the wife getting more and more aroused, the slapping of Mr Miller's hand against his thighs as he stroked himself with more urgency, the slow glazing of Sam's eyes as she fell further into the moment, it took mere minutes for the muscles to coil through Chase's thighs, the cramping to begin in his calves, the tight lifting of his balls that warned of his readiness.

At a high-pitched gasp from Mrs Miller, the first wave of euphoria bulleted through him. As her body bucked and backward-thrusted, cum shot from him fast and hot, filling her warm mouth with seed and relieving him of the pressure that had built throughout the session.

Over to his right, low, hard grunts came from Mr Miller, too, and as Chase opened his eyes that'd closed, the man's outline jerked in the recognised spasm of ejaculation.

Nodding toward Sam told her to wrap the session up, and her arm movements slowed, the wind-down blessedly steadying Mrs Millers sucking and yanking, and when Sam stopped, the woman let out a groan that seemed as much from relief as regret.

Finally permitting himself contact, Chase guided Mrs Millers mouth from his cock, his body twitching once more from the sensation. Once free, she stared up at him through half-lidded eyes, her mouth hanging open like she didn't know what to do with it since its job was over. Chase couldn't help but notice that her husband looked slightly shell-shocked, too, when he spared a glance his way, like he couldn't quite believe what he'd sat through. Like he definitely couldn't believe that he'd succumbed, himself.

"Why don't you and Mrs Miller go and get yourself cleaned up, and we can discuss the results of today's session in my office," Chase said.

The guy didn't argue. Just nodded, unsteadily got to his feet, and crossed the room to his wife. Taking her arm with one hand and placing the other in the small of her back, he helped her climb slowly to her feet. Only then did she release Chase's cock, like she'd forgotten she held it.

Behind them, the door swung open and Raelyn walked in.

"Can you show Mr and Mrs Miller to the washroom?" Chase almost laughed at the polite smile on her face as she waved them toward the door. "And, Raelyn?" Waiting until she turned back, he added, "Please ensure Mrs Miller is provided with a dental hygiene kit."

After one of his early clients had attempted to spit Chase's cum into a sample bottle for self-impregnation, he'd made it a rule that all clients who got a taste of him be supervised until no trace of his semen existed.

"Certainly, Mr Walker."

As soon as the door closed behind the three of them, Sam blew a breath upward that blasted her overhanging hair. "I don't suppose you're up for a quick fuck, are you?"

He laughed. "Not even slightly."

Another rule he'd put in place:

He never fucked his staff

"You could always ask Rae, though," he added.

At the tilt of her head and the easy smile she gave, he suspected she'd do exactly that. Which meant he also knew exactly what the two of them would be doing the moment they had a break.

Naked, with his hair dripping water down his spine, Chase stood in the staff quarter of the clinic, observing the client washroom on Screen C. The hidden camera showed Mr and Mrs Miller, both of them stepping from a single cubicle, their bodies moist and glistening from their shower. In all honesty, Chase had questioned whether their barriers would slam back into place as soon as the session ended, and it pleased him to know they'd washed together. If he rewound the recording, he'd probably find they'd even washed each other. Some leap, considering he doubted they'd ever shared a shower in all the years of their marriage.

Across from him, Sam shimmied into a clean thong before straightening her fresh linen dress over her thighs.

"They did well today," he said simply.

She closed the small gap until standing next to him, squinting a little at the screen. Raelyn had told her countless times to get her eyes tested, but she never listened. "Better than expected?" she asked.

He nodded and reached up to towel off his hair. "A lot better."

Along one wall of the room, mirrored doors hid a wardrobe lined with outfits, and dropping the damp towel into the laundry chute on route, he made his way over. Checking his reflection, he gave a smile of satisfaction at what he saw. Body muscled, yet sleek. A face unlined by worry, and green eyes that shone from the anticipation of life alone. The flopping mop atop his head, usually a white-gold blonde, had been darkened by moisture, and combing his fingers through the strands, he slid open one of the wardrobe doors.

No contemplation was needed for which outfit to select. Each pair of trousers resembled those either side of it, and the shirts all matched, also. Drawing out one of each, Chase turned back to watch the screen as he dressed.

Although they didn't go so far as towelling each other down, the couple seemed to have trouble keeping their attentions to themselves. Each time Mrs Miller sent a shy glance her husband's way, Mr Miller responded with an easy smile. Almost as though the two of them stood planning what they'd like to do to the other and were letting each other know by way of silent communication.

Leaving his trousers unclipped, Chase started on the buttons of his shirt, while the couple onscreen began the task of dressing themselves. Though she did so with her back to her husband, Mrs Millers glanced back at him over her shoulder plenty of times, and each time she did, her husband was already staring, already watching. Already smiling.

Chase tapped the screen. "This. This is exactly how a couple *should* be looking at each other after eighteen years of marriage."

"Which is exactly why I'm not married," Sam said, pouting. "Because I can't get a guy to look at me like that after one week."

"So, quit fucking them all on the first night, then."

"But I like fucking," she said with a smile, and Chase had to laugh.

Sam's love of sex, and being very fucking good at it, had been what'd qualified her for the job at the clinic in the first place. Both she and Raelyn were experts in the field. Hell, he'd booked them as a package deal on several occasions, in the days before the clinic, and when he'd needed staff he could trust to accompany him on his new venture, they'd been his first choice. So much so, he'd happily paid over the odds to have them released into his employ, and to ensure their filthy fucking pimp stayed off the radar.

After tucking his shirt in, he secured his waistband, reaching for a slate-grey tie, as Samantha slipped a foot into a heeled shoe.

"You almost ready?" she asked, balancing on her elevated foot to pull the other heel on.

"Give me five minutes before you bring them through," he said.

Once alone, he buzzed over his hair with the dryer, before combing the strands into place. While unruly if left—a look he preferred when on his own time—his hair was always worn sleek and tidy for work, if only to upkeep the professional profile for which he strived.

Six minutes later, he sat propped on the edge of his desk, as the door opened and Rae ushered Mr and Mrs Miller into the room. From the lack of eye contact, the switching expressions, the wife looked like she didn't know whether to smile or laugh, or be completely mortified at the prospect of facing Chase after what had occurred in their session.

"How're you feeling after your shower?" Chase asked, when they swayed to a stop a couple of metres in front of him.

"Refreshed," Mr Miller uttered, while his wife merely nodded.

"Good. So ..." His gaze scanned over their faces before dropping toward their linked hands between them. "I felt that today's session went very well. Do you agree?"

They mumbled their agreement, but at least both of them smiled as they did so.

"I'd like to book you in for one week from today for the next step in your plan—would that be convenient for you both?"

Mrs Miller glanced up at her husband before looking back to Chase. "We can make it convenient."

He had to stifle his grin. "Good. And between now and then, I want you to exercise restraint."

Their eyebrows rose slightly.

"I want you to practice your communication skills. I want to you continue to let each other know exactly what you want, or need." He pushed up from his desk, both sets of eyes on him as he took a step closer. "If you feel like fucking—and you will feel like fucking ..." He rounded the couple, stroked a hand down Mr Miller's arm as he reached him, and as their eyes locked, he held the other man's gaze for a longer moment than necessary. "Then, you make sure your partner knows. I don't care where you are." He circled them again, and while neither of them turned to follow, the tilting of their heads told him they were wholly aware of his presence and position. "I don't care who you are with ..." Stepping before them, he twisted until he faced them and stared directly at Mr Miller. "If you feel like drinking from your wife's cunt ..." He stepped in until his body met Mrs Miller's and leaned in until his lips met her ear. "Then, you damned well find a way to tell her," he whispered, smiling at the shiver that rippled through her.

"However," he said, turning away from them and giving them space. "I want you to *not* act on these impulses."

Ready for it, he swung round until he could see the confusion on their faces. Not giving them chance to argue, or question, he continued, "I want you both to spend the following week knowing the desires of your partner, yet not giving in to them. If it gets too much, then by all means, go ahead and pleasure yourself. *But* ... only pleasure yourself when alone."

"And what the bloody hell's that going to achieve?" Mr Miller asked, frowning.

Chase smiled—because he'd asked the very question he'd wanted him to. "If, Mr Miller, you follow my advice, by the time I see you again next week, you will have spent an entire week knowing how the other feels, and you will have spent an entire week *thinking* about your wife carrying out everything she's shared with you. So, when you come for your next appointment, you will be prepared. You will be ready." *You will be fucking willing*, he didn't add. "Do you think you can do that?"

"We'll try," Mrs Miller said.

Chase couldn't help but chuckle to himself as the couple walked from the room, as her husband pulled her body closer to his and slipped his hand across her waist.

One week? They'd be lucky if they lasted the hour.

Black letters spelled *Private* across the gold-toned nameplate of the door Chase stood before. A door to which only he held the key—one he kept locked away in a drawer of his desk.

Closing his eyes, he thought of what lay beyond the door, and his cock instantly hardened. He thought of what he wanted *to do* beyond the door, and his balls twitched in approval. In his mind, he calculated how much time he had before his next client would arrive. If he had enough moments spare even just to enter. Maybe enough seconds to begin what he would finish later.

On the verge of truly considering fetching the key, the tap-tapping of shoes warned him of an approach. Spinning away, he rounded the corner back into the staff quarters, just as Raelyn came waltzing in.

"Your six o'clock is here. I tried buzzing, but you didn't pick up."

"Because I'm not at my desk," he said with a wink. "Besides, they're early."

Her shoulders twitched into a shrug. "Maybe they're eager."

Across the room in the staff lockers, a series of intermittent hums sounded out. His phone. He strode across and, after tapping in the code, swung open the door to the one he'd allocated himself. Positioned on top of everything else in there, his mobile glowed up the entire interior, and a quick glance at the screen told him who was on the other end.

"You can take them through to my office," he told Raelyn. "I'll be there in a moment." Barely offering her any attention with the request, he swiped his thumb over the screen, bringing the phone to his ear as her heels tapped their way out and along the corridor. "Ma?" he answered.

"'Bout time you answered this phone. What's the point of

'avin' it, if you never answer? Do you know 'ow many times I called?"

He drew the phone from his ear and quickly checked his notifications before answering, "Seven?"

"Don't be smart with me, young man." She quieted. Probably to steady her breath, judging by the quiet puffs he could hear. Around ten seconds later, her voice calmer, she asked, "'Ow are you, Son?"

"I'm good."

"I miss you. 'Ow's work?"

Work. He almost laughed. When he'd first opened the clinic, he'd told his mother his dream was to provide a specialised therapy, and thanks to the subtlety of his explanation, she'd drummed it into her own head that he was some kind of qualified doctor, and that he spent his hours every day making everyone mentally well again.

Who the hell was he to correct a mirage she was happy with?

"Work's going well. It's good."

"I really miss you. Did you get yesterday's casserole?"

"It was delicious." His words were an assumption. He hadn't gotten home until late the night before, after meeting up with an old colleague and continued friend. They'd both landed at a local Italian to eat and talk and drink. The casserole had been the last thing on his mind by the time he made it back and fell into bed. "Your best yet," he added, because he knew she liked the praise.

"Yes, well, I sent over a lasagne for tonight. I was goin'a do curry, but you always complain 'bout those ..."

He always complained because his mother had a habit of creating curries full of heat and little else, and his breath always stank of fire and fucking brimstone afterwards. Not a good way to conduct up close and personal consults.

"I told you, Ma. There's nothing wrong with your curries—

they're delicious. They just don't agree with me." He rubbed a hand across his brows. Because he knew he'd have to cut the call short, and he knew his mother wouldn't like it. "Listen, I really have to go ..."

"You always 'ave to go. *I just 'ave to go do this, Ma. I just 'ave to be somewhere else, Ma ...*"

"But I'll come by the weekend ..." He paused, making sure she'd finished complaining and had heard him. When she didn't argue, he promised, "I'll come by Saturday morning, and we'll do breakfast together."

"We'll 'ave sausages," she said, all complaint gone from her voice. Planning food seemed to be the biggest part of her life, sometimes. "And I'll get some bacon in ... and the 'ens at number twenty-two have just laid a new batch of eggs ..."

"Sounds great, Ma. I'll see you Saturday. Love you."

Ending the call before she could get out of control, he went to tuck the mobile back into its spot, but paused before unfolding his fingers around the device. It wouldn't hurt his new client to wait two minutes more. After all, they'd shown up early —Chase was on time.

Bringing his phone back beneath his chin, he flicked through to the security cam app he'd installed. As soon as he tapped the screen, a real-time image flickered to life—of the corner of a room lit only by a dimmed uplighter, beneath which a small cot had been set. Mostly an image of what lay atop of the cot.

With her hands behind her, her feet tucked up to her butt, all of them bound to one another, a woman lay still. With a swipe of his finger and thumb, Chase zoomed in on the still figure, checked her chest for breathing—slow and steady—and her flesh for any puckering that'd mean the room's temperature would need adjusting. With everything as it should be, he let his gaze land on her face, smiling to himself at the parting of her lips.

He had plans for those later.

Tapping a small icon in the corner of the screened image, he brought the phone closer to his mouth. "How are you feeling?" he asked.

Onscreen, the woman's head snapped up toward the intercom by sense alone. Because she couldn't see. The mask she wore prevented that. "I'm comfortable, Sir," she replied.

"Good." After closing down the app, Chase screen-locked the mobile and secured it back inside his locker.

A quick check in the mirrors showed a cluster of errant hair making a break from conformity, and he worked his fingers through the strands, patting them back into place, before scanning his suit for marks. Every inch of the fabric was as pristine as it should be— except for the bulge of excitement poking against his trousers.

Sticking a hand down into his boxers, he made some quick adjustments, and reminded his cock, and his brain, that his fun would come. He just had to be patient.

After enough seconds for his body to get the message and settle down, he turned toward the door in the farthest corner of the staff quarters.

As he did so, he realised he probably should've asked Raelyn for a reminder of who his six o'clock was. He could just about recall Sam mentioning it was a new client, but nothing else. New clients were the most exciting, for Chase. Those initial visits where he tried to get their measure.

What did they need?

How far would he be able to push them—what were their boundaries?

Would they even come back for round two, or would they shit themselves and leave only dust in their frenzied wake?

Pushing through the door, he stepped directly into his office. As he closed himself in, his gaze swept toward the head of hair he could see above the back of the chaise. Strawberry blonde, the tones appearing to be both golden and red at the same time, draped over shoulders too slender to belong to a male.

A female, then.

Her lack of movement told him she hadn't heard his entrance.

So, a nervous female. Only nerves could make a client close in on themselves to the extent they'd miss another presence in the room.

Not wanting to startle her as he took the first steps toward his desk, he cleared his throat loud enough to be heard.

The client twitched in her seat. Her chin jerked up. A moment later, she twisted her head toward the sound, and the eyes that met his were such a clear blue, they appeared almost transparent enough to dive right into and lose himself forever.

Chase's hip bashed the corner of his desk, hard enough that his torso half buckled. Just catching himself before he could turn into a complete arse, he swung to the right, ordered his suddenly spazzy body to his own chair, and sank his butt down.

Though he felt slightly more in control with the small distance and a desk between them, that slipped a little as soon as he looked back to those eyes.

Fucking beautiful.

She frowned. "Excuse me?"

He hadn't said the words out loud. He knew he hadn't. Yet, as soon as she spoke, he knew his lips had formed them. His throat had uttered them, even if too low for her to have made out.

Clearing his throat again, he sent a quick glance toward his desktop, where one of the girls had left a note with the client's details on. "Abigail O'Shay?" he asked, his gaze lifting once more.

"My friends call me Abi," she said simply.

Unsure if it was a statement or invitation, he asked, "What would you like me to call you?" and silently cursed himself for the suggestive undertone in his voice.

She frowned again, her almost questioning reply of, "Abi," sounding like it should have been obvious.

"Abi ..." His gaze performed a rapid assessment. Corduroy jeans hugged her thighs, topped by a boho blouse that she'd tied almost to her throat. Her clear, pale complexion spoke of a healthy lifestyle while complementing her hair, and those eyes of hers, so fucking captivating, stared wide and about as unsure as he'd ever seen from someone in that chair. Few words, beyond unnecessary compliments, sprung forth as description of his newest client. Innocent. Wholesome. *Virginal.* He leaned back in his seat. "Do you understand what it is we do here?"

Twisting her fingers in her lap, she nodded.

"And how do you think we can help you?"

Her lips parted, but then seemed to freeze. Her whole body seemed to freeze. Like a creature acknowledging imminent and unavoidable danger.

Of course, his fucking brain focussed on the 'O' of her mouth and how it might look stretched even wider, all fucking accommodating, and before he could talk himself down, he'd shot up from his seat.

She watched him as he grabbed a more portable chair from over by the bookcase, her head as much as her gaze following him when he carried it across the room and set it down a few feet in front of her. Sinking his butt onto it, he rested his forearms across his knees, putting him at eye-level with the girl.

"Let's start again," he said, and at her quiet, "Okay," he held out his hand. "Chase Walker."

She took the offering, her skinny, wholesome fucking fingers making a feeble attempt to enclose his own. "Abi O'Shay. It's nice to meet you, Mr Walker."

Up close, he could see the tiny flecks of hazel speckling the blue of her eyes, surrounded by arched lashes of reddish gold. The small mole on the ridge of her left cheekbone. Freckles that tried to hide themselves without a decent bout of sunshine to give them the confidence to step forth.

"Maybe we could start with you sharing a bit about yourself," he said. "You put on your paperwork that you're twenty-two. Is that correct?"

She nodded. "Yes, I turned twenty-two a few months back in June."

Twenty-two placed her only a few years younger than himself. Not that it mattered. Not that it *should* matter.

"I, uh ... I work at a bakery," she added with a small shrug.

"One that sells their goods to the public, or one that mass produces for everywhere else?" The question was completely irrelevant to anything they'd do at the clinic, but mundane questions with easy answers, rather than him diving straight in and poking around their sex life, often helped put a nervous client at ease.

"To the public," she said, her shoulders relaxing a fraction of an inch. "I work front of store."

She sounded proud of the fact. Like she'd had to climb her way up the ranks to be able to serve people. Like she enjoyed it, even.

"Hobbies?" he asked.

"I go to church on the weekends."

Who the hell listed church as a hobby? "Anything else? Something you do just for your own gratification, maybe?" Chase knew exactly what he liked to do for his own gratification, but he doubted using it as an example would help with getting her to open up.

"I bake," she offered with a shrug.

So, she baked for a living. Baked for fun. The girl seriously needed to expand her horizons.

Though, the rapid flash of an image in his head, of Abi O'Shay in nothing but a waist-high apron, her nipples serving a delicious dose of strawberry frosting, suddenly made the activity seem a whole lot more appealing.

Even his cock liked the picture, the way it stirred in his shorts.

Fuck. Chase needed to shake it down, real fast.

Clearing his throat, he asked, "Boyfriend?" *Girlfriend?* Hell, maybe she had both.

Which was a pretty idiotic thought—because she wouldn't be sitting on his chaise, looking all fresh and sweet, if she was advanced enough in her sexuality to be performing threesomes.

Not to mention the fresh image didn't help with quieting his cock.

"Fiancé," she said quietly.

His gaze instantly dropped to the hands she wove together in her lap. He hadn't missed it—she didn't wear a ring. Out of choice? Or was her *fiancé* too tight to buy one? Or too poor?

What the hell did he care?

"So, how long have you and your fiancé been together?" he asked, his gaze lifting back to hers.

"A few months."

A few months? And they'd already discussed marriage?

"He goes to my church," she added, as if she'd read the questions in his expression. Like she thought that explained it all.

It didn't. "You're marrying him just because he goes to your church?" Chase tried his hardest to measure his tone, but couldn't be sure he succeeded.

"No. Goodness, no." She breathed out a quiet laugh, and her eyes lightened until they resembled the surface of the sea beneath the sun's rays. Something Chase tried not to notice. "He's a good man," she added.

"Do you love him?" Fuck, he wanted to bite down on the question as soon as he'd uttered it. At the same time, he felt the urge to watch for her reaction to it, which he found in the slight tightening of her eyes, the almost imperceptible pull back of her head.

"He's a good man," she repeated. "My parents approve ..."

As she trailed off, she averted her gaze, and Chase had to wonder. Had to fucking wonder how much of the engagement was even her bloody idea. Usually, what his clients did outside of their sessions was none of his business. He made sure it was none of his business. So, why did what she'd told him so far bother the fucking crap out of him?

"Why, exactly, did you come here today, Abi?"

"My friend told me to come," she said.

He blinked. "Your friend told you to come?"

"Yes. Rebecca Shannigan?"

Definitely not the name he'd expected her to utter. Chase had helped Rebecca Shannigan almost a year before. She'd come to him as a horny fucking nympho who'd met someone she actually liked and no longer just wanted to fuck everything with a pulse that was willing and able. Trouble was, she had no idea how *not* to fuck. Her new partner had confessed to being little different, and Chase had spent every week for almost five months teaching the two of them to discover the emotional side of sex. The pleasure of the intimacy when a couple made love instead of fucked. It had taken time, but they'd slowly come to appreciate that as much, if not more, than the high of a quick bang with little interaction. The two of them had left his practice with the promise to return if they slipped from their new regime, and as he hadn't seen either of them since, he had to assume the sessions had worked.

When Rebecca had first come to him, though, she'd been a mess who'd dressed like a hooker with attitude, and fucked like fucking was crack and she was an addict. Studying the woman in front him, the prim way she sat with her knees pressed together, the almost shy way she dipped her head after speaking, as if she felt the need to hide, no way on earth would he have placed the two of them in the same room together, let alone pegged them as friends.

Chase never said a word, though, or even acknowledged recognition of the name.

"She said you're the best there is," she continued. "She promised you'd be able to help me."

His stupid fucking cock jumped about again at the mere thought of what that help could comprise of. Masking his features and willing the gentle swelling away, he asked, "What kind of help do you think we offer here, Abi?"

A pink tinge blushed her cheeks, spreading up from where her throat met her blouse line like wildfire with an abundance of fuel in its path.

"Okay, I'll rephrase the question," he said. "What is it that you think CW Consults can do for *you*? What kind of help are *you* asking for?"

She held his gaze for only a moment before dipping her head. The movement caused a narrow curtain of hair to slide forward, and Chase had the urge to tuck it back. He couldn't help but wonder what, or who, had stolen her confidence, because a face like hers shouldn't be hidden. It deserved to be shown. To be seen.

"Take your time," he told her, and he meant it. With her as his last client of the day, he didn't have to usher her out of the office by a deadline. Hell, he could take all night over the consult if he wanted to. And fuck, did a part of him actually like the idea of that. "Try starting at the beginning," he suggested.

She nodded, even if the action did seem an unsure one. "My wedding is in less than four months." She slowly lifted her head. "And I don't ..." She glanced away again. "I don't want to be a failure on my wedding night."

He let the statement sink in before asking, "You're a virgin?" He tried to hide the surprise in his voice, even as his gaze dropped straight to her crotch. A crotch covered in smooth stretchy fabric, and he couldn't help but wonder, just for a moment, what kind of underwear a virgin wore. Because he'd never fucked a virgin. Had never fooled around with a virgin— at least, no one that'd admitted to being one.

He'd definitely never had a virgin step through the doors of his clinic and ask for help.

Catching her nod, he ordered his eyes to lift, but couldn't help studying her for a few seconds more before asking, "Does your fiancé know you're a virgin?"

"Yes," she said, her attention returning to him. The flush in her cheeks had heightened to cherry red.

"I'm not being judgemental here ..." *Fucking liar*. He was being as judge-fucking-mental as a high court wig-wearer looming over a chavvy delinquent. "But I fail to see why your fiancé would have a problem with that." No man would have a problem with a woman they were going to sleep with—were going to *marry*—being a *virgin*. Not unless they were a fucking idiot.

"Oh, no ..." She shook her head slightly. "It's not like that. It's just ..."

"It's just, what?" he prompted, when she didn't continue.

"It's just that ... from what others have said ... about him—I heard he has *some* experience—"

Chase just bet he had—especially if Abi had heard it from others and not from him. Bastard probably fucked about all over town, while he expected Abi to stay pure for his own gratification. "Did you consider asking him about what you heard?"

"We talked about it, but he just said I shouldn't listen to gossip."

Which probably meant there was sure to be some truth in the tales Abi had been told. Chase needed to change tact before he could tell his new client that he already didn't like the wanker of a bloke he hadn't even met and send her running off in tears.

He also needed to change tact before he could assess why he was suddenly hating on a guy he'd never met before and who probably behaved no different than any of the guys he'd grown up with.

"Okay, let's focus on you. Why does it mean so much to please"—*this arsehole*—"your new husband?" So much for changing tact.

So much for losing his damned attitude.

"Isn't that what every new wife wants?" she asked.

Answering the question with a question. Chase got the impression she wasn't used to focusing on herself.

"Maybe," he said, and seriously needing to focus on what she'd come to him seeking, rather than what he'd decided sounded like a shitty set-up in her private life, he asked, "What skills do you have so far?"

Her brow creased. "I don't understand the question."

"What sexual experience have you had?"

"None!" she said her eyes widening. "My mother said sex outside of marriage is a sin!"

Only if you're born female, by the sounds of it, he thought.

"Sexual experience doesn't have to include anybody but yourself," he explained. "Have you ever touched yourself, Abi?"

Her head was already shaking.

"Pleasured yourself?" he added, actually enjoying the purpling of her cheeks as she blushed even more.

"My mother said a lady touching ... *down there ...*" She whispered the last two words. "... is a sin, too."

Chased smiled as he ducked his head forward until she met his eyes. "Before we go any further, I just want to clear something up, okay?" Waiting for her nod, he continued, "The only time consensual sex is a sin is if you don't enjoy it."

She squinted her eyes slightly, like she was searching for the lie in his words. "But, my mother ..." She trailed off as Chase shook his head.

"With all due respect to your mother ... she's wrong. In this, she's wrong. Our bodies can provide immense physical—and emotional—pleasure, Abi. Why would we be given such bodies, if we weren't meant to experience that pleasure?"

She dipped her gaze. "I don't—I don't know. I've never ..."

"I'm going to teach you." Reaching out, he tucked a finger beneath her chin, lifting until he could see her eyes again. Fuck, he could look into those eyes for hours and never feel turmoil again. Another thought he had to shake off. "Before you try to understand the male body and what might work for them, you need to first understand your own and what works *for you*. Because there is nothing more beautiful to a man than watching a woman enjoying physical pleasure."

"Really?" She almost whispered the word, and he nodded.

"Really." He withdrew his hand, let it hang casually back over his lap like he hadn't just overstepped a boundary. Like he didn't want to touch a whole lot more of her than just her face. "So," he said, clearing his throat a little, "the plan we'll draw up for you will revolve around you. Okay?"

"Okay," she said, though it sounded more like a question.

"We're going to figure out what you need." *And not what your fucking knobhead of a fiancé needs.* "We're going to help you cross the barriers that are preventing you from discovering that for yourself."

"Are you going to make me touch myself?" she asked.

He gave a half shrug, with an equally half shake of his head. "Not make. We don't *make* the clients do anything here. We merely guide them, and whether or not they accept that guidance is up to them."

"And if I choose not to … not to touch myself?"

"The clients here are always in control of their sessions. *Always* …"

"But?" she asked, like she'd sensed he had more to say.

"But we really need to get you past this first hurdle before we can progress in your needs." Getting her past the first hurdle had nothing to do with his own needs, he told himself. "We need to get you to a point where you don't treat your body and what it can provide as something to be ashamed of."

"And when would we start this … this plan?"

"If your wedding is in four months …"

"A little less than," she said.

"If we have three months-ish," he said, inclining his head, "we should probably set up a weekly schedule beginning next week."

"Okay," she said, though she didn't sound exactly sure.

"Raelyn or Samantha will set that up for you."

"Do I leave now?"

He smiled. "Yes, we're done here for today. But I have some homework for you."

"You do?" Her features darkened into an expression of dread.

Pushing to his feet, he motioned for her to join him, which she did. Placing her less than a foot away. Her eyes less than a foot away. Lips he really wanted to see popped open again into the perfect 'O' more than close enough to touch.

He took a step backward. "I want you to recite that *sex is not a sin*. Physical pleasure is not a sin. It's okay to touch yourself. And it's okay to enjoy it."

"Sex is not a sin," she repeated, then added, "Do I have to say this out loud?"

Chase gave a soft laugh. "In your head works well, too."

She breathed out, finally smiling what looked like a genuine smile, and the way her chest quivered the fabric of her blouse, the way her eyes paled even further while glistening at the same time ... hell, Chase suddenly had the urge to bring next week's appointment all the way forward to right fucking then, just so he could keep her for longer. To see how far he could get her to go with just another hour to play with.

He really needed to get her out of there before she could fuck up his head any more.

And before the rapid swelling of his cock became obvious.

He stepped toward the door. "I'll walk you out."

Both Rae and Sam looked up as he opened the door to reception.

"Appointment needed?" Sam asked.

"Yes, can you book Abi in for next week." Not stepping aside, he waved her forward and caught the subtle whiff of lilies on the girl's hair as she slid past. "Sam will take care you of you," he told her.

At the slightest of head movements, he glanced back toward the desk, where Rae stared right at him, a single eyebrow raised. With Abi's back to him, he shrugged, mouthed *What?*, but she merely narrowed her eyes before planting her smile in place as the client reached the desk.

Usually, Chase closed the door at that point. Retreated back into his office. Worked the finished appointment out of the kinks in his muscles. Except, with a single tap of her toe against the floor, he found his gaze shooting back to the profile of Abi O'Shay. The way her blouse hung freely and her un-hunched body showed the true fullness of her breasts that she'd done a decent job of concealing.

Her toe tapped the floor again, before creating a pattern of tiny beats, and each movement jiggled her ass. An ass he'd missed assessing during her appointment. A fucking grade-ten ass on the scale of decent rears.

Taking a card from Sam, Abi swung around and headed toward the exit, and Chase was damned if he could drag his attention away from the way her hips swayed side to side. The girl could hypnotise a man with those alone—yet Chase got the impression she had no idea just how fucking sexy she was.

"You're drooling," Sam said, just as Abi pushed out through the doors.

"Fuck off, Sam," he told her, ducking back into his office.

As soon as he'd rounded the door, he shuttered himself in, leaned back against it. Let his head drop back as he closed his eyes and tried to ignore the stirring semi poking its head against the inside of his boxers.

A semi he suspected Rae had very much seen, with the way she'd been staring at his fucking crotch.

"Shit," he muttered, because a low throb had already begun in his balls.

Despite his effort to close down the part of him that wanted to clear out the offices so he could bring out his toys, Chase was far from sure he'd succeeded.

Chase's semi had turned into a full-on erection, thanks to the paperwork he ordered himself to do. Paperwork that involved a plan to bring Abi O'Shay out of her closeted shell.

Although the plan was of the slow and gentle progress variety, his head seemed insistent on placing himself into every scenario, leading to a totally wet and wild girl by the end of her therapy. A totally wet and wild *woman* who couldn't wait to practice her new found fuckdom on anyone willing.

And Chase was certainly willing—in his head, anyway.

Fuck. Either his imagination had to take a vacay, or his dick was going to explode from mental images alone.

He jumped at the sudden in-swing of the door, his head snapping up as Raelyn strode inside, carrying a paper bag and wafting spicy scents through the room.

She marched directly to his desk, plonked the bag down in front of him, and leaned over the desktop until less than two feet away. "Since when did you start calling the clients by their first names?"

He frowned. "Since never."

"Since this evening," she said, straightening. "This just came for you. Try eating at home once in a while, instead of buying this junk. I heard your mum's ravioli is to die for."

"I do eat at home." Just as he'd be eating there once he'd finished at the office.

Once he'd worked off some steam.

She didn't respond, just gave an abrupt nod and spun herself around. "You locking us out? We're off for the night." She asked him like she already knew he wouldn't be leaving straight away.

Maybe his efforts to discreetly shut himself inside didn't go as unnoticed as he'd assumed. He had no intention of getting up and proving her right, though. Hell, he couldn't stand just then, anyway, unless he wanted her to spill an opinion on how fucking hard he was.

"Goodnight, Rae," he said instead, ducking his head back to his note-taking like he had far more important things to get on with than feeding her curiosity.

Which he did. He just needed the two of them to vanish before he could get on.

Leaving his door open—a usual occurrence so late in the day

—she headed back out into the reception. With his head ducked low, Chase pretended to be working while he watched them beneath his brows, as they gathered their bags and switched out their shoes. A few minutes later, they headed for the door with their hands linked and their bags swinging, and the swoosh of the exit doors told him exactly the moment he was alone.

Shuffling the papers into a neat pile, he slipped them into the top drawer of his desk and retrieved the office keys from the next drawer down. It took barely any time at all to head out there, secure the place, dim all the lighting so anyone peering in would assume the place to be deserted.

Back at his desk, he unlocked the bottom left drawer and withdrew a ribbon-bound key he'd been thinking about for most of the day. After grabbing up the takeaway food and slipping the key around his neck, he took himself off to the staff quarters.

Once in there, he stripped off, shoved his work clothes into the laundry chute and took a rapid shower, stroking a hand over his solid cock as he soaped himself up.

Yeah, he was ready. More than fucking ready.

Stepping from the shower, he didn't even bother to towel himself dry before he rounded the corner to the locked door with nothing but the cooling food in his hand.

Using the key from around his neck, he let himself inside, pausing just long enough to turn and re-lock the door behind himself.

The space he occupied would never speak of much to anyone who made it past the first door. Nothing but a six-by-two-foot space with dark grey walls and claret carpet, a small filing cabinet at the far end, and a second door directly ahead. Using the same key, he unlocked the second door, and as soon as it swung inward, revealing what was inside, he smiled.

"Good evening," he said, stepping to the room.

"Good evening, Sir."

He took a moment to secure the second door before lapping his neck with the key's ribbon, and drawing in a deep breath, he turned to face what he termed his Toy Box.

In contrast to the small space he'd just passed through, dark grey carpeted the floor, and a deep, wine-red coated the walls. Chains strung from one of the walls. Hooks clung to another, whips and paddles all hanging from them in a long row of choice. On a third wall, beside the only other door, Chase had mounted shelves, which he'd gone on to fill with anything that'd caught his eye over the years since he'd created his private space.

Beneath those shelves, he'd set a chair that was as deep and padded as the one in the client office that Mr Miller had chosen earlier. Beside it, a hard, wooden stool to suit his less self-indulgent moods.

Both of them faced his self-designed contraption. A deep, wooden structure that took up centre stage, one solidly constructed of railway sleepers. Resembling a roughly-hewn, empty picture frame tall enough to accommodate even himself, it stood bolted tightly to the floor, secured to the ceiling via steel cables, and offered up enough adjustable leather cuffs to hold as many as three bodies in place.

Chase had never found a need for more than one.

As soon as he'd reassured himself of the order of everything else in the room, that was right where his gaze went next. The current toy. Exactly as he'd left her, exactly as he'd viewed her earlier, on the small cot in the darkest corner of the room, she lay hogtied and ready. Ready for him.

"Thirsty?" he asked, his cock ready to leave him behind if it wasn't offered relief soon.

"Yes, Sir."

Not far from the exit, a small fridge had been set into the wall, and from there, he withdrew a bottle of water.

Then he approached the speaker.

Naked from head to toe, laying on her side, she strained against her bindings to lift her face toward him. Chestnut strands of hair that had passed its wash-by date feathered out from her head, and a red, double-layered silk mask hid eyes that Chase knew to be pale brown.

As he got within a few feet, her lips parted, as if she sensed his nearness. "I've brought you some Singapore chicken," he told her.

"Thank you, Sir."

Setting the bag and the water down, he leaned over her body, pleased to see the wetness already present at the juncture of her legs as he worked the ropes around her ankles. Once he'd freed them, he stretched out each of the limbs, giving a gentle massage to her thighs and her calves until the taut muscles had loosened, before he swung her legs around to the edge of the cot, leaving her arms tethered behind her.

"Do you need to use the bathroom?"

"Yes, please, Sir."

"Can you walk?"

"I think so, Sir."

She whimpered a little when he pushed her torso upward until she sat, but quickly stifled it by pressing her lips together, and wrapping an arm around her back, Chase helped the woman to her feet. Her movements were slow and stiff as he walked her toward the far wall. Pushing the second doorway into its room beyond exposed a small bathroom, and Chase guided her inside and to the toilet. Once he'd sat her down, he stepped outside long enough for her to relieve her bladder, before heading back in and cleansing her with a washcloth and water from the small hand basin.

"Come," he ordered, and led her out from the bathroom and back to the cot.

He massaged her shoulders as he sank her butt back down, working for a moment at the knotted kinks at the base of her neck. Stepping closer, he gripped his cock and swept its tip over her lips, and they immediately parted even further, her chest rising and falling with the sudden hastening of her breaths.

"Do you want this?" he asked her.

"Yes, please, Sir," she said, her lips brushing the sensitive skin of his swollen crown.

"You may taste it."

Her tongue slipped over her lower lip. "Thank you, Sir." As he watched, she slid her tongue out farther, worked it beneath his thick shaft. Curling it around the underside of his cock, she slicked its entire length as her tongue retracted back into her mouth.

"Did you like that?" he asked her.

Her head gave a small nod.

"How much do you want to feel my cock inside your mouth? How much do you want to taste my cum?"

She squirmed, but only slightly, as though she hoped he wouldn't notice. "I really want to taste you, Sir."

"You will," he promised. "If you behave."

Taking a step back, he knelt before her and selected the bottle of water. Drips snaked their way over the woman's chin as he tipped the bottle against her lips. She didn't complain, though, and he offered no apology. He never apologised.

He allowed her to empty half of the bottle before setting it aside and studying the woman yet again.

As though awaiting what might come next, she sat quietly, lips no longer dry from her days of capticity, but glossy with moisture, and Chase opened the paper bag. From the carton inside, he drew out a piece of sticky, sweet-scented chicken. The woman's nose twitched as he drew it toward her, her lips parting as he brushed the food over them. As she accepted the offering, her tongue darted out, stole the sauce from his fingers.

Chase froze in place, a body created of rigidity and ice.

As if realising her mistake, she frowned. "I'm sorry, Sir. Forgive me."

If Chase had come to the room in need of arousal, he would have taken one of the paddles down for the insubordination. Smacked her until welts formed and she cried out in pain. Taught her that she should never take without permission

His cock was already too hard, though. He needed to get past the preliminaries as soon as possible.

"This time," he said. "Next time, you will be punished."

"Thank you, Sir."

One piece after another, Chase fed the chicken to the woman, and as he did so, he wondered how much longer he would keep her there. How much longer she'd hold up before she begged for release.

She'd already been with him for nine days.

As soon as the food tray had emptied, he carried the rubbish across and dropped it by the door, ready for disposal.

Although not big, her breasts stood firm and proud, her nipples poking at the air, thanks to the room's temperature Chase had set to just the right side of cool without freezing her to death. A narrow waist led to full hips, and those full hips dipped inward toward a crotch that'd been hairless when she'd first arrived—a crotch Chase had had minimal contact with during the nine days he'd held her.

Just another element of the control he so fucking craved.

"Are you ready?" he asked her.

"Yes, Sir," she said.

He reached out a hand and enclosed her throat within his fingers. Tight enough to support. Tight enough to restrict. "Stand."

Her legs trembled on her push to her feet. Although she didn't grumble, she didn't quite manage to suppress a whimper at the movement, nor with each of the following steps she took as Chase led her toward the structure in the centre of the room.

Within the wooden frame, he positioned her to face him before rounding her until he stood at the structure's rear. From there, he studied her naked ass. The almost healed striations from where she'd been punished four days prior. The bruising left behind by bites on her shoulder. He also untied the rope holding her hands captive.

Selecting one of the leather cuffs hanging down from the upper side of the frame, he worked her left arm upward and enclosed her wrist within the restraint, ignoring yet another small whimper as he did the same with her right arm. After rounding the frame to her front again, he crouched down and repeated the process, strapping each of her ankles into two cuffs at each of the bottom corners of the wooden device.

Straightening, he watched her features for complaint. For acquiescence. Aside from a slight tightening to her brows, probably from her arms being stretched upward after being behind her all day, her features seemed still.

"Do you want to feel pleasure?" he asked her.

"Yes, Sir." Chase didn't move, but stared hard at her, as if she would feel his expression, and as if she had, she corrected herself. "Yes, *please*, Sir. Please, I would. Sir."

Smiling to himself, he went to the shelving at the back of the room, from where he selected a small black device with wires coiled atop it and carried it back to the woman.

He reached up for the cuff around her left wrist and, loosening the pin holding it in place, slid it down the side of the frame until level with his chest, where he re-secured it. Although she didn't grumble, she didn't quite manage to suppress a gasp at the sudden movement, nor when Chase did the same with her right arm.

Each of the thin wires he uncoiled led to a small clamp. Taking the first one, he opened the thinly-padded teeth. As he folded them over the woman's left nipple, she let out a breath, her lips staying open while he prepared the second clamp. With its clenching over her right nipple, she released a soft moan.

"More?" he asked.

"Yes, please, Sir," she whispered.

"Legs," he ordered.

She spread her thighs as widely as the frame would allow.

Reaching down, Chase watched her face as he slipped a finger along her folds and located her clitoris. Already swollen, the sensitive flesh all but begged for attention, and pinching it between his finger and thumb, he tugged it outward, affixed a third clamp around it with little finesse, his cock jolting toward the woman when she let out a gasp.

"Down," he told her.

As he'd directed, she sank her knees to the bottom supporting beam he'd had embedded into the floor, her arms cinching above her head again in their restraints, her cunt positioned over a urinal that'd been plumbed into the flooring beneath her.

If Chase had been about pleasuring her alone, he could have left her standing, but without her arms extended for support, he doubted she would have remained standing for long. Not once he clicked the device's switch from off to on.

A small bracket had been attached to the left side of the frame, and Chase worked the device into it, uncaring of the sounds she emitted when doing so tugged at the clamp near her cunt.

"Open your mouth for me, and you will be rewarded."

The woman obeyed, and Chase stepped forward until the

heat of her breath washed over his cock and made it swell almost to its full proportion.

"Do you want to be rewarded?" he asked.

"Yes, please, Sir," she said, before opening her mouth wide once more.

Gripping the back of her neck with his hand, Chase guided her mouth forward. As soon as she reached him, her lips folded around the swollen head of his cock and her cheeks contracted with the suction of her mouth.

Tipping his face to the ceiling, he closed his eyes, expelled a held breath. "Good," he praised. "More."

With his cock in her mouth, he barely understood the compliant reply, but the vibration from her throat just made him even fucking harder, and he tugged her head farther forward, shoved his cock in a little more.

"Good girls always get rewarded," he said, and at her garbled reply, he stretched a hand toward the black device, not even bothering to open his eyes as his fingers glided over the familiar buttons until he'd found the one he wanted. With only a light compression from his forefinger, the woman's body jerked and her mouth tightened around his cock.

Leaving the clamps humming over her puckered flesh, Chase tightened his hand around her nape, threaded the fingers of his other hand through the hair of her crown, and held her exactly where he wanted her as he thrust his cock deep into her throat.

The gagging sound she made had him pulling back and slamming into her again.

Then again.

The mewling cries she made when he retracted for the third time had him fisting his hand even tighter within her hair, while the twisted flexing of her fingers, telling him the clamps were treating her exactly as planned, made him wish he'd taken the time to select a butt plug, as well.

Not that it mattered, anymore. Chase calculated she had around three minutes until climax, which meant he had only a little more himself.

With her head held firmly within his grasp, her mouth gaping and hot and wet, so fucking wet, he drove his hips forward, crammed his cock in right to its base, his eyes opening as he lowered his chin to watch the exact moment she came. To see the stretch of her lips, the strain of her cheeks. The fucking vulnerability of a woman who'd allow herself to be treated in such a way.

Except as his gaze fell on the woman, he no longer saw hair a shade of chestnut. No longer saw the lightly bronzed shoulders like those before him.

Instead, his mind imagined pale hair carrying hints of ginger wrapped around his fingers. Eyes of the palest blue closed tight beneath that mask. And envisioned breasts fuller than he'd first realised bouncing about with each hit of pleasure against her core, each slap of his balls against her chin.

It didn't take a genius to recognise the woman in his mind, as the first spasm hit his body and he grunted out a cry alongside the violent eruption from his cock.

Abi fucking O'Shay.

EPISODE TWO

"I hope you're ready for this." Chase Walker couldn't help but smirk at the other guy in his office. Six-foot-four, with a head shaved bald enough to glisten, and muscles that flexed with so much as a nod, he'd probably seem scary as fuck to anyone who met him on the streets, but Chase had known Jones for enough years to know different. He still remembered the skinny, lanky kid from school, who'd been awkward around girls and had a gift for chemistry.

The local gym and boxing club was owed a lot of thanks for the body Jones had grown into. He no longer had trouble getting girls. Or guys. And since he'd found his new passion in life, chemistry had taken a back seat for him.

"I'm ready." His voice was a whole lot deeper than it'd been in school, too.

"I'll bring them in, then," Chase said, already making his way across the room.

The first things he saw on opening the door into reception were his two assistants, Raelyn and Samantha. Both of them glanced up, Sam stretching her neck to the left a little as she peered past Chase into his office, sending a small smile and wave to the man in there.

Shifting his gaze to the right landed it on his waiting clients. The whole purpose of Jones being invited along to CW Consult for the next hour.

A woman with bobbed hair a dark, cocoa brown and a slight plumpness to the face that housed stunning indigo eyes, and a man carrying little fat on his frame, topped by a mop of greying mousiness. Both of them wore the clinic-provided robes and terry-cloth slippers, and both of them already stared his way.

"Mr and Mrs T," he said. The couple had insisted on the abbreviation since their first consult—a common practice for them, apparently, due to the too-often mispronunciation of their full name Titcomb. "How are you both?"

Unlike a lot of the clients who arrived for practical sessions, the couple bounced to their feet like a couple of kids on the promise of ice cream. "Excited," Mr T said, though the twitchy smile he offered hinted that he'd brought at least some nerves along for the session.

"That's what we like to hear." Chase waved them forward. "Come on through."

Waiting until the couple had filed through the door, he closed the four of them inside, watching for when the clients took in the visitor. Waiting for their reactions.

They hadn't asked what the guest would look like when they'd scheduled the session. And Chase hadn't offered the information. He knew the exact moment Jones had been processed, though, by the double blink Mrs T gave.

Dressed in tapered black trousers and a black muscle vest, Jones stood with his feet apart and his crossed arms bulging. Tattoos snaked over his biceps, as well as peeked up one side of his neck. As a complete package, he looked like he belonged at the door to a nightclub, rather than in Chase's office. Uncivilisation wrapped in civilised threads.

With his grin barely contained, Chase led the way forward and gestured for them to follow. "Mr and Mrs T, I'd like to you meet my associate, Jones."

Jones merely cocked his head to the side, his eyes narrowing as the couple stepped closer. He made no effort to take the hand offered by Mr T. Didn't even bother unfolding his arms. The guy had a reputation to uphold, after all—one he hadn't earned by playing the amenable friend.

"As we discussed last week, Jones is the owner of The Club," Chase went on.

Mr T glanced between Chase and Jones. "*The* The Club."

"Yes," Jones rumbled, and the couple's heads bounced up toward him as if shocked that he'd spoken. Ignoring them, Jones turned to Chase. "Let's do this."

"Ready?" he asked his clients, and at their ardent nods, he led them toward a second exit.

Out in the corridor, more doors led to four options. Chase pushed open the first door on the left and stepped back. "After you."

As soon as their backs had turned, Jones sent Chase a grin full of wicked promise before following them inside.

Mr and Mrs T had first visited the clinic looking for adventure with no fucking clue how to access it. Luckily for them, Chase knew where to find it *and* had a key to the door. As with any clients who came to Chase with specific requests, however, Chase had spent the past few weeks assessing their eligibility and willingness.

Mr and Mrs T had passed the first test of fucking with an audience—which had led them to the next test: Fucking with the audience of a stranger and responding to third party interference.

The ensuing appointment would be an interesting one, for certain. Because nobody could ever bank on the kind of mood Jones might be in.

The room Chase followed the three of them into looked like something from a hotel created purely for sex. Or a boudoir adapted for the clinic's needs.

The bronze-dressed bed stole the stage, complementing the caramel theme of the room. Golden drapes hung from the wall near its head, making the bed appear majestic—as well as hiding the iron hoops attached to the wall for those who preferred bondage. Distressed bedside drawers held toys and accessories within easy reach, while to the bed's left, a replica of an antique sex chair drew the eye. Set slightly apart from all of those, near the foot end of the bed, a large soft rug covered the floor in front of an open fireplace, complete with faux-burning logs.

As Chase closed the door on them all, Mrs T crossed the room toward the sex chair.

She ran her fingers over the fabric and along its frame, coming to a stop at one of the curled ends that protruded upward like horns. "How is this used?"

"However you want it to be." Chase gave them both a moment to scan the room, watching with interest as Mrs T paused to experience the texture of almost everything in there.

Mr T approached the bed before anything else, pulled open one of the drawers at its side. Closing it, he tipped his head, his hand reaching out, and he swept back the drape to reveal one of the two hoops affixed to the wall.

"Today's session will work slightly differently," Chase told them after a few moments. "Any interventions will be led by Jones. Any advice will be given by Jones. Any interactions will be made by Jones. My presence for the session will be to observe, and I will step in only if I believe, at any point, the session has become uncomfortable for anyone involved."

"But you're staying in the room?" Mrs T asked.

He pointed toward the most shadowed corner, where a red moulded stool had been set up, in complete contrast to the rest of the room's furnishings. "Right over there."

"And this session is recorded, as well as observed?"

"It is, yes. Any other questions?"

At the shakes of their heads, he glanced toward Jones and inclined his head. Once he'd received a nod of confirmation in return, Chase took himself over and settled onto the stool.

Handed over to the wall of intimidating muscle, the couple seemed nervous at last. They should have been. Only a complete exhibitionist with a big dose of arrogance would miss the size of the step they were about to climb.

"At this point in the session, there is only one thing I'm going to tell you." Still hovering near the door, arms crossed, feet apart, Jones narrowed his eyes on the couple. "Yellow."

Mr T swallowed. "Yellow?"

"Is that like a *safe word*?" Mrs T asked.

"Yes." Jones still didn't move.

"But ..." She glanced between Chase and Jones. "Are we doing BDSM here today?"

"We're doing whatever the fuck we end up doing here today." His smile was pure wickedness when Jones took a step toward the woman. "Let me explain something to you. At The Club, there are no rules. There are no restrictions. There are only safe words. If you are fucking, somebody will want to watch. Or they will want to fuck, too." He turned to Mr T. "If you are eating cunt ... somebody will want a taste. Or want you to taste *them*. If you are on a device that has restraints ... somebody *will* want to use them. The *safe word* is the warning to any party involved that they are overstepping a boundary you are *uncomfortable* with. If you can't learn to use a safe word, then you are wasting my time bringing me here today." His glance passed from husband to wife. "Are you wasting my time? You better fucking speak up now, if you are."

Mrs T shook her head—a little too quickly.

"We can use a safe word," Mr T said.

"Okay, then repeat it. *Know* it. Yellow."

"Yellow," the couple offered.

With a nod of approval, Jones moved across to a switch on the wall, his back to them as he dimmed the lighting in the room. "You two had better not still be wearing those robes when I turn back."

Mr and Mrs T both yanked at the ties holding their gowns closed, before shrugging them off their shoulders. Taking Mrs T's from her, her husband shuffled across and hung them from a row of hooks near where Chase sat.

Jones half-glanced over his shoulder. "Those fugly slippers, too."

Mrs T slipped hers from her feet and kicked them toward Mr T, as he removed his, leaving the two of them completely naked.

"Good. You know what to do." Still fully clothed, Jones turned back to face the room, re-folded his arms over his chest, and stared at the couple.

Mr and Mrs T stared right back.

Eyebrow quirked up, Jones smiled and inhaled long and slow. Exhaled. Chase knew he could stand there like that, not talking, barely moving, indefinitely. As far as the guy was concerned, the couple were paying him, and that gave him good enough reason to stay.

As if the silent standoff had finally gotten through to them, Mr and Mrs T looked away. Toward each other. A good foot or so taller than his wife, Mr T shifted to stand behind the woman, his chin above her shoulder. She tracked his movements with little more than a twist of her head.

As the man brought his lips down, Chase thought him about to kiss his wife, but instead he sank his teeth into her shoulder. She moaned as he scraped them over her skin on release.

"Open your thighs," he ordered.

She did, and her husband slid his hand over her shoulder blade and traced the length of her spin to the curve of her ass. Chase expected him to slip around to the front of her from there, but surprising him, Mr T soaked his fingers with his own saliva and worked them between her butt cheeks, and Chase knew the exact moment he'd found her anus by the almost surprised gasp she gave, as her body jerked forward and her hand made a grab for her husband.

Using his free hand, Mr T pushed on her torso until she bent forward before him. Keeping that hand in place, he spread her ass open with the other, and pressed his thumb into the tight opening. In response, his wife let out a quiet moan, and as her body swayed a little, Chase could see how fucking hard the man already was.

"On your knees," he ordered.

The woman complied. Her hands came out to support her frame.

Following her down, Mr T gripped the nape of her neck and pushed again. "Lower."

She spread her arms outward, dropping until her cheek pressed against the caramel carpet beneath her.

Placing a hand on each cheek of her ass, he stretched them apart until he'd exposed her anus. His stiff cock strained toward the tiny opening, but Mr T made no effort to fuck her there. Instead, he dipped down and swiped his tongue over the seam of her ass.

His wife twitched toward him, and he nibbled at the

surrounding skin, his tongue shooting out again for another lick. Opening his mouth wider, he sucked at the flesh, moved a little lower, sucked again. Giving a low groan, Mrs T chased his tongue with her ass, but not once did he go as far as her cunt. Not once did he penetrate her with so much as a finger.

His tongue lapped upward again, his thumbs brushing over her anus. She pushed back against him, gave a small whimper that sounded like complaint. As if in admonishment, her husband whipped his hand against her ass in a sharp slap, and she gave a small cry, her body jolting forward.

She quieted, barely containing the swivel of her chasing hips through his next round of licks and bites, and her husband finally rewarded her. The slide of his fingertip into her anus set her moaning, her fingers curling over. He pressed into her further, and she grabbed at the edge of the rug.

"More?" the man asked.

Her cheek rubbed against the carpet with her nod. "Yes."

Another slap of her ass resounded through the room. "More?" he asked again, rotating his finger against the rim of her ass.

Her eyes closed as her breaths hastened. "Yes, *please*."

Mr T withdrew his finger a little, smoothed a hand over her naked back, then forced that same finger into her ass down to the final knuckle. The woman cried out, a sound full of pleasure and little discomfort.

Brushing his free hand along her spine took it to the curve of her ass, and he swept over there and dipped between her thighs. Just a gentle exploration there before he brought his hand back out, fingers glistening with wetness. Lifting his gaze toward where Jones stood watching, he took those fingers to his mouth, folded his lips around them. Closed his eyes as he slowly drew them into his mouth.

Jones didn't need any more invitation than that. Unfolding

his arms, he grabbed the hem of his shirt and tugged it up over his head, putting the black swirls of tribal ink that splayed over his left pec and shoulder on display. He chucked it aside, every muscle in his arms and chest flexing with the simple movement. Fuck, even his stomach muscles clenched into his hard-earned pack.

Mr T's eyes opened onto Jones unbuckling his belt, and the man visibly swallowed. Chase watched him closely. Wondered if he'd back out already, before things had even remotely got interesting.

Gaze still on Jones, the man slid his finger back out of his wife's ass and rammed it straight back in again, faster, harder, and she gave a gasp that caught in her throat. "Do you want me to fuck you?" he asked her, fingering her ass a third time.

She groaned, her hips pushing toward him as if impatient. "*Please.*"

Mr T wrapped a hand around his cock as he stared toward where Jones pushed his trousers over his legs. He stroked its length, while Jones kicked off his shoes, slid his trousers from his ankles, placed them aside. As Jones straightened, revealing himself in all his commando glory, Mr T shuffled closer to his wife, his eyes tight and intense.

Women had often praised Chase on the size and beauty of his cock, but Jones resembled a fucking masterpiece as he stood there, naked, and enclosed his thick, hard length within a hand that was as muscular as the rest of him.

The next swallow the husband gave seemed full of want, as he positioned the head of his cock at the entrance to his wife's cunt. He didn't seem able to remove his gaze from the slow strokes Jones gave to his phallus, as he gripped hold of his wife's hip and slammed his cock into her until his groin slapped her ass.

She moaned into the carpet, her back flexed against the invasion, a moan that didn't abate when her husband drew back, slammed into her again.

Watching them, his expression dark, Jones continued the slow working of his hand along his shaft. Long, lazy strokes upward, followed by equally long ones down to its base.

Returning his gaze, Mr T thrust his hips back and forth, his finger still fucking his wife's ass, as the woman gripped at carpet fibres and moaned out her pleasure.

Jones let the man continue for a good two minutes before he prowled toward the couple like a predator starved of food. Bypassing the wife, he headed straight toward the husband. Rounded his body until he stood behind the man. Dropped to his knees, aligning his solid cock with the guy's ass, and his chest with his back.

As if testing his willingness, Jones gripped the other guy's ass, massaged his cheeks with rough squeezes of his hands. As the head of Jones's cock prodded between those cheeks, though, Mr T stiffened, gave an uneasy glance over his shoulder.

Jones didn't cease, but wrapped an arm around the other man's torso while dipping his other hand down between them and gripping his cock in place. When the husband's rhythm faltered, Jones leaned in close until his lips brushed his ear. "You know the rules."

Mr T frowned with his muttered, "Yellow," and he relaxed some with Jones's response of, "Good."

The man turned his focus back to his wife, but Jones didn't move away. Didn't remove his arm from around his waist. He positioned the length of his shaft between the other man's ass cheeks, letting the flesh hug his hard thickness as he began a slow undulation of his hips.

A quiet, "Fuck," left Mr T's lips, as he returned to fingering his wife's anus, and her sounds of pleasure recommenced.

Hitting his thighs against hers as he began thrusting his hips once more.

Jones tightened his hold of the man. "Slowly." Gripping the man's hips with his hands, he forced him to allow Jones to set the pace. Each nudge from Jones's cock within his cheeks pushed Mr T against his wife, as Jones held him exactly where he needed them both for himself.

It didn't take long for Mr T to figure out the rhythm, and Jones let free a groan. Daring to release his hold, he leaned in closer to the guy, his arm reaching around his waist again and holding him against himself, as he brought his other hand around to Mr T's front. Stretching down toward the other man's groin, Jones splayed his fingers over his crotch. As his fingers brushed over Mr T's cock, the man groaned, a sound that deepened when Jones circled his shaft. Uncurling his hand once more, Jones let each thrust of their hips slide Mr T's cock over his palm. The tips of his fingers pressed against the swollen outer flesh of Mrs T's cunt, and she moaned, pushed back against them, her hips twitching into a tiny rhythm in search of more.

With the demanded pace of their bodies, the three of them rocked into each other. Each drive of Jones's cock within those ass cheeks urged Mr T into his wife, and each demand of her cunt against Jones's fingers took the man right back to where Jones seemed to want him.

Just watching them gave Chase a big fucking hard-on that had his balls aching and his mouth pooling and his fists clenching to join in. Especially when the woman made a grab for her right breast and twisted her nipple in a way that had her crying out and the scent of her wet cunt filling the room.

"Don't stop." The plea sounded full of desperation. "God, please don't stop."

Chase had no idea if she begged for Jones's touch or her

husband's cock. Probably both. She toyed harder with her nipple. Pulled on its tip, digging the ridges of her fingernails into the tender flesh, building a pattern that had panted cries spilling from her and her entire body trembling with want. Her parted lips released every sound, and Chase pictured himself filling that mouth, imagined the heat within, the sucking moisture over his shaft with each plunge to the back of her throat.

His cock roared inside his shorts with the thoughts whirling in there. His sac hardened when the woman's cries heightened and her eyes screwed shut, and she worked her nipple harder, faster, her entire body seeming to tense.

The next sound to leave her wailed through the room. She dismissed her breast and gripped at air, her fingers flexing and opening, before her chest heaved with the rapid breaths gasping from her. She hadn't even finished whimpering when Jones pushed away from Mr T, rounded them both, and snatched her up from the carpet.

Leaving her husband on his knees with his cock dripping her cum.

Jones carried the woman around the bed to the sex chair. He set her down on the upper reclined seat, lay her head against the padded cushion. Lifting her left leg, he hooked her knee over one of the leg supports, before doing the same with her right leg. Once he'd positioned her there, knees bent, legs splayed, her cunt on full show and still pumping out cum in the lowlight, he turned and beckoned to her husband.

No hesitation marked Mr T's climb to his feet. At the chair, Jones grabbed him by the hips, kicked his legs apart so he stood with a foot each side of the chair's lower section, and pressing his chest to the man's back, he urged him forward toward his wife's waiting cunt. Reaching a hand around, Jones gripped the man's cock and guided it toward the wet pussy.

Mrs T let out a soft moan as he entered her, and Jones

rounded the chair, took each of her hands and wrapped her fingers around the curved bars protruding upward from each side of her head.

Buried deep within in his wife's cunt, Mr T looked toward Jones, as if awaiting permission to continue. Without speaking, Jones rounded the seat to him and, taking him by the hips, drew him out of her, before using his own pelvis to ram him back in. Once he'd set the couple at a steady pace, Jones took a step back, ran his hands over the other man's ass. Squeezed. Massaged. Slapped the left cheek hard enough to sting. Hard enough to leave an imprint of his hand.

Mr T cried out, but his hips bucked harder, burying him deep into his wife's pussy. After tugging the man's cock in and out of his wife a few more times, Jones spanked his ass again, smiling as the grunted cry filled the room.

Wrapping a fist around his own cock, Jones circled the couple on the chair, not stroking, just holding, his eyes tight as he watched the couple fucking. Each time he passed Mrs T, he reached out and pinched a nipple, a sharp cry lifting her chest high each time, but with both buds erect as hell, and her breaths shallow and carrying quiet moans, Chase suspected she gained only pleasure from the attacks.

On his third lap of the couple, Jones stilled behind the woman's head. Stepping up onto the padded footplate placed his solid cock above her face. She glanced up at the thick length, gave a lick of her lips. Even stretched up with her chin and swept her tongue over its tip.

Chase's breath shuddered from him as he thought of another tongue lapping over his own cock. *Fuck.* His body screamed for him to go join them, but he couldn't. Not that time. It would defeat the point of the exercise. He'd just have to have wait.

With the palm of his hand, Jones nudged the woman's face

away, and he reached for her husband, took the man's hand from where he clutched his wife's hip and pulled it toward him.

He wrapped the fingers of the man's hand around the upward, curving support, and stretched over for the other hand, placed that one around the opposite support. The move took Mr T closer to his wife, drew his body over hers.

It also took Mr T a whole lot closer to where Jones stood, and Chase knew what to expect next even before Jones slid a hand around the back of the other man's neck and encouraged him toward his waiting cock.

Breath held, Chase listened for the utterance. The safe word that would stop Jones from taking the act any further.

It didn't arrive. Mr T opened his mouth, and Jones crammed his cock into the guy's mouth with little consideration for breath or comfort. The man's lips whitened as they stretched to accommodate Jones's girth, and he gave a grunt as Jones delved deeper. Gagged as the large cock tapped the back of his throat.

Below him, Mrs T reached up and ran a finger over her husband's lips, before stroking along Jones's cock on his withdrawal.

"Keep fucking," Jones said, his voice a low rumble.

The man slid his cock from his wife, plunged back in, as Jones slipped his cock from his mouth and drove it back in. Each thrust he gave of his hips, Jones matched, until they became a circle of joined bodies, from cunt to cock to mouth, to touch as Mrs T continued her strokes of Jones's cock with one hand, adding the occasion lick of her tongue, and stroked her clitoris and her husband's cock with the other.

Deep, animalistic grunts filled the room with every thrust. Equally deep moans and higher-pitched gasps came in contrast.

Chase hardly noticed how his legs had spread. How his lips had parted. How his own hastened breaths matched those of the threesome screwing across the room. Fuck, even his backside flexed in time with the man's as he banged into his wife over and fucking over.

Jones let his head fall back, twisted his fingers around the strands of Mr T's head. His teeth clenched as his grunts grew longer.

Fucking beautiful. All of them, their faces twisted into desperation that bordered on ecstasy. All of their bodies taut and striving for release.

Chase gripped the chrome handles of the stool, as Mrs T's body arched over the chair, and he did little to contain his groan.

Jones cut his gaze on a direct path his way. Met his eyes. His lips curved into a knowing smile as he slammed his hips forward harder. Faster. Giving fresh grunts with each slap of his groin against the other man's face.

Chase would be lucky if he made it through the after-meeting without pausing for relief in between. His cock had swelled so hard, pain began mixing with desire. If they didn't finish soon, he might even beat them to it.

The threesome kicked up the fucking, until slaps of skin on skin resonated around the cries and the groans and squirming of bodies.

Chase had to white-knuckle the chair to keep his body seated. Watching intense fucking could get to him every damn time.

Mrs T stiffened, a rigid display of pure pleasure, before her body began a slow curl outward and her back arched even higher. A low wail leaked slowly from her throat, before she cried out and clutched at her husband's hips in a frenzied attack.

Around Jones's cock, Mr T's grunts grew louder, and Chase knew the exact moment he ejaculated by the judders of his body, the rhythm of his hips completely lost as he offloaded his pleasure into his wife's cunt.

As if in response to the two of them, Jones stilled against his mouth. His grip held those lips enclosed over the full length of his cock. A draw back of his hips followed by a fast slam forward had Jones's face twisting and a groan spilling free. He pumped in and out a few more times, his movements jerky. Uncontrolled. His head fell back, eyes closing, as further moans left him.

The room quieted but for the panting breaths of everyone in there. The three bodies relaxed, except for the heaving of their chests and the tiny after-tremors rippling through them.

They stayed like that for a few long minutes, before Jones freed his cock from the man's mouth and took a step backward.

Chase took that as his cue to hop down from the chair, all too aware of the hardness banging against his trousers. "Everyone okay?"

Jones didn't bother answering, and Chase hadn't expected him to. He strode across the room toward his discarded clothing, as Mr T slipped his cock free.

The man seemed shaky on his feet when he turned toward Chase, his eyes still a little glazed as he nodded. He held out a hand, which his wife took, and waiting until she'd swung her legs free of the supports, he helped her to stand.

"Mrs T?" Chase asked.

She smiled, the expression full of post-coital smugness. "I'm okay."

A quiet knock hit the other side of the room's door, and Raelyn followed its inward swing.

"Raelyn will take you to the shower rooms. Dental hygiene kits will be made available. Once you're ready, we'll convene back in my office to discuss today's session."

"Did we pass?" Mr T asked.

Chase didn't bother looking to Jones for direction—he knew he wouldn't give it before he was ready. "We'll discuss that once everyone has had a chance to refresh."

~

C hase tapped his forehead lightly against the wall beside the shower enclosure. Steam had misted the usually clear glass, but he could still see Jones's nakedness through there.

"You sure you don't need to shower?" he said from within.

Chase quit with the head torture. "I don't."

"I'm pretty sure you gizzed in your pants in there."

"I didn't."

Jones's head peeked around the glass. "Then, you definitely need to get in here and offload."

Chase couldn't help but smile. He might have considered the offer, if it hadn't been Jones making it. "I can handle it."

"You know I can make you feel good."

Chase didn't doubt it, but, "I remember you making the same offer to Johnny Jackson."

Jones let out a deep laugh and ducked back inside the shower.

Johnny Jackson had gone back to Jones's place a few years earlier, after a heavy night of clubbing. Nobody had seen him for a week afterward, and it'd taken six months for any of them to find out why.

The poor guy hadn't been able to walk.

"You haven't been to The Club lately," Jones called over the spray.

Chase pushed away from the wall. "I've been busy."

The water shut off and Jones reappeared, his cock once more hard and ready. Seemed like an almost perpetual state for the appendage. "You better fucking come with those two," he said, jerking his chin toward the door.

"They passed, then?" He grabbed a towel and tossed it to Jones.

"I like them." He didn't say anything else. He didn't really need to.

Chase smiled. "They'll think all their Christmases have come at once."

"Not if you don't plan on coming in with them, they won't."

No, they wouldn't. It was a rule of The Club. Nobody could simply show up there—even if they figured out where its location was at. Any new members had to go on the guest list beneath a representative. A sponsor. A long-standing member willing to get them through the door and vouch for them.

As Chase was the one introducing them to The Club, he had little choice but to take them there for their first visit.

"I'll be there."

Drying the length of his cock, Jones nodded his approval. "Tuesday. Ten. I'll add you all to the list." His gaze dropped toward Chase's crotch, where his stiffness still begged for release. "You really should sort that out."

"See you in the office," he told him, and headed for the door.

Ten minutes later, Jones stood at his side in his usual crossed-arms stance, and Mr and Mrs T faced them with anxious expressions on their faces.

"The Club will be open on Tuesday at ten pm."

At Jones's words, the couple's eyebrows lifted.

"You may attend on a probationary invitation," he continued, "so long as all pertinent paperwork has been completed and returned to me by noon tomorrow at the latest."

He reached down beside Chase's desk, the black leather briefcase he lifted seeming incongruous against the rest of his appearance. From inside, he withdrew a couple of packages and handed them to the couple. "These are the agreements for The Club. In them, you will find a club disclaimer against responsibility beyond its control, and a confidentiality clause. Read the agreement fully, initial each and every point in the designated boxes to show you understand and agree, and then sign, print your name, and date at the end. You must both fill in your own, individual paperwork. Once you've done them, hand them over to Walker. As your sponsor for the invitation, he will ensure I receive them by the cut-off time. Also in those packs, you will find payment details. Membership must be paid in full, in advance. You will arrange that within forty-hours, or the invitation becomes null and void. Any questions?"

"What do we bring with us?" Mr T asked, as his wife came out with, "What do we wear?"

Jones stared down at them. "You bring nothing. You will be wearing nothing. Anything beyond that will be provided by The Club." He turned toward Chase. "You have clean records for them?"

Chase nodded. "On file, yes." A requirement for treatment from CW Consult: Every client had to be tested for STDs, and their results come back clean before Chase would accept them for his programme.

It was also a requirement for The Club.

"I'll need a copy," Jones said.

"I'll have Sam fax them over."

With a nod, Jones clicked his briefcase shut and swung the carrier down to his side. "Tuesday, then. Don't be late."

Sitting in the padded armchair of his Toy Box, Chase watched as the woman's tits bounced up and down. Even with the after-meeting, Mr and Mrs T's session had left him with aching balls and a cock in dire need of ejaculation, which had led to him grabbing the room's key and sneaking away during the first break he got between clients.

Strung by her arms from the wooden frame Chase had had

specially made, the woman straddled another piece of furniture he'd ordered to his specifications. A low, sturdy stool that provided little comfort, but pleasure could certainly be found in the solid artificial cock that protruded from its centre.

Releasing whimpers of pleasure, the woman fucked the smooth lance like she'd spent the entire day in need of orgasm. Lips parted, she faced him, even though the blindfold prevented her from seeing his own actions. Almost as ardently as her breasts, her hair flicked around her face.

Chase tried not to dwell on the reddish shade to the strands. Or what it might mean that he'd instantly zoned in her, the second he'd spotted its sleek glossiness glinting in the flashing overhead lights at the fetish club he'd attended.

The woman he'd held previously had ran her course. Twelve days was a good stretch for Chase to last before growing bored of a new toy, and he'd paid her well before releasing her back to her life.

In front of him, the new woman worked her hips up and down, her face twisting in pleasure. Each slide up of her cunt left the makeshift cock slathered in her juices. Each slam back down had her crying out and panting hard.

Watching her, Chase tightened his grip around his own cock and squeezed as he worked his hand over the shaft. His bicep burned with how fast he yanked the foreskin down to the base and back up again. His grunts hit the air with the hastening of his own breaths.

His mind skipped back to the threesome he'd watched. The reason he'd needed to enter his Toy Box to begin.

And the pale-shaded redhead opposite him was the reason he'd stayed.

He studied the parted lips as he hand-fucked himself faster. Imagined those lips belonging on another pale redhead. Imaged those cheeks swollen to accommodate his cock. The hot wetness of within as she took him in fully and sucked and licked and groaned in the kind of desire that came only from pleasuring another.

He knew when his balls tightened that he didn't have long to go. Neither did the woman, judging by the way she tilted her hips slightly with each slap-down of her pussy. The way her cries had altered to whimpers—ones that spoke of a desperation to come.

Closing his eyes, he let his head drop back, her sounds washing over him as he pumped his hand around his cock. His jaw clenched with the effort, and for just a moment, he allowed himself to wonder, for the hundredth time in a week, just how it might feel to have Abi O'Shay's cunt gripping hold of his cock and pumping him free of strain and tension.

Cum shot from him in a violent eruption. A cry barked from him as his body bucked in the seat. He stroked again, sending out another spray, and again, until his body shuddered and his grunts left him breathless, because anything but a torturous orgasm would've fallen short of what his body needed right then.

When he opened his eyes, the woman had quit bouncing. Only her tethered arms held her upright as her chest heaved against her heavy breaths.

Chase hadn't even noticed her finishing. She might as well not have been in the room, for the all enjoyment he'd taken from watching her personally. All she'd served to do was plant fantasies in his head about a certain client of his. One he'd no right fantasising about.

He'd only met her once, for fuck's sake.

Suddenly just as frustrated as he'd been on first entering the room, Chase blew out a breath and pushed to his feet. At the wooden frame, he unbuckled the cuffs secured about the woman's wrists. As her body fell forward, she struck out a hand to support herself.

Looking down at her, Chase realised he felt little toward the woman. Little empathy for the redness circling her arms. Certainly very few fucks, if any, about whether or not she'd even orgasmed.

He was tired of it all, he realised with a frown. Or maybe he was just tired of himself.

Either way, as he gathered her into his arms and carried her toward the private bathroom in there, he already knew the woman had run her course.

"I've been looking for you everywhere."

Raelyn's voice penetrated the foggy steam, and Chase turned toward the panel separating them. Through the obscured glass, he could make out her form on the other side.

"Just needed a quick shower," he told her. Mostly because he hadn't bothered undressing to go palm his cock. He hadn't even bothered trying to catch the cum he'd shot, which had left him making a break for the showers via the laundry chute before either of the girls could spot him.

"Hmmm." The utterance sounded like she knew exactly what he'd been up to, even if she didn't know where. "Well, your early bird client just showed up early again."

Chase rubbed at the glass and cleared a circle to peer through. "Who?"

"Ms O'Shay."

He knocked the shower off and stepped from the enclosure.

"Yeah, I figured that'd get you moving."

She turned away, the ponytail she'd pulled her raven hair into swinging aside, and Chase grabbed for the towel.

"You want her in your office again?" she asked as she walked away.

A simple sentence, but one that set his cock stirring again. Rubbing at it a little too hard with the towel, he told her, "Keep her out in reception. I'll get her when I'm ready." At least that way, he couldn't be set off kilter when she sent one of her intense stares his way. That way, he'd be the one in control.

Glancing back, she offered another, "Hmmm," before vanishing around the corner and leaving him alone.

Sometimes, he hated how easily she and Sam could read him.

~

B ack in his office, Chase swung open the door to reception. Usually, his attention went straight to his team, but he couldn't help the quick glance toward the visitor seat first.

Sat upright, body tense, Abi O'Shay stared down toward knees lifted by the pointed positioning of her toes against the floor. Just as when he'd first met her the week before, she seemed completely withdrawn into herself and one-hundred percent unaware of his presence.

Chase wished he could say the same in return.

An embroidered cotton skirt covered her lap in peach, to just below her knees. Beneath that, legs that begged to be stroked, made of creamy flesh Chase imagined to be soft and smooth beneath his palms. A simple white blouse dipped over her chest into a modest V, and she could hunch her torso as much as she liked, but Chase just knew a gorgeous pair of breasts hid beneath. Something he intended to discover for certain before his work with her was done.

Something he really shouldn't have been thinking at all about one of his clients.

Suddenly realising what he was really seeing, Chase frowned.

Abi O'Shay didn't wear a clinic robe. And she should have been. She was booked in for a practical session.

He cut his gaze across toward the curved desk, behind which sat Rae and Sam. Raising an eyebrow, he gave a tiny nod toward the client, but received only an equally tiny headshake from Sam in return.

Meaning Abi had declined the robe.

What else would she be declining? he wondered.

He turned back to her. "Abi?"

The young woman jerked in her seat as her head whipped around to face him.

Out the corner of his eye, he just caught Raelyn mouthing *Abi*, but Chase could only look at the uncertain smile Abi offered as her gaze landed on him. He didn't give a damn what the girls thought about his use of Abi's Christian name, anyway.

"Would you like to come in?" he asked her.

She didn't so much as nod as she pushed to her feet. He stepped back as she reached him, allowing her access, and sent a quick glance toward the desk, just catching Sam's mouthed, *See you soon*, before he closed the two of them inside.

"Take a seat," he offered.

As he'd done during their previous meet, he fetched over a wooden chair and set it down opposite the chaise, while she sat herself on the padded lounger.

Lowering his own butt down until at eye level with her, he asked, "How are you feeling today?"

She smiled in a way that it couldn't be counted as a smile. Gave a nod that couldn't class as a nod. "Okay."

"Have you thought about our last appointment much over the past week?"

"I have." Small answers. Small voice. Chase suspected

getting her to participate in any form over the next hour would be a challenge.

He stretched his fingers. Relaxed them again. "I obviously didn't scare you away, as you're here now."

Her smile seemed more genuine the second time. "You didn't scare me."

"But ...?"

She drew in a deep breath and slowly released it. "I think I'm probably more scared of myself."

Chase frowned. "In what way, Abi?"

She reached up and scratched at her head before tucking her hand into her lap. "Because I'm scared of this whole ..." She waved that same hand about. "I'm scared I might ..."

"Do it wrong? Mess up? This isn't a test."

She shook her head, and the beginning of a smile crept over Chase's face at the rush of blood across her cheeks.

"You're afraid you might like it?"

She dropped her gaze toward where she tapped a thumb and finger together atop her skirt.

"Please look at me, Abi."

She lifted her face, but didn't meet his eyes.

He ducked until he could see the startlingly pale blue of hers. "You enjoying today's session, or any of the following sessions, is actually the best case scenario."

Her brow scrunched a little, but she didn't argue.

"Okay?"

"Okay," she said quietly.

"Nobody is going to force you to do anything."

"Okay."

"You're totally in control of every session you attend here."

"Okay," she said again.

She sighed, and his gaze absorbed the movement of her chest for a moment, before skimming down the rest of her body to the emerald green, embroidered ballet pumps she wore on her feet. Although he could work out for himself that she'd remained in her own clothing as a result of her concerns, he still mentioned, "You declined the robe." Though a statement, it sounded more like a question.

She gave a small nod. "I just didn't feel ready to ... to be naked ... around strangers ... yet."

He offered a smile of reassurance. "That's perfectly acceptable."

"I wore a skirt, though." She flicked at its hem slightly. "In case I felt ready to ... you know."

In his mind, he rubbed his hands together like the horny bastard he was. In reality, he simply said, "That's a great attitude to step in here with, Abi. You're going to do just fine."

She let out a shaky laugh. "This feels so weird."

"What does?"

"Sitting here. In an office. Contemplating doing ... whatever it is I'm supposed to be doing ..."

He could understand it seeming so, if that was where her head had gone. Turning up to an office for an appointment, and sitting, twiddling with your cunt while being watched from the other side of the desk. "Not in here," he said to reassure her.

She finally met his gaze herself, a 'What?' balanced in the formation of her lips.

"The practical sessions aren't carried out in my office," he explained. "We have more natural settings available for those."

"Where are they?" she asked, glancing toward the door like she expected him to take her on a field trip.

"Right here. In our premises." He pointed a finger toward the floor. "How about I take you through to the room we'll be using today, so you understand a little better?"

At her small nod, he straightened to his feet and waved for her to follow him as he crossed the room toward one of the exits. Pushing through it took them into the corridor lined with doors. Bypassing the one Mr and Mrs T had used earlier, and a second, unmarked door, Chase led Abi to the third door on the left.

"Dark Room," Abi said, reading the gold-toned nameplate.

Smiling at her, Chase pressed down the handle and followed the door on its inward swing to step inside.

Within was lowlighted, making the circular bed in the centre of the room easily visible, as were the fur blankets draped over its mattress. Sam had selected those. Chase could still remember how pleased she'd been to show off the satiny softness of the silvery grey throws.

In a deep lilac that bordered on pale slate, the walls continued the mood of the room. Other than a dresser of drawers, hiding an array of accessories, and a rug before a fireplace, similar to those in the other bedroom, the Dark Room held no other furniture. Just an expansive gilt-framed mirror over the mantle.

"It's a bedroom," Abi said from beside him.

He smiled. "It is."

"I like the bed," she said, pointing a slender finger.

"That helps." He gestured for her to step forward, waiting until she'd neared the bed. "Please, take a seat."

She did as he asked, bouncing a little when her rear met the mattress. Smoothing her hands over the soft blanket, she gave a visible swallow.

"Before we go any further, I need to run through a few details," he said, waiting for her gaze to lift before he continued. "Your session here today will be observed ..."

"We'll be watched?" she asked.

"Not we." At her frown, he smiled. "Given your needs,"— which really meant *nerves*—"I'm going to have a female associate assist you for today. We'll evaluate the session once it's ended, and then we can assess what you're ready for when you arrive for your next appointment."

"Okay," she said quietly. "But you'll be watching?"

"I will be observing the session, yes. However, please don't worry, because there are options on offer to help put you more at ease. And you'll remain completely in control the entire time. You won't be pushed to do something that makes you uncomfortable." Waiting for her nod of acknowledgement, he said, "I'm going to let Samantha in now. Don't be nervous. You've already met her."

Knowing she'd be there on cue, Chase crossed the room and opened the door to admit Sam. Dressed in a sixties-style A-line dress, she bobbed into the room with her blonde hair swaying, the picture of fun that Chase knew she could be.

"Don't look so nervous," she said Abi's way. "We're going to have a good time."

Abi just stared at her, and Sam laughed.

"Trust me. We'll treat it like a girls' sleepover."

"I've never been on a sleepover," Abi said, those lines showing across her brow once more.

"Well, you have some catching up to do, then." Sam glanced toward Chase. "No guys allowed at our sleepover. Sorry."

"I can take a hint," he said, turning to Abi. "Any questions before I go?"

She shook her head.

"Then, I'll be right next door. Any time you feel too uncomfortable to continue, all you have to do is say, and we can terminate the session. Otherwise, I'll see you once you've finished."

"Thank you, Mr Walker."

His mind absorbed her quiet politeness, as he headed out of the room and rounded to the next door along. Unmarked, unlike the others, it made no suggestion as to what lay within, and the small space was almost black when Chase stepped inside. He flicked on only enough light to navigate by, to avoid any glare hindering his observations.

Observations he had little doubt he'd take pleasure from. Especially if Abi ended up enjoying her session.

A wheeled, swivel stool sat in the centre of the room, enabling the seated to choose from both views on offer.

One wall supported a generous screen that showed almost the entire sex-themed bedroom they'd used earlier in the day. On the wall opposite, Sam sank down onto the bed next to Abi through the one-way window, disguised in the Dark Room as the mirror above the mantel.

Easing his butt onto the stool, Chase flicked a few switches, bringing more illumination into the room as screens came to life over the end wall. While the window allowed the prime view of the bed, its circular shape didn't always mean the clients took the position he needed them to, so he'd had the screens installed as backup. A way of gaining a three-sixty window from which to watch—no matter the lighting or darkness of the room.

"Do you know anything about sleepovers?"

At Sam's voice coming through the speakers, he turned back to the window as Abi shrugged.

"I watched *Grease*."

Sam smiled. "That's ... old school. The sleepovers I went to involved eating a whole lot of stuff we shouldn't have been eating, and talking about stuff we probably shouldn't have been talking about."

"Like sex?" Abi asked.

"Definitely sex. Mostly about words we'd heard, and what they meant, and how the acts they referred to could possibly be carried out. And we'd compare boobs and bums—" At Abi's horrified expression, she held up her hands, stifling a giggle. "Don't worry, we're not flashing each other today. I'm just going to guide you over the barrier of being able to touch yourself."

Her smile resettled before she continued. "I'm going to ask you to trust me. That I'm helping you, and there's no need for embarrassment between us two girls, and that this is an important bridge for you to cross. Can you do that for me?"

Though nerves lined her face, Abi nodded. "I'll try."

"Okay, then, we'll get started on that. Do you mind me sitting here next to you for this? If I'm right here, I can talk and show you through it, or we can sit on opposite sides of the bed, if you'd prefer? I'll just talk as I'm doing, and you can follow along."

"I think opposite ... seems less awkward."

"That's fine." Sam pushed up from the mattress. "You stay here, and I'll shimmy 'round to the other side."

Chase had to smile at the manoeuvre—it meant he still had Abi right opposite where he sat watching. Still had the best view in the house.

"Now, it's up to you, but you can either remove your skirt, or hike it up. Even just leave it where it is," Sam said as she repositioned herself with her back to Abi.

"Do I have to take off my underwear?"

"Not this time. A woman can still enjoy herself even with her clothes on. I'm going to show you that today."

Abi's shoulders relaxed a little. "Are you taking your skirt off?" she asked Sam, and Chase sat up straighter on the stool.

She was actually going to fucking play.

"Just hiking it up enough to be comfortable. That doesn't mean you have to," she added over her shoulder. "Do whatever feels best for you."

Abi released a heavy breath and nodded. "Okay."

"Good, so ... take a few deep breaths and shake off that tension ..."

Abi did as Sam had instructed, even stretched out her shoulders from side to side.

"And I want you to slide a hand beneath your skirt ..."

Sucking her bottom lip between her teeth, Abi slipped her right hand beneath the hem of her skirt.

"And you're going to slowly explore the shapes of the flesh you feel beneath the fabric with your fingers. Okay?"

Abi mumbled something that sounded like consent, her frown folding low as her arm lifted her skirt just enough for Chase to see the brush of her fingers between her thighs.

"Make sure your legs are parted enough so you're not struggling to reach," Sam said behind her, and Abi's knees spread as though controlled by the words.

A slow smile spread on Chase's face as he took in the creamy flesh hiding in the shadows. The tendons pulled taut along her inner thighs, like a couple of arrows pointing the way to the pale cotton of her underwear. Underwear she probed at with a look of utter concentration on her face.

"The flesh down there will feel almost like it's in two halves. You feel that?"

"Um-hmm."

At the base of where those two halves meet is your vagina. We're not going to be exploring that today. Instead, I want you to work your finger between those two halves. Just a little, so you can trace its seam."

Abi's lips parted, despite the creases across her brow deepening, and her breaths hastened, but more from concentration than pleasure, it seemed.

"Stop frowning," Sam said, like she knew, and Abi breathed out a quiet laugh.

"Who says I'm frowning?"

It was the closest thing to sass she'd shown, and Chase wanted to applaud her.

"I do," Sam said, smiling. "Now, relax."

"Relaxing," Abi muttered.

"Okay, I want you to slide your finger slowly upward until you reach your clitoris."

"What's a clitoris?" Abi asked.

"You'll know when you find it."

Leaning forward on the stool, Chase studied Abi's face. He didn't need to watch her fingers brushing over her folds. He wanted to see her expression when she realised she liked it.

As if in reward, her lips popped open as a whispered, "Oh," drifted out, and his cock swelled with pride.

"You there yet?" Sam asked.

"I'm there," she said, her voice soft.

"In case you haven't already figured it out, this beauty is a pleasure spot. Women can orgasm from playing with this tiny little thing alone."

"Okay," Aby breathed.

"I want you to try it. Flatten your fingertip over its peak and just move your hand in small circles."

Behind Abi, Sam's chin lifted a little as her elbow danced with each movement of her hand. She'd be wet, Chase knew. Wet and ready for release by the time she left the room.

Facing him, Abi stared down toward where her fingertips played across her clit, hiding her expression from him. As if she needed to *see*, her other hand bunched up her skirt hem and lifted it higher. Exposing her explorations. And the wet patch already formed on the fabric of her underwear.

A wet patch Chase really wanted to taste.

Fuck. He had to shove a hand into his shorts and adjust his cock from seeing that alone.

"How does that feel?" Sam asked.

At Abi's quiet, "Okay," Chase grinned as he tucked his shirt back in.

Her shoulders had relaxed into her toying. Her chest fluttered up and down with her breaths. And her fingers prodded at that nub of hers in firmer motions than she'd started with.

All evidence that it felt more than okay.

"When you're with a man, they nearly always reach for this spot to pleasure a woman," Sam said into the quiet. "But a woman can get pleasure from it while barely touching it at all."

Abi didn't bother with a response beyond a slight tilt of her head in Sam's direction.

"If you lie back on the bed, I can show you how," Sam offered.

Chase held his breath. Stared hard at the way Abi's shoulders stiffened at the suggestion. The way her fingers quit moving. As her face lifted, he could see the pink flush heating her cheeks. More evidence of her arousal.

Surprising the hell out of him, she kicked off her shoes, shifted her sweet little arse back on the bed, and sank her back down to meet the mattress.

She didn't lift her head as Sam stood and rounded the bed, but a quick check on one of the monitors showed her gaze shifting to the side and tracking the path of the other woman.

Reaching where Abi's legs overhung the bed, Sam lowered to her knees. "Shimmy back a little further." Waiting until Abi had done so, she took each of her shins and lifted Abi's legs until her knees had bent, placing her feet on the edge of the mattress. "Okay, relax your knees to the sides, but stop before it becomes uncomfortable."

"Like at the doctor's surgery," Abi said.

"Exactly like that, but without the embarrassment."

Her knees dropped as directed, and her skirt slipped over her thighs until Chase had a really fucking great view of her covered pussy.

"Now, find that sweet spot again," Sam instructed, waiting as

Abi slipped her finger against her folds and guided it upward toward her clitoris.

"Got it."

"Okay, I want you to take your finger a little higher, until just above that spot …"

Abi's finger swept a little higher. "Here?"

"You'll know if you're in the right place once you start," Sam said. "So, twist your hand around until your fingertips are pointing downward toward the new spot." Once Abi had done that, she continued, "And holding all of the fingers of your hand together, I want you to almost undulate them, like a wave, until the tips of your fingers press down on that spot. How much pressure you apply depends on how much *you* like, so just practice a moment."

Her first attempt seemed a little clunky, as if she was thinking too hard about it, and Chase almost wanted to go back in there, brush her hair away from her face. Help her to un-tense those muscles he could see starting to tighten again.

"Relax. Just let your fingers do their deal. Try again."

The joints of her hand only slightly looser, she tried pressing down a second time.

"How does that feel?"

Abi shifted on the bed. "I'm not sure."

"Would you feel more comfortable if I left you alone to try this?"

"I might," Abi said. "You're making me feel really self-conscious sitting down there."

Sam let out a low laugh. "I hear you."

As Sam pushed up from the floor, Abi's hand shifted away from her groin, and she lifted her head that time, following the movements of the other woman.

"I can dim the lights, make it feel more private, if you think that will help you concentrate." Pausing at the door, Sam glanced back, and Abi gave a small nod. "How dark do you like to go?"

Of course, Chase's dick took the question to a whole different level.

"As dark as they can?" Abi said, sounding unsure.

"Okay, well, I'll leave you alone for a little while, but I'll be back once you've finished to see how you got on."

With a tug on the door, Sam stepped from the room.

As soon as the door closed on her again, Abi's head dropped back to the bed. About the only body part moving, aside from her blinking eyes.

Yes, Chase knew she wanted the lights dropped. And that he should've given that request already. A part of him, though—the part that had him staring hard through the hidden window like he could control her actions—really hoped she'd be bold enough to restart without the cover of dark.

The door to the observation room clicked open and Sam invaded the moment, her gaze instantly flicking toward the room on the other side of the wall. "What are you waiting for? Dim the lights, *Mr Walker*."

He reached for a dial, and his slow turn of it created a graduated loss of light in the bedroom. "You could have gone for a break," he said casually. "I could have manned in here until she's done." What he really wanted was to tell Sam to fuck off and leave him to his most-probably-creepy observations.

"I want to watch," she said simply, before pressing a button and leaning in toward a mic. "Say when it's dark enough."

Her voice spilled through into the room Abi occupied, and the girl lifted her head for a moment before lowering it back to the bed.

The room grew as dark as a bedroom with regular curtains shielding its windows. Only once it reached severe blackout stage did Abi's voice call out an okay.

Beside the dimmer dial was a button marked N.V., and Chase depressed it with his finger, switching all cameras and the viewing window into night vision mode. No matter how more secluded and private the clients might feel their sessions were, it was just an illusion. Those on the other side of the glass could always see.

For a long few moments, Abi didn't move, aside from the rise and fall of her chest. almost as if she tried adjusting to the lack of light.

Or as if she'd lost her steel.

"Think she'll continue?" Sam asked, coming to stand beside him.

He leaned forward over the control board, taking him closer to the glass. "I don't know. I hope so."

"I'll bet." Sam's shoulders straightened as soon as she'd uttered the words, and she leaned in almost as far as Chase. "Oh, hello."

Yeah, Chase had caught it, too. The almost subtle flickering of Abi's fingers over her clit.

"I just won me twenty quid," Sam said.

Chase frowned. "You bet on Abi?"

"Yep."

"You're sick, you know that?"

"Says the guys who's probably been hard since the second he stepped in here."

"You can be quiet now." His voice came out a low rumble.

No way would he admit to her that she'd been right. He had been hard. Hell, he'd gotten hard most nights over the past week, just thinking about the session and what it might bring.

And as Abi massaged her fingertips across where she looked to be already swollen, his cock shot to its feet and waved all the fucking banners.

Like a couple of scientists spying on a specimen, the two of them watched in silence for a while, as Abi once more tested the undulation of her fingers against her fleshy mound. As she probed around and traced the seam of her cunt.

When her fingertips reached the pooling of her juices across her underwear, she brought her hand away and stared toward it, like she might see what the fuck she'd found down there through the darkness.

She didn't keep her hand away long, but placed it right back down there. No hesitation. And Chase knew she was starting to like it.

So did his cock. And his balls. And the part of his head that got a high from knowing they'd brought her to that point, the part that buzzed harder with some weird kind of static the more he watched.

Pushing off the stool, he nudged it away. Taking himself closer. About as close as he could get without pressing his damn nose to the glass.

He knew when she'd hit the right spot for her when she sucked in a quiet breath and shifted her legs against the soft throw. Spreading those thighs wider. The muscles of her cute ass tightening and lifting her into her ministrations.

He also knew when she'd found a rhythm that worked for her by the tightening of the tendons in her forearm, and the dipping of her chin as all the muscles in her body coiled into the mode of working together for a common goal.

"That's right, you've got this," Sam whispered beside him.

Reminding him that he wasn't alone as his hard cock skimmed against the lip of the control board he leaned into.

The fingers of Abi's free hand curled over until she gripped a wedge of the silky throw. Her head tipped upward, chased by the arching of her spine.

"She's close," Sam said.

Chase turned away from her. Stepped across to the screens.

He didn't need to see her body twisting with pleasure, or her fingers going crazy across her cunt.

No, Chase wanted to see her expression. He wanted to *know* her pleasure the moment she experienced it.

Screen three showed her face. The wideness of her eyes as if she was caught up in the shock of what her body could offer. The rigid roundness of her mouth as her chest rose and fell faster with her shortened breaths.

Fuck, that mouth. Just something about that mouth made him want to—

"God, she's a beautiful comer," Sam said, her shoulder brushing his. "Isn't she?"

Yes, she was. Even with the tension pulling at her features, as she concentrated probably harder than she'd ever concentrated before. And definitely with the way her pale hair splayed about the innocence radiating from that heart-shaped face of hers.

Chase had no intention of voicing that opinion, though.

"I bet you have a right boner right now." Sam's hand brushed over his pelvis, but he jerked his hips away from her.

"Fuck off, Sam."

"I'll bet your balls are all tight. Want me to help with that?"

He sidestepped again at her second grab for him. "Touch me again, and you're fired."

"You won't fire me. You need me."

"Yeah, about as much as I need a wasp sting in my fucking ear."

"You're such a bitch when you're horny." She folded her arms and turned back to the screens, as Abi's breaths grew faster still and tiny moans began spilling from her mouth. "Why don't you just find a pretty lady to fuck and get it out of your system? When are you going to quit torturing yourself?"

"When are you and Rae going to realise you're the perfect

match for each other and quit screwing any cock with attitude that walks your way?"

He heard the pop of her lips opening, and smiled to himself when no words followed. Thankful for the moment's quiet, he zoned in on the whimper that flew from Abi's mouth, and the way her body began curling back in on itself.

As a round of judders wracked her slender frame, her long, low groan broke free and killed the otherwise quiet of the viewing room, before her body suddenly stilled.

With her hand still pressed against her cunt, Abi lay there, her shoulders slowly sinking back toward the bed, her knees once more relaxing to the sides. Her breaths continued to rush from her, as she stared toward the ceiling, and Chase couldn't tell if she was basking in the afterglow, or feeling horrified by what the fuck she'd just done.

Allowing her a few more minutes to steady her breaths, Chase waited until she'd slid her fingers away from her clit and began pushing up from her rigid position before nodding to Sam. "Time to head back in and work your girly magic."

She turned for the door. "You're a dick."

"Doesn't matter," he said, gaze trained wholly on Abi. "You still love me."

"Jerk," she muttered, and pushed outside.

In his office, Abi sat before him, her eyes downcast and her hands in her lap. The high colour of desire no longer tinted her cheeks, only that of embarrassment having taken its place. She obviously had no intention of kick-starting the after-talk. She'd only responded with body language since she'd accepted his offer to step into the room.

"How did you feel today's session went?" Chase asked after almost a minute of quiet.

She shrugged, those slender shoulders sliding the fabric of her blouse over her breasts.

Chase ordered his focus away from the peaks of those mounds. Away from the rosy-pink nipples suddenly invading his brain. "Would you like to know how I think today's session went?"

The twitch of her shoulders told him she'd considered shrugging again, but then a quiet, "Okay," whispered past her lips.

He leaned forward until his elbows supported him atop his knees, taking his face within a foot of where she dipped hers. "I think you did great."

He waited, and as he'd hoped, her head slowly lifted, her gaze along with it, and as she met his stare head on, her eyebrows made a gentle journey upward. "Really?"

"Really." He smiled. "You were open to instruction, to trying something new. You accepted Samantha's assistance with dignity and grace, and you were ..." *Beautiful in ecstatic repose ...* "successful. You were successful, Abi."

"I did it right?" she asked.

"There isn't any right or wrong in this, as I already explained. It's merely about what *works* for you. Did you feel where you took today's session worked for you?"

Her cheeks lit up in a flash of purple, a horrified glint darkening her pale blues before she darted them away from him. A moment later, she seemed to compose herself, and although she didn't return his gaze once more, she nodded.

He hadn't really needed the confirmation, and maybe asking her for it made him a bastard, because anyone witnessing the way she'd pleasured herself would know she'd fucking enjoyed it. A lot. "I'm pleased you think so. You've taken a giant leap today, and I'm"—*really fucking happy I got to be a part of that* —"satisfied that you'll be ready to try the next stage of your plan, at your next appointment."

A stage that should involve no underwear. No messing about. Only a heap load of self-indulgence that would set his cock roaring.

That made his cock whimper at the thought alone.

He straightened on the chair and crossed his legs over the sick bastard in his pants.

"In the meantime, if you get any moments alone, at all ..."

"You want me to practice?" Her gaze shot back to his. "You want me to practice what I learned today?" Her voice held a quality of manic-ness, and Chase worried he'd scared her for a moment, until he registered the eagerness in the slight widening of her eyes, and the way her shoulders no longer shadowed her chest as it thrust into the light.

She fucking liked the idea of being ordered to play.

He fucking liked the idea of giving that order.

"Yes," he said. "That's exactly what I want you to do. Between now and next week, any time you have a moment of privacy, I want you to try what you've learned until you know the exact spot that brings you the fastest pleasure."

And he'd try not to spend the next week imagining her doing exactly that.

"Okay," she said, snapping him back to the moment, and he nodded like one of those dogs on the back shelves of cars.

"Good. Well." He shot to his feet. "I'll show you out, and they'll get you booked in at the front desk." He waved her forward, wanting her to hurry up.

Because the faster he got her out, the faster she'd rebook, and the faster he'd get those undies off her when she came back. Not him, personally. Just off. In general. Her sweet pussy peeking out and showing off just how much she really enjoyed discovering what her body could do.

He yanked the door open and stepped aside. "Until next week."

"Bye, Mr Walker." A small smile quirked her lips as she passed him, and he could've sworn her farewell held a massive dose of tease.

"Are we rebooking?" Rae asked from the desk.

Chase nodded as he watched the gentle swinging of Abi's skirt with each step she took. As he remembered exactly what that skirt covered. As his cock knocked on the door he'd done a good job of keeping closed through the entirety of her appointment.

"Bye, Abi," he said, shutting the door too fast so it banged into its frame. Chasing the barrier, he knocked his forehead against the wood. Closed his eyes. Tried to ignore the ache in his balls that felt like someone was twisting them all up in a knot. "Fuck." He butted the wood again. A third time. "Fuck, fuck, fuck."

He'd had sex machines and hot as hell women—and men— step through his doors over the past few years. He'd watched orgies, and kink galore, BDSM. Watched the fucking of mouths and cunts and anuses for hours on end.

And he'd retained his composure through each and every one of them.

Abi had merely touched herself and his brain felt scrambled. The innocent little baking-for-fun virgin would unravel him if he didn't get his shit together.

"Fuck," he muttered again, and head-butted the door once more for good measure.

The girls had gone home. Front entrance was locked. Lights had been dimmed.

Chase stood in his Toy Box for the second time that day.

Despite his raging hard-on, he hadn't undressed before letting himself inside.

He hadn't showered.

No, fully clothed, he stood staring down at the woman lying atop the cot, half on her front, half on her side, her breathing soft yet deep. The eye mask slipped to reveal long delicate lashes the same shade of reddish blonde as the hair splaying about her head. Her right breast gently hugging the thin mattress beneath.

Beautiful. She truly was.

Yet, she did shit for Chase, he realised in that moment. His already stiff cock should've been stirring at the sight of her. Should've been screaming like a fucking banshee to get out of his pants. And while it ached like a mofo, Chase already knew she'd never bring the relief it needed.

He just didn't want to address the reason behind that.

At fucking all.

His steps quiet, he retreated across the room to the small, usually-locked space that separated his Toy Box from the rest of the offices. At the far end, he pulled open one of the locker drawers and gathered up the pile of clothes in there. A handbag. A few pieces of jewellery. Stacking them over one arm, he carried them back through and planted them down on the cot near the woman's feet.

Leaning in, he placed a hand on her raised shoulder and gave a gentle shake.

It didn't take much for her stir, and she blinked up at him, her frown heavy across her brows. Probably because she'd never seen the room fully illuminated before, had never been woken that way by him before, and hadn't a clue what the hell was going on.

"Sir?" she asked quietly, blinking harder.

"Your belongings are at the end of the bed. We're going to get you dressed, and I've already arranged for you to be taken home."

He didn't wait to see her reaction. Or to hear any objection she might make. Just swung her legs around until she sat and started working underwear over each foot. As he drew the fabric close to her cunt, its glossy shine telling him how much she'd have appreciated a final pleasuring before departure, his balls tightened until painful, the desperation in his cock strong enough to make his legs want to limp.

He shook them off, though. He'd just have to tend them himself.

After assisting the woman with the last of her clothing and handing her the small pile of belongings, he guided her toward the exit and out into the entrance.

On the other side of the locked foyer doors, a shadowed figured stood beyond the broad panels of glass, one of which Chase swung open.

Dressed in a pressed suit, the guy waved for the woman to precede him, before sending Chase a nod.

Without moving away, Chase watched as they called the lift, as they stepped inside the brightly-lit cube, as the doors sucked closed on them and took them from sight—almost as if he needed to be sure that she left.

It was the first time since creating his private space that he'd let a Toy go before having a replacement lined up.

Definitely the first time he'd walked away from potential relief.

And there was absolutely no way he'd be analysing *that*.

EPISODE THREE

Hair a dark henna red, shoulders stiffly held back, and anxious eyes of dark amber aimed at him from amid coffee-toned skin, Jordan Ness sat on the chaise in Chase Walker's office in nothing but the clinic-provided robe and terry-cloth slippers. At least, that was the name she'd booked in under. If he listened to his staff, Raelyn and Samantha, she looked an awful lot like a certain celebrity who'd been avoiding the limelight a lot of late. One who'd early on earned a reputation for saying yes to any offer thrown at her and following through.

Of course, the couple of blocks of muscle, who accompanied her for each appointment and drowned the reception area chairs, didn't help with the assumption the two of them had drawn.

"Did you practice what we discussed last week?" Chase asked from behind his desk.

"I did, yes."

"And?"

Ms 'Ness' had visited CW Consult a fortnight before for assistance from Chase. After realising that she'd begun *watching* females a lot more than males, she found herself questioning her sexuality. In her words, she thought she might be *turning gay* after being a happy 'straight' for thirty-three and a half years. Especially as she hadn't been able to bring herself to sleep with any guys for over a month—which, apparently, wasn't like her, at all. Something his fellow staff agreed on.

At her first consultation, Chase had gotten the impression she'd expected him to be able to tell her either way with a single glance. It had taken an hour of patience to explain that sexuality wasn't as simple as that. And that people could often be attracted to more than one gender. They could also find beauty in a gender that was in no way sexually appealing to them.

So, she'd enlisted him: to help her discover whether her attraction to females was the 'real deal', or she was just having an enthusiastic appreciation for the appeal of the female body.

"I watched them," she said in answer to his question. "I watched them all, and when I finished with them, I *bought* some more."

Or had someone go out and buy them for you, Chase thought.

DVD's. Chase had given her three DVD's of light lesbian porn to study during her two week break between appointments. The non-sleezy variety.

"How did you find them?" he asked, resting his forearms on the desk.

She sighed, the gesture ending on a smile. "Hot."

"Anybody can find porn *hot*, Ms Ness. How did your body react to them—how did you find *yourself* reacting to them?"

"I masturbated," she said, matter-of-fact. "A lot."

"No feelings of guilt? Deprecating self-worth?"

"None. Not even in the slightest."

"Did you use a vibrator?"

She nodded. "Yes."

"Should you not consider, in that case, that watching them made you crave a man, rather than the women the porn made you fantasise about?"

"I didn't insert the vibrator," she said, her smile smug like she'd just won a round against an adversary. "I used it for stimulation only."

"So, how *did* watching lesbians in sexual situations make you feel?" he asked.

"Satisfied." Her smile broadened. "And eager to watch another." Her eyebrows twitched upward. "Horny as hell."

"And have you been involved in any sexual encounters with a woman, or women, since I last saw you?"

The confidence in her stare lessened a little as she shook her head. "No."

"What about men?"

"A couple of guys have tried." She shrugged, meeting his gaze again. "I wasn't into it."

"Okay." Pushing up from his chair, he rounded the desk to the other side and propped a butt cheek against its top. "Do you remember what we said this week's session might involve, on the grounds of your homework being a success?"

Her smile grew crooked. Possibly a little sordid, too. "Of course I do."

"And are you happy to proceed with the pre-discussed exercise?"

"Of course I am."

"Maybe you'd like to follow me, then."

She all but sprang from the seat in Chase's direction, and he had to contain his laugh. God, he fucking loved an enthusiastic client. Almost as much as he loved ones with barriers to break through.

One of the doors leading out of his office took them to a corridor and more doors. Chase pushed through the first on the left, into the room full of sensual promise and toys for almost every occasion.

The usual bronze bedcovering in the sex-themed bedroom had been switched out for a gold one that matched the drapes and accented the caramel walls. As did the distressed drawers that held sex toys aplenty. Facing the bed, the fireplace overlooking a shaggy rug remained unlit, while the antique replica sex chair in the corner of the room still made a formidable statement, even though shadows hugged it.

The client stilled beside him as her gaze traced every item in there. "Wow."

"This is where today's session will be carried out."

She blew out a slow breath and nodded. "Okay. Nothing like my room at home, but ... okay."

"If you'd like to take a seat?" He indicated a soft, armless chair that'd been placed in there earlier, and as Ms Ness lowered herself into it, Chase took a pew on the end of the bed facing her. "There are a few important points to run through before the session begins." He waited for her nod before continuing. "The session will be carried out by two females. How much you participate in the activities is entirely up to you. Whether, or not, you remove your robe is entirely up to you. And how you decide to let the two women know how much you want to participate is entirely up to you."

"That last bit's unclear," she said.

Pressing his fingertips together, he leaned in toward her. "Well, you can either specify anything you would like them to do, or you would like to do, as and when you want it to happen. Or, if you're uncomfortable with making a bold request ... you can agree on a safe word. What this means is that everyone within the room will act on instinct, but if anything happens that you're uncomfortable with, or you sense something is about to happen that makes you feel unsure, then speaking the safe word will end any activity, unless you give the okay for it to continue."

"Okay, got it."

"However, if you decide to use a safe word, rather than verbal prompting, throughout the activity, you must specify as such, as well as your consent to it, at the beginning of the session."

"For legal reasons," she said, and Chase nodded.

"Yes, for legal reasons. It's often best to choose a word that wouldn't ordinarily come up, at all or for any reason, during a sexual encounter. So, calling out something like *breast* or *finger* might be misconstrued, and so could be ineffective. Something mundane and completely non-sex-related is always best."

"Right," she said. "Any suggestions?"

Chase shrugged. "Something simple like a bug, or a car brand?"

"Bug ..." She shuddered. "Ugh, yeah, but no."

He smiled. "Any nerves, at all, before we start?"

"I can't tell," she said. "I feel jittery, but I'm ... excited. I think."

"You can feel nervous and excited at the same time."

"I guess." Nodding, she glanced about the room as if wondering when the hell things were going to get moving.

Chase was more than capable of getting the message: He wasn't what she'd come for. "Okay, so ... do you want me to stay for the session? If I stay, I'll be tucked away over in the corner where you'll barely notice me." He pointed toward the red stool stuck in the darkened corner behind her. "Or I can leave the room and give you more privacy."

"But you'll be watching, either way?" she asked.

"It's policy here for all practical sessions to be observed, to protect both the client and staff, so yes, I will be watching."

"In that case, I'll go with the privacy."

"Not a problem." He pushed up from the bed. "If you'd like to make yourself comfortable, I'll send in the ladies who'll be leading the session."

She blew out a breath, sinking back into her seat, as Chase made for the exit and slipped outside.

Raelyn stood in the corridor, just to the right of the door, a second woman at her side. Fawn. She worked for an agency—one Chase happened to be well acquainted with—and when Chase had called the woman in charge with a request, she'd told him she knew exactly who send.

Rae's long dark hair had been pulled out of its usual pony-tail and spilled over her back, her smoky-grey eye-makeup accentuating her hazel irises. Beside her, Fawn's hair almost matched Rae's in shade, but her indigo blue eyes made him wonder about a dye job. Not that it mattered. They were both semi-tall. Both curved in all the right places. And, dressed simi-larly in little black dresses and no shoes—probably no under-wear, too—they matched the description of Ms Ness's preference Chase had jotted down during a previous appointment.

"You ladies ready?" he asked once he'd checked them over.

"You betcha," Rae answered, to Fawn's, "Good to go."

"I'll be watching." He reached for the handle of the next door along. "Ask her for the safe word. I think that's how she's swaying."

"Will do," Rae said, and as she tugged down the handle into the bedroom, he stepped inside the observation space.

Flicking on low lighting as he went, he crossed between the large screen on one wall and the window into the other bedroom on the other wall. Pausing at a control panel, he clicked a few switches, and the screen popped to life with a huge image of Rae shutting herself and Fawn inside the room with the client.

Pressing a few more options, he split-screened the room so he could view both the bed and Ms Ness's position side by side.

"Hi, my name's Rae ..."

"We've met," the client said, which they had. Rae manned the front desk whenever her assistance wasn't needed during a session, so pretty much every client who visited for the services of CW Consult knew her face.

Rae nodded to her companion. "And this is Fawn. Our job is to try establishing a connection between your own desires and the sexuality of females when placed together in a situation such as the one that will be occurring here today. Did Mr Walker explain how this session will play out?"

"I'm aware of the plan, yes."

"Okay, so, are we working with a safe word? Or do you have—"

"Trifle," Ms Ness cut in, and Raelyn's eyebrows arched.

"Trifle?"

The client shrugged. "I bloody hate the stuff. Figured it'd make as good a safe word as any."

Rae smiled. "Trifle it is, then. Are you ready to commence?"

"I'm ready."

Rae paused, almost as if she studied her to make sure of that statement and only moved on once satisfied. Crossing the room, she headed for the wall switches, and a twist of the dials lowered the lighting to something more comfortable. More intimate in tone. As she turned back, her gaze didn't swing as far as Ms Ness, but settled on Fawn. And the smile she gave promised of goodness. And badness. And everything in between.

Like she'd suddenly been put on a stage in a men's club, Rae swung those hips of hers in the other woman's direction. Fawn watched every step, her chin jerking high, as if giving the order to approach. As Rae reached out, Fawn's lips had already parted. Her tongue already scraped across her upper teeth.

Taking Fawn by the hip, Rae pulled her toward herself, drove the fingers of her free hand up into Fawn's trailing hair. A good few inches taller, Rae tugged back Fawn's head before melding their lips together in a kiss that was as possessive as it was sensual.

Lips breaking apart until only their noses touched, Rae brushed a hand across Fawn's back. A moment later, she guided the zip of her dress all the way down and spread the rear of the garment into two halves, exposing the upper hills of Fawn's ass.

With little warning, Rae grabbed hold of Fawn's hair again, and reclaimed her mouth with heightened hunger. While holding her in place, she worked one strap of the dress from a shoulder, before switching hands and doing the same with the other.

The dress sagged only as far as where Fawn's chest bumped upward with each of her breaths, and Rae slipped a hand inside, pushed the dress down further. Putting on display a real pretty pair of breasts with rosebud nipples.

Reaching behind himself, Chase gripped the edge of the stool and rolled it closer to the screen. As he propped his butt up onto the seat and got comfortable for the show, the dress slid the rest of the way down until it pooled around Fawn's feet, and Chase had to take a moment to admire the beauty of the body it exposed.

Dipped waist. Breasts lush and plump without being too large. Soft rounded hips, and legs toned to a firm finish without appearing muscular.

No wonder his contact had set a high price for her.

Dipping her face, Rae drew one of those pert nipples into her mouth, and Fawn's body swayed into the action, her lips parting on a sigh. An arm around Fawn's back held her securely into Rae's lapping as she tongued the stiff flesh. Giving a low groan, Fawn gripped onto Rae's shoulders, as she brushed her attention over to the other breast.

Chase checked the image on the left of the screen. Of Ms Ness. The rapt way she stared toward where Rae drew that nipple into her mouth, then licked, drew it in then licked. He smiled when she fidgeted in her seat a little.

Movement from the girls drew his gaze back, as Rae swung Fawn toward the bed, kicked her legs back against the mattress, bent over the other woman's body until she had little choice but to sink backward and let the downy blankets catch her fall. Taking a moment to spread the woman's thighs wide, Rae stepped back away from her. A smile curved her lips as her gaze dropped toward the junction of Fawn's thighs, and reaching behind herself, she peeled down the zip of her own dress and shrugged it from her shoulders.

Although her back was to the client, Rae twisted far enough to stare back at her over her shoulder as she shimmied the black fabric over her torso, her waist. Putting her curvy ass on display as the dress floated down over her legs to the floor. "Like what you see?" she asked, her smile bordering on devilish.

"Yes," the client said. A simple response betrayed by the softening of her voice.

Glancing away, Rae approached the bed once more and sat in a coquettish pose beside Fawn's spread legs so she half faced Ms Ness. With her stare fixed back on the client, she slowly feathered a hand the length of Fawn's inner thigh, all the way up to where her cunt all but contracted for just a touch.

Without penetration, Rae continued her journey straight over that glossy pool and traced the seam of flesh, flicking over Fawn's clitoris and bringing her fingers to her mouth. Sucking over them with her lips, she closed her eyes, let out a low hum, her gaze going right back to Ms Ness when her lids lifted again.

Retaining that eye contact, Rae slipped a hand around the

knee beside her and, lifting Fawn's leg, hooked it over her lap. Putting that juicy cunt on even greater display. Like a fucking offering. Hell, it almost tempted Chase, so it had to be doing something for the client.

Leaning into her arm turned Rae's body closer to Fawn and farther from Ms Ness, but, lips parted, she glanced back over at the client as she took those fingers of hers straight back to Fawn's cunt and slipped the first finger inside. The other woman lifted her hips into the insertion. A quiet moan escaped. Followed by more small sounds of pleasure, more chasing of hips as Rae slowly withdrew then slid back in again with two fingers. Withdrew and glided back in with three fingers.

Pushing up until her elbows propped her, Fawn swept her gaze from where Rae finger fucked her in what had to be agonising slowness, to where Ms Ness stared between the two women and the ministrations happening before her. Like she didn't know where to look yet wanted to look everywhere at the same time.

As Chase studied the client, he noted the early hazing of her eyes that came with any sexual arousal. The way she straightened slightly in her seat, the movement brushing her thighs together. Probably a purposeful act. Her tongue dented just the inside of her cheek as she prodded there, almost a conscious action, as if to make herself more appealing to those she sought to bag.

Yeah, she liked what she saw. And she wanted what she saw. The biggest question was: would she take it?

Shifting her weight to one elbow, Fawn trailed a hand down her body, over her stomach, her pelvis, until her fingers curled around where Rae's pumped in and out of her. Until her own fingers where wet. Drawing them back again, she spread the seam of her flesh, exposing herself even further. Slathering that wetness all the way up to her clit, which she rolled between a finger and thumb before finding a rolling rhythm across it that her body seemed to like, judging by the way she ground into it and her breaths hastened.

"Faster."

At the breathy order from Fawn, Rae complied. Her hand drew back and drove back in, and the whimper she received told that Fawn approved. She drew out and back in again, her arm flexing as she quickly found a flow that had her palm slapping against Fawn's crotch each time she thrust into her. Her own breaths soon coming faster as she watched where Fawn's fingers danced in a frantic fashion across her clitoris.

Opposite them, Ms Ness clenched her hands in her lap. The knuckles whitening. Her entire body rigidly tense, as though she worried a single movement might make the mirage of her fantasies disappear.

A long drone of a cry came from Fawn. Her fingers worked faster, harder, over her swollen peak. Rae's fingers slammed faster, harder into her.

At the pinnacle of climax, a sharp gasp blasted from Fawn and her body arched backward, her breasts thrusting up against the air, but her fingers continued strumming, Rae continued pounding into her, and as a wail announced her orgasm, her legs contracted, cum spilled from her cunt, and she shot out a hand to steady Rae's movements.

Chest heaving, she relaxed her spine, the muscles throughout her body visibly softening against the mattress. With a tug, she pulled Rae down to her, the hand she slipped into those dark strands bringing Rae's mouth to her own, and they kissed. Long and slow. Sensual and lazy. Their lips sliding across each other's. Melding into each other's. Fawn's tongue licking out as Rae drew away and turned toward Ms Ness.

Showtime.

Their movements languid, the two women rolled up from

the bed, their approach toward the seated client almost as lazy. Bending down had Rae's breasts swaying forward, and she reached for a hand and drew Ms Ness to her feet.

Slipping behind the client, Fawn brought her hands around and worked the tie of the robe she wore. Freeing it set the robe swinging open, displaying the tanned skin beneath, and Ms Ness's breasts trembled as their peaked nipples broke out of their confines.

Leaning in, Rae drew one of those stiff buds into her mouth, while Fawn slipped the robe from the client's shoulders. Switching screens, Chase watched how Ms Ness leaned into the caress. How her hand half lifted. Her fingers half curled. As if she wanted more but lacked the confidence for the request.

Taking her hand once more, Rae walked back and led Ms Ness with her. As her legs bumped the foot of the bed, she sank down and kicked back. Shuffled her butt over the blankets. Spreading her thighs wide created a gap, and she patted the bed between them. An invitation.

"Sit," Rae said, as if to eliminate doubt from the offer.

Ms Ness hesitated less than a second before spinning herself and parking her ass between Rae's legs. Rae's arms slipped around her waist as soon as she had, and she drew the other woman against her chest. Reached down farther and nudged at her thighs, until Ms Ness took the hint and parted them as far as Rae's own legs would allow.

Lifting her gaze, the client stared up at Fawn, questions in her eyes. What am I doing here? What the hell's going to happen?

Will I enjoy it as much as I hope?

Taking hold of the client's left leg, Fawn stretched it wider and hooked it over Rae's knee. She did the same with the other leg, before dropping to the carpet in front of the exposed crotch.

A quick flick of a switch gave Chase an angle his main

cameras couldn't catch, and yeah. As he'd suspected. The client's pussy sparkled with want.

Sticking with that angle, he watched as Fawn gripped hold beneath Ms Ness's thighs and tugged her forward until her ass hit the bed's edge. As if to test the reception, she brushed just her fingertips over the spilled wetness, and the client gave a quiet gasp, the sound forced like she'd held her breath for moments before it broke free.

Not bothering with any more preliminaries, Fawn dipped her head between the client's thighs and gave a long lick of her tongue over the glossy folds, before clamping her lips right over the clitoris in a way that had the client jerking against Rae.

Lifting her head only slightly, Fawn peered up at her. "You like?"

Ms Ness nodded. "Yes. Yes, I like."

Not another word needed, Fawn dived right back down and wrapped her mouth over the client's cunt.

Body sagging, almost in relief, Ms Ness let her head fall back, and Rae guided it to her shoulder, propping it there as her hand swept over the client's stomach, down lower, until she toyed where Fawn licked. As she feathered back over skin that had definitely been kissed by the sun, she detoured to a breast. Cupping it with a hand, she plucked at the hard nipple, and Ms Ness gave a low groan, arching up into the touch.

With Fawn lapping and suckling at her cunt, Rae stroking and teasing her flesh, it didn't take long for an already aroused Ms Ness to sink back against the supporting body completely. Head tipping to the side, she lazily reached up an arm and circled Rae's neck, drawing her lips down to her exposed throat. Giving a low grumble of satisfaction when Rae accepted the direction and sucked the skin there into her mouth. Her other hand, she allowed to creep the length of her body until her fingers brushed over Fawn's head and tangled in the looser strands at her crown, as she guided the other woman into the pattern of tonguing she obviously craved.

And any doubts Chase might have had about her full participation vanished in a beat.

Eyes drooped to half mast, lips almost swollen around the low moans drifting out between them, and her body undulating toward the caresses of the two women, Ms Ness couldn't have looked more contented. More at home. Like she'd finally found exactly what she'd been seeking and was only too happy to drown in the erotic reality of her fantasies.

Hell, it was a sight to watch. An honour to be able to watch. Because even though her face twisted with the concentration of female climax, even though her body contorted itself against Fawn's willing face, his client shone bright like a woman experiencing the best fucking moment of her life.

Chase knew when she drew close by the tightening of the muscles through her legs as her knees lifted and her toes flexed and her moans of pleasure deepened. As though she didn't want to break that spell, Rae quit with her explorations of her body and brought her hand to Ms Ness's breast. Gently rolled her nipple between her fingers before giving a slight tug. Repeated the movement. Growing faster.

And the client's entire body seemed to dance to her orgasm. Her hips rocked against Fawn's mouth. Her body bowed her breasts high into the air. Her hands slammed down to her sides and gripped at the bedding. Twisting the sheets into a knotted mess as her cries blasted through the speakers into the small room with Chase.

It had taken less than three minutes for Ms Ness to splash Fawn's face with cum.

For seconds following, she stayed there, supported by Rae, her eyes closed as her chest pumped high and low with her breaths. Lips gently nuzzling at the woman's jawline, Rae trailed her fingertips over her flesh in lazy circles, while Fawn pressed soft kisses along her inner thighs.

"More," she finally whispered, the request barely audibly over her breathing. "Let me give something in return."

Opening her eyes, she twisted in Rae's lap and pushed at her chest until Rae settled into her back. Ms Ness rolled onto her knees and hooked an arm beneath Rae's thighs. Encouraged her to move higher up the bed.

"Okay?" Rae asked, peering down at the woman.

Nodding, the woman swept her hair back from her shoulders and dipped her face to Rae's pussy. She gave only a few licks of her tongue to begin. As if unsure. As if testing what Rae liked, what she herself liked, but when Rae released a sigh, she lapped harder, delved deeper between the fleshy folds on offer with the stiff tip of her tongue.

The hesitation Chase had expected didn't show its face. Hell, even a lot of guys got intimidated about going down on a woman for the first time, but his client had dived right in there like she couldn't fucking wait to sample the goods.

Score for Ms Ness.

Wrapping an arm around each of Rae's hips, she slid her knees backward, until her body arced into where she tasted and her ass prodded high into the air. An invitation, if ever Chase had seen one.

Rather than give it to her as she seemed to want it, Fawn took hold of the client's hips and tugged her sideways. Lifting her face from Rae's crotch, she glanced back over her shoulder, as Fawn forced her onto her side. Frowned when she was pushed down onto the bed and onto her back. Reaching over, Fawn offered a hand to Rae and helped her to her knees, and as his assistant shuffled over the blanket toward where Ms Ness peered up at her, Chase had to wonder how the woman would cope with what he suspected they had in mind.

Again, though, she didn't flinch. Not once—as Rae brought those knees forward until either side of the client's head. As she leaned over Ms Ness's body and braced a hand beside her torso. As Rae lowered her cunt down to her face.

Stretching back and gripping Rae's hip, the woman drew her down closer and, opening her mouth wide, accepted the awaiting pussy between her lips.

Rae let out a sigh, her lids half lowering with that first pull on her sensitive nub.

Facing them both, Fawn lifted one of the client's leg and hooked it over her own, and she worked herself tighter into the junction of the woman's legs until their legs scissored each other's and their cunts met. Bracing herself on an elbow, she began a slow undulation of her hips, brushing her pussy across Ms Ness's, her clit across the solid tendon of the client's inner thigh.

A muffled moan came from between Rae's thighs, and it took only seconds for the woman's hips to start rocking in response to the pussy working at her folds. For her to bring her thighs in closer and hug the leg she brushed her clitoris against in search of joy.

For seconds, Chase watched them. Just observed. No analysis. He always found so much beauty in pleasure, whether that of his own or others, and he couldn't help but admire how sex performed in a way that was never truly intended could work so fucking well.

From a simple missionary position between man and woman, to orgies that debased and explored avenues never meant for sexual stimulation while offering arousal in its higher forms. The true evolution of man.

With her pussy being swallowed, her fist digging into the bed for support, Rae fondled the breasts the client pushed up toward her. Tugged at the stiff nipples as she ground her own hips, gave her own moans of pleasure.

With her face wholly occupied, her throat bobbing as she swallowed like crazy, Ms Ness grabbed at her other breast, tweaking and twisting, adding to her own pleasure as she fucked the hell out of Fawn's inner thigh.

Fingertips digging into the soft flesh of the client's hip, Fawn forced her to remain where she needed her as she stimulated herself against the ridge of the high junction, as her hips thrust forward and rolled back, as the wet sounds of two happy cunts colliding spilled out.

Absolutely. Fucking. Beautiful. A few more minutes, and there'd be a trifecta of fucking ecstasy.

With his cock as rock solid as it always got during a session, Chase shifted on his seat, unbuttoned his flies to let himself breath, and settled in for the rest of the show.

∼

Below Chase's office, a narrowboat created ripples through the River Thames as he took a much-needed break. Hands in pockets, he pressed his forehead to the window, the density of the glass preventing him hearing the engine of the vessel as it chugged away from the city.

He closed his eyes against the view, breathed in long and slow, his exhale just as regulated, and willed the remainder of his stiffy to take an epic walk in the other direction.

Mr and Mrs Miller had left from their latest appointment almost fifteen minutes earlier. His dick didn't run on any timescale but its own, though. Especially when Mr Miller had come in prepared for his attempt at communicating to his wife. Prepared with cuffs and feathers and body oil. And he'd shown his wife exactly what he'd wanted to do with them.

Chase would never have guessed the guy had it in him. The session had certainly left him shocked as hell.

Hard as hell, too.

Hence the need to calm his cock the fuck down.

The door to his office clicked open behind him, the quiet tap of heels coming no closer than the threshold. "You okay?"

Smiling, he pushed off from the window and turned toward Raelyn. "Peachy. What's up?" He knew he didn't have another appointment for at least twenty minutes yet.

"I need the bathroom." She jerked her head toward the reception behind her. "Watch the desk for me?"

Chase strode across the office toward the door she held open, already looking around her into the empty space. "Where's Sam?"

She rolled her eyes. "I already told you, Walker. She finally gave in and booked an eye test. Remember?"

He may have had a vague memory of her saying something to that effect. Himself saying something like *'Good—about bloody time.'*.

Grunting, he stepped around her into the fronting of C.W. Consult. "Go, then, while it's quiet."

Leaving the door of his office open, she took that route through to the staff's private area of the floor. An area equipped with lockers. A bathroom and shower. Viewing screens of most areas of the offices.

It also led to Chase's secret Toy Box he hadn't bothered to fill since he'd sent his last 'toy' home.

Cricking his neck, like that could banish his urge to give in to those particular needs, he made a lazy walk to the desk Rae and Sam usually sat behind when not assisting in client sessions. Sleek and elegant in design, the polished wood curved around the two chairs it obscured, with barely a sharp edge in sight. Chase pulled out the cushioned seat he knew Rae would've just vacated and sat his rear down in front of the screen she'd left active with an image of Tom Hardy.

Lips twitching, he reached for the mouse and clicked the image away, slid the cursor across the files listed on the left, and pulled the daily appointments spread up.

Four pm would be his next booking. He double-tapped there, and when his eyes scanned over the name of his next client, his nostrils flared on his inhale, his lips curving as he breathed out.

Abi.

Abi, whose session would be filled with her explorations of her body. Of letting go of her inhibitions as she owned a self-induced orgasm.

Hopefully.

Would she remove her underwear second time around? Hell, maybe she'd remove everything.

Aaaaand ... fuck his cock for getting all up in his face again.

The air-rush of a door opening had his spine snapping straight and his head flipping toward the entrance.

He sat frozen for a moment, as the young woman herself stepped through the glass partition. She stopped short as soon as her gaze landed on him.

He shot to his feet. "Abi ..." He ordered his arse back down again as soon as his cock banged to be let out.

"Mr Walker?" She took a few steps forward, a frown appearing as her gaze skimmed over the reception area. Probably looking for anyone but him. "I ... I wasn't expecting to find you ..."

"I'm just watching the desk for a few minutes." His hand slapped down on the desk like an exploded punctuation to the announcement, like he had no fucking control of his limbs on that side of his office door. "You're early." He frowned at himself. "Stupid thing to say. You're always early."

"I like to be on time."

She crossed the bridge dividing her from the desk until she stood directly across from him. Peering down. Making him peer up. Except her breasts expanded and retracted as she breathed, and he had a really hard time focussing on anywhere but those. So much so, it took him a few seconds to recognise the basket of nerves she'd carried in with her.

"Everything okay?" he asked.

Her fingers twitched, and she took a deep breath as if she needed to steel herself to share her thoughts. "I actually can't make today's appointment."

His frown crept back in as the disappointment slammed into him and his dick made a slow wilt south. "You can't?"

She shook her head. "My mother .... She's making me go me shopping for ...." She pinched the bridge of her nose, waved her arm back down to clasp hands.

Chase hadn't even seen her that agitated when she'd turned up there to masturbate for the first time in her life, and seeing her like that then, just over having to cancel on him, had his brows edging lower.

Her discomfort kicked up a notch as she twisted her hands together. "I have plans to fulfil for the ... wedding."

For some reason, her explanation felt unfinished. Like she had more to tell him. That time when Chase got to his feet, he didn't give a damn that his semi erection might be on show. "That's okay. We can just reschedule." He shuffled paper about on the desk like that'd solve the problem of her leaving in a few moments. Because his head really didn't like the idea of that happening. "Can you make it tomorrow?" he asked, already tapping at the screen with the mouse. "We can squeeze you in for five ..."

"I won't be coming back," she said quietly. "I—I can't come

back. I'm sorry, Mr Walker. I'm ..." She swayed on the spot, as if she didn't know whether to stay longer, or just go.

She went. Just turned away and went. Her feet like a Geisha's, as she speed-walked for the door, yanked it open like she had a fire up her arse, and swung herself out into the landing of the floor they occupied.

As soon as she vanished from sight, Chase's body jolted him out of whatever trance he'd been gawping from. "Shit."

He almost threw himself out from behind the desk and jogged for the exit. Hauling the glass panel inward, he searched the landing for her feminine frame and sent up a silent thanks when he spotted her over by the lifts, tapping her toes against the tiled floor.

On the wall above her, yellow lit the floor number on fire and a quiet ping sounded out.

His dive toward her was something fucking epic. "Abi, wait!"

Her entire body jerked at his shout, and as she turned toward him, the lift doors sliding open to accept her, she seemed poised to bolt and make a run for it.

He strode-jogged across the tiles, his hands held up in a plea for her to stay put. He quit a foot shy of a collision and danced back on his toes, his hands coming to rest at his hips as he let out a heavy breath. "You want to tell me what's going on?"

She hugged her arms across her chest. Covering what, only moments before, had done a decent job of distracting him, and he noticed for the first time the soft sweater she wore and the way it clung to every line of her body. The leggings the desk had hidden, which highlighted every curve of her legs.

He forced his focus to her face. "Look, shoot me if I'm wrong, but you don't look completely happy about cancelling your appointments with us." He sniffed in another breath, relaxed his shoulders. "So, do you want to talk about why you won't be coming back?"

Her eyes glanced away, then back to him. Even in the windowless foyer, the blue of them appeared as translucent as the ocean. "The thing is, I've been using my savings. To pay." She tapped her toes against the floor—something Chase had already begun recognizing as a nervous trait in her. "I had a trust fund that passed to me when I turned eighteen, and I've been saving it for ..." She shrugged. "I don't know. Something important."

"And this was important to you." He didn't ask it as a question, because the answer was obvious even before she confirmed with a nod of her head.

"If it wasn't, I would never have even considered something like this." Her face tilted up toward his. "No offense."

"None taken. But that still doesn't explain the cancellation."

She nodded again, her gaze dropping with the movement. "Mother opened my post."

Okay, they were getting somewhere.

"And my bank statement."

"Does she usually open your post?" Chase asked, frowning again, again, again.

She gave a half shrug, half nod. "I'm usually pretty good at intercepting it. But the postman was running late, and I'd already left for the bakery, and ..." She let out a weighted sigh. "She was there waiting for me on my lunchbreak, demanding to know how I'd managed to spend hundreds of pounds in just a couple of weeks."

"Is that really any of her business?"

"According to my mother, while I'm living under her roof, it is."

"Did you tell her the truth?" he asked, curiosity poking through the annoyance he felt on her behalf.

She laughed, but it sounded more sad than amused. "My mother isn't the kind of woman you can tell you're seeing a sex therapist and expect to stay on her Christmas card list."

"So you lied?"

The creases of her lingered smile ironed out as she nodded. "I lied. Outright lied. I told her I'd spent the money on a wedding gift for Michael."

"Sounds pretty close to the truth, to me," Chase said.

He patted himself on the back when another laugh blew free on her sigh.

"I guess it does," she admitted, sobering again as quickly as she had the first time. "But I still can't come back. Because if she sees another statement like this one, it won't be explained away quite so easily."

"And you can't use your income." Another statement—because no regular bakery would pay a wage to cover his fees.

She shook her head. "She'd still see, either way. And I'd still have to explain myself, and ..." Her gaze locked with his for a moment, as if she willed him to figure it out on his own and save her having to admit, yet again, that her parents ruled her life.

"Which is why you're not coming back?" he asked instead.

She gave another nod. Another dip of her chin. "I'm really sorry, Mr Walker. You have no idea how ... how ..." She flicked her fingers up as if searching the air for the word. "... *mature* I've felt since visiting with you here. But I ..." Her gaze lifted to his again. "I've got to go. Sorry. Bye, Mr Walker."

Not even bothering to recall the lift, she spun for the stairway door, pushed through, and vanished from sight.

It took all of Chase's willpower not to shoot after her again.

After ten minutes of Chase just standing there, just staring like an idiot at the door Abi had disappeared through, the reception door created a quiet *whoosh* sound behind him.

"There you are," Raelyn said at his rear. "What're you doing out here?"

He slowly turned toward her, but didn't meet her eye as he said, "Abi cancelled." He crossed the small landing and squeezed past her into their premises. "She's not coming back."

The statement gave him about three seconds' reprieve, before her heels tapped after him. "What do you mean, she's not coming back?"

"She's not coming back, Rae," he said again, still striding for his office—maybe saying it enough would help it sink in.

"Like, ever?" she asked.

Stopping at his door, he half-spun toward her. "Yes, Rae. Like, ever. She cancelled. We lost her. She's not coming back. That clear enough?"

"Yes, it's clear enough." She said it quietly, but more like she could gauge his mood than because he'd hurt her with his tone.

Drawing in a deep breath to balance himself, he asked, "Do we have any more clients today?"

"No, she was the last one," she said to his profile, and he nodded.

"Then, pack up for the evening. Collect Sam from the opticians, or wherever she's gone. We'll call it a day."

"You have the T's this evening." More words cautiously spoken. "Don't forget them. Jones will flip."

"I didn't forget." At least, he hadn't—up until the point Abi O'Shay had walked in and blew him off kilter.

Though, why the fuck should he care that he'd lost her. As a client. Every client left eventually. None of them stayed forever.

He hated that her dismissal stung more.

Maybe The Club was exactly what he needed to shake his arse out of the funk it'd climbed into.

"Are you going tonight?" he asked, finally bringing his gaze around until he could see her.

"Maybe. Depends on our mood later."

Of course she and Samantha would only consider it as a package deal. They always did.

Giving her a nod, he turned for his office. "Go on home, Rae," he said, and as he marched into his own space, he felt certain The Club would knock some of his shit into place.

The Club could make a person forget their own name.

~

C hase didn't want to think about Abi O'Shay. He didn't want to think about how disturbed she'd seemed on finding him behind the desk, instead of Rae or Sam. Or how distressed she'd seemed when she'd turned away from him and done a runner.

Or how perfectly her sweater and leggings had moulded to her body.

He definitely didn't want to think about losing her. As a client. Only as a client. Because she wasn't actually his. Never was. Never would've been.

Instead, he forced his mind into the moment. Blanked out the flash of pale, pale eyes that stared out at him from his mind. And forced himself to act happy to see Mr and Mrs T, as they stepped from the rear of a black vehicle with rear-tinted windows—one of The Club's.

Smoothing her dress over her legs, Mrs T made a scan of her surroundings, her eyes full of an uncertainty Chase understood.

"Not what you were expecting?" he asked her, as her husband rounded the vehicle to where they both stood.

"Not exactly," he said, placing a hand against the small of her back.

Cracked concrete supported their feet, made darker by an earlier rainfall, while warehouses bathed them in shadows. Not one of the buildings showed activity. Nor light. At least they all had their windows intact and didn't look derelict, or like they'd be full of vermin. A couple of them, Chase knew to be active during the day. Others were waiting for their leases to be snatched up, but at the rates the owner charged, he doubted they would be in the immediate future.

"Come on." Turning toward the one directly behind him, he motioned for the couple to follow. "And don't worry. This is merely a façade."

Mrs T's heels seemed loud against the empty ground space, as the couple fell into step beside him, and Chase had to smile at the effort they'd put in. With her hair pinned like she'd had it specially styled, Mrs T wore a pale evening gown that draped low over each shoulder and cinched her waist. Equally as well turned out, her husband wore his dark suit and bowtie well, the cut of the fabric to the standards of a reputable tailor.

"How are you both feeling about this evening?" he asked, as he brought them to a pause before a corrugated door. "Nervous?"

"A little," Mrs T admitted.

"But mostly excited," Mr T added, and his wife nodded.

"Good," Chase said. "You should be both." He knocked a hand against the metal, creating a resonant boom throughout the building.

Little noise beyond a quiet shuffle came from the other side of the door before it groaned open. In the created gap stood the equivalent of Gibraltar Rock. In a suit. One that barely fit, while fitting everywhere perfectly at the same time.

"Do you have a key?" Even the voice that came from the rock sounded like an earthquake.

"The key is to a door to a curious world, where curiosity never kills the cat," Chase said in a serious tone.

"Name?" he asked, equally as rough and rumbly,

Despite knowing the bouncer would recognise him on sight, Chase still answered, "Walker plus two guests."

"Guest names?"

"Titcomb and Titcomb."

The tower of muscle stepped back, his chest puffed out as he permitted them entry, and Chase took the lead past him and into the dark space within.

The door groaned just as loudly as it closed, and the four of them would've been in total darkness if not for a flicker of light off to the right.

"Follow the torch," commanded what had become a mountain of shadow in the darkness.

Reaching out, he felt for Mrs T's hand and clasped on. "Don't get lost," he warned and guided them toward where the wall-mounted firelight beckoned them forth.

As they neared, the shape of a cloaked figure stepped from the wall, the blackness of the fabric matching the shade of the mask covering what had to be a woman's face, if the frame of the body was anything to go by. She didn't speak. Just turned and walked away.

At Mr and Mrs T's glances of confusion, he gave a reassuring nod. He already knew they were expected to follow, and so fell into step behind the swish of the floor-long cape.

Lifting a hand, the figure paused them all before a blockage. A moment later, a metallic screech sounded out as the panel holding them back worked free, and a second cloaked and masked figure stood waiting to greet them.

Without a word, Chase stepped through the next section of their route, a flicker of his fingers beckoning for the trailing couple to do the same, and as the metal squealed shut behind them, he awaited instruction.

"Welcome to The Club," the figure said in a low tenor. "You will proceed to the changing rooms and remove any clothing you are currently wearing. Only the garments you will find on offer in the changing rooms are permitted beyond this point. Once you are prepared for the evening's festivities, you may deposit any personal belongs you would like to be kept safe with the changing room assistants. From there, you will be given directions to your destination. It is important you listen carefully to any instructions you are given." He stepped back and waved for them to continue. "Proceed."

A few metres farther in, a right turn took them to a curtained opening, and Chase pushed through into a space containing five boxed-in cubicles, each of them cordoned by a heavy drape that currently stood open and exposed only emptiness within. Not that Chase had expected anyone else to be in there. Jones often insisted on a staggered arrival from his guests, for those who preferred to maintain anonymity.

To the right of the area was a windowed desk, behind which stood two masked females. The one on the right smiled as Chase glanced over. "Please use one of the cubicles provided to remove your clothing."

Inviting Mr and Mrs T ahead of himself, he waited until they'd each chosen a section and slid the curtains closed, before heading to the next one along.

Hangers had been left dangling from the few coat hooks in there, and shutting himself inside, Chase removed everything, from shoes, socks and trousers, tie then shirt, and the shorts he preferred over underpants. Naked, he arranged everything on the hangers and, with his personal belongings scooped up, carried them out, across to the window, and to the waiting women.

Lips painted a glossy red, they both smiled again at his approach. The one on the left slid a card and pen across the counter toward him, as he lay everything before them. "Identification number," she said.

All members, or guests were given a personal number in the information packs they received. And all members were expected to memorise that number—or risk losing whatever they handed over for safekeeping. Once a person, or persons, identity was confirmed at the first door, names were left behind inside The Club.

Chase jotted down his number, and she retrieved the card and pen, before carrying all of his belongings off toward a row of lockers. Chase watched as she pulled one open, placed his clothes inside, then slid the card with his ID number into a pocket on the front of the door once she'd closed it.

"Anything else?" the other woman asked.

"Yes, can you send the next two guests on to me? I'll be at the selection table."

"Certainly," she said smiling. "Have a lovely evening."

Allowing a small nod, Chase made his way around to the side of the locker desk, along a dark and narrow corridor. Every area a guest passed through led directly to the next. The entire setup always ensured no guest needed to double back on themselves. Far less chance of meeting other arrivals that way. Far less chance of recognition.

The corridor opened up on the left, where a long table draped in a white cloth took up most of the ten-by-six space. Masks had been spread out over the whiteness. Masks that'd been split into two choices. Red. Or black.

As he always did, Chase picked up a black one. Gender neutral, the mask held no beaded adornments, nor any feathers or crap a lot of the masks on the market seemed to come with. Made from a silky fabric, the accessory had been created simply, dipping down low over the nose, a little flexibility in the softer cheek sections, and rounded in a sleek curve where it raised over the forehead. Exactly as Jones had requested they be made.

As Chase slipped his onto his face and fitted the elastic

around the back of his head, Mr and Mrs T padded around the corner.

He braced himself for the appraisal. Knew it was coming, even before the couple's gazes crawled over his naked body from head to feet. Every guest at The Club got checked out by every other guest in attendance. Luckily, he'd grown used to being eye-mauled a long, long time ago.

Mrs T seemed to have trouble dragging her attention from his rear. "Red for the ladies and black for the men?" she asked.

"Nobody is singled out in such a way here," Chase told her. "You only select the red if you're comfortable with being kissed on the mouth. The black is to let other guests know not to pursue that activity with you. The colour is merely a way to inform other guests of your preference."

Her gaze skipped up to his own mask. "Which should we choose?"

"Whichever you're comfortable with. You might not, necessarily, go in there each wearing the same colour, even."

Before Chase had even finished speaking, Mr T had selected a black mask, which he began fitting over his face. Mrs T seemed more considerate in her choice. As if she needed to weigh up both options before deciding one of her fates for the entire evening. After a few moments, she stepped forward, her fingers folded over the strap of a red one, and smiling to herself, she placed it around her eyes and stretched the elastic over her head.

"Ready?" Chase asked.

She nodded, as Mr T said, "We're ready," and Chase led them through to the final preparation.

A heavy-looking door had been padded and studded, and looked a whole lot of soundproof. Like something from *Men In Black*, in his dark suit and shades, a dude almost as big as the first guy they'd encountered stood guard. Half smiling, he offered a nod of greeting, and Chase met his outstretched hand with his own in a masculine clasp.

"How're you doing?" the bouncer asked.

Although no names were ever used throughout the evening, Chase knew the bouncer's name, and the bouncer knew his. Another of his old school buddies. It always amazed Chase how many of them had fallen into the sex trade, in one form or another. Personally, he blamed Roy's Gym. The place had a whole lot to answer for.

"Good," Chase said, as the guy tugged him in and slapped a hand against his shoulder. "You?"

"I'm still breathing. It's always a good sign." He let his chuckle run its course, before reaching for the gold-coloured knob of the padded door. "Okay, lady and gentlemen, the word of the evening is *scarab*."

"Scarab. Got it." Chase rolled his shoulders out and stretched his arms out behind his back. With a quick flex of his neck either side, working the kinks out there, he gave the bouncer a nod. "Okay, let us in."

Unbothered by Chase's regular ritual, he twisted the knob and swung open the door, to reveal a low-lighted room coated in hints of red.

Behind him, the bouncer wished Mr and Mrs T a good evening as Chase stepped into the room, and a moment later, the door closed them in. When he turned to face the couple, their gazes seemed to be drinking up every detail on offer, their bodies held rigidly still, aside from the twist of their heads.

"Welcome to The Club," Chase said. Where rich folk gathered to act out their desires. Sordid. Depraved. Downright filthy. If fantasies were a ticket for access, The Club was the plane journey to the destination. "This is the Red Room," he explained, glancing back over the space.

A bed the size of a small island dominated the centre of the room on a shallow platform, while around it, ornate chairs had been set as if for a prominent view of the bed-stage.

Already, a woman lay with her head overhanging the edge of the mattress, her lips parted and arms splayed. From speakers overhead, quiet music seemed to float on the air, but she could still be heard as she groaned out her enjoyment at another woman's lips clamped over her cunt.

Still fairly early in the evening, only one spectator seat was occupied, where a man sat glassy-eyed while staring at the show, his hand fisted around the hair of a woman between his knees. Her head bobbed as her lips slid over his swollen cock.

With his dark blond hair, his face still unlined from age or financial concern, the man could easily have been Chase not so long ago. For a moment, Chase mentally placed himself in the same position. Placed his own gaze on the tongue fucking going on. Placed those lips around his own cock.

Yes, his shaft thickened at the thoughts. Just not as much as it seemed to whenever he placed a certain ex-client into his fantasies lately.

A client he had no right to be thinking of then.

Putting a guiding hand on Mr T's arm, he gestured for them to follow and continued on toward the open doorway on the far side of the room. Through it, an unlit corridor stretched off into a blackened hole he couldn't make out, and Chase walked them between the walls until they reached a doorway leading off.

The couple peered around the frame and into the room. Spiralled carvings decorated the oak arms of a four-poster bed in there, upon which a man lay with the tendons stretched though his neck as he tugged at his cock like something possessed. At the foot of the bed, with his legs sprawled across the seat of a tapestry-covered chaise longue, an elderly guy with loose skin matched him stroke for stroke.

"The Green Room," Chase said, though he didn't need to

explain why. All rooms were named by the colour that glowed out from the wan bulbs fitted into each fixture. He stepped back from the doorway. "Shall we?"

Mr T took a few seconds longer than his wife to turn away from the masturbation scene, glancing back once more, even as Chase motioned them forward.

The next three rooms also held beds in one form, or another. The fourth had been set up like a Victorian lounge, chairs placed around the room, footstools strategically set before a handful of the seats, an unlit, faux fireplace across one of the walls. On another wall, a full-length mirror had been hung, for those who enjoyed to watch even as they participated, and buckets of ice claimed the space of the few side tables in there.

"The yellow room," Chase told them before moving on to the next.

The next few rooms held sex chairs, fucking stools, whipping stools, an array of pleasuring—and paining—accessories. Most of them waited to be used—waited for more guests to arrive. In one of the rooms, a woman kneeled, her wrists and ankles hogtied behind her, while a man fucked her face hard enough to leave it swollen.

In the next room along, a woman swung in a sling that'd been strung from the ceiling, her knuckles white where she clung to the suspension ropes. Short, sharp screams erupted from her, in time with the pistoning hips of the man fucking her. And in time with the grunts bursting free from his throat.

Jones. Chase would recognise that flexing arse anywhere. And the tattoos he could see snaking over his back.

The way Mrs T took a step forward into the room told Chase she'd recognised him, too, from their practice session at his clinic. He suspected the two of them would be seeking Jones out before the end of the night. He just hoped they'd be prepared to face the guy in his own domain.

"Almost done," Chase said, catching the way Jones's head twitched in their direction when he spoke. "If you'll follow me, I'll show you the bathroom."

The bathroom stood on the right, through the next door down. An eight-man hot tub stood central. A woman sat with the water lapping at her nipples, her head resting back against the rim of the tub, while her fingers lazily twirled the stem of a glass. Chase knew the glass would only contain water, though. 'No alcohol' was a rule of The Club. Every member had to be lucid and yielding of their own will, not that of any kind of drug.

In the corner of the bathroom, a shower stall had been set up. Along one wall, a counter held a row of five sinks. On the opposite side of the room, toilets had been panelled in, in case of bodily needs.

His gaze skimmed back to the woman in the tub. Her hair flowed over the edge, dampened only slightly by the moist heat in the room, but Chase could still see the reddish highlights woven through the blonde strands. Could still imagine those same tones in a different head of hair.

As if she knew she was being watched, the woman arched her back until her breasts completely broke the surface and those peaks stiffened beneath the room's air. Chase couldn't help but stare at them. Couldn't help but drink in the pale softness of her skin as the water trailed over it, while picturing a different pair of breasts in their place.

A shot of lust tugged at his cock and flexed his balls at the thought.

Maybe the evening wouldn't go so badly, he told himself. He just had to do what he always seemed to do lately.

Stick a certain female in place of whomever he toyed with.

For a moment, his mind entertained joining the woman in the tub and doing exactly that. Until the woman lifted her lids and turned toward them, and eyes way too dark to act as Pacific blue locked onto his. She slid a hand into the water, her gaze unmoving as her body rocked enough to set the surface rippling.

"All guests are strongly advised to cleanse between each activity," Chase said, turning away from the subtle invitation. "And cleansing after anal sex is compulsory."

In the corridor, only two more doorways remained. The one at the very end of the row held a lock that Chase suspected had been secured, as PRIVATE had been stamped across its front.

The other held no such boundary. Through the widened opening, Chase could just make out the outlines of shapes he recognised through the shadows in there.

Mr and Mrs T stepped forward, and Chase instinctively followed, until all three stood in the opening and stared into the room.

"What's this room called?" Mrs T asked quietly.

"Sick," Chase said before he could stop himself.

She turned to him, her brows arched. "Really?"

He breathed out a low laugh and shook his head. "No, it's the Blue Room." Partly because of the lighting in there, though the bulb cast a gloomy midnight feel across everything in there, rather than offered illumination. Partly because few people left there smiling. It was definitely a room that had to be built up to, which was probably why it stood empty right then.

"Okay," he said, steering them away. "Are you comfortable enough to explore alone, or would you like me to accompany you for longer?"

Mrs T glanced up at her husband, her hand folding over his arm. "I think we're ready."

He peered down at her, and as if she'd communicated something in her look, he nodded and turned back to Chase. "We're ready," he echoed.

"Okay, just remember the rules. Respect everybody here, and everybody here will respect you. Do not attempt to kiss the mouth of anyone wearing a black mask—they've made a choice you have to uphold. Cleanse, as suggested. You'll be grateful you did, come morning. Do not interrupt the activities of other guests unless you are serious about participating, and respect any denials to participate. If there is any equipment you would like to try, but are unsure of its uses, ask. There will always be someone happy to assist—but be prepared for them to want to join you. Remember the safe word—you may need it. And most important of all ..." He took a breath and worked up a smile. "Enjoy yourselves. The Club is all about pleasure, after all."

"Oh, we will," she said, taking her husband's hand.

Leaning into the wall beside him, Chase watched as the two of them sauntered off along the corridor. Despite not really being in the mood for the evening's events, he couldn't help but smile at their enthusiasm, the tiny hop in their steps that told him they couldn't wait to dive in and come out wet. Another success on the client front for CW Consult.

A dark shape stepped from one of the rooms farther along, his head twisting toward where the couple had just passed his doorway. He stayed that way for only a few seconds before turning toward Chase, and his long, muscular legs made covering the floor space easy work with his intimidating strides.

Reaching Chase, Jones pressed a hand against the wall, propping himself there as he dipped his face the couple of inches to look into his eyes. "Lonely?"

Chase's lips twitched. "Not for you."

He shook his head and tutted. "Such a picky bastard." Rolling away from him, he leaned his back against the wall, his chest creating a profile against Chase's view of the shadows moving about farther along. "Wanna tell me why you look bored here tonight?"

"I'm not bored," Chase muttered.

"Well, you look it, and it's bad for business."

"I'm not bored," Chase said again.

Jones turned back to him and stared right into his eyes. "Preoccupied, then."

Chase glanced away. Jones's eyes had a habit of penetrating and burning brain cells without him even having to try.

"Who is she?" he asked.

Chase didn't answer. He didn't have an answer. Or didn't want to have one, anyway.

"You want to talk about it?" Jones asked.

With Jones? Chase almost laughed, but managed to curb it as he shook his head. Wasn't like there was really anything *to* talk about. Not like he'd been seeing Abi—not in the personal sense of the word. Not like she'd been one of his Toy Box selections. He didn't even know, himself, why her leaving the clinic had bothered him so fucking much.

"You want me to fix you up with a good distraction? Got an old friend coming later who loves to be dommed."

He thought back to the last two girls he'd released from his private room. How quickly he'd grown bored of them. How much his head had argued that they hadn't been what he wanted. Not anymore.

He pushed away from the wall, sidestepping Jones. "I'm good," he promised, and with a slap to his friend's shoulder, he forced himself in search in of 'fun'.

Back in the Red Room, Chase watched the comings of the members in there like some kind of fucking wallflower afraid to bite the bullet. He'd stepped into almost every room since shrugging off Jones, and had felt out of place in every one of them, as thoughts he had no right to be thinking, and definitely didn't understand, rampaged through his head and distracted the fuck out of him.

Over the past few months, he'd lessened his visits to The Club because he'd found entertainment enough in the women he hand-selected for his own personal amusement. As he'd perused the offerings of the evening, he had to wonder whether his usual happy place still held the appeal for him it once had, at all.

How the hell could one person change so much in so little time? And without a fucking good reason?

From his spot near a table of water glasses, he sipped on one of his own, holding the fizz in his mouth before swallowing, while some guy with a chest like a concrete slab rammed his cock into a wailing woman on the bed-stage. Her fingers gripped the edge of the mattress. Through the gaps in her mask, he could see her eyes tightly closed.

He glanced around at their audience. The same man who'd been sat there when he'd first arrived still claimed his same spot. Chase recognised him from earlier club visits and knew he had a preference for the shows other members put on. During that particular performance, muscular thighs supported the kneeling body before him, a definite male head replacing the female one of earlier and bobbing over the man's cock as he sucked like a fucking pro.

Opposite him, a woman bounced on the lap of some older guy, judging by the slight wrinkles claiming space on his otherwise toned body. With her back to him, she faced the stage, her gaze fixed on the rough screwing of the couple while her tits jiggled like they were trying to break free.

A few seats across, two women shared a love seat. One sat with her legs spread wide, a foot propped up onto the cushion beside her, an arm pinning the other woman back against her chest as her fingers fucked in and out of her cunt. The one getting the best deal jerked into each stroke, her juddering chest prodding her hard nipples up into the air, while her fingers grasped at the armrests either side of her.

Chase cut his gaze back to the couple on stage, as the woman's wails deepened into the kind of cries that could clench his balls without them even having to be touched.

Sure enough, his cock stirred with the biggest interest it'd shown all night. Even more so at the way the woman rocked back and forth with each thrust of the man's dick into her from behind. Her head lifted toward the roof, heavily-painted red lips poised around the sounds spilling from her. Lips poised in the perfect shape for him to climb up there and cram his own cock straight into her mouth.

"Fuck it," he muttered, and setting down his glass, he trod a path for the stage.

Almost as though she sensed an approach, the woman up there dipped her head, her eyes opened, and as her sights settled on him, her tongue swept over her glossy lips as they curved into a smile. The eagerness in her expression almost had him turning right back around and ducking out. He didn't want someone only interested in putting on a show. When he shared his cock with another, he needed their grunts and screams to be real. Not to feel like he'd just been fucking manipulated into his decision.

Nearing the two steps leading to the bed, he considered climbing them, anyway. Fuck how he usually felt. Because how he'd been feeling lately wasn't anywhere bloody close to his years-old reception to fucking and fun. He should just throw himself up there and fuck her mouth swollen. Fuck her throat 'til she could scarcely breathe. Remind himself of who he was.

Instead of lifting his foot, though, he swung it right past the steps. And kept right on, for the love seat and the two women who seemed to be watching his approach from beneath their heavy lids.

Reaching for the back of the seat beside the women's shoulders, he leaned in close, his hand folding over where those fingers pumped in and out of that cunt and stilling them. "Want to find a room?" he asked, quiet enough that only they'd hear, just loud enough to breach the music that'd shifted to some weird techno shit.

They studied him. Gazes dancing over his face. Down his body. Lingering where his stiff cock told them of his interest. The one in front tilted her head to the side as the other's lips met her ear, her focus skimming back up to his face as she listened. Removing the fingers from her pussy, the first woman pushed to her feet, giving Chase his answer, and as she took his hand, leading him away, the second woman latched onto his other hand and the three of them made for the corridor.

It took four attempts to find a bedroom not already claimed. The one they slunk into had no ceiling lighting. Only tiny specks glowed out from the black walls, leaving the room a shade of midnight with a starlight effect. Low visibility was exactly what Chase probably needed right then. Maybe if he couldn't see so well, he wouldn't visualise. Maybe he just needed to feel to go with the flow.

A flat square bed, as low as a futon, had been set in the centre of the room, and the women guided him to there. He did a quick assessment of the first woman as she swung to face him and sank down onto the bed. Cropped, spiky hair that feathered up and out around the red mask she wore. Nipples, two dark circles that stood out against her pale, slender body. As she lay back, she pulled him down with her, until he fit against her side, and in turn, he drew down the other woman until she lay opposite him.

Long strands, almost black in the shadowed space, draped

over the fleshy tits that pointed up at the two of them. She also wore a red mask—Chase wondered why he hadn't noticed that sooner. So long as they both understood what his black mask meant—he didn't need any complications.

Short-haired woman peered up at him. "How do you want us to play?"

For a half-breath, he considered gliding a hand along her body. Seeing if that skin felt as soft as it looked milky. He got no further than a twitch of his fingers, and instead, gripped hold of her thigh, rolled her toward him, turning her back to her companion. Once he'd got her on her side, he lifted the same thigh high until her legs split and her pussy poked out. Repositioning himself, he could see the glisten of anticipation weeping from her cunt.

Weaving his other hand into the long hair of the other woman, he tugged at her head, until she took the hint and followed his guidance toward the wet opening. He pushed her face between her companion's thighs from behind, and she gazed up at him from the front, as if awaiting further order.

The short-haired woman went to reach down, but Chase's order of, "Do not move," had her stopping.

Turning back toward the other one, he gave a gentle nudge to her head. "Drink from her."

She did as commanded. Her lips opening wide, before she clamped them over the awaiting pussy, and the woman before him let out a soft groan. Chase held mouth against cunt for a minute more, waiting until a steady rhythm had been set and the breathy moans kept the short-haired woman's mouth ever-open, before he untangled his hand from the long strands of hair and lowered the thigh down until it rested over the pussy-eater's arm. Turning his attention to the one getting all the attention, he took hold of what hair he could, lifted her head until she had little choice but to support herself on an elbow, and thrust his cock between those parted lips.

He closed his eyes as she opened wide and allowed him fully in. Let out a held breath, when her mouth closed around him and her throat worked, and the cheeks of her mouth suctioned around his shaft.

He could've happily stayed like that. Kept his eyes closed to the view. Just let her mouth give what his cock was craving. Except, like a fucking idiot, he lifted his lids, and his eyes narrowed at the lack of long hair. Lack of long, pale, sunset coloured hair. And he yanked out his cock and rammed it back into until her grunt blasted out around his flesh.

Not that she seemed to mind, with the way her hand reached for his hip, clasped hold of there, and with a gentle push away of his body, her lips slid along his length. Right before he could slip from her completely, she grasped him harder and hauled him right back into her.

Closing his eyes again, he tried letting himself believe he was somewhere else. Possibly with *someone* else. And gave himself over to the wet sucking of the short-haired woman, the dig of her fingernails into his skin, where she demanded his thrusts. The way the bed began swaying, swaying him with it, as her hips began a steady thrust into the mouth that sucked on her with equal fucking vigour.

The bed jostled more, and Chase's eyes opened to a guy climbing onto the foot of the bed. His gaze skipped from where Chase's cock got worked by the woman's lips, to where her cunt got worked by the other woman's greedy mouth, finally landing on the rounded curves of the free arse, where she'd positioned herself on spread knees as she pushed deeper between those thighs like she hadn't fed for fucking months.

Broad, muscular, his black mask hiding half of the face

beneath his well-trimmed hair, he gripped hold of his cock as he shuffled closer on his knees to the untreated pussy. Reaching out with his free hand, he brushed a palm across the cheeks of her ass, and as if she'd been craving some contact, the dark-haired woman pushed it higher. A signal of welcome. Come fuck. Come play.

He slipped his hand between her thighs, and her body jerked into him. Chase kept his gaze on them, as the lips around his cock sucked harder. Watched as the man brought his fingers back wet, as he licked the length of them whilst his palm stroked over his shaft. As he took those same, still shiny fingers and rubbed them around the woman's anus.

Chase waited for her protest. Anal sex was one of the biggest safe word inducers. She merely rolled her hips back at him, as if impatient.

The guy didn't seem to need more confirmation than that. Ducking his face in close, he gave a long lick across her puckered opening, and the woman groaned against her friend's cunt in response. As if spurred by the sound, the guy licked more viciously at her. Hard, intentional laps of his tongue, his saliva dripping freely across her skin. Once he'd saturated her anal crease, he pushed up, and shifting closer, he positioned the head of his cock at the entrance to her ass. Finally, wrapping a hand around her hip, he forced himself slowly into her body.

With the invasion, her muscles stiffened throughout her legs, her fingers grasped at something to cling onto. Wrapping a hand around her companion's thigh, she dived hard into her pussy feeding, the fleshy folds she delved inside muffling her groan as the guy withdrew his cock, stifling a second, louder groan when he pushed inside her a second time.

As if being fucked in the ass had set a new pace all round, the short-haired woman banged her pussy faster against the tongue lapping. Gripped Chase's hip even harder as her head nodded, her mouth swallowing him up, her cheeks massaging him as hotly as any wet cunt could. And once more, Chase relaxed into her ministrations. Let his head drop back and focused on the ceiling, until only the heat of that mouth and the grunts and moans and sucking danced through him as stimulation, and his cock strived for a whole new level of rigidity.

He knew when the first contact had been broken, by the heightened volume of the dark-haired woman, by the frustrated growl that vibrated around his shaft, and he glanced down to see the other woman clawing at the bedsheet, her head stuck in as stiff a position as the rest of her body. Her mouth seemed stretched to accommodate the sounds diving free of her throat, while the guy behind her drove his cock in faster and harder, his face screwed up into a blend of concentration and nearly-there.

As the movements of the mouth around his shaft slowed, Chase slipped his hand around the back of her head, urged her on. If she stopped, he'd lose his momentum—definitely not a step back he wanted to take.

She did as commanded, but released her hold on his hip and slid her hand along her own body. Over her stomach. Her hairless crotch. As soon as she'd reached her clitoris, both swollen with need and glossy with saliva, she started working herself. Her fingers dancing across the stiff peak, her body once again rolling into the stimulus. Beside them, the deep male grunts grew louder. The woman's cries had hit the high whine of desperation. Chase just focused on the wet strokes over his cock. And the manic strumming of fingers over clit and cunt.

Except, the more he stared at them, the harder he got, the more a different pussy crept into his head. One with pale hairs that curled around the soft folds. A different set of fingers. More delicate. Less experienced ...

Like his thoughts had hit a switch in his brain, he began shutting down from the moment. He needed to get out of there.

Before he went limp, or failed to ejaculate. Or something else equally fucking mortifying.

Because thinking of Abi, while fucking the face of a woman whose pussy was getting sucked on, by a woman whose ass was getting fucked, made him feel like a real sleazy fucking dirt-bag. The worst of the fucking worst.

But as he went to pull out of the woman's mouth, her hand snapped free of her cunt and hauled him to her again. Her mouth sucked harder. Wetter. Faster. Her fingernails piercing his flesh with her demands and her teeth scraping his length in her fervour.

And his stupid betraying dick kicked back into life, his body begging him to stay, no matter how much his mind tried to make his renewed grunts sound like *No*'s. No matter how much his head suddenly wanted him to be anywhere else but right there in that moment.

Like it mocked him in its disobedience, his cock grew harder and harder, setting into a solid mass of need-to-fucking-come. His balls tightened and twisted into rocks of give-us-a-fucking-break.

He barely had chance to state his case to his body, before it was jerking the hell all over the place, and his hand was slamming down against the bed to catch the forward throw of his torso, as his hips smacked against the woman's face and fucked, fucked, fucked every last drip of cum straight to her throat.

She bordered on gagging by the time he let her slide her mouth from over his dick, but she still smiled up at him like she'd just been given some kind of prize. Still watching him, she trailed her fingers back over her body. Back to her pussy. Opening her legs wider, she stared at him as she glided her fingertips between her folds and delved into her cunt.

If she expected Chase to step in where her friend at left off, she was shit out of luck.

Pushing away from her, he made for the edge of the bed. The guy's muscles had begun the intense cording of someone about to ejaculate. The long-haired woman had evolved to giving out the continuous wail of a woman in multi-orgasm.

Gripping hold of her hair, Chase sent her face back to the pussy she was supposed to be eating, and by the time he'd climbed from the bed, the woman he'd left behind had her fingers tangled into the long head of hair, as she fucked that face like she had a mission she couldn't afford to fail at.

His legs felt jellified as he stepped out of the room, and he leaned against the corridor wall for a moment, his breaths still irregular. His dick still bouncing around as if searching for its next sucker. Resting his head back against the wall, he closed his eyes, scraped his fingers through his hair.

The fuck, the fuck, the *fuck* was wrong with him?

His mind felt tugged in too many directions at once. And none of them were the same path his stupid fucking body wanted to take. Personally, Chase preferred his body's choice. He just needed to get his head in with the program. Needed to purge his fucking thoughts of a girl he barely even knew.

And when pleasure didn't do the job, there was only one alternative. An alternative almost guaranteed to work.

C hase rarely stepped inside the Blue Room of The Club. If he felt the need to role play, he preferred the privacy of his own space. For him, role playing, or being Master wasn't about putting on a show for spectators. Not about theatricals. It was about connecting with whomever he'd pared with through a mutual level of respect and understanding.

He'd definitely never stepped inside the Blue Room in the

mood he'd adopted right then. Never seeking the high others raved about.

The blue-tinted space was the biggest of all the named rooms. From front to back, small sections had been cordoned off, like office cubicles but higher for privacy, a little larger, too. Not total privacy, though. Every slot stayed bared open to any brave enough to follow the route that led between them all. So long as they understood they might get invited in to whatever scene they witnessed.

Chase glanced into only a few.

Four naked bodies hung from hoops embedded into the rear wall, the second guy along shallow breathing as a club-approved attendee scored the sharp edge of a blade across his torso.

A woman with her hands pressed flat to the wall, her tits bouncing as some guy fucked her from behind, her head bowed toward where a second one knelt in the space before her body and sucked at a dildo she'd attached against her clit.

In another, he just caught the struggle between a man and woman as he forced her to the wall and grabbed at her flesh, while she attempted to push him away. Amazing how many women fantasised their own rape.

Chase spared them more than a glance, as the very thing he'd gone in search of loomed out of the shadows ahead.

The biggest space in there, and the darkest, the final spot stretched from one side of the room to the other. Centrally placed, two posts had been affixed from floor to ceiling. Chains hung from them. More chains swayed down from the ceiling, a cuff attached on the end of each. At the foot of each post, more cuffs had been attached. Around the walls of the space, dark shapes lined the walls. Chase suspected them to be the tools that created the screams and cries often heard drifting from the Blue Room.

As he'd hoped, nobody occupied the spot he sought. He

doubted it would last for long, though. Especially as he crossed straight toward the two vertical beams until he stood between them. It'd been the reasoning for its positioning. Anyone brave enough to step into the shadows could be visible almost as far back as the door, and everyone a person passed in the Blue Room would be able to guess at their destination. Because anyone looking for oblivion didn't pause to play. Nor to watch.

Head easy on his neck, fists flexing at his sides, he wondered over the sanity of where his body—and mind—had led him. He counted up a list in his head, of all the reasons he should've been spinning his butt right around and beating a path out of there before anyone came.

Just as his resolve truly began to waver, fingertips brushed against his back. Over his butt. Around his hip. The rattle of a chain sounded to his left.

He didn't look up as the chill of metal slid across his stomach, an arm coming around and taking the chain's end. A hook clicked on his right, and the chain pulled taut in a diagonal line across his front. Another clink to his right, and a second chain clicked into place over his back. Creating a heavy, metallic X, with him trapped between its lines.

Fingers folded around one of his wrists, and his arm was tugged upward until above his head. The leather of a cuff slid around just above the joint, the tightening of it pressing against his pulse. His other arm was lifted and tethered beside it.

As a hand knocked his foot to the side, hot breath hit the back of his thigh. In more silent commands, his ankles were bound, one to each post. After a quick tug on each to check their security, hands brushed over the back of each calf, his thighs, pausing where the lower half of the chains had been draped. The warm breaths reached the back of his neck, lingering there long enough to create a gentle sweat across his skin.

"I never, for even one second of my life, imagined I would ever see Chase Walker stood between these posts."

Words spoken too low for anyone else to hear, but Chase recognised the voice, and he muttered a curse beneath his breath.

Jones's saunter around to the front of him was slow, probably a little torturous, too. His face came in close. Lips curved at the corners. Eyes glinting with some kind of malicious excitement. "Definitely you," he whispered.

"Fuck off, Jones," Chase hissed back.

He pushed in closer still, until his lips brushed Chase's ear. "You know the rules of these posts. Standing between them doesn't make you the master. It makes you the fucking slave."

His heart thumped against his ribs. "Don't make me go scarab on your ugly ass."

Jones pulled back until Chase could see his eyes again, and he held himself steady as the darkness within them seemed to suck Chase's truths from his brain. Because Chase had never once resorted to a safe word. Pride played a small part in that— the bigger one played by the fact that he didn't usually offer himself up in positions where he might need it.

Jones took a step back like he'd found the resolve he'd been hoping would be absent, his hands lifting to brace against the bars each side of Chase. "And if I promise not to lay a finger on you, personally?"

"Does that include via the extension of any props?" Chase asked, because he knew Jones could be brutal once his brain switched over to lust. He'd seen it happen to others. The thought of it happening to himself was scary as fuck.

He gave a small nod. "I won't lift a finger to you. You have my word."

Chase blew out a short breath, wrapped his fingers around the chains supporting his tethers.

"But I'm staying," Jones said. "I am totally fucking sticking around for this."

Before he could respond to that, Jones pushed back and nodded to a spot somewhere behind Chase. "Crop, whip, or paddle?" he asked, turning back.

Crop, whip, or paddle. He let the words roll around in his head. None of them sounded appealing—unless it was his own hand holding them. All of them would deliver what he needed.

"Crop," he said.

A slow smile crept over Jones's face, one Chase really didn't like the look of. "Number four," he said, and a shadow moved to Chase's right, toward the back wall where the first of the accessories hung.

As the dark figure moved back toward him, he gripped even tighter to the chains. Gritted his teeth against what he knew was to come. Clenched every muscle through his legs like that'd somehow help him stay grounded.

No more than a foot away, Jones stared hard at him, his eyes flickering as if he searched for any hint of doubt. "Ready?" he asked, and Chase nodded.

A sharp sting slapped against his ass, sending his hips bucking forward. Fire rapid-spread across his butt cheeks. And Chase had no chance of capturing his whimpered grunt as it shoved free of his throat.

Jones tipped his head, studied him again, the taut cording in his arm telling Chase he gripped his cock without him even having to look down and confirm. "You good?" Jones asked, worry diluting the beginnings of lust that brewed in his eyes.

Chase blew out a sharp breath and nodded.

"Again," Jones ordered.

The shock of a second *thwack* spliced through him, and his body jerked as a hissed breath pierced outward between his teeth.

"Again," Jones said, his voice a command, and as pain lanced across Chase's butt for the third time, he leaned in close until the tips of their noses brushed. Until the soft hairs bristled across Chase's chest from their nearness.

Chase lost sight of the room with the fourth hit. A tingle flooded his spine, his skull, into his shoulders, as the pain teased his sense receptors with the promise of more. And as a softly-blown breath caressed along the side of his neck, his body stirred in response. His head tilted into the tenderness, craving it as an antidote to the pain, despite his brain knowing Jones provided it.

His moans drooled out, long and deep, with the next two slices of pain across his ass, neither of them quite abating, even as the heat of Jones's breaths travelled over his chest. His stomach. Both of them merging with the groans he heard below him. Ones he knew had come from Jones. And his cock sprang forth with the jolting of his hips. Hard. Needy. Ready for something Chase had no fucking intention of giving it.

His knees unlocked with the whipping slap that followed, his arms screeching out their protest in the heat blooming through his shoulders as they were yanked tighter still, until only an endless brightness filled his vision.

Even through the all-consuming pain, though, he felt the hot breaths, so heavy along his stiffened shaft. He could visualise the nearness of the lips blowing them free. Visualise the parting of them in anticipation. Could imagine them brushing over the tight, tender flesh, despite them not once touching him. The way his hairs danced over his thighs told him more than just that mouth danced dangerously close to his skin. And he suddenly wanted them all closer. Wanted them so much closer than teasing. Than the promised restrictions allowed.

His hips jerked his cock forward before even the next strike had landed, fire engulfing the muscles of his arms as they did so.

Once more, only steamed air and the offer of heat he couldn't quite reach came as reward. And once more Chase thrust forward as best his unsupportive legs would allow, only to be denied any contact. In response, the pressure in his groin boiled, his balls knotting hard at the teasing.

At some point during the ministrations of the crop to his rear, the pain ceased to register. At some point, his brain let go of the space his body occupied. Claimed a new space to reside. One where only brightness shone over him, and a lightness to his soul he hadn't realised he craved. In that space, soft hands caressed his thighs. Even softer lips stroked his chest. And the heat engulfed his cock, tantalising the flesh there, making him harder and fucking harder. No more groans of pain left him, only moans of want and need, until his world narrowed down to the pathetic efforts of his body to reach its destination and the almost pained sounds of a desperate man.

~

S omething soft and warm supported Chase's chest. Something really fucking heavy crushed his thighs. And something cold and wet, really wet, slid over his ass.

Jerking, he tried to push up, but dropped back down with a hiss at the crazy pain that lanced his butt cheeks and seared his shoulders.

"Lie still."

Jones's voice. Behind him.

Chase tried pushing up again, but his arms didn't want to play, and his ass started crying.

What felt like a hand pressed between his shoulders blades. "I said, *lie still*. I'm fucking helping you, man."

Chase blinked until he had some focus to his vision. Took in the black satiny fabric he could see stretched out from beneath his squashed cheek. The small glow from a matt-black sconce on a gold-painted wall opposite. "'The fuck am I?" he asked, his voice gravelly and dry and scratching at his throat on its way out.

"The Club," Jones said, still behind him. "My room." Chase knew he'd have meant the private section. Where no guests were permitted.

Something spread over his butt and more coldness spread there, but he didn't seem to have any energy to investigate beyond asking, "'The fuck is that on my ass?"

"It's a salve. You're pretty ripped up, you fucking idiot."

As soon as Jones spoke the words, his skin stung like a mofo, his hands clenching in response—until he stiffened. "Wait— who the hell's putting that shit on me?"

Jones's quiet laugh held a whole lot of darkness, and Chase pushed back with his hips, giving a sharp cry at the inferno raging across his butt.

Jones pushed between his shoulder blades again, forcing him back down. "Relax, you moron. If I was going to fuck you, I'd have done it already. With a better lubricant than antiseptic cream."

The hands feathering over his butt shifted upward until they pressed down either side of his spine, and Chase attempted a jerky roll to the side. "Will you quit fucking touching me?"

"Will you quit fucking fighting. If you don't get some circulation back into your shoulders, you're going to be outta work the rest of the week. Now, stop fucking bitching, bitch."

"I ain't your bitch," Chase muttered, but he ceased pushing.

"You acted like my bitch tonight," Jones shot back.

Chase's body planked at the words. His mind bulleted backward in time. To the points of the evening where he'd been floating in ecstatic bliss. The points he couldn't even remember what the hell was happening, or what the hell he was doing, or giving a shit about either, beyond how fucking happy his entire being had felt.

He swallowed. Hard. "What did we ..."

"Relax." Jones kneaded the muscles in Chase's left shoulder. "I promised no touching. I wouldn't have broke that."

Chase settled a little, his face squishing back against the sheets, but only for a half beat. "Some other bastard fuck me?" He definitely felt fucked. His ass felt fucked. His brain felt fucked.

"Nobody fucked you. You know me better than that."

Chase did know him better than that. No way would Jones have let anything like that go down in his club without full and alert compliance. Chase let himself relax again, even went so far as closing his eyes, as Jones's knuckles dug into the fleshy muscle below the bone of his shoulder.

"Who is she?" Jones said, as he had earlier, cutting back into the brief quiet.

He frowned. "Who?"

His hands stilled against Chase's flesh. "Whoever has you this fucking wound up in knots, you dickhead."

Chase didn't answer, but his eyes flickered open.

"I know her?" Jones asked, when no answer came forth, and Chase shook his head as much as his body would allow. "She a client?"

Chase swallowed. He really didn't want to answer that question. Mostly because he couldn't without lying. "There isn't anyone," he said. Going by the bare bones of it, that was as close to truth as he could get.

The air in the room seemed to go as still as Jones did behind him, before his muttered, "Fuck," broke free.

As he pushed off and away, Chase gripped tight to the bedding at the pain burning back through his rear. Even the slightest movement seemed to blur his fucking eyes and make him want to blart like a baby.

Jones came around to where Chase's face twisted to the side, his body silhouetted by the weak light and looming over him. "I thought I told you to stay the fuck away from clients."

"Nothing's happened," Chase said, trying to push up and regretting it as soon as he did.

"After Nicolette, you'd venture there again?" He fisted his hands in front of him like he didn't know how to release his frustration, then settled on thwacking Chase round the back of the head. "The fuck is wrong with you?"

Chase just about reached where he'd been smacked and rubbed there. "Nothing's happened," he said again. "Nothing's going to happen. She's not my client anymore, okay?"

Jones stayed quiet for a handful of seconds, his breaths controlled. His body stiff. His voice came out deep when he said, "Don't make me pick up those fucking pieces again, man."

Chase closed his eyes and took a steadying breath before reopening them. "Can you get me home?"

"You're a stupid bastard."

"I know," Chase said. "But can you get me home. I don't think I can walk yet."

"That's the best way to leave here," Jones said, his tone a little lighter. "I'll give Daryl a call."

Chase woke in his own bed with only a vague recollection of how he'd got there. Cheek pressed to the soft blankets beneath them, lids resting over his eyes, arms about as relaxed as they'd been in weeks at his sides, he tried not to replay his evening. Not what had gone down. What he'd subjected himself to. Definitely tried not to catalogue how much he still hurt.

The last one was a little harder to achieve, though. Sure, whatever Jones had rubbed all over his butt seemed to be soothing the worst of the burn, but it still held enough heat to remind Chase of the fucking idiot he'd been.

Again, he shook the thoughts off. Tried to concentrate on something else. Groaned at himself when his damned brain flitted on a direct path to Abi.

Opening his eyes showed him his room. The white walls that appeared a moody grey beneath the moonlight. The sparse, equally white furniture dotted about the room. The surface of the Thames lapped at the lower rims of the portholes opposite him, and Chase lay there watching it gently rise and drop, teasing like it wanted to play, the clear view through the glass showcasing two different aspects of the world in a single glance.

Just like people. Nobody had only one layer. Everyone had an entire storybook to live out. And Chase had never wanted to read a client's pages as much as he wanted to read Abi's.

But just like everyone had more than one facet, every problem had more than one solution. And as the answer to Abi O'Shay's rushed into him like some kind of spectral possession, Chase couldn't help but smile. Because he suddenly knew what to do.

EPISODE FOUR

C hase hadn't sat since he'd arrived at the office. Partly
from the jittery energy buzzing through him. Mostly
because his arse hurt too fucking much, despite
Jones's best efforts to ease any discomfort. So, when the tippety-
tap footsteps of the girls broke through from the main entrance,
he was on his toes and striding as best he could before they'd
even reached the front desk.

They both stared at him, as he thrust into the reception.
Probably because he walked like he had a hot poker up his ass.

Raelyn's eyebrow made a slow journey toward her dark hairline. "Rough night?"

Ignoring her, he nodded toward the desk. A silent command
for them to get there already. "I need a mobile number for Abi
O'Shay. Stat."

He spun away and hobble-marched back into his office.
Where he couldn't sit down. Something he refused to admit was
his own bloody fault.

Within a few minutes, Samantha joined him, creases across
her brow and confusion in her eyes. "Rae told me last night that
Abi O'Shay walked."

148

Chase nodded and beckoned for the slip of paper in her hand. "I'm going to fix it."

"Why?" she asked, her frown deepening. "We don't have to fight for clients. They come to us. Isn't that what you said not long after we opened?"

"Because she deserves this," he said, snatching the paper free from her hand. When she didn't take the hint, he turned away from her, rounded his desk, and sank down onto an arse that really didn't want to support him. Hiding his wince, he gritted his teeth against the burning pain and grabbed up the receiver of his office phone, the stare he sent toward Sam pointed enough for her to get the message. He pretended not to notice the muttering beneath her breath as she headed for the door.

Half-limping, Chase ducked back out into reception feeling a whole lot lighter, and bee-lined for the curved desk that hugged his two-woman teammates. They both quit in their mumbling, and in their key tapping, as he leaned over the desk toward them.

"I need you to get some paperwork together."

Rae's eyes narrowed. "What kind of paperwork?"

"The kind of paperwork a client would fill in when their treatment is being put through the NHS."

Suspicion all but spat from the eyes of the two women. "Since when did the National Health Service pay for sex therapy?" Sam asked.

Chase's lips popped with his expelled breath. "They probably don't."

"Then, where are we supposed to find the paperwork for it?" Rae asked.

"Make some."

"What?" they said together.

He nodded toward the screens in front of them both. "Make some." He pushed off the desk. "And make it convincing," he ordered, as he spun back for his office.

"Are you fucking insane?" Rae asked to his rear, alongside Sam's, "Isn't this illegal?"

Pausing in his doorway, he twisted back with a smile. "Probably," he said to Rae. "And I doubt we'd get in trouble for giving something away for free," he told Sam. "Either way ..." His smile widened. "I don't really care."

~

Another day, another dollar. Or pound, in Chase's case. Across from him, Robin White sat on the chaise longue in a white robe and slippers, the top of his thick, dark hair faded by the sunlight pouring through the room wide windows.

Mr White had a collection of dolls at home. Not china dolls. The mannequin-looking, life-sized dolls. They were his company. His mealtime companions. His partners in masturbation. Except, they never responded when addressed. Never touched when invited. No matter how much Mr White tried including them in his activities, they merely stared, stared, stared.

And yet, he was having trouble giving them up. Which was probably why he sat sweating and looking fit to bolt during each of his visits to CW Consult. Probably why he looked as if he was choking on food whenever he spoke ill of them—or anytime Chase asked if he was ready to move on.

"It's your first practical session today," Chase said, leaning forward slightly.

Mr White nodded, resembling a smack-head in need of a fix

as he did so. His white robe gaped over his chest, thanks to the belt being tied high and tight above his rounded stomach.

"How do you feel about that? Do you think you're ready?"

His toes twitched, where they peeked out the front of the clinic-provided slippers. His fingers flinched in his lap. "I have to be, don't I." A statement, not a question.

"Why do you feel that way?" Chase asked.

"Because I can't keep going like this. It's ... it's *lonely*."

He fidgeted about on the seat. Chase just watched until he'd ceased, until he stilled his rear against the woven fabric. "Have you tried conducting human interactions since our last session?"

"I, uh ..." Back to the wriggling.

"Have you placed yourself in a situation where you might meet someone you could try talking to?" Chase pushed.

"I went to McDonald's on Tuesday. For lunch."

"Did you speak to anyone there?"

"I—I placed my order."

"Okay." Weaving his fingers together, Chase studied his client's face as he asked, "Were you served by a male, or female?"

His eyes met Chase's, but only for a second before flitting away. "A female—a woman."

"And what were your thoughts about the woman serving you?"

"She ..." He breathed out a laugh, but sobered as fast as he'd let his guard down. "She had really nice breasts."

"That's a pretty normal thought process for a guy, when faced with a woman they find attractive."

He shook his head, frowning. "She wasn't attractive. She just had ... really nice breasts."

"Okay." Chase's fingertips tapped together as he studied him again. "I want you to think back to the woman. Try and explain what about her made her unattractive to you."

The client was quiet a moment, his gaze cast aside as his brow tugged low, before he said, "She wouldn't stop moving."

Chase gestured for him to elaborate, to continue.

"I just wanted her to stand still and serve me, but she kept bouncing around. She kept moving. From side to side. Her hands busy, busy."

"Serving a customer usually requires a person to move, Mr White."

"And she wouldn't stop talking," he added, like Chase hadn't spoken. "And then she started singing *while* moving around ..."

"That made you uncomfortable?"

"Yes!" The word almost erupted from him. "Yes," he said, more softly. "It made me uncomfortable."

The way he barely sat still himself, with his fingers constantly dancing and his knees tapping together, and his eyes darting about, Chase suspected almost anything that involved another human made Mr White uncomfortable. "Are you keeping your appointments with your psychiatrist?" he asked him.

Another of those jerky, manic nods.

Chase already knew a fraction of the client's background. A mother who'd never shut up, always talking or yelling or singing or crying. A mother who'd smothered him to the point of suffocation. Who'd constantly made him tango to her tune and clung to him so much, the relationship had bordered on sensual.

That same mother had committed suicide and attempted to take her son along with her on the journey.

No wonder the man craved quiet and serenity.

"Good," he said, offering a small smile by way of praise. "And are they going well for you? Do you feel they're helping?"

"I don't know." He shrugged. "But nobody in therapy knows if something is helping until it's actually helped." He gave another quiet laugh, the gesture relaxing his features long enough for Chase to see the man beneath the stress and tension.

"I guess not," Chase said, his smile widening. "Okay," he said, moving on, "have you been thinking about what today's session might entail?" Sometimes, Chase found not divulging the details prior to a practical session, forcing the client to go into it blind, helped with progress. Mr White was one such client.

"I've been thinking about it." More eye darts. "A lot."

"And do you have any idea what you might expect from today's appointment?"

He shook his head in a gentle side-to-side sway, his, "No," slightly drawn out.

"That's okay. While the rules were explained to you upon registration, I'm going to quickly run through them again."

Over the next few minutes, Chase counted his way through the upcoming procedure and how it would work from Mr White's perspective: Any third parties had to be treated with respect; The client should feel comfortable at all times; Any time the client wished to stop, they had only to say, or indicate as such; And all sessions were observed, sometimes recorded, for the benefit of both the clients and the clinic.

"Any questions?" Chase asked as he closed the spiel.

"No questions," Mr White said.

"So, are you ready to try your first practical?" At the erratic nod of his client's head, Chase pushed to his feet. "Then, please follow me, Mr White."

Mr White's mouth seemed stuck. Not quite fully open. Not quite closed. But in a grimace that wasn't really a grimace—more an *oh, my* kind of look.

"Mr White?" Chase asked.

The man seemed to struggle with turning toward Chase. "Where did you get her?" he almost whispered, and Chase smiled.

"We've loaned her especially for today's session." He glanced toward where the female sat in the bedroom's chair. She didn't move. Didn't speak. Didn't blink. "Is she to your liking?"

He nodded so hard, his teeth clacked, as he twisted back toward the room's other occupant.

Small in frame, slender in body, the woman wore only a silvery bodice above undies secured by the ties hooked over her hips. Sheer, smoky-grey stockings clung to her legs, her bare feet arched into where her toes pressed against the flooring.

"Would you like to name her?" Chase asked.

Mr White chewed on air for a moment, before his lips formed around the name, "S-Sophia. She looks like a Sophia."

Chase could see that. High cheekbones seemed to accentuate the almond shape of her burnt umber eyes, and hair the colour of roasted chestnuts tumbled over her shoulders and along her spine. "Sophia is here today for your personal use. What you use Sophia for is your choice, so long as you remain within the boundaries of the clinic rules."

"She's ..." A quick dart of his tongue moistened the client's lips. "She's fully functional."

"Yes," Chase said, tucking his hands into his pockets.

His hands twitched at his sides as he gave another jerked nod. "Okay."

"Remember, I'll be in just the next room, observing the session in full." While he'd toyed with the idea of remaining in there with the client, Chase doubted Mr White would get anywhere close to performing in his presence. "So long as you treat the guest with respect, the session will be permitted to continue in full. Do you understand?"

"I understand."

"Okay, then. I'm going to depart the room." After one last glance toward the woman, checking for a reaction to his leaving, he twisted the handle of the door and stepped into the corridor outside.

The next door along led to the observation room, and Chase let himself in to where Raelyn already waited. She sent him a small smile as Chase closed the two of them inside.

Coming to stand beside where she already had the screens running, he asked, "Any thoughts? Vibes?"

Occasionally, just occasionally, Chase couldn't predict how a client's session would run, and mostly, that uncertainty occurred when the client had very particular requests, quirks, or needs.

Rae shook her head. "None bad. He seems kind of sweet. Just … I don't know, like, seriously edgy with it."

Chase agreed. Most of what made Mr White different was his ever-present nerves. Even then, beyond the viewing window, he seemed almost afraid to approach the female in there. Chase dreaded to think how far the client would've run already had he realised just how 'real' the female was.

"Maybe he's waiting for the nod," Rae said, as if sensing the same trepidation Chase did.

"Worth checking," he agreed, and he leaned into the intercom. "Mr White …"

The man's entire body jolted at Chase's voice entering the room.

Softening his tone, he continued, "You are free to begin when you're ready."

The heavy breath he expelled alongside his nod made his cheeks wobble. He took a hesitant step toward the woman, his eyes twitching, head tipped to the side. Like he needed to be sure she wouldn't bolt up and yell *Boo!*.

Robe still intact, he moved closer still. Just as Chase half-expected, he didn't go in for the invasive gropes of the body before him, but lifted fingers to her face. Traced over those impressive cheekbones, along the line of her straight nose, ending on her lips, which he seemed almost fascinated by in his study of them.

His hand shook as he feathered it over her jawline and traced the curve of her throat, veering off for a shoulder. That same hand trailed the length of her arm, until his fingers wrapped around her wrist, and he lifted it, taking her hand closer to his face. Touching. Inspecting. The wonder in his expression softening his features so much, Chase wished the man could always feel the way he must have in that moment.

For minutes, Mr White explored the woman. Not in a creepy, invasive way, but in a way that held respect and patience, despite the desire finding home in the man's eyes. From her chest to her thighs, all the way down to her ankles and feet, his hands seemed to examine every inch of her body, until he pushed to a stand and wrapped an arm around her back, worked the other beneath her knees, and lifted the woman from the chair. As he tugged her close against his chest, she didn't so much as flinch. Just held her arms and legs rigidly still, her expression as impassive as it had been on the client's arrival.

"He's more eager than we thought," Rae muttered, as the client strode across to the room's bed. Rather than climb on from its base, he rounded to the side, where he propped a knee up onto the mattress and lifted the woman away from his body, before lowering her down onto the blankets beneath.

Still, she adopted the same stance as she had when seated. Legs raised and crossed at the ankles. One arm still settled into her lap—the other at her side where Mr White had placed it.

Climbing fully onto his knees beside her, the client took one of her ankles, his other hand just above the thigh of the same leg. Almost as if he was afraid of breaking her, his caution was visible as he carefully straightened the leg, before giving the same treatment to the other, until she lay there with both legs straight down over the mattress. He turned his focus to her arms. The right one, he lifted high, above her head. She almost resembled an erotic ballerina in pose, as he curved it slightly inward, bent her fingers into a delicate curl. Her left hand, the one he'd already familiarised himself with, he rested against where her stomach peeked out from beneath her bodice.

Chase couldn't help but notice the small outward darts of the man's tongue through each of his movements, and as the client paused, he wondered what step he'd take next. Where he'd go with the options laid out before him.

"Fifty quid says he fucks her today," Rae said beside him.

"He won't." Chase spared her a glance before turning back to where Mr White's fingers hovered over the bindings of the woman's corset. "Poor guy is scared stupid."

"You'll get him past that."

Chase loved the confidence in her voice. "That's the plan."

She leaned in closer to the glass separating them from next door. Mr White's fingers trembled as they moved closer to that bow between her breasts. "Think he'll do it?"

"Just wait and see, Rae."

They didn't have to wait more than a handful of seconds, though the client's hand had still to steady itself as he took a length of the black ribbon and pulled the bow loose. As if steeled by his ability to take that first step, he hooked a finger beneath the simple knot and freed the ribbon of that, too, before tugging free one X of fabric after another, along the entire front of the corset.

Letting the withdrawn ribbon flitter away, he slid a hand beneath the base of the bodice, pressed his palm against the woman's stomach, and a heavy and impressive erection poked free as the skirt of Mr White's robe slipped from over his thigh.

Beside Chase, Rae let out a quiet whistle. "Mr White has quite the package."

Mr White had more than that. His cock would've filled any lower paid porn star with a massive dose of penis envy.

Hell, even Chase questioned his size, and he'd never had any complaints.

"Who would've thought it?" she added.

"He's a dark horse," Chase said, his lips twitching.

"A fucking stallion."

Stemming a laugh, he tried focusing on the room, as Mr White laid open the woman's corset. Exposing her taut stomach. Her breasts. He wondered if the man would notice the puckering of her nipples, despite the oft-comfortable temperature of the room. If he did, he didn't show it. Just headed right for the binds of her undies and untied the bows there with a lot less hesitation than he'd shown with the one on her corset.

The client's tug down of the dainty fabric revealed a pussy naked of hair. Chase half expected him to snatch the underwear out from under her and fling it aside, as he had the corset's ribbon, but the man simply unfolded it downward, tucked it between her thighs.

Surprising the hell out of Chase, he lifted his knee and nudged it between the woman's legs, forcing them apart. Eyes narrowing, Chase stepped a half-inch forward, his entire body on alert for what might come next, but no more force followed. Mr White simply settled his other leg between the woman's and, leaning forward, rested a hand against the mattress beside her arm.

"Want to pay up now?" Rae asked.

He shook his head. He wanted to tell her she was wrong, but Mr White's body language had already started arguing the case for her. His erection strained toward the woman's crotch. His breathing had hastened, a heaviness to it drawing his chest in and out. With hesitance, the client guided his hand toward his cock. Toward the woman's naked cunt. And Chase couldn't call which one he'd touch first.

As if second guessing his decision, the man's hand hovered a fraction from the woman's clitoris. A finger-curling shy of cupping her pussy. He stayed that way for a good few beats, before his hand inverted and gripped the length of his solid shaft, and Mr White's entire body rippled with the shudder that ran through it.

One long stroke down then up, and his body shook again. The man still seemed undecided about whether to just pleasure himself or seek it in the depths of the woman beneath him. Though, when he continued his steady strokes, lowered his face, and rubbed his cheeks over the woman's breasts, Chase suspected his path had been chosen.

～

Even post-session, Mr White seemed twitchy and withdrawn, but his cheeks glowed in a way they hadn't before. "You never told me," he said, his eyes slightly accusing as they briefly met Chase's.

"Told you ...?"

"That the doll would have a heartbeat."

"How did the presence of a heartbeat make you feel, Mr White?" By Chase's calculation, it'd made him feel a whole lot of calmness, because Mr White's round of masturbation was possibly the most peaceful and serene he'd ever witness. The most heartfelt, too.

Mr White shrugged and looked away, and Chase shuffled forward in his seat.

"I want you think about it," he said, his voice firm. "Your female friends at home do not have heartbeats. Correct?"

Waiting for the barely-there nod he received, he continued, "So, how did that make a difference to how you felt today?"

His fingers twisted in his lap. His toes turned inwards in his bulky boots. "Warm," he said on a heavy breath. "It made me feel warm."

Chase smiled. "Warm is a good way to feel." His smile widened when Mr White nodded his agreement. "Another question."

The client glanced his way. He always resembled a teenager caught cock fiddling by his parents, whenever Chase started asking him to respond.

"Why do you think there was a heartbeat today?"

The man's eyes squinted, as if he didn't like the question. A small twitch kicked in at the corner of his left eyes.

"Mr White?" Chase prompted.

"She was real." He picked at the cuticle of his thumbnail. "Wasn't she?"

Chase nodded. "She was." He paused, mostly to poke for a response to the confession, but no anger or sense of betrayal clouded the client's features. "How soon into your session did you know the woman was, in fact, a woman?"

"When I ..." His stare dropped, his fingers taut around one another. "When I touched her," he said, without looking up.

"Are you willing to tell me how you knew?"

"When I touched her ..." His hand lifted and stroked at the air, like he still imagined the moment. "Her body responded."

"How did it respond?" Chase asked.

"Her hairs. They danced." Though he didn't lift his face, Chase just caught the small smile shaping the man's lips. "It felt nice against my skin."

"Is that why you continued with the session?" Chase asked. "Even once you knew a woman was in there with you?"

"I wanted—" Dropping his hand back to his lap, he licked his lips. "I wanted to see if I could—if I'd be able to—"

"Perform?"

Mr White nodded.

"You wanted to see if you could still perform when with a real woman, instead of one of your dolls at home?"

"Yes," he said quietly.

"Do you think you performed well?"

He glanced toward the window, what sounded like a soft laugh exiting on his sigh. "I liked it. Does that count?"

"It depends. Did you enjoy it more than your usual sexual routine? Did you find it more fulfilling?"

He smiled. Chase always felt like he'd hit some kind of imaginary target whenever Mr White smiled. "Yes. Yes, I did."

"Good. Would you like to discuss your next session before you leave?"

"Will I be doing the same again?" he asked, and Chase caught a glimpse of hope in the man's eyes as they briefly snagged on him.

"Well, I wanted to give you some homework to try, and then your next appointment can be decided once we have the results of that. How do you feel about trying something at home?"

"I—I don't know. What would it be?"

"There's a website especially for men and women who like to live their lives as living dolls, and for those who like to date living dolls—Raelyn will give you the online address before you leave." As he paused for breath, he expected protest, but received none. "I want you to join the site, create a profile for yourself. And I want you to try talking to people on there—not physically, but via a computer. So, no face-to-face interactions—I wouldn't ask that of you until you know you're ready. It's simply typing what you want to say into a keyboard. A lot of people find talking easier that way. And I'll ring you in a few days to see how you're managing that." He tapped his fingertips together as he studied the tightening of every feature across the client's face. "Do you think you might be willing to try something like that, Mr White?"

~

I t had taken some gentle persuasion, but in the end, Mr White had agreed—though, only after receiving a crash course on how to navigate the site, and advice on what he might do, or say, once there himself. After his willingness to continue with the session, even knowing a live woman shared the room with him, Chase had little doubt his client would be moving forward in his life, if only eventually.

Chase still found himself considering how Mr White might do with the task he'd been set later that afternoon, as he sipped on his water while studying the waterway below his office, while awaiting the arrival of his next appointment—one he'd been anticipating all day.

The intercom buzzing through his office had him snapping back to the room, and he marched for his desk and pressed the small button that connected him to the front of house.

"Yes?" he asked.

"Your five o-clock is here," Sam said through the speaker.

He checked the clock on the far wall. Twenty minutes early —as usual. "Thanks, Sam," he said, and tucked the water bottle back into a drawer on the desk.

After a moment of checking that his trousers hung straight, the creased fronts lined up correctly, the hem of his shirt had been tucked in securely all around, Chase adjusted his tie and cut a path across his office. Try as he might to stem his grin, he completely failed as he swung open his office door and peered into the reception area.

Sat in the same spot where he'd very first seen her, as rigidly still as when he'd first seen her, and just as fucking stunning, Abi O'Shay turned his way, those eyes of hers poking a response out of his cock that could've damned him to hell. He had to swallow down the gathering of saliva in his throat as she locked him into some kind of silent standoff he didn't quite understand.

As she pushed to her feet, the smile on her lips made her look far from the nervous girl he'd first met. And gone were the innocent skirts and flouncy shirts. In their place, Abi wore tight, tight jeans that rose high over her waist and did an amazing job of plumping up her breasts, which already strained against the confines of the low-buttoned blouse she wore.

Chase didn't dare glance at Raelyn or Samantha as she stepped toward him with her hand outstretched and his stupid grin widened—he didn't want to see the eye rolls and head-shakes he knew they'd be throwing his way.

"Mr Walker," she said, slipping her hand into his. "It's good to be back."

"It's good to have you back." Keeping hold of her hand, he guided her into his office and closed the door on his nosy employees. He didn't want to analyse his satisfaction at her being back in his office as he led her across the room. Or how much her hand being wrapped in his made his lips want to curve up a whole lot higher than he was letting them. He also didn't want to analyse his self-satisfaction over him being the reason she was back there to begin.

Waiting until he'd settled her onto the couch and he'd sank his own butt down facing her, he finally released his hold of her as he noted, "You chose not to wear the clinic robe again?"

She gave a nod that showed her awkwardness at the question. As she did, Chase could just see the higher swells of her breasts bounce with the action between the V of her blouse. He suddenly had no problem with saliva as his mouth dried up like a dead tree.

"I was hoping today that we'd progress a step," he managed. In fact, he'd been hoping for it *all* day, but he kept that to himself. "Do you not feel ready for that?"

"Oh, I do. I just ..." She picked at the seam of her jeans, drawing Chase's gaze to the inside of her thighs. He let out a sigh as he remembered those same thighs widened the week before. Her hands between them. Stroking. Exploring. "Wearing my own clothes into the, um ..."

"Practical session," he offered, ordering his eyes back to her face.

"Yes. Wearing my own clothes makes it feel a little less ... clinical? More natural." Her shoulders lifted in a small shrug. "I feel less ... I don't know ... intimidated by it, that way."

Her eyes locked with his, until he struggled to look away. He hated to think what his mouth was doing, as the corners curved up into something barely resembling a smile. He probably looked a complete fucking moron just staring at her like a goof. "That's perfectly fine," he managed through his rubber lips. He cleared his throat and glanced away. "Maybe, if you're ready, we could get started?"

"Okay," she said.

"Okay." Nodding, he climbed to his feet and, waving for her to precede him, headed for the corridor that housed all their private rooms.

S am stood next to Chase in the observation room. He mostly just wanted her to fuck off and let him perv alone. Especially as, through the viewing window, Abi O'Shay fumbled with the buttons of her jeans as if she had every intention of following their directive to strip from the waist down.

Sam had dimmed the lighting in there, but just like it hadn't the last time, it did little to impede the spectators' view.

For a moment, with one hand poised over her partially-opened waistband, Abi glanced toward the expansive mirror on the wall. Her eyes cutting like a laser through the barrier until they burned into Chase's own. Almost as if she knew exactly where he stood. Watching. Waiting.

He kind of loved that she might be seeking him out.

Without lowering her gaze, she pushed down on the denim, and ivory lace came into view as she worked the jeans over the remainder of her legs and kicked them away. As she straightened, Chase couldn't help studying the high line of fabric over her hips, the way the lace dipped into a V toward her pussy.

He drew in a deep breath and released it on a sigh, ignoring the turn of Sam's head in his direction. He didn't want to know what she thought about his rapt fucking attention to the happenings in the next room, anyway. Not when Abi still hadn't looked away and held him as captive as if he'd been bound by chains and his head braced in place.

Her fingers folded over the thin cloth hugging her hips. Her chest seemed to heave upward as she breathed through the panic that flitted into her eyes.

"You can do it," Sam muttered beside him, voicing his own thoughts.

As if afraid of changing her mind, Abi shoved the underwear straight down and off.

Leaving her standing there in nothing but that tight blouse and whatever it hid.

Chase hated that they'd agreed she could keep that much on. Because staring at calves that spoke of much walking, and milky thighs that led the way upward to where Chase could see the delicate hairs licking at Abi's cunt, he realised it wasn't enough. Nowhere near enough.

Chase wanted to see all of her.

"Tell her, if she's comfortable with it, she can remove her shirt," he told Sam.

"You tell her that, and she'll never come back."

"She will." For some reason, he was sure of that, even if he felt ungrounded by everything else that involved Abi.

"It's too soon for her," Sam said, leaning into his personal space. "Quit thinking with your dick and think like her therapist."

Forcing his attention from the scene in the other room, he turned toward Sam, took in the sternness of her eyes, the *don't fucking argue with me* set of her mouth.

She was right. He knew she was right. He just didn't want her to be.

Turning away from Sam, he clicked the intercom button, but he didn't speak for a few seconds. Afraid of telling Abi to do exactly as his cock demanded.

After a rough throat clearing, he asked, "Abi, are you okay with me leading the session today? I think it will help for you to learn to respond to a male voice rather than female for your progress."

Her eyes flitted toward the room's speaker and back again, almost as if she questioned her own judgement on where he might be standing behind the glass, and she nodded. "Okay."

"If you become uncomfortable with my leading the session, at any point, simply raise your hand, and Samantha will take over from me."

Another nod of consent, before her body half swayed, half twisted toward the bed, as if she knew where she had to go so why not get on with it already.

"While I think it will be for the best to keep your shirt on ..."

Liar, Sam mouthed at him.

He ignored her. "... you might be more comfortable if you unbutton it. At least partially, from the bottom, so you can shift it to the sides should it become restricting, at all."

Her gaze returned to the mirror as he released the communication switch. If not for the slight twitch at the corner of one eye, Chase would have said her expression held attitude, as she reached down and worked free the lowest button on her shirt. The second. And third. Exposing a stomach as pale as her thighs and very slightly rounded.

He expected her to stop there.

She didn't.

Her hands worked the next three buttons, until lace that matched her underwear peeked out as the blouse slipped from the high mounds of her chest.

"Well ..." Sam almost breathed the word beside him.

"Yeah," Chase said, not wanting to note the slight roughness to his voice.

"She's enough to turn me on."

"Of course she is, Sam. Even scummy dickheads turn you on."

"Says the guy who gets a hard-on at every single practical session he runs."

Not like the one he had right then, he thought, as he opened his mouth to tell her to fuck off, but realising that Abi still stared their way as if awaiting instruction, he depressed the button connecting him to her. "Can you see much in there, Abi?"

"I see enough to move around. It's not quite so dark as last time."

"Once you feel ready, then, I'd like you to get comfortable."

"On the bed?" she asked, turning toward it again.

"Or the chair. Wherever you feel you'll relax better."

"Take the bed," Sam whispered beside him.

Chase suspected she only wanted Abi to head that way because of the surprise she'd left there for her. He had to admit, though, he really wanted her flat on her back, too, if only for the added view it would offer.

Almost as if she'd heard the prompt, Abi twisted farther toward the bed and took slow steps in that direction. Her hand came out as she neared, and she braced it against the bed's edge, before lifting a knee onto the covered mattress. Sliding her other knee on to join it gave Chase and Sam a prime shot of her arse, as her shirt hem slipped higher up her back, followed by a tiny glimpse of her pussy.

Chase's throat dried to cracking point just from him looking. He'd never wanted to be in a room with a client more. He'd never wanted to lick a client more. Or fuck a client more. Like, right there, in that exact position, her back arching, that cherub face of hers peering back at him as she took him all the way in and moaned out every ounce of her pleasure ....

A low groan eked past his throat before he could stem it.

Blanking out the quiet laughter coming Sam, he focused on the window. Like he could focus on anything else. Not with how hard his cock had swelled. He almost wanted to disregard the fact that Sam was in there with him and just relieve the fuck out of himself. He wouldn't, though—mostly because he'd never live it down.

In the next room, Abi swung her hips round until she sat on that sweet arse. The movement bringing her knees up and open, offering a fuller view of where the hairs teased the tip of her clit. Finally, she took her arms back as support, in a way that thrust her breasts wholly free of that damned shirt, and Chase's throat dried so bad, he worried if he'd even be able to talk, as he drank in the sight of plump milky swells just balancing on top of her bra.

"Come to mama," Sam whispered.

Ignoring her, Chase gave another throat clearing that seemed to scratch just about everywhere it reached. "Are you comfortable, Abi?"

"Yes," she said, though Chase doubted she'd be sitting up for long. Especially if he had his way.

He clicked off the intercom. "Let's see just how adventurous she's feeling this week."

"You're sick," Sam muttered.

"My sickness pays your wages," he said, not even looking at her. Not that he could've. He didn't think he ever wanted to remove his gaze from the viewing window again. Or let Abi O'Shay go.

Maybe he should introduce her to the next bedroom along —where he could bind her to the bed and hold her hostage until he'd taken his fill.

He wondered how she'd respond if he showed her his Toy Box ...

He quickly squashed the mental images those provoked. Abi was the kind of woman who needed nurturing. *Deserved* nurturing. And tenderness. She was the kind of woman who'd make love, not the kind to fuck faster and harder than the body advised against.

And if he didn't quit thinking full stop, he'd be spraying in his pants and making a holy mess of the situation.

"Okay," he said roughly into the intercom, "can you remember what you practised last week—what Sam taught you?"

Abi nodded, her gaze once more scanning the one-way glass.

"I want you to start there," Chase told her, trying to ignore how his cock demanded to be let free. "I want you to touch yourself, Abi. I want you to make yourself wet," he added, before he could stop the words.

Abi's cheeks darkened, as if she blushed.

The response only seemed to poke at the fire beginning a slow burn through his body, and he closed his eyes, released a low groan. "This is fucking torture," he muttered.

"You love torture," Sam said beside him. "And your visit to The Club last night tells me you now enjoy *being* tortured. So, suck it up, Walker."

Chase kept his eyes on the window through her gossip prodding, though he should've known she and Rae would've turned up there at some point, if only to observe how the latest members had faired under Chase's induction. He just wished he'd spotted them before he'd lost sight of his senses.

In the other room, Abi showed a few seconds of hesitation, before she brought a hand around to the front of her, brushed her fingers over the high ridge of her pelvis, and breached the soft heat between her thighs. Her legs spread a little wider as she explored. Between the fleshy folds. Her palm flattening over her clitoris. The tips of her fingers just reached where the first hints of arousal glistened around the opening of her cunt.

"She's been practising," Sam said.

Exactly what Chase had been thinking. Because Abi's fingers seemed a lot more exploratory than they'd been the week before. They slid into each groove. Rolled over every mound. And just slightly dipped into the shallow pool of her cum before slipping all the way back up and circling her clit.

Straight back down, her fingers retraced their route. Tracing the rim of her vagina. Re-seeking the sensitive bud that already looked ready to beg.

Chase could practically feel it's lines against his lips as his tongue swept over them.

As she dipped down a third time, her gaze lifted toward the mirror. Back toward Chase. Somehow holding his gaze, even through the glass, she took the tip of her clitoris between her finger and thumb. Almost as if she needed to know she did it right, as she rolled the delicate flesh and gave a gentle tug.

Almost as if she hoped that he watched.

And he was definitely watching. He was watching so fucking hard.

"She's ready," Sam said beside him. "Move her on."

Trying to swallow enough saliva into his mouth to talk, he pressed the connector. "Abi, I want you to explore inside your vagina. I want you to try dipping your fingers into where you are most wet."

Giving a tiny nod, she guided her hand back down toward the juncture of her thighs, straight to her wet spot that grew glossier by the second. At first, just a fingertip entered, and Abi's gaze dropped from the glass toward where she touched herself. Jaw loose, brow slightly creased in concentration, she dared slide that finger in a little further, her chest fluttering with each breath she took.

"Good," Chase said, hating that his voice cracked on the word. "Now slide back out." He waited until she had, and leaned back in to speak, his tone deeper as he instructed, "This time, use two fingers. But gently." He didn't want to risk damage to an untouched cunt.

Using two fingers seemed to take more consideration for her. She took more time probing into her hot channel, slipping them all the way in until they could go no further, until knuckle hit the restriction of bone.

"How does that feel for you, Abi?" Chase asked.

He knew how it felt for him. Erotic and beautiful. Stimulating as fucking hell.

"I'm not sure," she said quietly.

"She needs to use the toy," Sam whispered.

"Not yet. She needs to find a good rhythm with this first." He turned back toward the darkened room. "Abi, I want you to practice this a little longer. I want you to create a smoothness to the insertion of your fingers. I want you to get used to how that feels. And most importantly, I need you to relax." He felt like a hypocrite, even as he said the words. He'd never been wound so bloody tight in his life. "Okay?"

"Okay," she said, though the word was little more than a whisper.

"Try lying back. It might help."

"Help give you a better view," Sam muttered.

"Fuck off, Sam," he said, watching as Abi rolled her spine down onto the mattress and lay her head back.

The tendons along her arm tightened with the extra stretch required to reach, as she once more probed into her cunt. Slid back out. In then out, not as slow as she'd begun, but still not fast.

"I want you to try curling your fingertips in the next time, just a little," Chase said through the speakers. After giving her a few moments to try it, he asked, "Do you feel the soft ridges just inside your vagina?"

Her head brushed against the bed with her nod, her lips only slightly apart in her focussed expression.

"That's your G-spot. You'll learn better how to increase your pleasure through it, the more you practice. For now, just keep doing what you're doing, but bring your other hand down. I want you to stroke over wherever feels good to you on the outside *while* exploring within."

She didn't move at first, and Chase wondered if he'd confused her with his request, but then her free hand feathered slowly over her body. Caressing the flesh of her bare stomach between her shirt flaps. Creeping closer toward where she gently lifted her hips as if her body already anticipated her own touch.

Yes, Chase thought, she'd definitely been practising.

Her lips popped wider on a breath, as her fingers relocated her clitoris. As they gave tiny strokes across its tip. As her other fingers slipped in and out of her cunt.

"How does that feel?" Chase asked her.

"Okay .... Nice."

She didn't sound convinced, though. And despite her body's evident efforts to respond, Abi's features remained guarded, as if she concentrated too hard, as if she questioned it too hard.

"Move her on," Sam said, her voice a little more insistent than the last time. "She needs to be fully distracted, or she's not going to hit peak."

Chase leaned into the intercom. "I want you to keep those fingers moving inside you. But with your other hand, I want you to reach up above your head. There's something there on the bed I'd like you to try."

On a screen to their left, Abi's hand stretched upward, sweeping across the sheets in a slow arc. As soon as she touched the small device, she paused, her fingers patting over it, curling around it. After a few seconds of touching, she picked it up and brought it down to her chest.

"Feel over it," Chase said. "Do you feel the end that has ridges around its rim?"

"Yes," she said, fumbling around the base with her fingers— a sight that made Chase want to yank off his tie and get air to his flesh.

"You need to twist that," he explained. "Use both hands, if you need to."

She slipped her fingers free of her cunt and used them to grip the small vibrator, while twisting the bottom with her other hand. As a quiet buzz filled the room, she jerked on the bed, and the toy dropped from her grip and landed on her stomach, where it continued humming across her skin.

"Don't be afraid of it," Chase said patiently. "It will assist you in feeling pleasure. When you're ready, I want you to take it in your hand and hold it in a way that feels comfortable to you." After a short pause, he added, "You only need one hand for this, Abi."

Understanding the directive in his remark, she took the other hand of hers straight back down to between her legs. Guided those fingers right back to her wet pussy. And dipped into the deep pool like she'd every intention of doing so all along.

Yes, Chase wanted to murmur, *just like that*. "How does the device feel in your hand?" he asked instead, once she'd broken back into her rhythm of in-and-out finger gliding.

"It tickles," she said. "A little bit."

Sam let out a giggle beside him that had his own lips curving.

"Good," he said. "That's good. You're going to use this in place of the hand that's holding it."

"I have to put it down there?" Abi asked, her eyes widening slightly in the darkness.

"Only on the outside. See how it feels to you—just when you feel ready to try it."

She adjusted her hold on the vibrator, seemed suddenly awkward holding it—though the small ones could often be more difficult to hold, and the one they'd supplied Abi with came in at only four inches long. As if satisfied with the grip she had, she shifted her hand lower. Before she'd reached her pussy, she took it closer to her body, brushed it over her skin as if testing the sensation it had to offer.

Her lips parted as it skimmed her hip bone. A tiny tremor rippled through her as it crept inward over her pubis.

Hitting her clit with the vibrator, she let out groan—one she slammed her lips over just as fast as she withdrew the device, as if she couldn't quite believe the sound had come from her.

"Good," Chase said. "You're doing good, Abi." *Real good.*

"Yeah, don't stop now," Sam whispered.

"Try again," he encouraged. *For God's sake, don't stop.* "But don't be afraid of it. You're experimenting. Discovering what pleasures you." What pleasured Chase, too, judging by his body's response. "However it makes you feel, it's perfectly natural. And completely acceptable to enjoy it."

She didn't even hesitate that time, before she dipped her hand back to her pussy, pressed the vibrator back against her clit. And her entire body curved upward in response, her groan equally as loud.

For a moment, she just lay there, her hands still, her chest shifting up then down as her breaths came fast. "It feels over-whelming," she said into the quiet.

Chase pressed the intercom. "Try adjusting its speed. The base, where you twisted to switch it on, try twisting it the other way. Just a little, though. You don't want to shut it off completely."

Abi didn't even bother removing her fingers from her cunt that time, as she adjusted with the vibrator's speed as he'd instructed. She also didn't bother awaiting his prompt before she took the device straight back to where her clit stood almost erect, finally making the demands for what could offer it relief.

That time, as the contact was made, her groan arrived softer. Her chest pushing into the air as her legs widened. As her toes curled against the sheets.

And the room spun around Chase as all blood left his brain on a rapid race southward.

"There she is," Sam muttered, jerking his mind back into focus. "She's got this."

"You need to keep those fingers moving." Chase practically growled the order. "Don't stop with the rhythm you've found."

Almost as if his very voice controlled her body, she slipped her fingers deep into her cunt, her thighs stretching wide until tendons pushed against skin, as she shifted her arm to the side, creating more room for her ministrations against her clit.

Shutting down the intercom, Chase prepared to relax himself in for the show.

For one so raw, she certainly seemed at ease with bracing the new experience thrown at her. Seemed to quickly find a method of self-pleasure her body responded to.

One to which Chase's own body reacted, too. His cock roared in his shorts. Though, his gaze latching on to where her fingers seemed to be growing slicker with every slow pump in and out probably didn't help any with that.

Or the way her soft moans rolled from her like they refused to be restrained.

Within minutes of finger fucking herself, of sending probably more stimulation through that sensitive bud of hers than she'd ever experienced, her body had arched up, her hips driving down against the mattress, her heels digging in until her cunt made tiny jerks into each thrusted plunge of her fingers she gave.

Along the line of her body, her breasts probed the air, nipples solid and swollen against the fabric of her bra, and Chase couldn't help but imagine them drawn between his lips. The deepened sounds he'd push from her as he sucked and nibbled and plucked .... He had to reach down and readjust the solid thickness of his cock, it ached so fucking hard.

"She needs to get that V inside her," Sam said, reminding him he had company, and when he glanced across, she stood as captivated as himself. "Learn what that baby can really do."

It took him a moment to register her words, and he turned back to the window with a frown. "She's not losing her virginity to a fucking vibrator, Sam." Not if he had any say in the matter, anyway. She deserved a whole lot better than that.

In the other room, Abi's moans heightened. Became gasped cries. Her chest pumping high in time with the pump of her fingers and the buzzing device she rolled across her clit.

"She's close."

Chase nodded. She was. And he planned to experience her end right alongside her.

Just as he had last time, he turned toward the screen that showed a close-up of her face, smiling to himself on finding her eyes wide open and as expressive as fucking hell. A dark tint coloured her otherwise pale cheeks. Her mouth formed the perfect oval around the sounds pouring from her throat, as her crown pressed down against the bedsheets. And when her entire body shuddered into climax and a forced whimper blasted from her, Chase couldn't help but wish he'd been the one to bring her that orgasm. That he'd been the one to make her cry out so fucking freely and tremble from head to toe.

He had to clench his hands against the urges rushing through him, because his dick really wished it had played some part in it, too. Fuck, he needed to get out of there.

As soon as Abi's body slowed to twitches and her cries lowered to unsteady breaths, Chase ducked behind Sam toward the door. "Bring her through once she's ready," he told her as he tugged the handle down.

"Where are you ..." Her words trailed off as her gaze dropped to his crotch, and her lips formed a silent *oh*.

Yeah, *oh*. Because if Chase didn't get his arse somewhere he could jack the shit out of himself, he'd be storming next door and mounting his client before she'd even fully reached the end of her orgasm.

The door slammed shut behind him, and he marched along the corridor, threw open the door to his office, and all but ran for the staff quarters housing the private showers. All while questioning his sanity over inviting Abi O'Shay back to his practice.

Because in that moment, Chase realised, he didn't want the barriers of her being his client to be there anymore.

∾

Water splashed over his back, as Chase pumped his fist around his cock. His arm burned with the effort. His body held rigidly taut as he concentrated all his energy where he needed it most.

Grout dug a groove into his forehead, where it rested against the tiled wall, his eyes dipped to where his hand slicked up and down like it had an engine powering the fuck out of it. His other hand, he held fisted at his side, tense and unmoving, as if having to use the tiniest bit of brain power on anything other than relieving his cock could somehow roundhouse him off the path to his goal.

Every muscle in his thighs ached with how tight he held them. His arse clenched with each thrust he gave into his hand.

Closing his eyes for a moment let him see Abi. See her body rocking into her own touch. Her expression as the pleasure took hold. Her lips. Those fucking lips. Soft and hot and round, so fucking round. He pictured his cock between those lips. Seeking her heat. Being stroked by her tongue. Her eyes wide in her eagerness to accommodate his needs—

Cum shot so hard from his cock, his body jerked, his knees almost giving out as he barked out a cry and juddered in his efforts to keep the orgasm rolling. To hand-fuck the juice out of himself until not even a single drop remained.

Grunts pushed out, his entire fucking face twitching as each additional spray hit the tile in front of him. By the time he'd stilled his hand, his whole body trembled as his breaths panted the hell out of his chest.

"Good. You've finished."

Still breathing hard, Chase closed his eyes and stifled a groan.

"You going to tell me what's going on?"

He should've known one of them would have something to say about his actions since he'd walked in that morning. Should've known he'd got off too lightly, after the efforts he'd put in to get Abi back on his list.

"I don't have time for this, Rae." He forced himself away from the wall. His hand shook as he reached for the showerhead.

"Make time," she said behind him.

Wishing he had more than a panel of glass to block her out, he sprayed himself clean before turning toward her. He stepped from the cubicle, all too aware of his cock bouncing around, still hard, still wanting. "Abi's appointment isn't finished yet. You'll have to talk to me later."

Her gaze dropped to his crotch, lifted back to his face. "Since when have you cared about making a client wait five minutes."

Five minutes? Chase doubted five minutes would be anywhere near enough time to cover the subject of Abi and why the hell he wanted her there in his clinic. He couldn't even cover it that fast if figuring it out in his own head with nobody to fucking argue with him. "I can't run over tonight. I have dinner with my mother." Not a lie. Even if it wasn't exactly a truthful answer to her question.

She stared hard at him for a moment—too long a moment. Her eyes probing and filled with suspicion. "I can find out if you're lying to me," she said.

"You want my phone to call her?" He jerked his head toward the lockers where he kept it.

"No," she said, her lips curving in a way that said she wasn't amused in the slightest. "But just so you know. This conversation ain't over, Walker." As she turned and headed for the door, she shot back, "Not by a long shot."

~

M a Walker lived in a ground floor apartment around two miles from CW Consult. An apartment Chase paid for. He'd had to negotiate hard to get the one she had, and paid through the nose for a private quarter of the garden to be made available to his mother alone.

Using his own set of keys, he let himself into the pale-painted foyer. White tiles gleamed bright enough to reflect his movements from beneath his feet. A large Monet replica hung on the wall to his left, after the door labelled '1', and on the other side of it, farther along the wall, was a lift to the two floors above. Straight ahead, a door led to a glass-boxed staircase, and on the wall to the right, two more doors to the other apartments of floor G.

The trainers he'd changed into squeaked against the tiles as he strode toward the one in the far-right corner. Apartment number 3. While the keychain in his pocket held access to that door, as well as the front entrance, Chase never used it. He hadn't let himself into his mother's home since he'd left her for an adventure of his own. For whatever twisted reason, he considered it disrespectful—no matter that she never paid him the same consideration in return.

Dipping his face to the peephole he'd insisted be adapted to his mother's height, he tapped the knocker against the wood and waited. He knew the second she peered through by the high-pitched, "It's my boy," that made its muffled way through the wood.

The door swinging open revealed his mother's round face. No matter how often he visited, she always beamed like she hadn't seen him in a year. Stood there a fraction shy of clapping her hands like he'd surprised the hell out of her and she hadn't been expecting him at all.

Letting out a huge sigh her whole being seemed to participate in, she let her gaze skim his entire length to his feet, then all the way back up again. "Look at you."

He took a step back, spread his arms out to the side. "Don't be daft, Ma. I look exactly the same as I did last week." Spotting the beginning of a headshake that always preceded a protest, he stepped into the hallway and, stooping to her five-two height, wrapped his arms around his mother's shoulders.

"I can't believe you're 'ere," she said, her hands patting at his back.

It was something she always said. Every time he visited. And it made him feel guilty, every damn time, that he'd dared leave it longer than a day between visits.

"I told you I'd come. If I say I'm coming ..."

"You come," she said, pulling back and taking his face in her hands.

Since he'd been a toddler, his mother had looked at him like she couldn't quite believe what she'd produced. She looked at him like he was her greatest creation. Made him feel like he was, too.

"Dinner smells good," he said, intercepting the tears he knew would arrive if he let her stare at him for too long.

"Roast beef," she said, turning for the kitchen, and he knew he'd redirected her thoughts in time.

Following her into the cosy room, he watched as she bustled across to the cooker top and stirred at what looked like gravy in a saucepan. The kitchen was another room he'd had set out how she'd requested. None of that 'fandangled modern rubbish'. Just plain old pine fronting, a granite top, and as close to a traditional range as they could get without all the work of running one.

"Sit down," she ordered, like she knew he stood there staring. "You must be tired after a day mendin' peoples' 'eads."

Most workers did feel tired after a full shift. Chase always seemed to leave the office feeling energised.

Or maybe that was just his perpetual hard-on egging him on.

And the fact he still hadn't got close to offloading Abi out of his system.

Doing as his mother said, he pulled a chair out from beneath the pine table and sank onto the frilly pad on its seat, thankful for the cushioning when his still-sore arse scraped against the underside of his boxers.

The window beside the pans his ma tended to looked out over her garden quarter, where some kind of vine clung to a trellis fence, and wildflowers bordered a small patch of grass. "That fella been coming to cut your lawn?" he asked, eyeing the overgrown green blades.

"Stop frettin'," his mother said, reaching for the oven door. "It's not his day 'til tomorrow."

"I wasn't fretting."

"Yes, you were." She turned toward him with a roasting tin in her hands. "You're always frettin'." Placing the tin down on a mat in front of him, she nodded toward the meat fork and carver knife she'd set out. "And you ain't no need to. I can take care of meself, you know." She twisted back toward the open oven door and pulled out a second tray. "I been doin' it for a long time. You 'ave to when you 'ave responsibilities ..."

By responsibilities, she meant Chase. She always meant Chase.

Letting her waffle on, he switched off to her regular lecture about the only reason Chase knew how to take care of himself and others being that he'd had a good teacher, and set about carving the meat. As always, his ma had cooked it to perfection —or just how he liked it, anyway. Not bloody. Not tough. Just the right side of juicy to curl away in slices beneath his guiding of the blade and melt against his tongue.

"And when are you goin'a find yourself a nice girl to take care of you?" she said, banging roast potatoes down onto the table.

"I thought you just said you'd taught me to take care of myself," he said without looking up. "Why do I need taking care of, when you don't?"

She moved about again and produced a bowl of cauliflower cheese. "'Cause you're a bloke. And all women know that blokes ain't no good at takin' care of 'emselves." A bowl of carrots joined the cauliflower, but at least she offered a wink with her words, and Chase couldn't help but smile.

"Is this the talk about the birds and the bees again, Ma?"

"Ha!" Her grin stretched wide as she brought more food across from the cooker. Anyone would've thought a dozen more guests were expected for the meal. "So, 'ave you?" she asked, clattering plates against each other as she extracted them from a pile in the cupboard.

"Have I what?"

"Found yourself a nice girl."

He tried really hard not to think about the only nice girl he knew. One he'd never have for a whole complicated haystack of reasons. One who was due to get married to some guy who sounded like an idiot—in Chase's opinion, anyway.

And Chase was helping to prep her for the event.

Sighing, he pushed the beef tray aside and made way for the plate she handed him. "I don't need a nice girl, Ma. I already have you."

Her hand clipped the back of his head as she rounded behind him on the way to her seat.

"What was that for?" he asked, rubbing the spot out of habit rather than because she'd hurt him.

"You know," she said, a sternness to her voice as she sat beside him, and she picked up her knife and fork with grit and determination in her expression. His mother's version of: End of conversation. For then, anyway.

For the next few minutes, she was blissfully quiet, as she divided out beef slices between their two plates, as she mounded up enough vegetables to fuel an army of soldiers in front of him and soaked them in gravy. Thankful for the break in inquisition, Chase grabbed his cutlery and shovelled up a forkful of broad beans. It was an eating ritual of his—eat the stuff he hated first, then work his way in to the good stuff. A way of dealing with his mother's insistence that he eat anything good for him, whether he liked it, or not. Because no woman likes a man too unfit to 'bring home the bacon', she liked telling him. Far too often.

"Remember that Naomi," his mother suddenly said into the quiet. Her lips squished around two baton carrots as she spoke.

Chase just glanced at her and continued eating. There never had been a Naomi.

"Or was 'er name Nancy?"

"Nobody names their kids *Nancy* anymore, Ma."

"Well, I can't 'elp it if I don't remember their names, can I?" she said, feeding a floret of cauliflower to herself.

Chase supressed the heavy sigh clogging his chest. His mother played the same game every time she brought her up. Tried to get Chase on board. Talking about her like the topic wasn't out of bounds. And it worked. Too many damned times.

"You were 'appy when Naomi was in the picture," his mother said, using her own made-up name for the woman. Like he couldn't have predicted the words. Words he had to listen to at least once a month.

How would you know? he wanted to say.

His mother had never even met Nic.

No, she just had just listen to you rambling on about her, his brain offered. *Had to watch you grinning like a moron, every time you did.*

"A bit posh, for my likin'," his mother continued on. "But she made you smile, didn't she? You was always smilin' when you was with Naomi."

Chase chewed on a too-big slice of beef. If his mouth was full, she'd forgive him his lack of response.

"Oh ..." His mother let out a big sigh, pretending not to be watching him out of the corner of her eye. "Why can't I ever remember 'er name?"

He pretended he didn't hear and ate a lump of veg. He knew she wanted him to help her out. Knew she wanted him to step in with the woman's name.

He wouldn't, though. He never did. Partly because there wasn't any point. But mostly because he knew his mother hadn't forgotten Nic's name. She'd never forgotten a single detail where Chase was concerned. His mother had the longest memory in the fucking world.

And, sometimes, that memory was the proverbial pain in Chase's sore and stinging arse.

For the first time in three weeks, Chase hoped his mother hadn't made dessert.

Dinner sat heavy in his stomach as Chase left the clean-faced apartment block. For the entire meal, his mother had waffled on, and on, and fucking on about Nic. What the hell did she expect to achieve by it, anyway? Not like talking about her would fix the past.

Besides, he didn't even want to fix it. Not anymore. He hadn't for over a year.

He just wished his ma would get with the programme.

Trying his best to push it aside, he checked the time on his phone—a little after nine—and weighed up his options for the rest of the evening: grab transport home, walk home, crawl home.

Or get fucked up.

His brain clung to the last on the list. The Club didn't open two nights in a row, so he couldn't go there. And the girls at the nightclubs got on his nerves with their needy chasing and clinging, like the whole night was a competition and bagging a guy was their prize. It saddened him how fast they came running at a simple nod of his head.

Not so long back, he'd have loved that ease. Not so long back, he'd thought it made him desirable.

He'd since grown to realise, it just made him as easy as the women he'd picked up.

Before he'd registered the unconscious decision, he'd moved. His feet treading pavement and carrying him at a clipped pace.

Toward home.

He probably should've called a taxi. Hopped on a bus to cover at least part of the journey. Except, after the round of bulleted questions being fired at him for the past couple of hours, he didn't want any kind of company, he realised. Even the kind that most likely wouldn't talk to him.

Rain had fallen while he'd been in his mother's place, and puddles remained as evidence of that. Beneath the lamplight offering an intermittent glow against the encroaching night, each shallow pool glistened out his reflection on passing, his shadow sweeping across the ground like an inverted torch.

He'd always loved the city at night. When central, everywhere seemed to shine as brightly as the streets did during the day—a unique kind of glow that no other city seemed to rival. When on the outskirts, where Chase made his trek home, the shadows felt like a cloak to hide beneath, a security blanket that trapped out the darkness of a person's mind and brought the kind of peace that only came with shutting out the rest of the world.

He loved the city even more once he reached the path alongside the Thames, almost thirty minutes later. Still a way to go, but at least he'd hit the homestretch. He'd hit the place he considered his own.

The quiet tune of the river always seemed to calm him. The cool breeze that danced across its surface to soothe. For the first time in days, he sensed his shoulders relaxing. And he began to forget just how much his bloody arse still hurt.

Up ahead, a lone figure cut onto the path, their slender shoulders hunched against the slight chill of the air. Chase paid them little more than a glance as soon as he'd established the lack of threat, not bothering to slow his pace to fall in behind them for the long stretch. It probably made him a sexist bastard, his assumption of a gentle-framed woman, but the streets of the city held far more meaner and fucked up occupants than a female walking alone.

Across on the water, a narrowboat had been moored, above which smoke chugged from the vessel's small chimney, probably from a fire offering warmth and homeliness. The undrawn curtains showed the lit interior, where a couple sat close together within the colourful space. Neither looked bored, or restless, or discontent.

Thinking of the more spacious home he, himself, headed toward, Chase almost envied them their cosy cubbyhole of a lounge that gave those living there little choice but to exist in close quarters. Though, had he ever met someone he'd wanted to share his own home with, let alone one so restrictive in space?

Weaving around the small, shrugging stroller, he kept on his route, his frown deep as he considered his own question. Maybe he had some kind of major malfunction going on—something that kept anyone from seeing him as a more permanent solu-

J.A. BELFIELD

tion. Anyone except Jones, anyway. And wasn't that Chase's own fault? His biggest bouts of thinking seemed to be done by his cock, not his head, after all. Not to mention the barriers he'd constructed from strong steel and grit and a whole lot of back-the-fuck-off.

"Mr Walker?"

The gentle voice cut into the quiet of the night, the tone alone ordering Chase's feet to a standstill.

His turn toward the speaker was slow, hesitant, as if he questioned what his own hearing had already deducted. Eyes squinted against the dimness of the evening, he took a step closer, his head ducking like that'd help his eyes to obey his order to snap him out of his tranced thoughts.

"Abi?" She said it like a question, pointing to herself.

Christ, how lost had he been inside his own head? "Hi," he managed, before clearing his throat. "Isn't it a little late for you to be out walking?"

"Isn't it a little late for *you* to be out walking?" she shot back.

His smile slipped free. "Touché. Except, I'm actually just on my way home." Unbidden, his gaze skimmed over her form, showing the same jeans she'd worn to her appointment earlier, the blouse he decided he liked a lot hidden by a toggle-fronted coat.

"Been doing anything fun?" she asked.

His gaze flicked back up, to where her damp hair hung around her face, the tendrils curled upwards at the ends, where their shade had darkened from the moisture.

How he imagined she'd look if she'd just taken a shower.

"Visiting my mother," he said, his voice suddenly a lot hoarser than he wanted it to be. Even once he'd replied, his mouth still worked, like he had more to say but wasn't sure what. Seeing her there, unplanned, unrestricted by protocol, by the walls and eyes of the office, had him off balance. Foot lifted, he

188

felt ready to bolt—because, for whatever fucked up reason, seeing Abi outside of his own ruled domain scared the ever-loving crap out of Chase. "Yourself?" he asked, once his lips had got back on board.

"Not much, really," she said, staring up at him with those pale, really fucking pale eyes. The limited light only seemed to enhance their translucent appeal. "Mostly just walking." She shrugged. "And thinking."

"About the wedding?" He wanted to kick himself for the question when her shoulders folded in around her chest.

"A little," she said quietly, glancing away.

He studied her for a moment. The way a deep sadness seemed to shroud her very soul—one he rarely noticed when in the office. Probably because all he thought about in there was how much of her body he might get to see. Because he was a sick, sick bastard with limited fucking scope.

"Are you okay?" he asked, finding himself more than interested in the answer.

She gave a nod, but it was slow, almost hesitant.

Part of him wanted to take her hand, drag her off somewhere they could find a quiet corner, and offer her his shoulders to offload that sadness of hers onto. They were broad enough—what would it matter if they carried that of others on top of his own?

The other part of him, the sensible part that'd built a business he'd grown proud of, reminded himself that he didn't do ... this. He didn't take an interest in clients' private lives outside of what he needed to know. He didn't let himself give a shit if they were unhappy anywhere outside of the bedroom.

With Abi, though, he did give a shit.

Even if he didn't want to.

The functioning quarter of his brain ordered him to ask, "Can I call you a taxi?" and before he could stop himself, he added, "You shouldn't really be out here alone at night." Again, with the caring shit.

"Because I'm a woman?" She turned back to him, hitting him full force with those fucking eyes of hers.

Swallowing, he nodded. "If you like, yes.

She breathed out a quiet laugh. "I'm a big girl, Mr Walker. I can take care of myself." Chase wasn't so sure of that, but he didn't voice as such as she twisted away from him, glancing back from beneath the lashes she'd lowered. "I'll see you next week?"

"You will," he said, his smile reappearing—like the thought of that alone sprinkled happy dust over his stupid head.

"Goodnight, Mr Walker."

Turning fully away, she headed back along the path from the way they'd come, her hips swinging effortlessly even with her coat weighing them down. Chase must have stood there a full minute, just watching the way she moved. The way each overhead streetlamp she passed radiated her in a halo of gold. As she grew smaller with each retreating step she took, the ache in his groin grew more and more obvious.

Again, Chase was painfully hard as fucking hell.

And, once more, Abi O-Shay was the bloody cause.

EPISODE FIVE

Thomas Johnston. Arms built from steroids. A chest the size of Buckingham Palace. And desirer of the dead.

Dressed in rumpled corduroys that his body did a decent job of ironing out and a sweater long gone baggy at every one of its cuffs, his thinning hair combed flat from its far-side parting, he smelled surprising fresh and appealing as he stared at Chase from his spot on the chaise.

"Do you remember what we discussed the last time you were here?" Chase asked, trying to hide his frown.

Mr Johnston nodded. "I told you things I've never told anyone else."

Probably because if he'd told them to just anyone he knew outside of CW Consults, Mr Johnston would've lost all his friends. Unless, of course, he had friends with the same tendencies. Chase didn't want to think about the path a group of friends like that might follow.

Whatever his sexual fantasies, though, Thomas Johnston hadn't acted on them. He'd booked himself in with Chase's clinic and gone in search of help—where he'd been surprised to discover that there just might be a legal alternative for the fetishes he'd so far resisted carrying out.

"That's generally what I'm here for," Chase said with a small smile. "Do you remember, at the end of your last appointment, I made a suggestion for continuing your therapy in a safe and controlled environment?"

Mr Johnston eyes sparkled for an instant: the look of a guy being given something he probably shouldn't have. "I remember. I've been thinking about it. About what it might be like. How long do you think I might have to wait?"

"Well, I had thought today would work," Chase said, straightening from his seat and rounding the desk. He waved a hand toward Mr Johnston. Mostly his attire. "Did the ladies at the front desk not invite you to the changing rooms to prepare?"

"Ah ... yes." He squirmed a little. "But I showered this morning, so ..."

"I'm sorry, Mr Johnston, but it's policy at CW Consults. All clients must agree to cleanse here immediately prior to any practical sessions, just as they are expected to wear only the clinic robes for those appointments. It was in the paperwork you signed when you became a client with us."

The man shot to his feet like his arse had been lit, his towering bulk a heavy contrast to his voice. "I-I could wash now. Get changed. I have time. I do have time?"

Despite his distaste for the man's eagerness, Chase almost laughed as he nodded. "I'll get Samantha to show you the way."

The room Chase stood in was usually set up as an office scene, but the desk and chair and filing cabinets that supported the theme had been pushed to the far corner of the room, a wide screen blocking them from view.

Also blocking them from view was a second set of screens, ones with a heavy, denim-blue fabric stretched between their metal frames. Those had been positioned around a specially made gurney, one wider than the regular beds found in hospitals, and reinforced against the clatters and squeaks often created by those, too.

On the gurney, a woman lay, with only a white sheet for protection against the chill blasting from the air conditioning in there. Skin pale, body rigidly still, lips a morbid blend of blue and purple. Chase tried not to stare at the damage to her temple, as the specialist he'd ordered in checked the prop over.

After a few more nods and quiet whispers, the man from Taboo Services nodded Chase's way. "Everything's ready. Should I ...?"

"Yes, if you wouldn't mind," Chase said, and the specialist took himself off toward a discreet corner of the room and positioned himself out of sight.

They waited only a few more minutes for Samantha to push open the door and usher in Mr Johnston. The soft fabric of the clinic robe barely contained his mounded chest, and the terry-cloth slippers strained around his feet that were, Chase noted, as muscular as the rest of him.

Sending a quick glance toward the awaiting scene, he had to wonder if the gurney would hold up.

The door closed at Mr Johnston's rear, and Chase studied his expression as he shuffled over. The way his eyes darted about the room as if trying to gain its measure. The way those same eyes stilled as his gaze reached the vicinity of the screen-enclosed gurney. His throat bobbed with a swallow. His tongue swept across his lips. And he turned to Chase with an expression of gormlessness like he couldn't figure out what was happening, or how the hell he'd got there.

"Welcome to your practical session," Chase offered. "Did Samantha explain to you how these work?"

He nodded, his half-open mouth making him look almost comical.

"Then, you understand that, for both your protection and of those involved, today's session will be secondarily observed at all times and, where it deemed necessary, recorded?"

Another mute nod.

"In that case, I see little reason in delaying. I'm going to take an unobtrusive seat over there." He pointed to one he'd set up in the corner of the room facing the inner 'U' of the screens. "And I think the best case here will be to allow you to commence as soon as you're comfortable, and then we can discuss your session in my office once you've had a chance to change. Any questions?"

His mouth finally closed for his headshake, and Chase withdrew a small foil-wrapped package from his pocket and held it out to his client.

"You will be expected to use this." He waited until Mr Johnston had taken it from him. "Failure to do so will result in the session being terminated, and may affect your eligibility for future practical sessions. Do you understand?"

He tucked the condom into the pocket of his robe. "I understand," he said, finally speaking.

"Okay, this session may commence."

His client went to step forward, but hesitated. "Is there a way I can do this without someone else in here?"

Chase shook his head. "I'm afraid not."

He nodded like he'd expected as such, and after a final glance at Chase, one that told him he really didn't like his presence, he lumbered over toward the setup.

The stool Chase had set up for himself elevated him for a better view of the session. Ahead of him, Mr Johnston stood at

194

the foot of the gurney. Not moving. Just staring. Almost as if afraid to believe he really saw what his eyes showed.

Adjusting on the stool until comfortable, Chase watched as, almost reverently, Mr Johnston circled the gurney, his gaze downcast toward the body atop it, his hands brushing just outside of the form beneath the sheets. Reaching the woman's head, he finally touched her, his fingers stroking around the deep gash there.

Moving alongside the gurney again, he gripped hold of the sheet's hem, drawing it down from the body, until she lay pale and exposed, and as if once more in disbelief of his situation, he paused at the foot of the bed, his hands coming up to link behind his head as he drew in deep breaths. For a moment, he closed his eyes. Like he needed the disconnect to gain control of himself. Like he never imagined he'd be stood before the very thing of which he fantasised. And in that moment, he represented a need no different to that of any other man out there, regardless of how Chase, or anyone one else, might feel about his urges.

Because he didn't look sleazy, as Chase suspected he may have. And he didn't resemble any of the pictures Chase had painted in his head, of a session such as the one he led then. No, Mr Johnston simply looked as though he considered himself blessed. Blessed to be standing there. To be given such an offering. Blessed to finally be given an outlet for his desires.

His hand reached out, and Chase couldn't help but notice its tremble as the man brushed over the woman's calf. Her knee. Gently moving that leg aside created a small gap, which Mr Johnston widened by shifting her other leg over. Although he hadn't spread her legs wide, he'd still placed her pussy on show, and the breath he gave as he stared down toward it shuddered from him.

Slowly, as if unwilling to jostle the frozen body, the man

climbed onto the foot of the gurney, one knee at a time. His thighs nudged against hers as he moved closer to the woman's core.

For the next six minutes, Chase quietly observed, as his client caressed the body laid out before him. Over high-ridged hips. A slightly rounded stomach. Breasts full in flesh but flattened from position, their tips puckered tightly against the cold.

No matter where Mr Johnston touched her, he did so with a tenderness Chase hadn't been expecting. Not just because of the nature of his request, but because of the man's size and gait. And Chase silently chastised his own preconceptions that'd set his client into a mould he didn't really deserve. Not when he'd sought help and hadn't simply acted out his desires regardless of respect or legalities or boundaries.

Ahead of him, Mr Johnston held himself rigid above the woman. His knees between her thighs. His hands aside each of her shoulders. His solid arms trembling as they supported him there. When his body lowered to hers, and his lips claimed the job of exploring the woman's body, Chase doubted his client would be holding out much longer.

~

After finally finding the sexual outlet he'd sought, Chase had expected Mr Johnston to return to his office refreshed and full of beans. Not edgy and twitchy, with a face full of shame, which was how he actually stepped through the door after cleaning up.

Inviting the client to take a seat on the chaise, Chase drew a chair closer for himself, waiting until they'd both settled, facing one another, before he gave the order of, "Talk to me."

The man's arms kept lifting from his sides, like he felt the need to gesture but didn't know how. "There's something wrong with me. Isn't there?" His voice sounded as full of hurt as his expression looked.

"What did you get out of today's session?" Chase asked, instead of responding to the client's self-accusation.

"This ..." He took a deep breath, his chest full of tremors as it lifted. "Me ... it's *illegal* ... for a *reason*." He hissed the last word, as if to say so had pained him.

"May I speak candidly for a moment?" Chase asked, and at the jerked nod of assent, he clasped his hands in a loose knot of fingers. "Everyone fantasises. Everyone. And whether they admit it, or not, I can guarantee you that around eighty percent of those who fantasise do so about the taboo. They fantasise anything from extramarital affairs to orgies, to sex with non-existent beings only the creator has heard of—some even fantasise of the very deeds they fear the most."

"Like rape," Mr Johnston offered, his voice a little steadier.

Chase nodded. "Amongst other scenarios. And yes, a lot of those fantasised about are dark and very much considered immoral or unnatural. *Illegal*. And yes, a lot of those who do the fantasising will never carry out a single one of those dreams. To have come to me when you did, and admit the feelings you were having, took bravery, Mr Johnston. And the fact that you came here searching for a solution, or a way to cure yourself of your thoughts, tells me you have a greater understanding of your situation than most. However, in my experience, fantasies don't vanish through mere will power alone. Nor do they evaporate with a few therapy discussions, where another person tries to figure out *why* you have these feelings, or tries to steer you toward a 'healthier' route of sexual needs." He did air-quotes for the word, his expression probably conveying exactly what he thought of that. "The fantasies in our mind are what we, if brave enough to admit to ourselves, truly crave. They are the darkest part of our soul. And yes, for some, they can be left untended with no diminishing effect on the individual's life. But with the correct understanding of an individual's needs, very often a safe and *legal* solution can be found, if only the individual knows where to look."

"But ... what I did today was *il*legal," the client insisted, and Chase shook his head.

"CW Consults would never condone illegal sexual practices within its establishment." He smiled, as much at the confusion blanking the other man's eyes as to reassure. "Have you ever heard of the term pseudonecrophilia, Mr Johnston?"

The deep grooves that appeared on his brow told Chase he hadn't. "What?"

"The kind of sex you crave is termed necrophilia." Chase paused, and the client nodded his agreement. "Pseudonecrophilia re-enacts the desired scenario ... except nobody involved in the situation is actually dead."

He watched as that sank in. As Mr Johnston's eyebrows went from crouching over his eyes to leaping up toward his hairline. "She wasn't *dead*!" He sounded almost affronted. "Jesus, no wonder she wasn't as cold and stiff as—"

Chase held out his palms. "Before you judge this, let's take a moment to evaluate it. During your practical session—and think only of during your practical session—did you once question whether the woman you interacted with was actually dead."

"Well, no, but ..."

"Why not?"

"Because ..." His mouth seemed stuck open, then he snapped out of it. "Because she *looked* dead. She *acted* dead. She—"

"And because of that, you enjoyed it. Yes?"

"Well ... yes."

"Because having the illusion of what we seek in our needs is often a successful solution."

"But ... it all seemed so real."

Chase smiled. "I'm going to introduce you to the people responsible for making today's session happen. Do you think you're ready for that?"

At the client's nod, albeit a hesitant one, Chase reached over his desk and pressed the intercom. "Can you show our guests in, please?"

A couple of minutes later, Raelyn swung open the office door, and the technician from earlier entered, alongside a woman who resembled the body from the gurney, except she had colour in her cheeks and the gash from her head had disappeared.

With her pale wispy hair tied back into a neat bun, she tapped her way forward in low heels, which she'd topped with tailored trousers and a sheer blouse. The smile she sent toward Mr Johnston as she sat beside him was obviously meant to reassure, but the man seemed stuck gawping. Only when she held out a hand in greeting did he snap out of it.

"Hi, my name's Colleen."

He gave a nod that made him appear dumb as he accepted her hand, his free hand lifting toward her head. With gentle slowness, he traced over the edge of her forehead, where the skin had been damaged earlier. "How?" he asked.

"Makeup," the technician said, hovering at the side of the chaise. He stepped forward, extended his hand. "Brian."

The two men shook, and Mr Johnston turned back to Chase with a look on his face that said *what the hell's going on?*

Chase gestured toward the new arrivals. "Colleen and Brian work with a company called Taboo Services. It's a company that caters to clients with specific, often unconventional, sexual needs. Like your own," he added, flicking a hand toward the client. "I invited them to join us for today's session, because I wanted to show you that there are healthy and legal alternatives to the outlet you seek. And for the same reason, I didn't tell you in advance, because I wanted you to enter into the session without a preconceived opinion of it."

Mr Johnston blew out a weighted breath, but he nodded. Nodded like he'd finally gotten on board with the stunt Chase had pulled. And like he didn't think it was such a shitty thing for him to have done, after all.

"And I invited Colleen and Brian in here with us now," Chase continued, "because I think you remaining in touch with them and trying their services over a longer period would be of great benefit to you. I truly believe they can offer what you need."

"Would it …. Would it be the same woman every time?" he asked.

"Our aim is to cater to the client's wishes," Brian said. "So, if a specific model was requested for every appointment, we would try to provide that—or if the client preferred a different model each time."

"Would I still need to come here for the appointments?" Mr Johnston asked, turning to Chase.

"Not unless you wanted them to be held here. If you'd prefer, you could arrange with Taboo Services for the appointments to be held somewhere else—somewhere you're comfortable with."

"Most of the time, appointments take place at our therapy centre," Brian said.

"Okay?" Chase asked.

"Okay," Mr Johnston said, sighing as he nodded.

"If you have any other questions, I'm sure Brian will have all the answers you need," Chase said.

"So, I don't need to come back here?" the client asked.

Chase smiled. "Not unless you feel you need to. Sometimes, there are others out there better equipped to suit a client's needs. Taboo Services and yourself are a perfect match, Mr Johnston."

For the first time since he'd arrived, his soon to be ex-client smiled.

"However," Chase added, reaching across his desk for a business card he'd laid there, "if you find yourself dissatisfied with Taboo Services, either now, or at any point in the future—if you decide they're no longer fulfilling your needs—I would like you to contact a colleague of mine." He handed over the card, waiting until the client took the name and number of a professional he knew and trusted. "Jonathan Ashbourne is a solid consultant. He'll get you to where you need to be to live a healthy, structured life."

"Okay," Mr Johnston said, studying the card. "Thank you, Mr Walker."

"My pleasure." Chase climbed to his feet—code for 'end of session'. "Good luck in your ventures." *Have a nice life*, he wanted to add.

Because Chase had high doubts that he'd be seeing Mr Johnston again. The man looked far too much like every one of his life worries had been taken to the cleaners and ironed out for good. It was one of the reasons Chase continued to do what he did.

The weather beyond the office window didn't seem to know whether to rain, or shine. One moment, bright sunlight filtered across Chase's desk. The next, clouds smothered its glow and shot rain on the earth. A lot like how Chase's mood had been lately. Because he never quite knew which way to swing anymore, either.

And Mr Johnston's appointment hadn't helped with that.

Chase hated that he'd spent the preliminary appointments with the man feeling a disgust he hadn't wanted to admit was there. He always hated taking a dislike to a client because of their tendencies. An opinion that always seemed a whole lot more prominent when a client managed to change his mind.

Sure, he still disliked the idea of sex with a dead being. As hard as he'd tried, he just couldn't find the appeal. However, Mr Johnston's eagerness to find a way through the legal and moral barriers in a way that didn't leave even himself revolted had helped broaden Chase's view on that whole area of preference. He only wished more of those who pursued a similar dream would take the initiative of seeking help.

Letting his head drop back against the high rim of his chair, he closed his eyes for a moment. Fuck, he felt tired. Filled with a weariness that seemed to be weighing him down. His lack of sleep didn't help with that, though, did it? Because, more and more lately, Chase seemed to lie awake with far too many thoughts whizzing a path through his brain. Thoughts that shot in from all directions and converged into a central mass of confusion that left him tossing and turning into the early hours then hand-fucking himself into an undeniable exhaustion when nothing else worked.

Not even bothering to open his eyes, his slid a hand across his desk for the intercom button.

"Yes?" Sam's voice.

"Sam, who else have I got today?" Maybe he could cut an appointment short. Skip out early. Find someone to help steer him toward an oblivion his mind badly needed.

"Ms O'Shay has just arrived for her four thirty."

Chase didn't know whether to smile or frown at the announcement. His cock definitely wanted to smile. His cock liked the idea of Abi being up next very much.

His head, though—that just felt confused. Confused by pretty much anything involving Abi O'Shay.

Sadly, for Chase's weak resolve, his cock won a round, as soon as he remembered what they had planned for her session.

"Would you like me to send her through?" Sam asked.

A big part of him wanted to tell her *no* and rush forth to go grab her himself.

The small part of him, the part that had him gritting his teeth against his urges, ordered him to keep his butt in his seat.

"Yes, please do," he said through the intercom.

Shoulders tenser than they'd been a moment ago—though, not necessarily in a bad way—and his mind a whole lot more awake, Chase tried not to stare directly at the door like he couldn't fucking wait for it open.

He couldn't, but that was beside the point. He had to at least pretend he didn't suffer with a massive dose of Eager Beaver—if only to himself. His gaze darted to his bookshelves. Back to the door. Across to the chaise longue. Back to the door. To the coving around the top of the walls. Back to the door. Toward where he tapped his fingertips against the underside of his desk.

The door opened. Sam pushed through first, taking enough steps into the room to widen the gap, and stood to the side for the client to pass through.

Abi.

Abi in a clinic-provided robe and terry-cloth slippers.

The sight was like a challenge accepted and smashed. Like an achieved climb of Everest.

And that smile Chase had been clinging so tightly to? Totally broke free and blew up the fucking room.

The lights had already been dimmed slightly in the bedroom they entered. The bed had been freshly covered. The carpets recently cleaned.

Striding across the rug, Chase sensed every step Abi took behind him. Which meant he already knew she'd be standing less than three feet away from him, when he turned to face her.

Even in the lesser lighting, her beauty shone out, as if to provide illumination to a space otherwise lacking. Swallowing, Chase tried to keep his focus on her face. If he let himself think too hard about what might, or might not, be under the robe, he'd likely get no words out at all. "Do you need me to run through everything for you?"

Most people didn't after attending a couple of practical sessions. Abi was amongst them with the headshake she gave.

"And you are comfortable with the plan for today?"

"I'm comfortable with it." Though she didn't waver as she stared up at him, he could've sworn he caught a slight twitch to give away her nerves.

While he didn't really want to see those nerves, their presence didn't surprise him. He'd have been more shocked to find them absent. "Okay," he said. "Where would you like me to position myself?"

Frowning, she peered around the room. "Somewhere I won't be able to see you?" Her gaze flicked back up to his. "Sorry, that sounds ..."

He shook his head, a smile spreading his lips. "It's okay. I understand what you mean." Twisting away from her, he reached for the room's chair and carried it to a corner of the room that would allow him a slanted view of her body. Better scope for seeing more of her at once. "Here?" he asked, sending her a glance over his shoulder, and she nodded, her hands tucked deep into the pockets of the robe.

"Can the lights be lower?" she asked, as he went to sit.

"They can, but I'd rather they not be quite as low as you're used to having them." He'd never see enough of her that way—something on which he didn't want to compromise.

On the other side of the room, he twisted the dial until a pale golden haze shrouded the room and he could just make out the features of Abi's face as she watched him.

"Do you need me to talk you through the session?" he asked as he headed back to his seat. "Or do you feel ready to explore on your own?"

"I'm not sure." She glanced across at the bed, drawing her lower lip between her teeth as she turned back toward Chase. "Maybe just if I need ..."

"Guidance?" he offered, and she nodded. "Okay, well, I'm going to place myself here. If I feel you could try something more than you're doing, I'll step in. Otherwise, I'll stay quiet and simply observe."

"Okay," she said quietly, her gaze retracing its route toward the bed. "Is ... is the thing I used before ..."

"The vibrator is on there, right where you found it the last time." And Chase, really, really hoped she'd use it, if only so he could hear those heightened cries of hers again.

With another quiet *okay*, and a small nod, she made hesitant steps across the room. The mattress depressed slightly as she lifted a knee onto it, followed by the other, and with her hands braced in front of her, she crawled farther onto the bed.

She stilled near the centre. Seemed undecided about what to do next. "Can I keep the robe on?" she asked after a few beats.

No, take it off. "Whatever you feel is best for you." For a little while, at least.

Her entire body seemed to take part in the sigh she released. Shuffling more fully onto her knees, she reached out across the bedding. She held the vibrator when she drew her hand back. Through the shadows, she traced her fingers over its shape, as though surprised at the appearance of something she'd only encountered in darkness. Perhaps she'd expected it to be larger.

Or smaller. Chase couldn't decipher her inner thoughts from the slight frown she wore.

Placing it back down on the bed, but closer to her own position, she glanced across toward Chase. "It feels weird with you in here."

"Weird, how?" he asked.

"I'm not sure." She shrugged, a dainty movement even with the bulk of the robe. "It's like ... when I just heard your voice, I knew you were watching, but it felt like—it felt like I was performing for someone who wasn't really there. Does that make sense?"

"Like the voice giving you orders was something you imagined for yourself?"

"Kind of," she said.

"You could pretend I'm not here now."

"It's not the same. Not really. It feels weird with you just sitting there and not saying anything." He wondered if she noticed how her fingers twisted into the blankets. "It feels ... I don't know."

"Did you like being told what to do?" he asked. He didn't want to evaluate his body's response to that possibility. Or the way his voice had suddenly deepened.

Her gaze locked with his as she answered, "Yes."

Chase's jaw locked as he fought against swallowing. "Untie your robe, Abi," he ordered before he could second guess his path.

The lines deepened across her brow. "But ... I'm naked underneath."

"Will you spend your entire life never discovering the simple pleasure of being naked while in the presence of another?" He could almost imagine Sam on the other side of the glass, her *What the hell are you doing?* barking up her throat. "Will you let your fear take that from you?"

Hurt seeped into her eyes. "No," she said. Except, she didn't sound so sure.

Chase wanted to make her sure. "Then, untie your robe. You unbuttoned your shirt the last time you were here. It's the same."

"Last time, I wore a bra underneath," she said, her voice a little firmer.

"That didn't stop you looking fucking divine." His own tone came out harsh, and the two of them sat staring at one another, Abi's chest trembling its way up and down like she struggled to interpret his words.

Or maybe she understood them just fine but didn't quite believe their presence. Chase could hardly believe he'd spoken them himself.

Unclenching his jaw, he cleared his throat. "Untying your robe will enable you to move it aside," he said, forcing calmness into his tone. "Otherwise, it might get in your way and restrict access to your body." Chase had seen first-hand how frustrated women could get over a simple piece of clothing stalling their lust. "You asked for my vocal guidance. I'm giving it to you."

She held his gaze for a long few seconds, releasing a quiet huff as she glanced away. Her fingers went to the belt at her waist. Fumbled with the knot she'd tied there. After working the fabric free, she pushed the two ends away, knocking the robe aside with them. As she twisted around to sit on her butt, the tips of her nipples poked free.

And Chase let out the longest of long fucking breaths.

"Do you still need me to tell you what to do?" he asked, when she glanced back toward him. "Do you need me to tell you to touch yourself, Abi?"

Heat blushed over her cheeks, but she held his gaze with her quiet, "Yes."

"Lie back," he ordered. He expected at least some defiance, but received none, as she uncurled herself down to the bed, leaving only her knees slightly raised. "Now stroke yourself. I want to know what pleasures you. I need you to show me what makes you feel good."

"Should I ... should I touch *in there* again?" She didn't look his way as she spoke.

"Yes."

Her lips parted as she reached down. As her fingers breached her pubis.

Chase almost wanted to shift his position, move his chair to where he'd have a better view of her cunt. If only to see how wet she could get with his commands guiding her actions.

He knew when she'd located a sweet spot by the heightened tone of her sigh. By the way her thighs lowered to the sides. Her hips nudged up so subtly, she probably didn't even realise she moved them herself.

"How wet are you, Abi?" He needed to know.

Her head rolled to the side. Those eyes of her landed on him, their paleness even paler. Their brightness even brighter. "Wet," she said, the word barely more than a whisper, shooting need into his already hardened cock.

"Use it," he said. "Spread it. Make your clitoris wet until it slides beneath your fingers."

She glanced away again as she stretched down. Her fingers dipped into her cunt, before she slipped them back out covered in her own juices and trailed a glossy path to her clit.

"Again."

She obeyed. Back in to collect her personal nectar. Back up to paint herself with the evidence of pleasure.

"Now faster."

Again, she did as directed. Her hand slipping to her cunt, gathering pre-cum, then back to her clitoris.

Chase couldn't help noticing how her fingers lingered longer each time. Inside herself. Around her responding clitoris. He also couldn't help but notice how her fingers had begun to curl each time she withdrew them from her pussy, meaning their tips would be stroking over her G-spot, heightening that desire of hers he could see building.

At that point, he should've been relaxing back into his seat. Letting the session take its course and leaving the client to find their own way. Except, his body wouldn't let him relax. Wouldn't let him lean back for even a second, lest he risk missing any part of the show. His arms corded tight, despite their casual placement over the chair's rests. His jaw locked tight against the roll of his tongue. And each of his thigh muscles clenched into a solid mass of *No!* as his hips tried shunting forward in time with the throb of his cock.

"Stop holding back," he told her, as she matched him in the set of her legs and the almost visible pinning of her ass against the bed. Almost as though she feared revealing how much she wanted what she could offer herself. As if she feared showing *him.* "Listen to what your body tells you. Obey its needs."

Her breaths hastened as she thrust her hips up to meet the plunge of her fingers. Toes clenching tightly against the sheets, she spread her thighs wider until the tendons pulled taut through each, forcing her shifting hips into a smaller rhythm that held an almost frantic appeal. Her free hand released its clutch of the bedding and hovered over her torso. As if she wanted to touch herself further but didn't know where.

Fuck, his cock hurt just from his watching her. His balls ached like a couple of bastards. Still, he wanted more. More from Abi. More for himself. More of fucking everything.

"Your breast," he told her, his voice scarcely clinging to control. "Your nipple."

As if she'd already pre-practised the act, her fingertips went straight to the rigid bud and rolled over its tip, her back instantly arching as if to beg contact from herself. Chase felt strangled by his own breaths as her entire body began a slow undulation into each of her ministrations.

"You're still holding back." He had no idea how he still managed to talk. He had no idea how he managed to cling onto the growing need in his groin, either. "I want you to show *me* how much you like your touch, Abi. I want to *hear* you." He really wanted to fucking hear her.

Almost as soon as he'd spoken, her lips released a gasp that deepened into a moan. Her back arched higher. Her fingers plunged deeper, the ball of her hand massaging her stiff clitoris.

And Chase knew he could look at her no longer. Because if he did ... he'd be stripping out of his bottoms and fucking that sweet virginity the hell out of her, consequences be damned.

Closing his eyes, he forced his body back in the seat, forced himself to only listen.

"Good," he murmured, when a deep groan boiling with need filled the room.

He pictured her hips driving upward, seeking solace for that need. Her heels drilling downward into the sheets. Letting his mind wander deeper, he caught on her cunt. Fingers pumping in and out, creating a waterfall of glossiness that spilled down to the crease of her ass.

"Use your thumb on your clitoris, Abi," he ordered. "Rub it as you stroke your insides. Rub it until you yearn your own touch."

He knew from the slight whimper when she'd hit it just right, and his cock swelled so fucking hard with a yearning of its own, Chase questioned if she'd notice if he just relieved himself there and then. If he hand-fucked the stiffness out of himself and eased the ache that burned right up into his gut.

Forcing his mind's eye up higher, he latched onto his conjured image of her breasts. Full and beseeching. Hard as fucking pegs. And Abi's hands massaging and plumping and nipping and toying. Those gentle sounds of hers spurred on by the sparks of pleasure he knew would be firing their way down to her pussy with every single pluck.

Above her heaving chest, that soft-shaped face contorted with the desperation to come. Mouth wide and expressive with every sigh, cry and whimper. Her eyes wide, so fucking wide. And one hundred percent on him, as if she needed the visual to reach her peak. As if the sight of him alone was her guidance.

Just thinking of her perfect, angelic face, he wanted to climb on that bed with her, grip that freefalling hair and yank her head back, show her what she could truly do with those lips. Teach her the most base noises of desire and how to create them.

As he imagined himself doing exactly that, pictured the thickness of his shaft sliding home into the heat of her wet mouth, he sensed the warmth of a body over his. The nudge of a thigh against his.

Letting his head fall back against the seat, he accepted the weight of another across his lap. Gripped tight to the arms of the seat as he imagined the trail of glossiness spreading across his legs as she straddled him.

Silky skin brushed across his cheek. The skin of her breasts. He wanted to grasp hold of its fleshiness, suck its tip deep into his mouth. Show her the joy she could gain from the affections of another. Instead, he held himself as rigid as his cock had grown in his pants.

Arms pressed in either side of his head, over his shoulders. A flat stomach aligned with his own. At the gentle rock of her hips, he was already moaning before her cunt had even made the first contact with his dick.

Not daring to move, not daring to even open his eyes, he held his breath. Waiting for her next move. Giving her full control.

Her hips shifted back, and she brought them forward again, sweeping her cunt across his solid shaft with a tiny upward flick that had the head of his cock flinching while crying out for more. His muttered, "Fuck," left his lips before he could tame it, another moan eking out when she repeated the move.

With each brush of her pussy across his hardness, her breaths hastened, her quiet groan merged with those he made. With each nudge against him, her breasts caressed his chest and made him wish like fucking hell he'd had chance to shuck his damned shirt.

"How does that feel to you?" he asked, his voice little more than a growl.

All he received in response was a heightened whimper, her hips grinding into him with an urgency that met his own.

"How does that *feel*, Abi?" he demanded.

"Good—" A gasp broke through her whisper. "It feels good."

It felt more than good to him. It felt fucking amazing, and within seconds his hips had found their own rhythm, rising up to meet her, to grind harder against her cunt as it stroked around his cock. His head tipped back further, his jaw locked tight against the grunts bubbling up his throat, and as the first eruption dived from his cock, his grip of the chair set it groaning beneath the pressure, his body bucking into the trailing releases that shot free one after another.

The breath he freed burst past his lips, his chest rising and dipping with those that followed, and he finally allowed himself a glimpse at the temptress who'd taken him across the finish so fucking fast.

Except, Abi didn't sit astride him, as he'd allowed himself to imagine. She still lay back on the bed. Her hips pushing her cunt into where he fingers plunged in and out, the fingers of her free hand tugging hard at her nipple and twisting with each drive into her pussy, and her lips circled around the stifled cries she gave on the pinnacle of climax. All while she stared directly at him.

With his hips still thrusting at air in a way he scarcely noticed, he allowed his gaze to lock with hers, forced a stuck swallow along his throat. "Let go," he ordered.

And her body arched into the orgasm that seemed to rip through her from head to toe. Like a ripple effect that had her entire body undulating into its force, as she allowed herself to ride the wave of euphoria rather than fight its demands.

The cry that spilled from her hit the highest pitch he'd heard from her yet, as her hips jerked into the spasm of her muscles. Quieting when her hand slowed its strokes of her cunt and she steadied the trembles of her body, until she lay there, a quivering form of panted breaths and heaving bosom.

It was only as a slight frown crept across her brow and she averted her eyes like he'd flashed her that Chase realised how much she might have seen. How much of him she might have witnessed, as he'd forgotten his surroundings and his role, his stern composure to which he held so tightly, as he'd laid himself bare, with a rawness he never allowed in his work.

Suddenly all too aware of the soggy mess inside his boxers, he pushed to his feet and tapped a knuckle against the glass of the fake mirror. "Sam will be in very soon." He barely glanced at Abi as he said the words, and by the lack of movement in his periphery, she paid him the same respect. "I'll see you in my office once you've had time to clean up." An act he dearly needed to get on for himself.

As soon as the door swung inward, and Sam stepped inside with a questioning glare she fired on a direct path for Chase, he pushed his way out into the corridor and made a beeline for the staff quarters. Something that seemed to be becoming habit wherever Abi O'Shay was involved.

~

Freshly cleansed and freshly clothed, Chase pushed forward a step when the door to his office swung open. He stared like a fucking idiot as Abi entered and Sam closed them in together. Stared like an idiot as Abi's feet quit moving and she just stood there returning his interest.

"Abi ..." He trailed off. Mostly because he didn't know what to say. Mostly because he didn't know how much she'd seen of his control slip and didn't want to give himself up any more than necessary.

"Mr Walker," she replied, and her gaze finally snapped from his, sweeping the room as a blush began smothering her pale cheeks.

He jerked a hand toward the chaise. "Take a seat. Please."

Her movements slow, she crossed to the low sofa and sat her arse down. Chase really didn't want to think about how that same arse had ground against the bed not so long before. He already had a big enough hole to climb his way out of.

His thoughts didn't seem connected to his brain much, lately, though.

Drawing his own chair closer, he sank down until eye level, his hands instantly entwining between his knees. His eyes seeking out some kind of signal for her feelings.

"Abi ..." His mouth seemed stuck on that one word, yet again —though what the hell was he supposed to say to her? *Look, I'm really sorry if you spotted my ejaculating in there, but you just have this effect on me my body seems defenceless against.*

No woman had gotten Chase so outside of his own command. Not even Nicolette.

"Mr Walker," she shot back at him for a second time, and Chase could've sworn her lips twitched at the corners before she glanced away again.

Clearing his throat, he straightened in his seat a little. Maybe even a tiny amount of extra distance might help with his focus. "How did you feel today's session went?" Safe question, safe ground. So long as he stuck within that territory, he could deal.

Except, the stare she sent him from beneath lowered lashes held a whole lot of intent he had no idea how to interpret. "How did you feel it went, Mr Walker?"

Okay, so she'd definitely seen *something*. The real question was *how much?*. "You breached a new barrier." So had Chase. "Pushed yourself that little bit higher." She'd pushed a whole lot harder against Chase's resolve, too. "Did you enjoy today's session?"

Her cheeks darkened to red. "Yes, I enjoyed it." Her lips full-on curved for an instant, before she seemed to curb the smile and stared off toward the window. "It was very enjoyable." Her gaze sliced back to him, all probing and direct. "Don't you think, Mr Walker?"

She was playing with him. She had to be. Otherwise, why the coy glances and shy smiles, and eyes full of an understanding she seemed to want him to be privy to? "My enjoyment of the session is not what we're here to discuss, *Abi*." He had no idea how he kept his voice level. Giving a sharp clearing of his throat, he leaned in a little closer—totally, one-hundred percent against his better judgement. "You've been practising for your sessions, I saw."

"You told me to," she said, almost defensive in her tone. "You gave me homework."

"Do you always do your homework?" He should've bit down on his own tongue before those words had left his mouth. Fuck, he sounded flirtatious and suggestive as hell.

"Yes, Mr Walker." Her lips inched up again, her left eyebrow doing the same. "I always have, and always do, complete my studies. It's important, don't you think?"

The direct way she stared at him, the expression she didn't even seem to be attempting to hide, Chase could've sworn she'd mentally climbed on a train designated for an eighteen-to-thirties weekend, because she'd have been smashing it out of the park on a trip like that. A trip for which Chase definitely wanted to board. Even her body sat poised without a hint of nerves—which only brought Chase's own to the forefront with what appeared to be a switcheroo of roles.

Abi, the controlled and poised one.

Chase in a mode of *What the fuck am I even supposed to be doing.*

He barely pulled off his swallow as he nodded. "Yes, very important, yes."

He waited for her to respond to that. She didn't. Just sat there with some kind of smugness hiding just beneath the surface of her features, a shine in her pale eyes he couldn't quite fathom. Fidgeting in his seat, Chase pushed up to sit straight. Away from Abi. Away from whatever spell she'd cast to set a subtle tingling throughout his body that tugged at his groin.

"Next week ..." he said.

Again, she didn't speak, but continued with her quiet studying of him.

He probably sounded like he had a cough on the way with all the throat clearing he did. "I think we should be ready for you to progress to the next stage of your plan."

Her eyebrow quirked up a fraction more. "And what is the next stage of my plan, Mr Walker?"

Something about the way she said his name had his body responding, and he rubbed his palms along his thighs like that'd distract him enough for his dick to calm the fuck down. "Nudity." He watched for her reaction. She barely even flinched.

"My robe fell all the way open today," she said, her expression unmoving, but Chase knew he'd relocated those nerves she'd been covering from the slight waver to her tone. For some reason, it offered him a little of his own confidence back.

"Your robe could be shrugged off all the way down to your elbows, and that still wouldn't classify as you being naked." Clutching onto the shred of returning control, he leaned forward again, trying his damnedest to hold back his smile. "And I didn't mean for only you to be nude, Abi."

Her eyes widened for an instant, before she narrowed them on him. "I don't think I quite understand what you're saying, Mr Walker."

He allowed his smile through, moulding it into something he hoped represented patience and understanding. "When you finally become intimate with a man ... with your husband ..." God, he hated that fucking word lately. "... he will most likely get naked to be with you. And there's a high chance he will like for you to be naked, also."

Because who the hell wouldn't want Abi O'Shay naked alongside them. Skin brushing on skin, heat transferring from one body to another, the kind of merging perspiration that only occurs during a hard round of satisfying sex ....

Chase did, and he wasn't even marrying her.

"Surely, you're aware of this?" he added.

Her hands twitched in her lap and her expression shielded over—like she was more than aware of it but had so far been burying the fact under whatever rock she could find. He wanted to smile at the slip in her façade. He didn't want to smile, at the same time. After all, wasn't finding her confidence what treating Abi O'Shay was supposed to be about? After two beats, her face lined, lips set with a tiny twist at their corners—almost as if she felt only disgust at the very idea.

"I mean, that's how most sexual acts are carried out between married couples." Chase had to wonder how much of her demeanour change had to do with the act itself ... and how much of it was aimed at the man with whom she'd eventually be getting unclothed. "But that's what we're here for. To prepare you for such an eventuality." He sensed his professionalism edging back in with each word he spoke, relieved to be back on less foreign ground.

"By my getting naked?" she asked.

"Yes. With another."

It seemed to be Abi's turn to swallow. "I'm going to be naked with a naked man?"

Chase nodded, watching her expression, gauging her reaction.

"Who?" she said, her voice pitched a fraction higher than usual.

Usually, CW Consult would bring in a third party. Get them to strip down and cover the kind of task Abi would be faced with. Because Chase never 'just got naked' with clients—not a single client had tried undressing him completely since he'd started the practice. What would be the point, when the rules clearly stated they couldn't ask him for anything resembling full intercourse?

Not a single one of his regular rules seemed applicable where Abi was concerned, though, and Chase didn't even pause to consider the consequences, as he threw out his, "Me."

That time, her eyebrows winged high into her forehead. Her chest shifted up and down with the few hastened breaths that followed. And as she visibly gained control of herself, her features resettled into a quiet calm, through which he could only just see the nerves. "Okay." She said it real quiet. Like saying it quiet would make it less out there, less explosive in her mind.

"Okay?" he asked, because he needed to be sure—though, of what, even he didn't quite know.

She nodded, a small gesture that told him she still processed everything he'd told her.

"Okay, then," he said, climbing to his feet and gesturing for Abi to join him. "I want you to continue with your homework," he said as he guided her across the room. His dipping back into what'd almost become a shaky subject for them probably made him a dick, but he didn't care. Reaching the door, he pulled it open and waved for her to go through, turning to Rae and Sam behind the desk as Abi pattered over to them. "Can you book Abi in for next week, please?"

As Sam nodded and started tapping on her keyboard, Abi sent a glance back toward Chase. "I can only do Thursday next week."

"Thursday works for me. Sam?"

A few clicks, then, "We can do Thursday."

"Well, then." Chase smiled—grinned—as he met Abi's wide stare. "I will see you then."

He would *definitely* be seeing her then. A heapeded-whole fucking lot of her.

He couldn't quite wipe the smile away as he turned back for his office.

~

Chase really should've been heading home. Taking some alone time to unwind.

Since his after-appointment with Abi, though, all he'd thought about was her, naked, and himself so fucking close to that soft skin of hers, and he knew he'd have just ended up jacking off half a dozen times in an effort to get his bastard imaginings out of his skull.

So, instead, he'd dragged his hide off to The Trafalgar to try and dull his rotten thoughts with a drink, or ten.

The noise of inside hit him as soon as he pushed on the door, voices and laughter and music bleeding through the smallest gap. Even for a Friday, the place sounded busy for that time of evening—it didn't usually fill until at least nine.

In the lounge of the pub, only a handful of tables hadn't been claimed, and bodies hovered around the bar in huddles of those who'd come with friends. Heading straight for them, Chase shouldered his way through until his feel hit the walnut fronting of the chest-high bar. Even once there, he waited over a minute for a barman to separate him from the crowd and saunter over with a smile.

"What'll it be?"

Chase only spared him half a glance as he ordered a pint, his gaze trying to see around the bar huggers as the tender grabbed a glass. He scanned the lounge, from one four-man booth to the next, from one age-old seat to the next, until his gaze landed on a familiar set of eyes, and he smirked to himself as he paid for his drink and carried it out through the bodies.

Halfway across the floor, his presence seemed to get noticed, and as those dark eyes swung around to land on Chase, a smile tugged across the face of the guy hogging a whole table to himself.

"What the fuck is this I see?" he said, as soon as Chase reached him. He pushed to his feet, his hand reaching out to clasp Chase's, his other slapping him on the shoulder. "Zookeepers must be slacking on the job if you've escaped your cage. How're you doing, man?"

"Still rollin' like a motherfucker," Chase said, and his friend let out a hearty laugh at the familiar saying they'd shared for years.

As with Jones, Chase had known Ade Atkins since school. Just another of their circle who'd hung in the same spots, got lost in the same activities, and trod the same path through the forest of a life filled with sex. Growing up, Ade's dark eyes had spelled of trouble and brought the girls running. His unkempt mop of chestnut hair had only added to his bad boy image, though he'd kept that a lot neater since the clientele he attracted had shifted a whole heap upward.

"Haven't heard from you in a while," Chase said as he sank onto the bench seat facing Ade across the table.

He gave a vague nod, but Chase couldn't help noticing how his eyes sliced away. "Been busy working. You know how it is."

Chase nodded himself, taking a swig of his beer. He did know how it was.

"What about you?" Ade asked. "Where the hell you been hiding?"

"Work mostly." And in his shower, wanking like it'd become his new favourite pastime. Mostly to thoughts of Abi O'Shay. He shrugged with a small smile. "Okay, pretty much just work."

"Hey, when business is good, you gotta climb on board the rollercoaster and scream that you wanna go faster, right?"

Chase pointed a finger his way. "Right."

The smiles they'd just shared faded, their eyes skimming away from each other. To anyone else, they probably appeared to have sank into a comfortable silence, but Chase had spotted the tight lines of Ade's shoulders as soon as he'd chosen his table to sit. Knowing if he pushed him Ade would clam up, Chase downed another shot of his drink and waited. It was how Ade had always been, growing up. Whenever he'd had something on his mind, or a problem he didn't know how to fix, he'd shut everyone out with a stony expression and hunched shoulders, only opening his mouth for support when he was good and ready.

It took almost seven long minutes of his blank expression before Ade swung his gaze back toward Chase. "I've been meaning to call you."

Chase noted the twitch of his fingers against his glass, but pretended he hadn't. "About what?"

"About work." His shoulders seemed to hunch over, but their shift only took Ade closer to Chase across the table. "About *my* work."

Chase didn't need telling about Ade's work. Because Chase had been in the same role prior to calling it a day and setting up CW Consult, so he knew exactly what it entailed—what it *could* entail. And usually any stories shared from his job involved laughter-filled recollections, not nervous, shifty-eyed explanations.

Swallowing, Chase asked, "What's wrong at work, Ade?"

"I, uh ..." He blew out a breath that popped his cheeks, his gaze sliding away before it shot back again. "I got assigned Nicolette."

Chase breathed in. Breathed out. He'd expected a tightening of his fists. A tensing of his shoulders. Maybe even a tremor to his inhalation. He got none of that—which Chase hadn't really anticipated, despite his adamant declarations of being over her. "Okay," he said slowly.

"I'm sorry, man," Ade said, lifting his palm toward Chase. "Mrs Pacton didn't give me a choice."

"Ade, I said it's okay."

"I fucking told her I didn't want the job, but she said if she had to reassign her to someone else, she'd reassign some of my other clients, too."

Reaching out, he gripped the back of Ade's head and stilled his face in front of his own. "Will you quit being a dick. I just fucking told you it's okay."

Chase, himself, didn't need the added confirmations that it was okay. He'd known as soon as he'd spoken the first one that he'd meant it. Because he was over Nicolette. Past her. Done and dusted and out the other side with a clean outlook and clean goals. Even if it had taken him longer than he'd have liked to get there.

Ade stared hard at him for a few long seconds. "You're really cool with it?"

"It's not like I never expected it to happen at some point. She replaced me the minute I'd walked, and she'll continue to replace each and every one of you as soon as she grows bored." It was the truth, a hazard of the job—probably why Ade didn't so much as flinch at Chase's words. "Besides, you're the best Mrs Pacton's got working for her now, so it was only a matter of time." He let go of his friend and settled back into his seat. "I'm cool with it. She's a good deal to land—you're lucky."

What he never mentioned was that the good deal part of the equation only applied to someone able to switch off their emotions from the job. Something Chase had done with ease, until he'd taken on Nic.

Something Ade did with ease, no matter who he got assigned.

Ade tipped his glass toward Chase before downing a gulp. "Thanks, man. I appreciate it." His gaze lifted, sticking to something behind Chase's left shoulder, his lips curving into only a fraction of a smile. "Shit's about to get disturbing."

From those words alone, Chase knew who'd just walked in and grabbed Ade's attention. He should've known he'd show. He always did on the odd occasions Chase ventured out—like he had his own satellite tracking everyone's movements.

A couple of minutes later, a fricking hulk of a shadow descended over the table, and a body thrust itself into the seat opposite Chase, giving Ade no choice but to scoot along the bench and make room.

Jones's smile seemed twisted as he set it on Chase. "Walker. You fucking remembered you have friends." He leaned in toward Ade. "This is a fucking momentous occasion."

"It is a momentous occasion," Ade agreed with a nod.

"So, down your pint," Jones said, turning back to Chase, "and get the fucking drinks in."

Chase sighed and did as ordered, preparing to worm his way through the thickening cluster of bodies. He could've argued with Jones. He probably should've done, but Chase knew from his tone alone that Jones had already been drinking before he'd even got there. And he knew arguing with him when like that would be a waste of time for anyone involved.

"Fuck me, your arse is fucking gorgeous," Jones shouted after him.

Chase sighed harder as everyone around him turned toward the yelling idiot, and then toward Chase like they wanted to check out his butt for their own benefit. Sounded like Jones had had more than first assessment suggested. Chase just hoped he'd gone with the soft stuff and nothing too hard. He hoped even harder that Jones wasn't really drunk at all and was just in a really fanfucktic mood and high on life.

He doubted it, though.

It took almost five minutes for the tender to realise Chase actually wanted serving and wasn't just trying to grab his attention for a lark, and with three pint glasses wedged between his fingers, he twisted and turned his way back to the table.

As soon as he broke free from the crowd, his eyes narrowed. Mostly on the way Jones stared really fucking hard at something —something Chase didn't want to check out because that kind of stare from Jones too often led to trouble. He also didn't like the way Ade had his head tipped in close to Jones and stared the same way, their lips mumbling. Because that kind of behaviour always spelled trouble for Chase specifically.

Cutting off their line of sight to whatever they checked out, he dropped the drinks to the table and slipped back onto the bench. "'The fuck are you two doing? Whatever the hell it is, it hadn't better involve me." He settled deeper into his seat, his steely eyes slicing from one of them to the other.

"Girl over there," Ade said, still fixated on something over Chase's shoulder. "Totally just fucking checked you out when you went to the bar."

He rolled his eyes. "Fuck off, you two. I'm not playing." Too many times, the two of them had gelled together in a *let's get Walker fucked tonight* campaign. He'd never met anyone who couldn't accept as much as they didn't that if he wanted sex he'd just get it himself, who couldn't accept that not every night had to be about getting lucky. If their stupid efforts didn't end in so much laughter and pissing about, he'd have probably found the whole thing tedious as hell.

"I'm not playing, either, man." Ade leaned in closer across the table like he had a secret to share. "I'm telling you straight. She totally eye-fucked you when you went for drinks. Look for your fucking self."

Shaking his head at the idiots, he twisted in his seat. Anything to shut them up. Once he'd got his butt far enough around, he scanned the lounge behind him, but other than the parting and re-meeting of bodies into their groups, he saw absolutely zilch to back up their stupid projections.

Lips curled into a smile that wasn't a smile, he turned back and raised an eyebrow.

They merely lifted their hands. "She was fucking there," Ade said. "If you looked when we told you the first time, you'd have seen her."

With a fingertip against each, he pushed their drinks across the table toward them both. "And if she was *that* interested, she'd have still been standing and staring her butt off. But she wasn't."

"Maybe if you'd been a bit more discreet in checking *her* out, she would," Ade muttered.

"Listen—" Chase curled his hand around his own glass. He didn't like the way Jones stared at him from beneath his lowered brows. "Just find someone else to fuck with, yeah? I came here for a quiet night out, so just give it to me."

"If I tell you someone is checking you out," Jones said, his voice low, "they're fucking checking you out, Walker."

That time, Chase's smile did break through, though it didn't hold much humour. "I know you like to always be right. Hell, you even *think* you're always right. But this time, you're not, so get over it."

"When you turned around, how many people paid you the slightest bit of attention." Jones's voice had deepened. Not always a good sign.

Chase heaved a breath in then out, before admitting, "None."

"And how many of them even so much as looked up when you walked into The Trafalgar?"

He rolled his eyes, but went with it—mostly because trying not to would be pointless. "None."

"And how many of them are looking at me now ..." He shot a hand across and down into Ade's crotch.

Ade jerked back, but whatever Jones did beneath the table must've held him in place because he didn't move more than that.

"How *many*?" Jones asked, when nobody spoke.

Chase glanced either side of their table, took in the way everyone just nattered on among themselves like nothing existed outside of their own groups. He looked back to Jones. "None."

"None," Jones repeated, and his arm slowly moved up and down. "Even if I hand-fuck him through his kegs beneath the table."

Beside him, Ade's jaw tightened. Lines etched outward from the corners of his eyes.

"Not a single person is interested in what we're doing."

"You can quit now," Ade said through his teeth.

"I'm not done." Jones's arm continued shifting up, down, the tendons pulling tight as he probably massaged the fuck out of Ade's cock beneath the table. "I have a point to fucking make."

Whatever the hell Jones did next had a groan pushing free from Ade and his hands gripping the edge of the table, but Jones didn't once remove his focus from Chase. His stare heavy and probing and full of a smugness that was present all too often in Chase's childhood friend.

A snorted breath flared Ade's nostrils. His knuckles bleached against the table-top as the muscles through his shoulders clenched tight.

"Still want me to stop?" Though he spoke to Ade, Jones continued staring at Chase.

"Don't you fucking dare," he rumbled.

If Chase hadn't been privy to Jones's games before, he might've gotten himself a decent hard-on from the show, especially as Ade's head shook like the guy was having a seizure. Instead, he just settled back into his seat and let the two of them get on with it. Wasn't the first time Jones had gone for Ade. Wouldn't be the last.

The wicked grin that split Jones's lips could've earned him a high seat in hell, as he pumped his arm up and down behind the table and Ade's body twitched like fucking crazy beside him. It took around thirty seconds more for Ade to jerk back against his seat and heavy breaths to pump from him as his hands fisted in front of him. Eyes closing, he rode out the orgasm like he and Jones had booked a private room and he'd just had the wank of his life.

"You fucking cocksucker," Ade muttered, his voice close to a growl.

Jones shot out a brief laugh before turning to Ade. "That was just a taster, sugar. Imagine how fucking good it would've felt if I'd got your cock out of your pants and sucked you as dry as a ninety-year-old nun."

"Fuck you, Jones."

"Was there even a point to this exercise?" Chase asked, reaching for his pint.

With that smug fucking smile on his face, Jones scanned the room before his gaze settled back on Chase. "Just like I expected. You can even jack someone off in plain sight of these sheep, and not a single one of them notice a damned thing."

"And the point is ...?"

"The point is, you fucking moron, if I tell you someone in here is checking you out, then believe it. Because she was the only one not *bleeting* and *bah*ing like every other sad bastard in here."

Chase just looked away. Away at nothing—anything, if it meant he didn't have to see Jones's big *fuck you* dancing a jig in his self-satisfied smirk.

Across the table, Ade shoved at Jones, shoving harder when Jones's dark chuckle rolled out. "Move, you dickhead. Thanks to you, I now have to go clean up."

"Only if you get rid of those kiddie boxers," Jones said. "Make yourself more ready for me when I treat you to a bigger taste of the Jonesenator later."

"In your dreams, Jones." He pushed, until Jones had no choice but to stand if he didn't want to land on his arse on the floor. "In your fucking dreams."

As Jones moved to the side, and Ade squeezed past him, Chase twisted for another glance behind, but still saw nothing fitting 'someone checking him out'.

"That's right, baby," Jones shouted after Ade. "Plenty more where that came from."

Before Jones could catch him scouring, Chase spun back and feigned nursing his drink.

Once he'd reclaimed his seat, Jones watched Chase as he took a long gulp of beer and set his glass back on the table. "He talk to you yet?" The banter of before had vanished from his expression, as had all mention of the 'interested party'. Only a deep seriousness stared out at Chase from Jones's eyes.

Chase didn't need to ask what he meant. "He did."

"And?"

Chase frowned. "And what?"

Jones seemed to probe right through to his brain with a level of intensity that added to his already intimidating personality. "You okay, Walker?"

Chase held his gaze, because Jones would never believe him if he so much as fluttered. "I'm good."

"Yeah?" Only the tiniest tic above his eyebrow gave away the depth of Jones's concern.

"Yeah," Chase confirmed.

Jones rolled back into his seat, his arms outstretched as he cupped his glass atop the table. His gaze lazily roamed the room, his head tilting as he checked out one corner after another. His easy dismissal of the conversation told Chase that even Jones believed he was okay when he'd said so—which meant it had to be true.

With his head tipped to the right, his gaze seemed to lock onto a spot beyond Chase's shoulder. "Incoming," he muttered, his voice low but deep enough to carry.

Chase rolled his eyes. He should've known neither of them would give up so easily. Despite his lack of enthusiasm, though, he couldn't help watching for whomever had Jones's attention to cross his periphery.

He knew when they'd reached him by the slight shift of

Jones's eyes, and as soon as they'd passed the table, Chase flicked his sights higher.

Straight onto a swinging ponytail of strawberry blonde hair.

Cropped denim shorts covered a swaying arse, from where satiny leggings stretched downward and coated a slim but shapely pair of legs. Letting his gaze skim higher, he took in the flick of hair, the way the yellowed overhead lights made the tips look like they'd been dipped in a vat of sunshine—and Chase was on his feet before he'd even registered his own command to stand.

Ignoring Jones's quiet laughter, he pushed off through the increasing bodies as the ponytail hid within the crowd. Along the full length of the bar. Through the arches that led to the back rooms and the restaurant. And through a second set of arches leading to the bathrooms.

No one lingered in the corridor between the four doors. The fire exit at the end definitely hadn't been opened because he'd have heard the clank of it shutting.

After ducking his head back out into the lounge long enough to double check he hadn't missed her on route, he pushed through into the men's, hoping to catch sight of her on his way back out.

Over by the five urinals, a row of five guys took a piss, but Chase ignored them all and marched right over to where Ade had his cock resting on the sink counter and his jeans gathered at his ankles. If any of the others in there thought it odd for a guy to be washing his tool in the men's bathrooms, none of them showed it.

"Looks like it got messy out there," Chase said, leaning against the counter beside Ade.

"Bastard got me good," Ade muttered.

"Seemed like you enjoyed it to me."

Ade merely shrugged. "He's good at what he does."

Chase nodded. Jones *was* good at what he did. Whoever he did it with. Even those who struggled to walk after he'd finished with them never had any complaints about the journey that'd put them there.

"You come to help clean me up?" Ade asked, when Chase hadn't moved.

He didn't want to reveal what'd really dragged him to the toilets, and as soon as a urinal came free, he pushed off from the counter. "No, I need a piss."

By the time Chase had finished relieving himself and cleaned up, Ade was done at the sinks, and the two of them pushed out of the men's together, but Chase couldn't stop the glances left and right as they did so. He also could stop the people-scouring as they wove their way back to the table where Jones sat waiting. Though, what he was looking for, exactly, he didn't want to investigate too closely.

As soon as they reached the table, Ade rounded to the side Chase had been occupying. "No way am I sitting next to that dodgy fucker again."

Before Chase could join him, Jones grabbed his arm and pulled him round to face him. In his other hand, he held up a twenty, only a ghost of a smile curling the corners of his lips.

"You could try getting off your arse and going yourself," Chase said, and Jones's smile widened.

"I could. But I don't want to."

Snatching the note from his hand, Chase swung for the bar and back into the four-deep gathering blocking his way. Elbows up high, he nudged through until his chest hit the bar and signalled the white-shirted young woman behind there. "Three Guinness and black—pints."

As she placed the drinks down in front of him, he handed over the note. "Keep the change."

Her brows shot up. Probably because she'd made as much as the drinks had cost. "Cheers."

Grinning, he grouped the drinks within his hands and backed away toward their seats. Served Jones right for being a lazy bastard.

Those around him parted more readily for a rear-facing body, it seemed, and breaking free of their confines, he spun for the table, cursing beneath his breath as a collision set the drinks spilling over his hands after his success at getting them that far.

"I'm so sorry. I'm sorry. Please forgive—" The feminine voice cut off with a quiet gasp. "Mr Walker?"

Letting his gaze slide to the left, he took in the satiny-clad legs, the small denim shorts, up over a cami that hugged a small waist and embraced a really fucking amazing pair of tits, all the way up to the palest of blue eyes all wide and staring back at him.

"Abi?" He couldn't help the frown. "What are you doing here?"

"Oh, I'm—"

"Friend of yours?" Jones asked, and Chase glanced over to find both him and Ade staring real hard at the two of them.

Sending a hundred, silent *fuck*'s up into the stratosphere, he attempted to school his features into something that didn't portray his panic as he sent Jones a small nod.

Bumping into Abi outside of the office when alone was one thing.

Bumping into her when with Ade and Jones was something else entirely.

"This is Abi," he just about managed, before nodding from her to the two of them. "Ade and Jones."

"Abi should join us." The statement came from Jones—of course it fucking did.

"Oh—" Abi's lips stayed open, her gaze slicing toward Chase like she sought out his help.

"I'm pretty sure Abi has friends of her own here she'd rather be with," Chase said.

Turning his smile on Abi, Jones asked, "Do you have friends you're here with?"

Her lips worked open and closed before she gave a gentle shake of her head.

"See?" Sliding out from his seat, Jones smacked a hand against Chase's shoulder, sending more Guinness to speckle his arms, but he never once took his sights off Abi. "You can sit next to me."

She seemed almost unsure of what to do for a moment, but after a visible swallow, she slipped past Jones and sank her cute butt onto the bench.

Chase seemed only able to stare at her, sitting there, among his friends—his friends from his very private life that he kept very separate to work. For good reason. He scarcely registered Jones taking the drinks from his hands and planting them on the table, not until a rough nudge to his shoulder sent him back toward the bar.

"Get your friend a drink, Walker. Where're your manners?"

Turning away as if on auto, he headed back for the bar, despite his body screaming for him to stay. To be close to Abi. If only to provide some kind of protective barrier between her and Jones. Because Chase didn't even want to think about what he might say to her in his absence.

His push through to the bar seemed to take twice as long the second time. As did grabbing the tender's attention. And being handed Abi's drink.

By the time he broke free and stood staring back at the table, Jones had boxed Abi in and all but loomed over her small frame, Ade grinned at her across the table as if deciding which part of her to start with first ... and Chase wanted to surge over there and beat the ever loving shit out of the pair of them.

Forcing himself to not do exactly that, he took himself to his empty seat, plonked himself down, and slid a glass of wine across the table toward Abi. "You drink white?"

"Sometimes," she said, her fingers rolling around the stem and drawing it closer. "Thank you, Mr Walker."

Chase sensed Jones's gaze shooting across toward him, but he didn't dare meet it. He didn't want to see the scrutiny he knew he'd find there. And watching Abi, as she quietly watched him, seemed a much more preferable option, anyway.

"So, Abi ..." Hell, Jones's tone sounded full of a suspicion Chase didn't want to hear. "How do you know our *Mr Walker* here?"

Chase swallowed. So loud, he had to wonder if the others at the table had heard. The only one paying him attention, though, was Abi, her eyes full of questions and panic, as if she somehow knew she shouldn't give Jones the truth. Staring right back at her, Chase willed her to lie—to tell him anything but the truth. Fuck knew, he'd never survive the verbal beating if Jones was fed that.

"At work," Abi said after a small pause.

"Your work, or his work?"

Chase held his breath.

"My work."

Trying not to let the air out on a rush, Chase exhaled.

"Yeah?" Jones asked.

Abi's gaze finally broke from Chase's as she lifted her face toward Jones and gave a small nod.

"And what is *your* work, Abi?"

Why the hell did the conversation suddenly sound like a fucking interrogation? "Leave her be, Jones," Chase said before he could stop himself, and Jones turned a dark smile his way.

"I'm just talking to her, *Mr* Walker .... And what *is* your work, Abi?"

Chase really wished he'd quit with the *Abi* and *Mr Walker* shit.

"I work in a bakery." Abi seemed to relax with that answer, as though relieved at being able to answer straight.

"Baking *buns*?" Jones said, his smile twisting into something sinister.

"And cakes," she said, her fingers toying with the stem of her glass.

"And is *Mr* Walker a customer?"

Chase gave an exaggerated sigh, mostly to let Jones know he was being a dick, but Jones didn't even stir in the way he studied Abi. Beside him, Ade sat with his arms resting on the table, watching the word parry opposite with the same interest Chase had seen him watch porn as a teen.

"Yes," she said, back to lying.

Jones's eyes twitched in the corners, the skin tightening almost slight enough to be missed. "Why *Mr* Walker, then—why call him that?"

"We address all our customers that way."

Chase wanted to applaud the smoothness of her answer. Almost as if she'd slipped into the role and suddenly had it all figured out.

"That so?" Jones spared Chase barely more than a glance before narrowing his eyes back on the girl. "So, why does he get to call you Abi? More to the point, how does he *know* to call you Abi?"

She stared up at him for a moment, her efforts to school her features visible in the way she clenched her jaw and held herself rigid. "Because ... my name is on my nametag." She tapped her chest as if to highlight where she normally wore it, but all she did was draw three lots of attention straight down to her fluttering tits.

That time, Chase's swallow was definitely audible as he fisted his hands beneath the table and fought the urge to punch his two mates for having the audacity to so much as dare looking. Reacting wouldn't make it better. It wouldn't make any of it better.

It would only make everything worse.

Jones was the first to lift his gaze, sending a new smile Chase's way, his eyes practically drooping beneath the weight of the suspicion they held, before he glanced back to Abi. "So, tell me, *Abi*, what does *Mr* Walker usually order from your bakery? What's his absolute favourite thing to devour?"

A smile slipped free from Abi, and she dipped her face, as if to try hiding it. "A French fancy," Abi said, her eyes lifting toward Chase for a moment. "But I have a feeling he has a secret craving for a plain old custard doughnut."

Beside him, Ade chuckled, and Chase tipped his head to the side as he studied her. He could've sworn her words held a deeper meaning than appeared on the surface. In fact, he could've sworn Abi O'Shay was fucking *flirting* with him.

"You know what I like?" Jones said, breaking the moment enough for Abi's attention to sway toward the bastard. "A good turnover." He dipped his face closer to Abi's, his smile dipping into predatory territory. "With lots and lots of delicious *cream*."

Before he could stop himself, Chase shot a foot out beneath the table and booted Jones in the shin. He glared at his friend as soon as Jones turned his way, but the bastard only grinned at him like he'd been heading toward that exact result all along. "Quit being a dick, Jones."

Jones merely laughed—Ade, too, the betraying fucker. "Lighten up, *Mr* Walker. I was just messing. Abi, here, knows that, don't you, Abi?" He twisted back toward her, and she dipped her face again, that small smile of hers putting in a reappearance.

As soon as he saw it, Chase hated that it was there. Hated that it was there for anyone besides himself. And he knew if he didn't get her out of there, Jones would coax a whole heap more of those smiles from her, and Chase would end up wanting to commit murder before the night was through.

"What's up with you today?" Jones said, like he needed to goad him further. Not an ounce of concern laced the taunting tone he used. "Why're you so fucking uptight, *Mr* Walker?"

"Maybe I'm just tired ..." *... of you fucking with me.* Though he didn't complete his thoughts, he suspected they showed within his features from the way Jones stared harder at him before he swung to face Abi again.

"Maybe you should take yourself home, then," Jones said.

Chase wanted to punch him. In the head. The balls. Definitely in the cock. Because he caught the hidden meaning behind his words. *Fuck off and leave us to it.* Only thing with that was, he'd most likely be including Abi in his side of the plans. Not because he wanted her, but because he knew—he fucking *knew*—he was pushing Chase's buttons every time he so much as looked at her. And that meant the bastard was testing him.

As much as he wanted to jump up, grab Abi's hand, and march her from the bar, away from the pair of them, he wouldn't give Jones the satisfaction of seeing him lose his shit over the girl.

Instead, he turned to Abi, feigning indifference as he asked, "You want me to call you a cab for home? I can wait with you until it comes, if you like."

"Are you leaving, too?" she asked.

His eyes flicked toward Jones, but only for a brief second. "I am."

Her release of breath was subtle, but Chase caught it. He also caught the wash of relief over her features. "Then, that would be great. Thank you, Mr Walker."

"Leaving so soon." Jones turned an expression on her that'd convinced way too many unsuspecting victims to bow to his needs. Because Jones one-hundred percent knew how to be charming when he decided he wanted to be. "But we've barely got to know each other."

Chase kicked him again, ignoring the subtle curve of his lips. "Move out of her way, Jones. Let the lady out."

With a feigned sigh, he pushed his arse backward until at the edge of the seat and swung his legs round. Pushing to his feet, he held a hand out toward Abi, and after a moment's hesitation, she took it, using the assistance to slide across the bench. Except, Jones having a hold on her meant she had to shimmy way too close to his solid mass to squeeze past. Which took her chest flush with his abs, and her face almost pressed against his chest, and had Chase shooting eye daggers at Jones to back the fuck off.

Jones held Chase's glare for only a beat before peering down at Abi with the sweetest of sweet fucking smiles planted in place. "It was *very* nice to meet you, *Abi*." Chase almost heaved a sigh of relief, until Jones added, "It would be *very* nice to meet you again."

"Over my dead body," Chase muttered, and before Abi could respond, he narrowed his eyes in warning to Jones as he took Abi's shoulder and guided her away from the bastard.

God, he hated the amusement lighting up her face as she turned his way. Hated the way she turned that same glowing face of hers toward Ade, too.

"It was nice meeting you, Ade."

He mocked a salute her way, his smile filled with enough wattage to light up the entire bloody street. "It was definitely nice meeting you."

A laugh spilled from her, stalling Chase for a heartbeat. Half of him wanted to stay right there and see if she'd laugh some more. The other, less rational half took Abi's arm and led her away. Away from the fuckers who'd brought that laughter forth. Toward where they'd be nowhere in sight.

On a mission to reach the door, he darted around people stripped down to shirts from the gathering heat in the lounge, tugging out his phone as he went. A couple of taps and swipes had him connected to a local taxi firm, and by the time he pushed the two of them outside and into the cooled evening, he'd got a car booked.

"Two minutes," he told Abi, as he brought her to a stop near the pub's perimeter.

The railings had been in place since forever. On one side, a small road separated them from where the Thames currented its way along, while on the other, what had traditionally been set up as an outdoor dining area had devolved into the role of smokers' gallery.

"You cold?" he asked her.

Despite her arms practically hugging her own shoulders, she shook her head, but Chase stripped off the sweater he wore over his shirt, anyway, and handed it to her.

"You look like you need it more than I do."

Outside in the increasing darkness, with just the two of them there, the girl from inside seemed to be shrinking away, and in its place, Abi's shyness he'd grown used to seeing began slipping back into position.

"Listen, I—"

"Your friends seem nice," she said before he could finish, and his laugh broke free.

Watching her wriggle into the knitted sweater, I couldn't help but smile. "They were being dicks tonight." He worked hard to contain his smile from growing as she tugged the sweater down to almost the tips of her shorts. "I'm sorry about them."

"You don't have to be." She held her arms to the sides, did a slight tilt of her hips. "Thanks for the sweater."

For a moment, his brain went *there*. Imaging Abi O'Shay in nothing but his damned sweater. All cosy and warm, and naked beneath.

He swallowed hard, leaning his forearms against the railings, if only to take her from his sights long enough to tame his mind. Even so, he admitted, "It looks better on you than it does me, anyway."

"I wouldn't be so sure about that," she said quietly—so quietly, he doubted she intended for him to hear.

He went to check her out, search her expression for any meaning to the words, but the blast of a horn from the small drop-off area had them both jumping up like they'd been electrified.

"That'll be your ride," he said, stating the obvious.

She smiled, but the gesture held a hint of sadness. "Then, I guess this is goodbye."

"Come on, I'll walk you down." Taking her arm, he led her toward the steps that descended to where the car waited.

"We could share the taxi," she said, "if you needed to get home, too."

More words his stupid head wanted to overanalyse, but he'd be damned if he let it go there. "I prefer to walk. I'll be okay."

With a small nod, she waited as he leaned in and opened a rear door on the car, then ducked into the seat, the interior light of the taxi lightening her eyes even further when she peered up at him. "Thank you, Mr Walker."

"You're welcome, Abi."

After closing her in, he headed around to the other side of the car and tapped on the driver's window. As it slid down, he extracted a twenty from his wallet and handed it over. "Take her wherever she tells you to."

Nodding, the driver slid the note into a bag he wore around his waist and worked the gears into first, and Chase sent Abi a small smile as she waved, before the taxi rounded the corner and disappeared from view.

"You fucking idiot."

The voice came from his left and had Chase's shoulders stiffening. He turned to see Jones staring down at him from the other side of the railings.

"The girl's a client." His eyes narrowed into the irritation they showed. "Isn't she?"

Chase sighed. Mostly because he didn't want to hear it—the exact reason he hadn't told Jones about Abi to start with. Because there *was* nothing to tell.

At least, that was what he kept telling himself, anyway.

"Not now, Jones, yeah?"

"Yes, now!" Jones pointed at him and strode to the steps, jogging down them until he stood only a few feet short of Chase. "It's her, isn't it?"

"What's *her*?" Chase almost snapped the words. Offense for defence, and all that crap.

"She's the one who has you all fucking tied up in knots." He pointed at him again. "I fucking told you there was someone. What the fuck is wrong with you?"

"You're talking shit." That time, Chase did snap. "No, she's not the fucking *one*. There *is* no *one*. Why the hell're you trying to figure me out, anyway?"

"Fine! Lie your arse through it all, but at least have the decency to be honest about her being a client. She is, isn't she?"

Chase's lips poised ready to lie, but Jones did his whole brain penetration act with those fucking eyes of his, and the denial died before it'd even formed. Averting his gaze for fear of what he'd see in Jones's, he nodded.

"Shit! Fucking, fuck, shit, shit!" The curses came out low, but Jones's tone still held all the intent of someone unsure of what the fuck to do. A long few seconds passed before Jones spoke again. "If I tell you something, will you listen to me?"

Chase glanced back to him, hating the worry he saw in his face—worry he'd put there. "I always do."

"Okay, will you *hear* me?"

His jaw clenched like he already knew he wouldn't like what Jones had to say. "I'll try," he said.

"Your *client*, Abi ... she might come across as all sweet. And she might come across as all innocent—"

"She *is* innocent," Chase cut in.

Jones nodded, but more as if in placation than agreement. "Maybe," he said quietly. "But know this—despite that air of innocence and naivety, the girl is real fucking dangerous, Walker. She dangerous to you. She's dangerous to what you've built for yourself. And dangerous ain't a place you need to be. Are you hearing me?"

Chase gave a tiny jerk of his chin—it was all he could manage.

"You damned well better have been," he muttered, and turned back for the steps.

Leaving Chase standing in the middle of the drop-off point, wondering how the hell his night had ended in such an ass-backward way. He'd only gone out for a bloody pint, for fuck's sake.

EPISODE SIX

C hase must've blanked out for a second. Or three. Or twenty. He blamed the couple sitting opposite him, who'd yet to quit sending digs at one another like it was anyone's fault but their own for the two of them ending up in his office.

All he'd done was ask what they thought CW Consult could do for them.

Sighing, he held up a hand, and when neither of them seemed to notice the gesture, he added a verbal, "Please. Stop."

The two stalled mid-sentence, their slow head turns toward him full of drama and indignance, like he had no right to be interrupting their blasted bickering.

"Thank you," he said, ignoring the duet of scowls he received. "I think we should start this session again. Okay?"

Despite the curling of lips, they both nodded, and Chase tried on a small smile he didn't really feel like offering out. The couple had already given him a headache, and he'd only met them a total of seven minutes before.

"Mr Maxwell ..." He turned to the man on the left of the chaise, the calmer of the two by the barest of fractions. "Maybe you could tell me which of you broached the subject of attending the type of therapy we offer here at CW Consult?"

Mr Maxwell brushed his hands over his pressed trousers before poking a thumb toward his equally well-pressed partner. "He did."

Beside him, Mr Ricci sniffed hard and gave a flip of his dark hair, but Chase kept his focus on Mr Maxwell.

"Why do you think he suggested the type of therapy we offer here?"

The sulking expression moved over for a new one that appeared almost vindictive, in the harsh glint of his eyes and the sharpening arch of his brows. "Because he likes to fuck anything with a dick, and, according to *him*, that's *my* fault for not being interesting enough a lover."

"Oh, for fuck's sake, Matty." Mr Ricci tossed his hands up before letting them drop back to his knees. "How. Many. Times are you going to bring that up? This—" He poked his hands toward 'Matty'. "This is the problem. Because you do nothing but whine about everything. All. The damn. Time."

"About you screwing everyone else? Well, *obviously*."

"But you do it when I'm trying to make love to you."

"*Make love.* Oh, purlease." Mr Maxwell twisted in his seat until facing Mr Ricci. "So, do you *make love* to all the guys you *pay* to have sex with? Because that's how you make me feel …. *Like a two-bit hooker!*" He almost screamed the last few words at his partner, and Chase had to pinch the bridge of his nose in an effort to stem the spreading ache there.

"Please," he said, holding up his hand again.

"*A two-bit hooker?*" Mr Ricci said over the top of him. "I've never treated you like *a two-bit hooker* since the day I met you."

"*Hellooo.* Money to *buy myself something nice*," he said, doing air quotes. "Gifts to shut me the hell up—*guilt* gifts."

"You take *gifts* for the boys *you* buy, Matty? *Nobody* buys gifts for the boys. Why the hell would we be paying them, if we're treating them like our fucking *boyfriends*?"

"So, you *have* been buying boys!"

"Now you're putting words in my mouth!" Mr Ricci pushed to his feet, hands on his hips as he scowled down at his partner. "I never even said that!"

"That's exactly what you just said!"

Turning away from them, Chase slid discreetly from his chair and quietly rounded his desk. Doing his damnedest to switch off the back-and-forthing creating havoc to what he'd hoped would be a good day, he opened his bottom drawer and pulled out a bottle of water. Across from him, the two continued in a *you did it, no, it was you* kind of pattern, and he turned his back on them and strode across to his window.

Below him, the usual water traffic chugged gently along the Thames. Off in the distance, the vast array of buildings created an intriguing stepped skyline that he rarely grew tired of studying. Taking a long swig of his water, he let his gaze skim from the old to the new, all of them great architectural designs in their own way, though he couldn't help but linger for longer on the old. For Chase, they held a mysterious kind of beauty— that man could build something so solid and magnificent in frame during a time that lacked in modern machinery or technology.

Behind him, the bitching heightened, and he took another long gulp of his drink. In all of his time doing what he did, he'd never had to step away from a client—or clients. He suspected every one of his other clients would've bloody well noticed he'd stepped away, if it'd come to that, too. Whereas Mr Maxwell and Mr Ricci didn't seem to have realised, at all. He couldn't tell how much of it was down to the heat of their moment, or how much of it was a simple case of immense self-obsession.

Wishing like crazy he had something stronger in his bottle,

he downed another mouthful, screwed on the cap, and turned back around. "Okay, that's enough!"

His barked order seemed to sever the air of the room, taking all other sound with it. Mouths caught open and eyebrows raised high, the two men stood staring at him like he'd grown a couple of extra heads with a few dozen horns to top them off.

"Sit down," he snapped, before they could think about retaliating.

The slight pause to their compliance told him they thought about doing exactly that, but with heaved sighs that spoke of wounded pride and sulkiness way more than resignation, the two of them twisted their butts around to the chaise longue and plonked themselves back down. Though, Chase noted the gap they kept between themselves as they did so—a gap that hadn't been there when they'd first arrived and taken a seat—and the cold shoulder each gave his partner in an obvious display of refusing to look at one another.

Moving closer to them again, Chase set his water down on his desk. "Mr Ricci, how long ago did you begin dating Mr Maxwell?"

"Four years, three months, and twenty-three days ago," he said with a sniff. Since he'd arrived, his thick, styled hair had flopped over his brow, making him appear a lot younger than the thirty-nine years his paperwork stated.

"And when do you feel the two of you began to develop issues in the relationship?"

His brow creased, like he struggled to work it out, or like he hadn't been keeping track. Beside him, Mr Maxwell shifted in his seat and tugged on each of his shirt cuffs before stepping in with, "Seven months and two days ago."

Retaking his seat in front of them, Chase pressed his finger-tips together, smiling briefly at the preciseness of both of their answers. "Whatever the issues are in the relationship, you evidently want to sort them out, otherwise you wouldn't be here. Is that correct?"

"Yes!" Mr Ricci said, to Mr Maxwell's, "Of course that's why we're here."

Giving a slow nod, Chase tapped the tips of his forefingers together, studying the men from one to the other. "Okay." He paused for a moment, before continuing, "I'm going to help you."

Their two sighs of relief sagged their shoulders by an inch.

"But on one condition," Chase added.

And their guardedness once more rose into place. Neither of them said a word in protest, though—or questioned what that condition might be. Score one for the clients.

"In order for you to be seen here at CW Consults, you must both agree to attend sessions with a relationship counsellor."

Mr Maxwell looked about to argue, but Mr Ricci beat him with, "But—"

Chase held up a hand before he could go any further. "Mr Ricci, the issues I've witnessed here today seem to go a little deeper than what goes on in the bedroom. And if I'm right, then trying to find a sexual medium between the two of you would be a pointless endeavour, because if there's tension outside of the bedroom, that tension is only going to leak into the bedroom, and eventually, sex will just be borne of and filled with bitter resentment. Is that what you both want?"

A couple of muttered 'No's and headshakes answered him.

"So, do you both agree to attend relationship counselling?"

"How long do we have to go for?" Mr Maxwell asked, his voice low and full of sulk.

"Before I'll see you here? Two months." Chase spread his hands, gave a small shrug. "And for as long as it takes after that, if the therapist considers it necessary."

The couple turned from Chase toward each other. In profile,

Chase could see the full pout of Mr Maxwell's lip and the doleful way he peered up at his partner, as Mr Ricci seemed to study every inch of his face. "We could give it a try," Mr Ricci said after a few beats.

In answer, Mr Maxwell gave a jerk of his shoulder and a handful of tiny nods. When he turned back to Chase, he lowered his gaze like a submissive being reprimanded. "Okay, we'll give it a go."

"Excellent." Chase pushed straight to his feet and swept a hand toward the door. "If you'll come with me, I'll have one of my staff arrange the appointment with the therapist for you."

"You're arranging the appointment?" Mr Ricci asked, climbing to his feet and taking the first step toward what Chase hoped would be peace and quiet for himself.

"Any referrals I make are only to professionals I personally know and trust to help my clients, Mr Ricci." Waiting for Mr Maxwell to stand, he led them both toward the exit. "Doctor Mandini is very good at what she does. Trust me. You'll like her."

Pulling open the door revealed Raelyn and Samantha sitting behind the curved Reception desk. Whatever expression Chase wore on his face must've told a story of the clients he'd just seen, because both women dipped their faces like they needed to hide smiles they couldn't quite supress. Either that, or they'd well and truly heard the entire episode, which wouldn't have been hard, considering the volumes the two men had reached.

"Sam, can you find Lena's number out and ask if she can accept Mr Maxwell and Mr Ricci onto her schedule?"

With a nod, she turned to her screen, already tapping away at the keys.

"Thank you so much for seeing us today, Mr Walker."

Chase took the hand offered by Mr Ricci. "You're welcome. Hopefully, we'll see you back here soon." Somehow, Chase smiled through the lie—a lie he hoped could be killed once Lena Mandini had worked her magic with them.

After a repeated gesture with Mr Maxwell, the two men wandered across to the desk, where Sam spoke quietly on the phone, and Chase couldn't help but feel relieved at seeing their backs. At knowing it signified them walking out of his offices.

Heated arguments sometimes came with the territory, especially considering the hidden passion of some of his clients, but petty squabbles of blame and shame? Nope, that had been a first.

Hopefully, it would be his last.

~

Chase managed a whole ten minutes of sitting with his head propped in his hands and his eyes closed, before the door to his office swung inwards and heels clopped against the floor.

"Rough session?" Rae asked to the top of his head.

Giving a hard rub to his face, he opened his eyes and nodded. "'Could say that. You hear them out there?"

"Some—and that was bad enough." Her pencil skirt hugged her thighs, but did little to hinder her swaying walk to his desk, where she propped a butt cheek on the ledge. "You busy now?"

"How long do I have until my next client?"

"Thanks to those two being kicked out early, almost thirty minutes."

He sank back against his seat. "No, then."

"Good." She pushed to her feet again. "Follow me."

She didn't wait to see if he complied, just strode straight for the door leading to the session room corridor. Sighing, Chase pushed away from his desk and followed behind the swing of her raven-toned ponytail. On the other side of the door, the corridor stood empty, as it should have, and Rae ignored all the rooms prepped for client practical sessions and pushed down on the handle of the door leading to the observation room.

Frowning, Chase watched as she marched inside and flipped on one of the overhead lights.

"In," she ordered without turning, and with little choice other than to kick up an argument he couldn't be bothered with, he stepped into the room and closed the door.

"What's up?" he asked, concern warring with his curiosity.

"Sit down." She nodded toward a stool, and he dragged it closer to himself and sank his arse onto it. Leaning over him, she pressed a few power switches and scrolled through lists on the screen, then she grabbed the back of his seat and swivelled him to face the huge viewing screen mounted across one of the walls.

On it, Abi O'Shay lay back against the bed in the room behind them, the image frozen as if awaiting the command to move forth.

"You watch her last session back yet?" Rae asked over his shoulder.

"Not yet." He didn't need to. All the bits he'd caught, the bits he'd actually had his eyes open for, had etched themselves into his brain and refused to depart.

All the parts he hadn't caught, his mind had recreated all on its own.

"Then, we'll watch it now." She tapped a button that set the picture into motion.

With her hand dipped between her thighs, Abi thrust her hips into the flick and dip of her fingers, her cunt meeting each plunge. Her clit getting attention each time her arse sank back against the mattress. It was a sight Chase had seen a few times since she'd began coming to his clinic. A sight he hoped he'd see again.

More than once, when alone, he wondered if he'd step into a

territory he had no right to and watch the damned Abi O'Shay recordings even after she'd moved on, but those thoughts came from a deep, dark part of himself he rarely investigated—for good reason.

"Watch ..." Rae said, leaning in closer over his shoulder, and he forced his eyes back into focus, his mind back from where it'd taken him.

Onscreen, Abi's chest thrust higher with the rocking of her body into her finger fucking. Lifting from the bed, her free hand hovered over her torso. Although Sam had muted the show, Chase knew the command would come any moment. For Abi to touch herself, to pleasure herself further.

And right on cue, her hand skimmed across to her breast and rolled across the rigid tip of her nipple. Her back arched into the contact, and Chase sat poised, eyes fixed on her face. Waiting for it. The moment he'd demanded she give in.

As Abi's lips popped open and her eyelids half-lowered, Chase released the breath he'd held. Her back arched higher, as she massaged the clitoris with the ball of her hand between the deepening plunges of her fingers into her pussy.

Shifting in his seat, Chase tried adjusting the swell of his cock without actually touching it. Without alerting Rae to just how hard watching Abi got him.

He stood little chance of that, though, when Abi adjusted her fingers as they fucked her own body and extended her thumb to press down on her clitoris. To flick across its tip. To circle the solid ridge that'd stiffened more and more with every caress of her hand.

"Quit staring at her cunt and watch her face, Walker."

At Rae's order, he forced his gaze toward where she'd tipped her face to the side, her brows pulled taut in concentration and her pupils as dilated as fuck. With her focus fixed on a singular spot of the room, her entire body quivered, her lips rounded and narrowed with every sound that had passed her throat.

Chase knew when she'd hit peak by the stretching of the tendons through her neck, the flex of the muscles across her shoulders, but not once did she close her eyes or shift her gaze from whatever held her so rapt.

Leaning in, Rae tapped a button, and the image on the screen froze. "What do you see, Chase?"

Frowning, he stared at the screen—like he hadn't been already. "Abi O'Shay," he said slowly, wondering what the hell Rae was getting at.

"What about her?"

His lips curved into a half-smile. "She just had a great fucking orgasm."

"How?"

His frown returned. "What do you mean, *how*? She gave it to herself—like *we* taught her to do."

"You're missing the point." Her chest pressed against his shoulder and she stretched over him and stuck her fingertip almost in Abi's face. "Look at her. You see her face. The way she's staring." Her body moved from his as she stepped back. "What do you think she's staring at so intensely that, obviously, made her come as easily as she did?"

Chase swallowed. Because he already knew the answer.

He suspected Rae already knew the answer, too.

He gave a dismissive shrug of his shoulders instead.

"Could it be this?" Rae said behind him, and the image across the wall blinked out, to be replaced by a full-blown view of Chase sitting in that damned chair with his eyes half-mast and staring right back at Abi, and his cock straining against the wet patch just visible on the outside his pants.

The stool Chase sat on spun until he faced Rae, and she

dropped down until her eyes levelled with his. "Tell me you didn't fucking gizz in your pants watching Abi O'Shay."

He had to force his eyes to remain steady. Had to force his lips to form the word, "No." He rarely, if ever, lied to Raelyn or Sam. Their working relationship had been built on trust and openness from the beginning, and he hated that he'd just crossed the line they'd scored together.

She whirled him back to face the screen and pointed straight at his crotch. "Then, what the fuck is that, Walker?"

If Sam had dragged him in there, demanding answers, he'd have barked back and probably bitten and offered up a few threats of job loss.

Rae, though, was a whole heap scarier than Sam and had a way of chewing at his leg until he held his hands up in surrender.

"Sweat?" he offered.

"Bullshit!" She swung him back to face her again. "What the hell do you think you're doing with this client?"

"Has Sam seen this?" he asked instead of answering her.

"If she has, she hasn't mentioned it. And I haven't told her. Yet, anyway."

"You planning on telling her?" Having Rae rag on him was one thing. Having the pair of him tag-teaming and nagging consistently and persistently would be irritating as fuck, and more than he wanted to deal with right then.

Letting out a heavy sigh, Rae straightened, finally giving him a little breathing space. "Probably not." Folding her arms across her chest, she stared down at him. "I'm serious, though. What the hell are you doing with her?"

"I'm not doing anything." Her mouth opened, but before she could argue, he held up his hands. "I'm not. I haven't touched her. I haven't crossed any lines ..."

"Yet," Rae said, flicking her ponytail away as it slid over her shoulder. "Listen, I know what you've got planned for her next visit, and I think you should cancel."

"You want me to cancel on Abi?" His head was shaking even before he said, "I can't do that."

"Then, get someone else in for it. Ring Mrs P and have her send someone over."

"There isn't time. Abi's appointment is *today*."

Rae's eyes narrowed to slits, like a couple of lasers spitting suspicion out at him.

He could understand her reaction. Chase never kept track of who he was seeing when. That was what he'd hired Sam and Rae for, amongst other things. He didn't even know, himself, when he'd switched to keeping track of Abi's next visit.

Rather than defending his slip-up, he gave a nonchalant shrug. "Look, if she turns up here today expecting one thing, and I throw her to the wolves, she'll regress. We can't do that to her."

Rae's second sigh seemed even weightier than the last, but her face softened as she said, "I'm worried about you, babe. *She* worries me. What if something goes wrong and it jeopardises the practice. Where will that leave us? What would we even do if we don't have this? What—"

"Will you stop with the worrying?" Pushing to his feet, he took her shoulder and gave a slight squeeze. "Rae, I got this. It's all under control."

She rolled her eyes in an award-winning performance of *yeah, right!*.

"Really. Two, maybe three more sessions, and Abi O'Shay will be moving on, anyway. I can do a few more sessions without fucking up." Waiting until her gaze met his again, he smiled. "I promise, Rae. I got this."

The wary nod she sent him said she trusted him on that about as much as he trusted himself.

A case of erectile dysfunction. A foray into BDSM that'd seemed more about beating the shit out of each other than respectively dipping toes into something new. And a female client who thought she'd gone there for some kind of clitoral stimulation that she wouldn't have to provide herself.

Chase had gently told her that if she wanted that kind of service, maybe she should move to The States and set up home in Colorado.

Almost subconsciously, his head tapped against his desktop as he rested it there. His day had pretty much gone from bad to bad, to fucking bad, bad, bad. Somebody, somewhere, had to give him a damned break. Soon.

Despite hearing the click of his office door, followed by the tapping of heels, he didn't bother lifting his head from where it rested against his forearms. Not even as those footsteps reached his desk and the tickle of being stared at hit the back of his neck.

"You awake, Walker." Rae.

"Yeah," he said quietly, his lips meeting wood with the movement.

He detected a small laugh on her exhale. Could almost imagine her smiling at his enthusiasm. Or lack of.

"Here's something to get you moving."

"What is it?" he asked, kissing wood again.

Her voice held none of her humour as she told him, "Your early bird's early again."

He finally lifted his head, wincing at the steely flint in Rae's eyes as they stared down at him.

"Don't fuck this up," was all she said, twisting for the door. "Stay there. I'll send her through."

Chase just stared after her back. Thinking of the session he had coming. Thinking of the promise he'd made to Rae.

Thinking what an impossible situation a combination of the two actually made.

She pulled the door open, and beckoned toward the hallway. "Mr Walker will see you now, Miss O'Shay."

He didn't hear a sound from her feet before she appeared in the doorway, her eyes downcast as she thanked Raelyn. Her hands clasped at her waist as she stepped into the room.

As soon as the door shut behind her, leaving the two of them alone, her face lifted, her eyes found him, and a smile grew on her face like he'd just given her the sun. "Hello, Mr Walker."

He found his own lips responding, stretching at the corners for the first time that day. "Abi." For a moment, he allowed his sights to venture lower. Over the press of her breasts against the underside of the clinic robe, the way the crossover of fabric gaped slightly to accommodate them. The belt at her waist high-lighted her slenderness, above where the robe hung to her knees and the pale legs led down to the clinic slippers she wore. Even in something as mundane as that, she managed to look about as perfect as could be.

Focussing back on the reason for her being there—for *him* being there—he gestured toward the chaise longue. "Come in and take a seat."

She seemed to have trouble controlling her twitching mouth as she made the steps forward and did exactly as he'd suggested.

Chase had trouble interpreting what the hell her lips were trying to do. Or what the smiley-shine of her eyes meant. What the slight swing of her steps were telling him ....

He pushed to his feet, all too aware of her watching him as he rounded the desk and propped himself against its front ledge. "How are you feeling about today's session, Abi?"

Her gaze seemed to be clasped directly onto him. She was growing bolder with her eye contact. "I'm feeling confident."

Yeah, Chase could see that. She held her spine straight, but more of an *I'm in control* pose than one borne of tension. Her hands toyed with each other in her lap, but more *let's get going* than *what am I doing here?*.

Chase took every tiny single bit of it in. "Do you remember what we discussed last week—about what this week's session would involve?"

She smiled a smile that held a whole lot of sass and sauce. Hell, even her left eyebrow arched like it played along. "Yes, I remember."

The way she said it, her voice low and soft and fucking inviting had Chase suddenly wondering who'd be leading whom in the ensuing session. He wanted to wriggle a finger beneath his collar and work the damned fabric looser— because, it felt way too bloody hot to be in there with her right then.

If anyone other than Abi sat before him, he'd have been questioning if he was being played.

Swallowing, he tucked his hands in his pockets so he couldn't give his uncertainty away. "Did you want to go through it before we start, or—"

"We could start ... and then you can talk me through it." She shrugged, an indifferent gesture that looked anything but.

Holy hell. Abi was actually fucking eager to get in the bloody shower with him.

Chase wanted to groan. To sneak off and strap some kind of torture device to his cock that could kill any urges before they could start.

Because, for the first time since he'd said the words to his friend and colleague, he truly worried he wouldn't be keeping that promise, after all.

~

"Oh, wow." Abi paused just inside the door to the clinic's session bathroom. Her eyes wide, she seemed to scan every inch of the room.

Chase could understand her reaction. They'd had the room fitted specially, not least to keep those kinds of practical's separate to the after-session washroom. And to anyone without the means to stay in top-dollar accommodation, the generous space probably screamed of opulence and money and a whole lot of OTT—because who the hell fantasised about sex in a crummy bathroom with dodgy piping and a shit stench coming from its loo?

Taking a few hesitant steps in, Abi aimed for the bath in the centre of the room—though it bore little resemblance to those found in most homes. Square in shape, its base sank beneath the shallow ledge surrounding it, and with the entire structure waterproofed by tiles, it probably looked more like a miniature swimming pool than a tub.

In line with it, a full counter stretched along one wall, its graphite top supporting the equally graphite washbowls atop it. And partially hiding the wall opposite was the only other fixture in there: a glass enclosure big enough to accommodate four.

"I thought we were doing this in a natural setting," she said quietly.

"A bathroom is a natural setting," he said, watching her.

She glanced back at him over her shoulder, the smile on her lips contradicting the disbelief in her eyes. "This isn't a bathroom, Mr Walker. It's bloody Narnia."

Chase let free a laugh, as much at her unexpected language as at her words. "Everyone should experience Narnia at least once in their life," he said, moving closer to her.

A frown flitted across her brow. "How am I supposed to relax in something this grand?"

For a moment, he'd entertained the idea that Abi could be wooed with riches, but the rapid switch in her demeanour had him questioning that assessment and panicking that he'd lost her before they'd even begun. Arm outstretched and leading the way, he strode toward the left. "Would it make you more comfortable if we restricted the session to the shower?" He peered back at her, but she still wore that damned frown. "It's no different to any other shower cubicle, other than in size. There's more than one shower head—no worrying about squeezing in to share the one jet." He let a smile out and hoped it covered the desperation he sensed creeping through him like a shifty fucking cancer. "And ..." He swung open the door to the enclosure, exposing the space within. "As soon as the warm water hits the glass, it'll hide all this crap out here, and you won't even have to see it. You can pretend you're just in a regular shower. In a regular bathroom."

"With a regular guy?" she asked, but at least her brows had eased up.

"With a regular guy," he said, his smile inching wider.

Her chest rose, dropping again as she released a long sigh. "Okay."

Chase wanted to fist bump the bloody air, but restrained himself. He did relax his gesturing, though, instead tucking his hands into his pockets like that alone could tempt Abi onto the chill train with him. "Good ... so, how would you like to proceed?"

"I ... I don't know." The nerves that'd been missing in his office seemed to have returned as she hugged her chest with her arms, the fingers of one hand toying with the neckline of her robe. "How did you envision it proceeding, when you decided on what we'd do for the session?"

Chase very much doubted Abi really wanted to know the answer to that question. Because none of the scenarios he'd envisioned would ever pass the code around which they conducted their sessions. Not a single fucking one of them.

And damn his stupid head for taking him there right then. Damn his stupid cock, too, for stirring as soon as he pictured a very wet and very willing Abi O'Shay, all fucking slippery with need and languid with willingness and want.

Clearing his throat, he tore his gaze from where she stared right at him through those pale, stupidly captivating eyes. "Well, either you could undress first and, once you're in the shower, let me know as soon as you're comfortable, and I will join you. Or, I can go in first, and you can join me once you feel ready to do so." He dared seek out her gaze again, once more getting sucker punched as hard as he did every damned time. "The choice is yours, Abi."

The choice is yours? Four simple words that had Chase holding his breath. Holding and waiting to see which way she'd go. He counted off five, excruciatingly long seconds in his head, while Abi stared at him, her eyebrows twitching around with whatever thoughts went through her head.

When her lips finally popped open, the tiny sound cut through the air like a fucking explosion. "You can go in first."

Chase swallowed. Half because her decision meant he'd be stripping off in front of her, and while he never usually had an issue with his body being on show, it suddenly felt a hella lot different knowing Abi O'Shay would be his audience.

And half because he couldn't be one-hundred percent certain she'd join him once he had.

"You sure?" he asked. Just to check.

She seemed to contemplate his question, but only for a half beat before she nodded. "Yes, I'm sure."

"Okay, then." Offering up what he hoped would be a reassuring smile, he reached across into the shower cubicle and spun a couple of the taps in there, backing out as two jets of water plummeted into its base. "You can use these hooks for your robe, when you're ready to remove it." He loosened his tie as he spoke, and as soon as he'd tugged it free enough, he lifted it over his head and hung it from one of said hooks.

For a moment, he didn't know where to look as he reached for the first button on his shirt. At Abi. Not at Abi. If he looked at her, made eye contact, what message would that send?

What message did he want to send? Not one he should've been, that was for damned sure.

Twisting his body slightly, he kept his gaze low. Studied the floor tiles as he worked his way through the rest of the buttons, until he was pulling the hem of his shirt from his trousers and shrugging it from his shoulders.

To the right of him, he sensed Abi fidgeting, could almost imagine her shifting from one foot to another, tucking a hand inside the opposite sleeve of her robe, entwining her fingers around one another. Still, he didn't so much as glance her way as he hung his shirt over his tie and flipped open the waist fastening of his trousers. Not bothering to take it slow—it wasn't a fucking striptease, after all—he shoved the fabric down over his legs as soon as he'd unsecured them enough, and kicked them off his feet along with his shoes.

Leaving him standing there in only socks and boxers. With Abi's heavy gaze all the fuck over him.

In his mind, anyway. And that alone was enough to have his dick twitching in his pants.

Angling his body even farther from her, he balanced from foot to foot and lost his socks, placing them inside his shoes, and his shoes beneath the hangers. Just his boxers to go. And fuck, if his stupid dick didn't spring its way out of them the second he slid them down.

Sending a silent curse down at his idiotic, overeager body, he tossed his underwear in a direct flight for the rest of his clothing, and as soon as they'd landed where he wanted them, he glanced back over his shoulder, just catching the jerk of Abi's head.

So, she had been watching him. Totally didn't help with his argument against his disobedient body.

"When you're ready," was all he said, before he stepped into the glass enclosure and shut himself in.

Inside, the heat of the water engulfed him. It had already created a fine misted layer over the glass, blurring Abi's form into a mass that almost merged with her surroundings. For a moment, Chase just stood there, staring toward where he knew he'd left her. Willing her to disrobe and get the hell in the shower alongside him.

In truth, they didn't really need the shower for the session. Any of the practice's rooms would've sufficed for them to get naked and give Abi a chance to discover how she felt about the male body being revealed to her.

In some dark part of his brain, Chase knew the chance to see Abi completely exposed and dripping wet all in one session held the real reason for the option.

Shutting the door on those thoughts, he reached for a bar of soap from a mounted dish. She'd never take that damned robe off as long as he was pulling a Norman Bates on her. "Abi, can you pass me something please?"

Her form swayed, like she glanced around. "What is it?"

"In the cupboard beneath the basins—can you grab me a sponge from there?" After all, throwing regular, mundane requests at her, ones that anyone might ask when taking a shower, could help put her more at ease. Knowing it was also a great way to toss in a nudge of encouragement, he added, "Feel free to grab one for yourself, too."

He didn't quite catch the pad of her feet, thanks to the spattering of the water around him, but he could see the glide of her outline toward where he'd directed her. He watched her as she bent, as she made her way toward him, and he wondered how she'd pass it to him. Would she look as she held it out? Would she even open the door—because maybe she'd just chuck it in over the top of the glass and back away like she'd been stung.

"Can you give me a moment?" she said through the panel.

"Sure," he said. "Whatever you need."

She stood as still beyond the door to the cubicle as she had in the centre of the room before he'd made his request. And he watched her just as hard as he had then, too, while, in his head, he silently counted off seconds. One. Two. Three ....

On eight, she moved, and he knew the exact moment she'd lost the robe by the stretch she made toward the hooks.

She returned to the shower door, and another six seconds passed, her body statuesque.

"Do you ... do you think you could, maybe, turn around. Just until ..."

"Sure." He did as she'd asked. Turned to face the rear corner of the stall. Putting his back on show. His ass the first thing she'd probably notice as soon as she stepped inside.

What would she even think of his ass?

Why did he even care?

Because he did. And there was no damned way around the fact, because he cared a whole fucking lot what Abi O'Shay thought of his body.

Standing there, it felt like someone danced a flaming torch across every one of his nerve endings. Every inch of his body seemed aware of the water skating over it, every muscle in his body seemed tensed and ready for her arrival.

His stupid cock was ready, too. Sticking up and out and hard, like it sought her before she'd even stepped through the door.

At the quiet click of the panel opening, his head twitched to the side. At the second click of the door, a heavy throb kicked in along his shaft.

Because she was there. Right there behind him. Naked and so fucking close to his own nakedness. A light tickle danced the length of his spine, like all the hairs there reached out to accept her, shouting their welcomes and invites to come closer.

"Okay?" He spoke low. Didn't turn. Didn't so much as glance back toward her.

The breath she let out shook—the kind of breath that could clog a person's throat. "I'm okay." She didn't sound so sure, though. "I have your sponge."

He allowed himself to turn to her then. Told himself he'd just reach for the sponge, that'd be it, he'd go back about his business.

Except, as soon as his gaze fell on Abi, it got stuck. Like real stuck. On her everything and everywhere. Hell, he didn't even *want* to look away.

The wideness of her eyes expressed their paleness even more than usual as she stared up at him, but he couldn't help but catch the flutter of her tits just below. Really fucking beautiful tits. More beautiful, even, than he'd pictured them to be. And more perfect than her slipping robe the week before had allowed him to see. All milky and full, and perky as hell. Tiny rosebud nipples that softened the longer she stood there, like the warmth of the water trailing over them soothed their distress.

His stupid, stupid, disobedient eyes dropped lower. Toward where she stood with her thighs pinned together, one knee slightly overlapping the other, like she subconsciously protected herself against his heavy scrutiny. And his scrutiny weighed a fucking tonne. Especially when he acknowledged the lack of hairs coating her pubis, the missing curls that usually licked at her cunt.

She'd shaved. She'd totally fucking gone and shaved. And hell, if that didn't go and make his dick all the bloody harder.

She held out her hand as if reaching to pet an animal whose temperament she couldn't judge. "Here's your sponge."

Forcing his gaze northward, he took the sponge from her. For a moment, he got caught on those bloody eyes of hers again, the way the pupils expanded into the translucency. "Thank you," he said, ordering himself to turn away. "There's soap up on your dish, if you need it." He lathered his own bar against his sponge. "Feel free to do whatever feels natural to you."

He sensed more than saw the gentle reach of her arm beside him. Sensed more than saw every movement she made. From the way she rolled that soap bar between her hands, to the jig of her breasts caused by the gesture.

Trying his damnedest not to go back to his staring malarkey, he swept the sponge over his chest, his shoulder, under his armpit like that'd remind him he wasn't performing a show to turn the girl on, but going through the motions to put her at ease.

A few minutes passed, only the beat of the water creating sound, only hands sliding over bodies, before he asked, "So, how does it feel, Abi, being in the same space as a naked man?" The question seemed a whole lot deeper than it merely being the standard style of question he asked every client after every practical session. *How did it feel to you?*

She didn't answer right away. Chase knew she'd have heard him. She probably needed to consider her answer—something he noticed she did often.

Eventually, she replied with a simple, "Aware."

His hand paused the sponge over his abdomen, but he didn't turn as he asked, "Aware, how?"

She gave a loud exhale, more a release of nerves than a sigh. "Aware of everything."

Chase thought for a moment she'd given as much as she intended, but after a short pause, she continued.

"When I first saw the shower, it looked huge. Now it feels inadequate. Like ... like us being in here, together, like ... *this* is so much larger than that. Does that make sense?"

It did make sense. The air within the cubicle felt charged with more than steam and water, and whatever it was had his body wanting to respond to every damned word and nuance she shared. "Yes," he said quietly and continued his sweep across his body, guided the sponge over his hip.

It wasn't enough, though. He wanted more. Wanted *everything.*

Or maybe he just needed to know he wasn't the only one suffering from a throbbing urge to fuck with the barrier of professionalism and a made promise in the way.

"Why?" he asked. "What is it exactly that makes you feel aware? *What* are you aware *of*?"

"You," she said, and his hand stilled again. "Of how close you are. Of how ... *undressed* you are. I'm aware of every movement you make and how you make it."

So was Chase. Everywhere he touched himself felt like torture, because where he most wanted to touch himself would likely set her running for the door and compromise it all. Fuck, he wanted to fist himself and relieve the ever-loving crap out of his cock, though.

"And I'm aware of myself." The quieted water on her side of the stall told him she stilled, too. He just caught the outward flick of her hand—something she did when trying to explain herself, to compose her thoughts into a sentence. "It feels like my senses are heightened. It feels ... it feels like, when I touch myself—wash myself, it feels like more. *I* feel it more."

"Where, Abi?" His voice had roughened, but he didn't care. "Where do you feel it more?"

"Everywhere."

She seemed to breathe the word, and Chase turned to her then.

Her hands had dropped to her sides and she stood there, exposed and dripping wet, chest high and trembling. Tiny soap suds still clung to her skin, ones Chase just knew would offer the perfect glide for exploring hands, as she stared up at him, lips slightly parted as if awaiting a response.

Her eyes got him the most, though. Pupils fully dilated, they shone like onyx with what he could only identify as desire—and Chase had his hand in her hair before he could second guess himself. Had his other hand cupped beneath her ass.

As he slammed her back against the glass, lifting her feet from the floor, she let out a soft grunt that held little objection. When he hooked her thigh over his hip, she still uttered no denial, but lifted her other leg, slipped it around until she hugged him with limbs far stronger and firmer than his appraisals had shown them to be.

"Mr Walker." Her voice was a mere whisper, but it did everything to him.

Everything.

Between her thighs, his cock basked in the heat pumping from her core—a core wet from a lot more than just the water coating her body. Burying his face into the crook of her neck, he allowed himself a moment. Nuzzled at the soft flesh there. Inhaled the light feminine aroma that seemed unique to her.

Her fingers dug into his skin as she clutched at his shoulders and gave a soft moan, as she whispered another, "Mr Walker." And he nodded to himself.

Nodded to himself because he knew he wouldn't be denying himself anymore.

He'd enter her body so deep, she'd scream out his name, and he'd thrust into her over and over until she'd never utter any other words during her moments of pleasure, except those he wanted, *needed*, to hear.

Mr Walker.

"Mr Walker."

He frowned at the lack of passion in her voice.

"Mr Walker, are you okay?"

Chase blinked. Hard. He almost took a step backward as he registered his position: exactly where he'd been standing just seconds before. As he registered Abi still standing right in the same spot, still staring up at him with questions in her eyes— except her desire had dimmed beneath the frown claiming her brow.

He swallowed down the urges that raged through his body and focused on her moving lips, the slight tilt of her head. "Sorry, did you say something?"

"I asked if ..." Her gaze flickered south, but only for an instant before she lifted back to him, a light blush covering her cheeks. "I wanted to know if all men look like that?"

His own attention dropped to where hers had gone. To where his cock hummed like a fucking lighthouse warning unsuspecting victims away from danger. "Only when aroused," he said, his voice scratching at his throat.

Lifting his gaze again, he just caught the intake of breath, the small flutter of her hand toward her chest.

"Are you aroused?" The question seemed bold coming from Abi, and as if in agreement, the colour darkened across her cheeks.

He wanted to lean in to her, take her face in the palms of his hands, but he resisted the urge as he responded, "Abi, I'm in a shower, naked, with possibly the most beautiful and intriguing woman I've ever had the pleasure of meeting. If I wasn't aroused by that, I'd be a client here, not the bloody therapist."

Her lips rounded as if in a silent *oh*, and she twisted back toward the spray of water, her gaze dipping slightly as she did so, though not before sending another glance toward his rampant hard-on.

"You should understand, though—that not all men look the same," he said, like that'd get her attention back on him. Because he needed it there. On him. Penetrating through to his very soul, like only she could *see* him. "Not all men are the same size."

His mind drifted to Jones, a really bad fucking example of what an average cock might look like. It just as fast flitted to her husband-to-be. The man she'd be marrying.

The bastard who didn't deserve her—in Chase's world, anyway.

Chase bet the fucker's cock'd be nowhere near as formed as his own.

Would Abi be disappointed when she saw it?

And thinking about Abi in the vicinity of that dick wearing nothing but a stiffy had his own solid shaft taking its first step toward limping out.

He barely registered the fisting of his hand against the tiles as he braced himself into the spray. He didn't even realise he'd curled his lip, until water squeezed through and into his mouth.

Discreetly spitting it down to the basin below, he glanced toward where Abi still focused away, her slender fingers lazily dabbing the sponge over her body like her thoughts were everywhere but on the task at hand.

In that moment, he allowed himself to admit what he'd so far refused to entertain. That he didn't want Abi to get married. He barely knew her, outside of his office. He'd spent his whole life moving in a circle so enclosed by stockades, and it was a circle the likes of Abi would never be a member of.

She was his polar opposite. On a whole other level of decent than he'd ever be—or been.

And once she left his services, he'd likely never see her again.

Yet ... he didn't want her to get married.

Especially not to the dickhead he'd never met but hated.

As those thoughts roiled around inside his head, Chase felt suddenly exhausted.

Even his cock had deflated some beneath the weight of his miserable ponderings and merely jigged beneath each tap of the water, instead of its usual performance of dancing like a drugged-out teen at a rave.

He pushed away from the wall, but only partially twisted toward Abi. "I think this will be enough for today's session. I'm going to step out and redress. You're welcome to stay in here for a little while longer—you can refresh in here rather than switching to the client bathroom." The way she frowned up at him had him swallowing, but not from dry throat. "Okay?" he asked.

She didn't speak, just nodded, almost as if she sensed his shift in mood.

Stepping toward the door, he couldn't help but reach out and fold his fingers around her arm, but only gently, more a caress than a grip. Almost like he needed at least some contact. At least once. Waiting until she met his eyes, because he somehow knew she would, he told her, "Just knock on the door once you've finished in here. Sam will bring you through to my office."

Again, she nodded in response, and releasing his hold on her, he pulled open the door and stepped from the stall. Away from the warmth. Away from Abi.

For the first time since she'd been coming to his practice, Chase wouldn't be running off to relieve himself. For the first time after one of her sessions, he didn't have a roaring hard-on.

And that was no one's damned fault but his own.

~

W hile waiting for Abi, he grabbed a coffee from the staff quarters. A strong one—because he needed something to give a boost to his weary head. With his butt sank into a padded chair in the corner, he stared down at where his arms draped over his knees, the nursed cup hovering central.

He felt done. Defeated and deflated—for no fucking good reason.

It'd been a long time since he'd let himself sink that way.

According to his ma, he'd always been an obsessive child. Even Jones had ribbed him, growing up, about how he couldn't let something go until he'd got a solid outcome, or resolution.

Hell, he couldn't even watch a film that ended with a non-ending, not without feeling pissed off. Those bloody things could drive him nuts for days.

He didn't even notice Rae's approach, until her feet crept into his sight line and stopped a foot short of him. Bare feet. Like catching him unawares had been her goal.

"You did okay today," she said.

He didn't glance up at her as he asked, "Did I?"

"Well ... up until the point where you looked like you wanted to pin her against the tiles and fuck the virginity out of her."

The skin tightened around his eyes as he winced. The cameras set around the session bathroom had been specially designed with heated lenses, to keep them clear of steam. He should've known at least one of the girls would've been keeping an eye on his behaviour.

"But you pulled it back pretty quick," she said above his head. "And, for that, I'm proud of you."

Her feet padded away. He thought she'd leave, but a quiet screech across the floor told him she had other ideas, and he

271

lifted his gaze as she settled into a chair. Placing them level with one another.

"I'm worried about you, babe."

He nodded, like he agreed with her, and let his gaze lower to his mug again. A mug almost full, the coffee barely touched. "I know."

"I really think you should get someone else in for the O'Shay girl."

He sucked in a heavy breath, then slowly eased it back out. "Since when did we start doing what's best for the team here, instead of what's best for the clients, Rae?"

"Today," she said, assertion in her tone.

He shook his head, but it was a half-assed effort. "I can't do that."

"Get Ade in."

"He's busy."

"He'll find time," she argued.

"He's busy *with Nicolette.*"

She quieted, like he'd thrown her. So, she hadn't known about Ade working with Nic? One thing she would know, though, was how much time Nic demanded of whomever she booked. "Get someone else in, then," she said, but his head was already shaking at the idea. "You have to," she almost barked.

"Listen, Rae. Abi has maybe a few sessions left before she'll be where she'll needs to be—hell, she might not even need that many." He dared glance up at her again then, where resignation and concern and disagreement all warred for space in her eyes. "I'm not pulling out on her so far into her plan. I can't do that to her."

"No matter what it does to you—how it will leave you?"

"Yeah," he said, releasing a sigh. "No matter what."

With his mug plonked down on the floor at his feet, he pushed up and strode for his office. Argument over. Because it didn't matter what. He never gave up on a client he could help. He always saw it through—that was what kept them filing through his damned doors.

∼

A bi already sat waiting when Chase stepped into his office. The slow-built confidence had vanished from her posture as he approached from behind, and in its place was the hunched shoulders of uncertainty.

Clearing his throat to warn of his presence, he rounded behind his desk. He contemplated sitting there, putting into practice the distance he'd need to start creating, but something within him once again overruled reason, and he continued right on past to the seat opposite the chaise.

Abi glanced up as he sank down in front of her. Worry lined the questions in her eyes, eyes that he met and held as he shifted forward and leaned in.

"Are you okay?" he asked quietly.

She gave a barely-there nod.

"You seem upset." She did, too, he realised, as he studied her expression deeper. Not only concern mudded the usual clarity of her eyes, but something that looked a lot like hurt.

"I'm okay." She glanced away, toward the window.

Chase should probably have pushed on with the after-chat, but he got the sense she had more to say, confirmed when she turned back to him.

"Did I do something wrong today, Mr Walker?"

It became Chase's turn to frown. "Why would you think that?"

"Because you seemed ... disappointed. Annoyed ... or something." She shrugged, despite his headshake. "And you left ... it felt like you cut the session short—like you hated it. I don't—"

"Hey." Reaching out, he folded his fingers over where hers fidgeted in her lap. "You didn't do anything wrong. Okay?"

Her gaze dropped toward where he touched her. "It felt as if I did."

"Abi, look at me." He waited until her face lifted again. "You didn't do anything wrong. I promise you."

She seemed to study him for a long few minutes, as if seeking out the lie in his words, then she released a sigh, her shoulders sagging with what looked like relief.

He retracted his hand, trying to ignore how cold even that small separation from her left him. "Now, shall we discuss today's session?"

Finally allowing a small smile to peek through, she nodded.

"Good. Then, we'll begin where we usually begin. How do you feel your practical went today, Abi?"

She seemed unsure again as she poked a small finger into the air like it had no sense of direction. "I think we just covered how *I* think it went. Maybe it's best to discuss how you think it went."

Chase couldn't stop the laugh that broke free on his exhale. "Okay, good point. So ..." He spread his fingers wide as he lifted his palms toward her. "We'll go through the aims of today— what we hoped to achieve for you. One: Being naked in close proximity to a man. We covered that, would you agree?" Waiting for her nod, he continued, "Two: Being in that same proximity whilst the man was naked, also. Again, we can check that off the list. However, the real question here is, how comfortable were you, being in that situation. Any concerns? Anything about it that made you feel threatened?" At the shaking of her head, he asked, "How about this: On a scale of one to ten, with ten being very comfortable, and one being very *un*comfortable, how did you feel during your session today, in relation to a naked man being so close to you whilst naked yourself?"

"Eight." She answered without hesitation, though she gave a slight pause before shrugging and adding, "Up until the point where I felt like I'd done something wrong in there, anyway."

Something that'd been entirely his fault. "Abi, I'm sorry I made you feel that way," he said, his frown moving back in. "It was never my intention to, I can assure you of that."

"Okay," she said, but he couldn't quite decide on the intent of the word.

He nodded, either way. "So, let's go back to what we spoke of during the session. About how being close to a naked man made you feel. You said *aware*—do you have anything to add to that?"

"Nothing to add, not really. Aware was exactly how being close to you that way made me feel."

Close *to you*. Not close to *a man*. For a moment, Chase allowed him to question if her word choice had been intentional—until he mentally shook his head clear of those thoughts. He already had enough complications going on up there as it was.

"And now?" he asked, focusing back on the there and then. "How do you feel after the fact—now that you've had time to reflect on your practical session and how you felt during that?"

She held his gaze for the longest of moments, those blue pools of hers seeming to penetrate straight through to his very soul, then she drew in a quiet breath that could almost have passed for a gasp. "Cold," she finally answered. "I just ... feel cold."

Chase's eyes tightened as he studied her, as he tried defining that answer. Had she felt cold because she'd left the shower? Felt cold because of his behaviour fucking everything up?

Or had the shower made her feel the exact way he did?

Being beside her, so close, so beautifully naked, had made him feel the warmest he'd been in years, and since the moment he'd stepped from the stall, away from her, he'd been filled with

275

a void even an inferno would struggle to heat—did she sense that? *Feel* that?

Clearing his throat, he relocated his brain long enough to ask, "Cold, how?"

Again with the staring, eye probing, brain penetration trick. Her shoulders lifted, then sagged with the second, long sigh she gave. "Can we talk about next week now, please?" She glanced away as she asked.

Chase wanted to tell her *no*. Wanted to demand she explain herself. Order her to describe what she meant by *cold*. He didn't, though—because what right did he have after being a Class-A wank-up in the shower?

Besides, he'd never forced anything on a client yet. It'd make him a totally selfish bastard to start doing so with Abi.

Realising his hands had clenched, where they hung between his knees, he forced his fingers to un-flex. "Next week, I thought we could do some demonstrations of how a couple can find pleasure together, without actually having intercourse."

That gaze of hers swung right back round. "We?" she asked, a slight squint affecting the outer corner of just one eye.

"Yes. Is that okay?" Part of him needed her to tell him no, despite an even bigger part of him hoping she'd say yes.

Her hesitant nod came before her verbal, "Yes."

He took in her expression. The small flash of fear quickly smothered by the colouring of her cheeks and a hint of a shine spreading over her irises.

"What would it entail?" she asked, when he hadn't continued. "What kind of ... demonstrations?"

He swallowed before starting, "There are many other ways to pleasure each other. some considered foreplay. And others, such as oral sex. Sometimes, a couple can reach climax without either of them touching the other, or themselves ..." Though, he doubted Abi would be anywhere near ready to explore something like that—not until she knew her body better, anyway.

Would she even get to know her body better, though, once she stepped from his offices? It wasn't like he'd ever be the one to tutor her through the steps of full intercourse. The bastard who'd be getting her would probably shove in his dick and take what he wanted, without a single fucking care for whether Abi enjoyed it, or not.

He jumped at a soft touch to his hand and glanced down toward where slender fingers hooked over the fist he'd made.

"You seem tense today, Mr Walker," she said quietly. Gently. As if she considered him in need of being approached with care.

Concern greeted him when he lifted his gaze. "Yes, I'm fine." He didn't sound so convinced, though. Clearing his throat, he ordered his shoulders, his hands, his everything to relax, noting the almost cautious retreat of Abi's hand as he did so. "Where were we ..."

"You were telling me how couples can—"

"Please each other without intercourse. Do you have any questions so far?" he asked, slowly regaining his composure.

"Which of those you mentioned would we ...?"

"I think we should look at how oral sex works."

"Oral sex?" She said it so deadpan, it sounded more statement than question.

He nodded, added a, "Yes," for clarity.

"We'll be having oral sex?"

Chase breathed out a laugh at her saucer eyes, and he had to wonder if she even fully understood what the act was. For some reason, seeing Abi more off-kilter than himself helped settle the disturbances to his usual façade. "Not performing—don't panic. I promise you, you've nothing to worry about. Next week, we'll just be *studying* how it works. How a couple can make it work *for them* as individuals, or through personal preference."

277

God help him, he'd never make it through the session if they took it any further than that.

Abi released a long breath. "Okay."

"And your homework between now and then ..."

Her gaze snapped back to his.

"I want you to be sure you understand what, exactly, oral sex is before you return for your next session. Okay?"

She gave a shaky nod. "I can do that."

"Good." He pushed to his feet, feeling more in control, despite the heaviness he sensed still weighing down his shoulders. "I'll see you to the desk, then, and Rae, or Sam, will get you booked in for next week."

~

Chase had spent a good fifteen minutes mentally banging his head against a hard surface once Abi had left his office. Despite his regained composure, he still couldn't quite shake off the cloak of darkness each time the realisation that she'd be gone soon—to some other guy—buzzed through his head.

And the cloak weighed a fucking tonne.

In an effort to ignore it, he'd gone through the motions of completing his notes on Abi's session, which hadn't exactly helped, and seeing Sam and Rae off for the day, though their piercing watchfulness hadn't exactly helped with his charade, either.

By the time he neared home, his head had hit a tizzy of flitting from seeing Abi with someone else's hands on her, and seeing Abi in the shower, exactly as she'd been earlier, staring up at him, staring down at him, that small fire he'd seen burning bright in her eyes.

With a sharp shake of his head, he rounded through a gap in

the wall lining the Thames. A handful of steps had been built into the riverbank, and he descended them to a floating gangplank that led to his digs.

Equally floating, from the bank side of the premises his home resembled a wooden slatted box, stained a dark oak, with a singular door and a couple of windows he kept private with shuttered blinds.

A narrow strip of decking ran the breadth of the structure, and Chase stepped onto there, feeling the gentle current of the water as soon as he had. With keys he grabbed from his pocket, he worked through the triple set of locks and pushed open the door.

As soon as he stepped inside and shut out the world, the ache that'd built in his shoulders eased a little, as the white glossy walls greeted him in the narrow hallway. After slinging his jacket over a rack on his right, and kicking his shoes off beneath that, he climbed a short set of stairs that brought him out into the corner of the main living space and flicked on the low-lighting around the walls.

With its open plan layout, anyone visiting could see straight into the lounge, the trio of sofas in a U of seating around a grey-washed coffee table, and along the polished flooring to the kitchen, the duet of parallel work units, the chromed appliances and glossy counters. Windows spanned the entire length opposite, covering both sections, smooth-gliding glass doors central and leading onto a broad deck that peered over the Thames.

Chase headed for his kitchen and the bottle of Glenmorangie beckoning from the counter. He poured a healthy shot into a tumbler he grabbed from a cupboard and bottomed it with ice from the freezer.

The first sip was always the best sip, the slow burn along his insides like a temporary antidote to the chill that could attack from within.

Setting his glass down, he tugged open the door to the fridge. On the middle shelf sat a foil covered dish, and he pulled that out, set it on the side and, after removing a sticky note from its top, worked it free of its makeshift lid. As soon as he had, rich meatiness sprang free to scent his kitchen, and he smiled. Despite his mood. Despite the shitty and despondent line of his shoulders. Because Chase fucking loved Ragu.

His gaze skimmed across to the sticky note he'd pressed to the counter.

Eat it with the crusty bread I left in the cupboard. His ma's handwriting.

Smiling again, Chase bunged the dish in the microwave and set the timer for three minutes, before grabbing up his drink and heading for the glass doors. He slid them only wide enough to squeeze through, so as not to invite the mozzies in for a feast, and crossed the balcony deck to the railings that overlooked the dark water below.

Thanks to the time of evening, the lights lining the river and those shining out from moored crafts skewed a clear vision of the view, but he knew from experience that, on a clear day, when the sun reflected against the water's surface, it could be both beautiful and calming. Sometimes sociable, too. The warm days always brought out the fair-weather boaters, and they had a habit of waving to every other boater they passed. For some reason, they seemed to place Chase into that category, like his living on the river auto-allowed him access to their club. Often, boats had drawn up alongside his home, those on board saying *hi* while secretly trying to carry out their true mission of peering inside, like his crib was some big secret they needed to discover.

He'd gone through varying phases of tolerance over the nosiness, from loving the attention, to hating their prying eyes, to indifference. Anyone so heavily concerned with the lifestyle of another was obviously trying to escape whatever needed sorting in their own lives, if only temporarily, and he'd never been one to encourage that—in others, anyway.

Swallowing down another sip of whisky, he let his head hang for a moment. Through the railings, he could see the gentle shift of the water, the tiny ripples catching what little light reached them. He focused on them, used their dance as distraction, to calm his mind that refused to shut off, to ease muscles that seemed intent on staying tense.

The ping of the microwave rang from the kitchen. With a heavy sigh, he pushed back from the railing, poured a healthy slug of whisky down his throat, wincing as the blast of heat roiled through him, and shut himself back indoors.

The kitchen's breakfast bar butted up to the floor-to-ceiling window, and he pulled his meal from the microwave, the wrapped bread from the cupboard, a spoon from the drawer, and headed across to a stool to eat. His ma had pre-buttered the thick crusty slices, and Chase piled spoonsful of Ragu on top, opening his mouth to accommodate each mountainous mouthful. His ma's cooking got him every time. He'd leave the office not even feeling hungry. He'd reach home and find what she'd left him and turn into a man starved and deprived.

More than once, as he wiped bread around the juices of his bowl, his gaze lifted to the glass window before him. The lighting within the space prevented him seeing much of outside, but he couldn't shake the sense that he was being observed.

Obviously, his open plan home and broad windows made him a prime invitation for being spied on, especially as dusk dropped and anyone out there had a better view than he did on the inside, but the sense of watchfulness right then had the back of his neck prickling and his eyes making overt attempts to catch what had him so on edge.

With his face lowered toward his bowl, he used the last of the bread to polish the sides, while his eyes studied as much beyond the glass as they could from beneath his brows. When, after a full minute of scrutiny, he found nothing visibly out there, he carried his empties across and deposited them in the dishwasher.

For minutes after, he leaned against the counter, the remnants of the whisky in his palm, his gaze travelling across the open plan space in front of him. Any other night, and he'd have sank into one of his sofas for a few hours, taken the bottle and glass with him, maybe turned on the flatscreen affixed to the far wall. He loved his job, but it often left him mentally exhausted, and he needed his easy ritual of winding down. Switching off and appreciating solitude after a day of having to talk to and listen to others, hours of having to observe and focus on everyone but himself.

Except, right then, his body didn't seem willing to shut down. Each time he so much as considered couching his arse, every piece of his brain scrambled up like static spaghetti and held him back and twitching in place.

Reaching for the bottle, he served himself another shot of alcohol. Maybe he just needed a little help. Maybe he just needed to liquefy those limbs of his.

Maybe he just needed to not give so much of a shit about whatever it was had him jittery as hell.

Resting his head back against the wall unit, he poured a large glug of whiskey into his mouth and swallowed, a low growl humming through him at the slow, downward burn. As soon as that'd hit south, he repeated with the second half of his drink, until he'd drained the glass and his body felt a little lighter—though, he didn't give any less of a shit than he already had, and that pissed him off.

He'd spent the past few years creating a life he could feel contented living, and he'd succeeded—he'd reached a point of happiness that had him bounding out of bed each morning and raring to go.

So, why did he feel so fucking *dis*contented of late?

Why couldn't he shake the sense that it was all about to go horribly wrong?

Releasing a low groan, he rubbed a hand down his face and reached for the bottle a third time. Carrying that and his glass, he made for the gap at the rear end of the counters, where the only other staircase led to the sleeping quarters, and not bothering to switch on a light, he descended into the shadows.

Partially hugged by the surrounding water, downstairs always seemed to have a surreal quality to any sound produced down there, though Chase suspected it was more his imagination than science causing the effect. A white wall greeted him ahead of the bottom step, the base of its porthole just tickled by the Thames water outside, and Chase rounded the newel post to the long corridor of below. Three white doors led off, two on the left, one right ahead. He passed the first, the guest bedroom, and pushed down on the handle to the second.

Ignoring the shower stall in the corner of the bathroom, he cut straight for the tub sitting central, stuck in the plug, and set the water pumping. Leaving that to run, he ducked back out and into the room at the end of the hall—his bedroom.

Decked in pale tones and made to look like a ship's cabin, it was Chase's favourite room in the house. He'd always wanted to go boating as a kid. Sailing, yachting, fishing—he didn't give a shit which, just so long as it was out on the water, unrestricted by walls and the rules that came with city life—but he'd never got to do any of them. His ma had always hated the water, and thanks to his father being an ever-absent figure in his life, he hadn't really had anyone else to take him. Then adulthood had crept in, and sex and high-rolling had taken up the majority of his time. The closest he'd got to fulfilling his childhood fantasies had been attending parties on moored yachts, where the biggest cause of the vessel's sway was all the shagging on board.

Maybe that'd been why he'd chosen to live where he did. Sure, he could've just gone and done what he'd dreamed of for so long. He had the means. He had the contacts. But what'd be the point without someone significant to share it with? And Jones, nor Ade, didn't fall into that role, regardless of how close they all were.

With tumbler and bottle set down on one of the bedside units, Chase gripped hold of the scruff of his shirt and tugged it up over his head. As soon as he'd shucked that, he worked the buttons of the jeans he'd donned to walk home, the fitted boxers he preferred over briefs. After bunging them all in a basket, he padded his way back to the bathroom, relishing the prickle of his bare flesh in the cool air.

Truth was, he didn't even need the bath. He washed after every client. Often washed at the end of every day, before changing from his work suit. But the water soothed him, and he felt the power of its calm as soon as he'd stuck even a foot into its shallow depths.

The water still spilled from the tap as he settled his butt down, that already in there just reaching his hips as he shuffled himself forward and lay back against the tub's sloped rim. The cold of the surface sent a chill skimming over his flesh, but he pressed back harder rather than withdraw. Beneath his chin, his nipples poked outward, two solid nubs of *what the fuck* at the assault, but their hardness only took Chase's mind back. Back to earlier, and the stiff peaks of Abi's breasts as she'd stared at him in the shower. The growing rigidity of his cock as he'd taken those details in—just as it grew then with the mere memory of the afternoon.

Closing his eyes on his body, he slid himself deeper into the rising water, but no matter how much he ordered his brain to the present, it defied him and stayed on the session with Abi.

Maybe if he only referred to it as a session, he could shut off any emotions he harboured for the girl. Compartmentalise it as *work*. Only work. A job. Nothing more. Nothing less. That was how he usually dealt—with any client other than Abi.

Except his dick seemed to respond to thoughts unrelated to those in his head.

Or maybe it didn't.

Because the more he thought about Abi—whatever thoughts he had about her—the more he noticed the low ache starting up in his balls, the more that damned vein throbbed along his shaft.

Fuck his cock. Fuck his stupid head. Fuck his weakness and unwelcomed emotions.

Even as he mentally berated himself, though, he recaptured that image of Abi standing naked and wet, her eyes totally hot with what he suddenly decided was want, and his hand reached for his pulsing hardness.

As soon as he gripped its length and squeezed, his head tilted back a little further and his lips popped open on an exhale. Like he'd held captive his own breath and it'd just gotten a taste of freedom.

Keeping his eyes closed, he slid his palm in a slow path upward. He could picture Abi so vividly. On her knees. Peering up at him all innocent and sweet—though, nowhere near as innocent as she'd been weeks ago, when he'd first met her. If Chase had his way, she'd become even less so. All he needed was a day—one day—to make it happen.

Ignoring the truth that that'd never happen, he mentally opened her mouth, braced her hands against his hips, so fucking delicate and small. He quickly dipped his hand into the bath water to wet it, and imagining the enclosing of it around his cock to be the wet heat of her mouth, he skimmed it downward. Down to the base. Rubbing his thumb across the head as he imagined her tongue tracing the same route.

It was a dangerous game to play, but Chase didn't care. Fantasies were about as close as he'd ever be permitted to get to Abi O'Shay, and he'd take those over nothing.

Besides, sometimes fantasies trumped all else. And Chase should know. He'd lived with them for years.

Lifting his hips to the stroke of his hand, he allowed himself to relax into his movements. Relax into each roll back of his foreskin, each roll up.

Before him, on her knees, Abi fought for balance, as he dragged the fingers of his free hand through her hair, forced her mouth lower over his cock, his cock deeper into her throat. With each grunt she gave, each squeak as she tried sucking in air, he conjured the soft fluttering of her hair across his belly, his hips. Imagined the brush of her breasts against his inner thighs.

"That's it. Just like that," he whispered—as if she needed guidance.

She probably would, he realised. And he'd be more than happy to take her on that tour.

Fisting his hand tighter into her hair, he forced her face down harder, faster, thrusting his hips up until he slammed hard into her mouth. The whimper she gave was like candy to a diabetic, and he withdrew and drove upward even harder, letting out a low groan at the rapid build of heat, the twisting tightness in his balls.

Fuck, he'd come fast and hard before, but laying there right then, he'd barely touched himself beyond a few strokes. And he was close already. So fucking close it hurt. All too often, that torturous ache would lead his actions, have him dragging it out and prolonging his release until he ended up as nothing but a panting mess desperate for ejaculation and willing to do anything to achieve that.

But right then, Chase already felt like a desperate mess, and dealing with the pain of withholding wouldn't help fix that.

Tightening his grip, he upped the pace, upped the friction. Pumped his hand up and down over his shaft so hard and fast, his body jerked like it seizured and his breaths sounded like they came from something wild and rabid.

It took twenty seconds. Twenty fucking seconds before his legs shot out and collided with the tub's sides and his shoulders clenched into one solid mass of muscle as his throat spewed out a pathetic high keening sound.

He snapped open his eyes, just as a holy fucking fountain of cum spewed from his cock before raining back down. Over his groin. His belly. All the fuck over the surface of the water and the sides of the bath. In an orgasm that left him panting and twitching and cursing beneath his breath.

"Fuck." His entire body seemed to be breathing hard, shrugging itself inward, as if worshipping some great moment it'd shared with his dick, and it took moments before Chase felt in control enough to uncurl himself, to straighten knees that'd flexed upward, to unroll shoulders that'd hunched so tight they burned. As soon as he had, his body seemed to slap back into position in the bath, and Chase lay there, his breaths still heaving at his chest, his body clinging to the surround spunk skimming the water's surface like mutant frogspawn.

"Fuck," he muttered again.

His head bashed back against the enamel, and he smacked it back a second time, a third, the entire time mentally screeching away for allowing himself to go where he'd just gone. For not being stronger and ordering Abi O'Shay the fuck out of his head.

'The fuck was wrong with him? Wasn't like he *knew* Abi.

Wasn't like he'd *get* to know her. So, why the hell couldn't he shut down where the damned woman was concerned?

Jones had been right, he realised. *Finally* realised.

And so were the girls.

Abi was dangerous.

To him. To his mental stability.

To the practice he'd spent years building.

He should've recognised that in her from the start. Maybe then he could've avoided it reaching the point it had. Some might call his interest in her a crush, but Chase recognised it for what it was.

At some level, he'd probably *always* recognised it for what it was.

An obsession.

But, as he'd told Rae, he'd only have to deal with Abi a couple more times, and she'd leave his services, be gone from his life for good. Badda-bing-badda-boom.

He could deal with a couple of sessions. He could deal with her walking away and marrying some guy he didn't even know and hoped never to meet because he couldn't promise civility if he did.

Shutting off the tap, he bust his arse out of the water until standing in the pool of his own weakness. *I got this*, he tried assuring himself as he stepped out and reached for a towel.

But deep down, in some dark corner his brain he didn't grant a voice to very often, he couldn't help but wonder who the hell he was trying to kid.

EPISODE SEVEN

R aelyn and Samantha sat on the chaise in Chase Walker's office, their eyes eagerly aimed at the box he set down on the floor in front them. While Rae's raven hair stayed tamed in a thick plait that coiled its way over just one shoulder, Sam's contrasting blonde waves surrounded her head, almost obscuring the scissors sticking up from between her fingers.

Chase held out a hand. "Nurse ..."

As soon as Sam had settled the scissors against his palm, he set about scoring through the thick tape holding the package sealed.

Neither Sam, nor Rae, spoke through the *zip* sound— unusual for the both of them. They all too often had far more opinions than Chase wanted to hear.

Chase was just relieved to have something to distract him, if only for a few minutes. His head had been far too full of stuff it had no right to be of late.

After snapping the lid free of the ends of the tape, he forced the top of the box open, folding each half against the sides, exposing what Sam called giant bubble wrap inside.

He grabbed the three linked rows of air-filled sacs and dropped them to the floor, and Sam rubbed her hands together.

"Here come the goods," she said, like the blooming delivery was addressed to her. Or *for* her.

In actual fact, it was neither.

"Maybe we'll get some of our own if they're any good," Rae said beside her, but her voice held enough humour that Chase knew not to take her seriously.

Drawing out the well-packaged products still didn't give much insight as to the box's contents, as each item had been individually bagged and wrapped.

"For God's sake, come on," Sam said, reaching out for one of the bags, but Chase snatched it away.

"I don't want all our scents and fingerprints on these. Don't you know felines have a decent sense of smell?"

At Rae's barked laugh, he finally smiled. Felt like he didn't dish anywhere near enough of those out lately.

"So, just open it already," Sam said.

Straightening to his full height, he drew out the first item to its full length. "Ready?"

"Yesssss."

Letting Rae's throaty chuckles and Sam's enthusiasm draw his mood into the game, he worked down the zipper at the front of the bundle, arms stretching fully apart to accommodate its length. Once he'd created a big enough gap, he worked the suit bag open, unhooking it from the rigid frame holding the shoulders of the garment within, and tugged the rest of the outfit free.

A limp lump of fabric sagged over the chest part of the outfit, and Chase lifted it up before breathing out a quiet laugh and turning to the girls.

"Well …" Rae's mouth seemed stuck around the word.

"It's …" Sam's lips worked for a moment before stretching into a grin. "Bloody awesome." She shot to her feet and reached

out for a touch. "Seriously, it's way better than I expected it to be." She glanced down toward Rae. "I thought it'd be all baggy and itchy and stiff, but ..." She rubbed the fabric of the collar between thumb and fingers. "... it's really soft and ... lush."

"It actually is," Chase said, at Rae's skeptical expression, and she pushed to her feet, also, her fingers reaching.

"Okay, it feels good. So, let's work this thing out. No zipper?"

"No zipper," Chase confirmed.

"So, the entire thing's stretch. And it covers feet. What about hands, how do those work?"

"They can either be worn and fastened into place by the small stud on the inside of the sleeve, or if the wearer wants to be able to feel, they can take them off and tuck them back, and fasten them there using the stud on the outside of the sleeve."

"You sound like a rep for the company," Rae muttered, before lifting up the hooded section of the suit. "So, this is stretchy and fitted, too. Comes straight over the head from behind." She stuck her fist inside it like a makeshift head. "And right the way over the face ..."

"With an optional teeth attachment that can be fitted over your own," Chase finished for her.

"Wow," was all she said.

"Hang on, turn it around, I want to see," Sam said.

Slipping the suit fully free from its protective covering, Chase let the plastic rustle its way down to the floor and spun the outfit a half turn, until the front faced him and the rear faced the girls.

As soon as he had, Sam grabbed its full, very silky-looking tail in her hands, stroking it all the way down to its tip. "This is beautiful."

"Sick," Rae said beside her before pointing to the suit. "That male or female?"

"Grey tabby, so should be female." Reaching down, Chase

worked his hand between the furry legs of the suit, fiddling through the fabric of the crotch until he'd found the opening. "Yep, female. Which means, the one still in the box should be a ginger tom."

"Can we look at that one, too?" Sam asked, her fingers visually itching toward the other item.

"After we've put this one back as it came, yep."

"Oh, my God, Mr and Mrs Worthington are going to be stoked with these."

"Mrs Worthington's gonna get stoked, all right," Rae muttered. "Right in her pussy pussy."

"I can't wait to ring and tell them they're here," Sam said over Chase's quiet snort. "Do you think they'll try them on here. Will we get to see?"

Rae's head was already shaking. "No," she said, prodding her finger toward Sam.

"No, what?" Sam could bat her lashes and pull an innocent act all she liked, but Chase—and Rae—had known her too long to be fooled.

"No, we are not getting some—I was *joking*. I don't want to be a bloody cat in heat."

"But—"

"No," Rae said again, sterner, before nodding to Chase. "Come on, let's check the other one. The sooner we get these back in the box, the better."

～

Mr and Mrs Worthington *had* loved the costumes. When they'd first visited CW Consult, they'd openly expressed their unusual interest in animals. At first, Chase had worried they'd come to ask for an outlet CW Consults couldn't provide—even his clinic had some lines drawn—but they'd gone on to explain how erotic they found the mating of certain animals, and how they'd even attempted to recreated a mating session at home. Initially, they'd come seeking help, assuming there to be something 'wrong' with their fetish, but Chase hadn't seen any issues with something that didn't affect anyone, or thing, outside of their own relationship and had, instead, taught themselves to embrace it. And, after a couple of failed attempts at purchasing role-playing outfits of their own that'd left them itchy from rashes, or sore from rough fabrics, Chase had offered to hunt down ones that could work. Between himself, Rae and Sam, and a whole lot of phone calls, they'd eventually found the resulting outfits at an outlet called 'Sensual Costume'.

Two hours earlier, the couple had turned up to try on their order. Two hours earlier, Sam had stood mooning over the sleek cut of the fabric and glossiness of the fur, and fawned over the realistic curvature of the tails. Two hours earlier, Sam had stroked Mr and Mrs Worthington so much, Chase swore they'd bordered on inviting her to join them for a pussy-themed evening at their home.

And two hours *after* their visit, Sam was still staring off into space and throwing out the occasional comment about soft fur and silky tails, and 'imagine how amazing it would feel to glide your naked body over *that*'.

Chase actually felt sorry for Rae, having to sit out there and listen to it—at least he'd had a couple of 'easy' clients in that time: a first-timer, which had just required his office for initial assessment, and an old-timer who'd thought he could turn up with his own selection of 'hired ladies' and use the room he assumed he'd booked himself into.

It had taken some delicate explaining to get him to under-stand that CW Consults wasn't a 'by-the-hour' hotel. And it had taken some sensitive, yet stern, herding to get the old guy back out of Chase's office. They'd only got him to leave their floor, completely, by Rae calling an alternative hourly accommodation and Chase arranging a car to take the horny bastard there.

As soon as he'd shunted them into the lift and hit the down button, Chase marched back into the foyer of the clinic. Planting his hands on the curved desk, he leaned in toward the girls. "Who has food?"

"You missed lunch," Rae said in response.

"I was updating client plans." He stuck out his lower lips and blew at an imaginary hair. "I don't even know how long ago that was—what time is it, anyway?"

"Three thirty," Sam said without looking up from whatever she was doing—probably ordering herself a cat role-playing outfit.

"No wonder I'm fucking starving." Not moving away, he glanced from one to the other, narrowing his gaze as he stared at each with more intent.

Rae let him go on for almost a full minute before she slipped her hand beneath the desk and brought out a plastic tub. "You earn more money than us. Learn to feed *yourself*, Walker."

"I would, but you told me to quit buying takeaway." He grabbed up the tub before she could retract the offer and strode for his office. Kicking the door shut at his rear, he lifted up the corner of the lid and peeked inside.

Rice and peas. That'd do nicely.

That'd do nicely indeed.

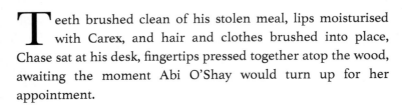

Teeth brushed clean of his stolen meal, lips moisturised with Carex, and hair and clothes brushed into place, Chase sat at his desk, fingertips pressed together atop the wood, awaiting the moment Abi O'Shay would turn up for her appointment.

He calculated the time in his head to be four forty-five. Fifteen minutes early for her booking. Five minutes later than she usually showed up.

His door had been shut to, so he couldn't see out to the reception for the exact moment she arrived. Which left him sat waiting for one of the girls to buzz through.

Knowing them, they'd leave him sitting an extra few minutes longer than necessary, just for the kick.

When the buzz came less than a minute later, it seemed to vibrate through the entirety of Chase's body, until it zipped its way out through his toes and had them pushing his arse back from the desk. He'd already rounded his desk by the time Sam's voice broke through.

"Your five o'clock is here, Mr Walker."

When he opened the door to Reception, he sighed out his relief at finding Abi hadn't changed into a clinic robe.

Finally, his head had ruled over his body with the instruction he'd given. Rae had overruled it, too, when she'd forbidden him to demonstrate oral sex positions with Abi, while she wore nothing more than a clinic robe with the potential to fall wide open and lay her bare.

Though, what Abi wore instead didn't exactly tamp down his already-twitchy dick.

A small skirt splayed around her hips, its hem draped over her thighs a good four inches above her knees. The blouse she'd donned held a gypsy appeal, patterned with embroidery a few shades darker than its red cotton, puffed sleeves making her shoulders appear higher than she set them, the soft collar dipping down to where the top button barely concealed the top swell of her breasts.

On her lap sat a small white box, and before he could stop himself, Chase asked, "You brought accessories with you today?"

Her eyes, already aimed his way as he'd appraised her,

J.A. BELFIELD

followed the slight dip of his own toward the box, and she breathed out a quiet laugh that lingered in the curve of her lips. "It's a gift," she said, pushing to her feet. "I brought you a treat."

A treat? Every time Abi showed up at his office and lost her inhibitions, it felt like a treat to Chase, but he refrained from telling her that. Ignoring the straightening of Rae and Sam in their seats, he smiled right back at her instead. "What kind of treat?"

Damn his betraying voice and its deepened tone.

Lifting the lid up on the box, she stepped forward until he could see inside. Dipping in a hand, he wrapped it around one of three balls of dough in there and lifted it up for inspection.

"Doughnuts?"

She nodded. "*Custard* doughnuts."

"You make these yourself?" Powdery white sugar already coated the fingers holding it.

"I did." She half-pointed toward the one in his hand. "You should try it."

Lips curving, he gave a nod. "Okay."

As soon as his teeth clamped over it and his lips brushed the sugary sweetness, a low groan left him, his lids lowering over his eyes. He took his time chewing, not even caring that everyone was probably staring at him, or that he could feel the sugar dusting his face. Swallowing, he opened his eyes again and smiled across at Rae and Sam. "That is one fine doughnut."

A pretty pink blush darkened Abi's cheeks when he turned back to her, and he couldn't help noticing the way she slightly dipped her gaze, as if both embarrassed and pleased by his praise.

"Where're ours, then?" Rae asked.

"Oh, well ... I did bring enough for three ..."

Abi twisted toward the reception desk, but before she could so much as take a step, Chase hooked an arm over the box and freed it from her hands. "These are mine," he said, pointing his half-eaten one their way before spinning for his office.

"Pig," Sam shouted after him.

Abi laughed as she followed behind him. She still smiled as he closed the door.

"You wouldn't be trying to distract me from this week's session, would you?" he asked as he carried the doughnuts across to his desk.

"I wouldn't dream of even trying," she said behind him.

After popping the box down, he spun and rested his butt against the desk's lip. Across from him, Abi took the chaise, and as she shuffled until she almost mirrored his pose on the edge of the seat, Chase noted the humour still playing across her features. "Did you do the homework I set?" he asked, like he needed to relocate the uncertainty he associated with the woman.

Rather than shy away from the probing question, though, she met his gaze as she answered, "Yes."

Biting off another chunk of doughnut, he studied her for a long moment, but not once did she back away from the direct eye contact, so much so, his every nerve ending seemed to tingle by the time he swallowed. "How does it make you feel about today's session?" he finally asked, feeding himself the last piece of cake.

"Curious," she said. A simple answer that had a far from simple effect on Chase's idiot body.

Brushing away the powder from around his mouth, he nodded. "Curious is good." Or it would be, had they met under different circumstances and sat across from each other in a different venue. Then Chase would reveal to her everything she held curiosity over, and then some.

Needing to feed the healthy dose of his own, he asked, "What was your source?" At her slight frown, he added,

"Where you got your information from to complete your homework?" In his mind, he imagined her sitting before a small screen, discreetly hidden beneath the covers of her bed, the volume down low. Would she have Googled? Would she have clicked the links a search like that would've brought up?

Would she have been turned on—enough to need relief she would have had to provide herself?

"I asked Rebecca to meet me for lunch and asked her—Rebecca Shannigan." She half pointed in his direction, the pink reclaiming her cheeks again. "She was a client here, if you remember me saying ..."

"I remember," he said. "What did she tell you about oral sex, when you asked?"

Her colour heightened, before a visible swallow worked its way through her throat. "She told me oral sex is pleasuring another person at their ..."

Her mouth worked a moment before Chase supplied, "Their pussy or cock."

She stared at him for a few long beats. "With your mouth," she finally added, her expression completely deadpan, and Chase had to contain his laugh that wanted to escape.

"Correct," he said instead. "Mouth, lips, tongue. So, knowing what the act, itself, would entail, are you still happy to explore the possibilities in today's session?"

"Yes." Her reply held none of the hesitation he'd expected, but came at him fast—a little husky, too.

The breath Chase gave released a whole lot of tension from his body—which had to be fucked up. In truth, he should've been hoping for her answer to be *no*. Because clothing, or no clothing, doing what he was about to with Abi O'Shay would place him in a tightrope situation. And he had no fucking idea how good his balance would be.

"Maybe we should get started, then," he said, trying to keep his voice level.

He must have succeeded, because Abi pushed to her feet looking more than ready to get started.

Knowing familiarity would help put her at ease, Chase led her through to the bedroom used for her earlier visits.

"So, I don't need to get undressed?" she asked, stepping into the room behind him.

"No," he said quickly—a little too quickly. For a moment, he wondered if she understood the effect she had on him. Closing them in together, he turned to her, and he had to order his brain away from the thought of her stripping before him—*for* him—as she stood staring back wearing an expression he couldn't decipher. "We'll only be exploring the different ways it can be performed—different positions. We won't actually be participating in the act itself."

Abi glanced away as he spoke, her eyes cast toward the floor. On anyone else, the gesture would've spelled disappointment. Chase had no idea what to make of it when coming from Abi.

"Okay," she said quietly.

"Right, well ... we should begin, then," he said, watching her closely. "Do you have a preference for where we should do it?" He inwardly cringed at his choice of words.

Abi's gaze swung back up to him. "I thought we were doing it in here."

"We are." He smiled—just about, anyway. His body felt on the verge of twanging, the closer it got to having Abi's face near his crotch. "I meant, would you prefer using the bed? Or we could take the floor." He gestured toward the thick rug set before the fake fireplace.

Abi's body swayed between the two choices as if she gave careful consideration to the decision. Giving a sharp nod, she said, "The bed."

The bed. Meaning he'd be on the bed. With Abi.

Chase had no bloody idea if that'd be better, or worse, than floor. Or maybe either way'd end up being an unholy nightmare.

Trying to school his features into an expression that didn't give away the war his head waged with his eager body, he waved a hand toward the circular bed just waiting and beckoning and promising a world full of torture. "After you," he said.

With a few glances his way, as if checking he approved, Abi crossed to the bed.

And Chase approved, all right. He approved a whole lot.

She lifted a knee up onto the mattress, followed by the other. As she shuffled on until about a foot from the edge, Chase wondered if she even realised the inward placement of each shoulder, the way each arm pushed at her breasts until their upper mounds fought against the buttons of her blouse. Had she any idea of her body language, or the effect she could have on a man?

Did have on a man.

"Here okay?" she asked, only innocence seeming to radiate from those stunning eyes of hers.

"Yes," he said. There, just as she was, was very much okay.

Fighting the urge to lose his tie and loosen his collar, he traced her steps until he stood before where she knelt. "Option number one for oral sex is a simple position." He had no idea what he was doing when he reached out and grabbed each of her knees. Sliding her around brought her to fully face him, and he slid a hand around each thigh, gently tugging until she took the hint and unfolded her legs. As soon as she had, he drew them forward, hooked her knees over the mattress, letting her feet overhang toward the floor.

Her gaze burned through him throughout the entire manoeuvre.

Allowing himself to be drawn right in by those oceanic

blues, he placed a hand either side of her thighs and lowered himself to the floor. His chest butted her knees as he crowded in around her—the closest he'd permitted himself to get so far.

"This position can work well whoever's receiving the pleasure, whoever is giving it." For a moment, he mentally argued that he hadn't planned to put himself in the giving position. At all. He reached for her knees anyway, gently encouraged them apart.

If he'd been expecting any resistance from her, he didn't get any. She just swung her legs aside like a damned invitation, leaving nothing but a few scraps of clothing separating Chase from her core.

"And with the woman, or man, in this position, it allows the recipient stability and a modicum of comfort ..." Clearing his throat a little, he continued, "And at the same time, it allows the man, or woman, giving pleasure easy access."

"The bed doesn't get in the way?" she asked, more innocence spilling into the room.

"Not unless you let it." When she frowned down at him, he slipped his arms beneath her thighs and pushed through far enough to grip her ass in his hands. At his sharp tug toward him, she let out a tiny squeak. Forcing away his smile at the sound, he balanced her on the edge of the bed, and before he could talk himself out of it, he grabbed the hem of her skirt and shoved it high against her waist. Confronting himself with the white cotton of her undies.

For a long moment, he stared at them—mainly at the wetness spreading across the cotton. And his entire mouth seemed to dry up as heat spread through his body and hardened his cock. "Pretty much unrestricted access," he said roughly.

"Okay," she said above him. He could've sworn her voice wobbled.

"If a guy wants to get closer still ..." He dared peek back up at her face and almost groaned at the way her lips had parted, the way her left hand had lifted toward his head like her soul already understood the motions of the act they discussed. Dipping his face again, Chase worked a shoulder beneath one of her legs, gritting his teeth against the audible hastening of her breaths. "By a man simply positioning a woman's legs over his shoulders ..." He shrugged his other shoulder beneath her other leg, but as he ducked his face closer to her crotch, his own breaths stalled in his throat.

Because Abi was *wet* wet. Really fucking *wet*. Far wetter than she'd been only a moment before.

His tongue swiped across his lips, before he finished with, "... usually does the trick." His voice bordered on being a low growl, and he knew if he didn't remove himself—and fast—he'd be acting in a way he'd never be able to undo.

A part of him didn't care—a big part. That same part wanted him to stay exactly where he was and show Abi the true high of getting her cunt licked out, the unadulterated pleasure of having her clit drawn so deep into someone's mouth, she wouldn't know whether to beg him to stop, or cry for more.

A feather-light ruffling of his hair had his body freezing all over. At first, he considered that her breaths had stirred the strands, but at the next brush of the hairs, he knew. She'd touched him. Without provocation, she'd taken one of those pretty hands of hers and initiated contact.

And Chase had no fucking idea what to make of that—or what to do about it.

As chastely as the touch began, it ceased. "You said there were other positions?" she said quietly.

He nodded, mostly because he didn't trust himself to speak. Pushing up to his feet took him away from the heat of Abi's body. He allowed himself a quick scan of her face, took in the way her eyes shone, the deepening of the colour tinting her cheeks. "Instead of the recipient using a bed for support," he said, glancing away, "they can use a wall." He pointed to the nearest uncluttered patch. "They lean back against the wall, but standing instead of sitting, and the same principle applies to the one giving what we've just looked at."

"They do it on their knees," she said.

His lips curved at her gentle tone, and he nodded. "And just as I demonstrated here." He pointed from the spot he'd just occupied toward the wall. "Depending on the physics of the couple involved, the whole hooking of the woman's legs over the shoulders thing works in that position, too." He silently groaned at his oh, so fucking eloquent wording.

"Physics?"

He turned toward her again then. "Yeah. Body weight. Strength. Endurance. Personal balance. Those kinds of factors."

"Have you ever done it that way?" she asked, and he could tell from the evident mortification drawing her features down that she probably hadn't meant to enquire out loud.

Even so, he answered, "Yes. I like it that way."

"Why?"

His smile slipped free again. "Because it gives me more control."

Her lips shifted, like she had more to say, like she wanted to probe further, but she quickly closed them as if changing her mind.

To make sure it stayed that way, Chase nodded toward the bed. "Lie back. Get comfortable." As she went to sink straight back from her position at the edge, he shook his head. "Legs up on the bed, too."

With her eyes on him, she obeyed, swinging her legs up and settling herself down on the soft throw covering the bed. "Like this?"

"Exactly like that." Climbing onto the bed alongside her, he slipped a hand between her rigid legs. "Except, these need to be more relaxed if you want a guy to get close enough to pleasure you—and if you want us to continue exploring positions today."

Once more as accommodating as ever, she drew her heels toward her butt and let her legs ease to the sides.

He gave a sharp nod. "Better." Moving into position at her feet jostled the bed, and he stretched an arm between her parted knees, his torso following, until he'd planted the hand down beside her hip and his face hovered over her pelvis. "Again," he said, peering up at her, "Easy access."

To demonstrate—or maybe because he secretly loved the personal torment—he dipped his head in closer, taking his nose to within an inch of her cotton-covered clit, his head brushing her skirt where it'd bunched around the tops of her thighs. And fuck, if the scent of her arousal hadn't begun to pulse its way free of her pussy.

Once more, all moisture vanished from Chase's mouth.

"This same position applies to both sexes," he said, all too aware of how much his voice had deepened. "Whoever's giving. Whoever's receiving." He couldn't help but ponder for a half-beat, whether it'd be more torturous doing as he was—or being the one lying on his back while guiding Abi into positions that'd have her mouth really fucking close to his erection.

Because he was definitely erect. His cock swelled into a solid mass, like it could break through his trousers using sheer bulk alone.

Daring to glance up at her, he found her gaze directly on him again. She'd scarcely looked away since the session began. And beneath that heated and inquisitive stare, her chest made a tremulous journey upward before bouncing its way back down.

Maybe she was as affected by their closeness as he was.

Fuck that. She *was* affected. Her scent, her colouring, her soaked undies. Why should he discount signs he'd never question on another woman? All signs he'd seen a thousand times before.

Abi O'Shay was well and truly turned on. And that only amped up Chase's own arousal by a whole heap of trouble.

Pushing up from her, he lifted her left leg and slid his own legs out to the side beneath it, and still she watched him, concentration creating a slight frown across her brow. "Whoever's at the giving end of the deal has more options for position from this angle. They can come on from the side, like this— allowing them to move the recipient's legs where they want, or need, them. Or ..."

He scooted out from beneath her leg, placed her foot back down against the throw, and shifted around to her side.

"Or the giver can just as easily come in from this angle."

Nudging her legs wider apart with his fingertips, he reached across her torso and braced a hand down on her other side. Using that for support, he crooked his other arm around her nearest thigh and pushed over her body until his face, once more, hovered over her cunt.

"It looks uncomfortable for you," she said, her voice carrying a definite tremor.

"Nobody gives a damn about comfort while they're doing something that feels right and good, Abi."

His voice came out sharper than intended, and for a long pause, neither of them spoke. Neither of them moved, either. Which left Chase staring down at a pussy he really fucking wanted but would never have.

"Often, in this position ..." He cleared his throat to rid it of the gravel it clung to. "If the woman is the recipient," he continued, "her lifting a leg up to hook over the giver's shoulder will increase the access because it tilts the pelvis upward."

Without provocation, the thigh he held onto lifted, before the weight of Abi's ankle hit his shoulder blade.

"Like this?" she asked.

Yeah. Totally like that.

Except, Chase couldn't quite get the words out, because all he could focus on was the proximity of her pussy to his mouth, and the lack of barrier, from her skirt sliding even farther out of the way. The dampness of her underwear had evolved into full-out saturation—hell, even the crooks of her thighs had begun to glisten—and Chase wanted nothing more than to dip his face a couple of inches so he could taste her.

Would her essence be as sweet as she, herself, appeared on the surface?

Or would it hold a whole unexpected level of darkness that could bewitch its taster as easily as Abi seemed to have bewitched him?

Not even trying to formulate a decent sentence, Chase grunted his approval, lowering her leg from his shoulder, and ordered his salivating tongue away from the goods. Pushing up until he knelt at her side again, he twisted until he faced her, hoping she couldn't see in his expression the thoughts he'd just had.

"Ready for the next position?"

She gave a short nod, her gaze still on him.

As soon as she had, he grabbed her hips, flipped her onto her stomach. Ignoring the way his cock surged at her squeak of surprise, he flipped his hands beneath her hips again and hauled upward until her knees supported her and she had to press her palms into the mattress to avoid kissing the throw.

"You could have warned me," she said, her voice a little breathy.

A bold statement for Abi, and Chase seemed only capable of a low rumble of laughter that was a whole lot darker than it should've been—telling him he should probably pull back from whatever depth his mind had devolved to.

"You'll thank me if you ever experience it this way." He moved down the bed until kneeling behind her, staring at the sweet mounds of her arse. Her skirt had slipped back into place with her new position, but Chase could still see the curves of her body, and all too easily remembered what hid beneath.

Being the fucking idiot he was, he took hold of each of her thighs, his fingers splayed enough to brush the undersides of her ass cheeks, his thumbs outstretched toward what he'd just denied himself. "This way allows the giver to find a position that works for him. He can either dip in close from where he is." He just caught her glancing back at him over her shoulder before he demonstrated by pushing in close. If not for her skirt, he'd have had the bridge of his nose crammed between her ass cheeks and his hot breaths breezing all over her cunt. "Or he can come in sideways." He dropped down until he'd propped an elbow between her knees and muscled a shoulder between her thighs, and his face halfway peeked beneath the hem of her skirt at underwear she'd definitely need to change before going home.

Shuffling down onto his back switched his point of view to a prime one. Chase wanted nothing more than to dive upward and steal a taste. Just one. What the hell would it even hurt, beyond giving Abi a short fucking thrill?

"How strong are you, Abi—you feeling sturdy there?"

"I'm stronger than I look."

Chase didn't doubt it. "Then, brace yourself, because you're about to take some of my weight."

"Oka—"

Grabbing hold of her ass, Chase hauled himself upward before he could talk himself out of it. With his arms clinging to her hips, his muscles gave a small pang of protest before settling into the task. Somehow managing to have aimed his head right beneath her skirt, Chase balanced with his mouth about a hairs-breadth from Abi's cunt.

"Depending on how long the couple can hold for ..." Chase deliberately let his lips brush the fabric of her undies as he spoke. He knew she felt it by the slight twitch of her hips and the quiet gasp he caught above his head, and he wondered if she peered down the length of her body. Watching him. Waiting. "... this can be a great position for the woman," he finished, a small thrill rippling along his spine at her tremor.

Resisting the beseeching of his mind for him to stick out his tongue and lick the damned goods, he relaxed his hold on Abi and dropped back to the bed.

She didn't move as he wriggled free and got back onto his knees, but she let out another sound of surprise when he gripped her hips and rolled her onto her back.

Legs akimbo, mouth a perfect 'O' of *what the hell*, she stared up at him as if waiting to see what he'd do next.

Fucking. Adorable.

"Up against the pillows," he said, taking hold again and guiding her. As soon as he had her propped where he wanted her, he stretched out each of her legs until he had them straight and tucked between his own.

Still, she just stared up at him. The surprise had left her eyes, though, making way for what looked very much like heated anticipation.

"This next position serves mostly the man in the situation." On his hands and knees, he slowly crawled his way up her body. He loved that she didn't recoil or complain, but just kept those damned hypnotic eyes on him the whole time. She didn't even try retreating when his face closed in on hers and he had to shift his hands to the pillow to continue, then the wall behind her head—giving her a close-up of first his shirted chest then lower abs.

"From this position, a man can guide himself into a woman's mouth. Or guide her mouth to his cock." To demonstrate, he tangled his fingers around her hair and gave a small tug toward himself. Not too much, though. He didn't want to scare her off. "Or the woman has enough access to make a man pray for all that is holy that she never stops."

Her quiet laugh breezed across his stomach, tightening the muscles there as warmth seeped through his shirt to caress him.

"Scoot down," he said, his hand pressing against her head where his fingers remained entwined.

She went to look up, but he held tight, preventing the action. After a moment's hesitation, she obeyed, and the wiggling of her body between his thighs was like the devil himself had thrown down a temptation, one upon which he expected Chase to act.

As soon as he had Abi's chin directly beneath the V of his groin, he relaxed his hold on her. Pressed both palm into the pillows above her head. Shifted his knees back just enough to alter the angle of his crotch. And a slight tilting of his hips took the swell of his throbbing cock to within an inch of the mouth he'd been dreaming about fucking.

For the first time since the session had started, Abi's gaze seemed distracted from meeting his. From the lowered state of her lashes, he guessed she held about as much awareness of his erection as Chase did.

"This position gives me a lot more control than it does you." He had no idea how he continued to talk.

He also had no idea when he'd switched from generic references to inserting himself and Abi into the equation.

"You like control," Abi said, her voice a mere murmur.

"Yes, I do. And when the positions are reversed ..." He rolled from over her. Lying back against the mattress, he beckoned to Abi, and as soon as she'd gotten onto her knees, Chase slid her closer to him. Over him. The entire time watching the nervous twitch of her lips—like she didn't know what to make of the game they were playing, but she liked it.

And they were definitely playing at something. Chase just didn't know which one of them led. Or which of them followed to see where it could go.

"Higher," he ordered, when she stilled with her knees tucked against the sides of his ribcage.

Holding his arms and shoulders in tight to his chest allowed her to shuffle closer to his face.

It also allowed his knuckles to brush against her wet undies, and he had to bite down on a dark chuckle of fucking glee at the jolt of her body.

"Keep coming," he said, trying his damnedest not to grin like a fricking moron at the way her hands slapped down above his head. The way her hips shimmied over his shoulders.

Her skirt held just the right length that when she breached the tip of his chin, it merely tickled his flesh with the swaying of her hips. Holding his breath, he kept his gaze riveted on her face, as she covered the final inch until only Chase's eyes peeked from beneath fabric, while his mouth breathed in the very essence of her pussy like he could taste it from scent alone.

He had to lick his lips to get them to work. "As I started saying … reversing positions gives you all the control."

"Something you don't like so much."

He studied her for a moment. She seemed so much more open to stating her opinion than usual. And Chase was pretty sure he liked it.

"I wouldn't exactly say that." In fact, knowing it was Abi's pussy hovering in prime position for pouring cum down his throat, Chase decided he did like it. A lot. "You control when you lower your … sex to my mouth." He wondered if she even noticed the almost unconscious lowering of her pussy toward his parted lips. "You control how much pressure there is between your pussy and my mouth." Again. She fucking did it again. Hell, even her arms trembled against the top of his head like she struggled to keep herself away. She'd be full-on sitting on his face if she kept it up. "You control the angle of the caresses. The licks. The sucking of your clit. You control every damned thing about the partnering, Abi."

Her cunt dropped over that final gap, and like he had no control over his actions, Chase darted out his tongue and took that fucking taste he needed.

Hoping she wouldn't notice made him an idiot, because Abi's sharp gasp pierced the room as she jerked back from him like she'd been electrocuted.

For five, long seconds, he and Abi stared at each other, his hands itching to slide right up under her skirt, grab her arse, and yank her back to him.

Above him, the placement of her arms pushed her breasts forward, making Chase all too aware of how heavily she breathed. And all Chase could think about was, if a tiny, stolen taste set her breathing so erratic, how hard would shoving his tongue into her cunt have her panting?

With her skirt still covering most of his face, she wouldn't see his tongue sliding across his lips, or the smile teasing at the corners of his mouth as the shock in her eyes un-misted, leaving only a very clear desire in its place.

"There are a lot of positions for this," she said, breaking the stare-down. Her voice sounded as husky as he'd expected it to.

"There are probably a whole lot more," he said. "All anyone has to do to find them is be open to ideas and experimentation."

"Are we experimenting?" Her tone made the questions sound like a flirt but inexperience got in the way of her pulling it off.

Chase's cock still pulsed hard, his hips twitching upward like he had no control. "Not today," he said, questioning his own wording as soon as it was out. Like only 'today' stood in the way of pursuing all the Abi scenarios he kept in his head, as if 'tomorrow' the rules would be different and he could fuck her as high as the heavens and make her scream his name until hoarse. He had to mentally shake his head clear before continuing, "But there is one more position we're going to cover before we wrap up."

Her lips curved slightly. Like she was glad the session wasn't about to end.

"The next position allows the involvement of both ..." ... *of us* ... "parties." Chase loved that she hadn't bothered moving away to listen, but just stayed there with her chest hovering above his face, and her pussy slowly sinking back down just below his chin. "It allows both ..." ...*of us* ... "parties to receive the pleasure while giving it."

When she still didn't move, he breathed out a low laugh. "This isn't the position we need to be in for it, Abi."

Her eyes sparked as that colour shot back over her cheeks, and pushing against the pillows, she lifted her leg from over him until she knelt at his side. "Where do you want me?"

Anywhere and everywhere, balanced on the tip of his tongue. "Depends." Flexing, he sat up and offered a small shrug. "Do you want to be on top, or bottom?"

"What's the difference?" she asked.

"One allows you the most control. The other—you relinquish some of that control." He probably should've explained which position covered what, but the dark side of his brain that craved what he shouldn't have didn't *want* her to choose the easy option. While having her pussy pressing against him had been fucking awesome, it didn't quite compete with the absolute hotness leaning over Abi would produce, knowing he had her exactly as he wanted her.

Would want her.

If he could even have her.

Which he couldn't.

Kicking his stupid voice of reason out of bed, he studied the shifting expressions on Abi's face as she seemed to give the decision serious consideration. Her brows bunched inward. Her eyes, while managing to stay on him, flickered side to side.

After a few shuddering rises of her chest, she said, "Bottom?" like she didn't quite understand what she was letting herself in for.

And she didn't—or wouldn't, if they planned to actually go ahead with fucking the fuck outta each other's faces. Which they weren't.

Nodding, he thumbed toward the bed. "On your back, then." His deepened tone made the direction sound a whole lot dirtier than it was.

Without argument, she tipped herself into her butt and unrolled herself over the mattress. "Like this?"

He waved toward the foot of the bed. "Farther down," he said. Holding up a hand, he stopped her about halfway, her calves just about overhanging the bottom lip of the mattress.

With her head tilted up, she stared at him as if seeking approval, and Chase had to drag his focus away from how the position raised her hips from the blanket a little, how even the dipping down of her shoulders did shit to disguise the rapid rise and fall of her chest. It also did absolutely nothing to hide how fucking deliciously dishevelled she looked in comparison to when she'd first stepped into the room.

Her hair still clumped together some where his fingers had taken hold. Her clothes scarcely covered where she'd probably hoped they would when she'd dressed that morning—like she no longer cared that the button attempting to contain her breasts barely clung to its partnering hole. Or whether, or not, her skirt covered her ass. Hell, even an inch of her stomach showed between the two halves of her clothing. Almost as if, since the beginning of her session—since the beginning of *all* her sessions—whatever barrier she'd placed between them had suddenly been smashed down.

Though, maybe sitting on a guy's face, however briefly, could have that affect.

And he was staring.

Giving his head another sharp shake, Chase got to his knees and manoeuvred until kneeling behind Abi's head. As he did so, her gaze followed him, and she peered up and back at him as he continued to stare down at her.

"Welcome to the sixty-nine," he said, before stretching his way over her torso until his chest hovered over her stomach, his cock over her face, and he had a prime view of her pussy folds through her increasingly translucent underwear.

Almost unconsciously, her legs relaxed to the sides. As if those instincts of hers were once again putting in an appearance.

"As I said ..." His gaze latched onto a fresh spill of wetness across the cotton covering her cunt. "This position allows both of us to give *and receive* pleasure."

Her heels scraped across the bedding. Toward her arse. He watched as the action took her knees high, lifted her pelvis. When they ceased moving, her thighs wavered close enough for him to rest his head against, and he had to wonder over the point of the shift. Had she done it with intent?

Because on any other woman, he'd have seen that as invitation.

On Abi, he had no fucking idea what to make of it all.

The softest of touches feathered over his cock, and Chase nearly shot off the bed with how hard he jerked.

Tucking his chin in tight, he peered between the length of their bodies—and his frown slammed down on seeing her hand poised a needlepoint away from his zipper.

He opened his mouth, his lips even began forming the question, but his gob crammed closed when she took hold of his belt and unfed it from the buckle. It was like his mouth had even less sense than his brain did, as though seeing where the hell she might be going was a good idea.

It wasn't.

It was a really fucking stupid idea.

So, why the hell couldn't he get his damned voice to protest, or his body to move away.

Probably because his dick was chuckling his ugly little head off in devious glee.

The leather of his belt hung in front of Abi's face in two halves. "My friend told me about this position," she quietly.

Chase probably should've answered. Hell, even something like, *Oh, yeah, what'd she tell you?* would've been better than his mute staring from his rigid body that suddenly felt alive with an anticipation he had no right to be feeling.

"I wondered if you would show it to me," she continued.

The buzz of his zip cut through the air, and he finally got his act together enough to ask, "Abi, what are you doing?" Arousal thickened his voice as much as it did his cock. Arousal from what, though? She'd only undone his trousers, for frick's sake.

"I need to understand what it's really like. With someone I trust." Again with the soft voice. "I want to *know*."

His cock acted like it wanted to K.O. his boxers out of the way at her words. His teeth ground beneath the effort of remaining still. "I'm not sure you're ready for that."

His cock probably wanted to punch Chase in the head, too—just to shut him up.

"I have to be ready," she said.

The wedding. Right. How could he forget about the fucking wedding?

Yet, when her hands edged beneath his clothing, gliding against his bare skin beneath, Chase about forgot his own name.

"Abi ..."

Cloth rubbed against flesh, as she pushed his clothing down just enough to release him. Between their bodies, Chase could see the length of his overexcited cock bouncing down above Abi's face.

It took all his resolve to tell her, "This isn't something you want to do now. Here." *With me*, he almost added. No matter how much Chase wanted to do it himself.

Her breath washed over him, setting his nerve endings aflame. Her fingertips teased at the sensitive skin of his inner thigh.

One breath—slow, steady. A lot steadier than he'd have ever expected from her.

Two breaths.

Three.

"I do." Though she spoke scarcely above a whisper, Chase heard her just fine.

"You should think it through," he said, closing his eyes against the torture of having to say that.

Why the hell was he trying to talk her out of what he craved. What he needed. He'd never be questioning it if it were another client lying beneath him.

Though, any other client, and he'd have never gotten into the sixty-nine with them to begin.

"I did," she said. "I thought about it all week, since Rebecca told me about it."

All week? A part of him wondered who, exactly, she'd placed in each scenario her mind had toyed with.

"I've thought a lot about what it would be like," she said, her voice bordering on sultry, leaving Chase wondering if her desire to continue truly did match his own. A single fingertip stretched up and brushed over the head of his cock, making it twitch, the ease with which it slid across his flesh telling him he'd already leaked some pre-cum. "I'm ready to find out."

His focus downright refused to shift when her tongue poked from between her lips and headed for the tip of his hardened length. The instant it made contact, a tiny groan eked out on his released breath.

"Abi ..."

Her tongue shot out again, less hesitant, expanding to its full length as she curled it beneath the underside of his shaft and licked over his swollen head. Pausing, she asked, "Is this right?" For the first time since she'd shocked the hell out of him, she sounded unsure.

That probably should've been where he took advantage and told her if she had to ask, she wasn't ready—or some other bullshit to stop her roaming along a path that would probably be too rocky for her. Completely shunning the practical side of his brain, he murmured, "Anything that involves your mouth and my cock cannot possibly add up to anything less than right."

She released an audible sigh, one that blasted his flesh with heat and had his cock jumping about again. "Okay," she whispered, almost to herself, and wrapping a hand lightly around his rigid shaft, she licked at him again.

At which point, Chase swayed on his limbs and had trouble swallowing.

Lick after lick, she treated his cock like her personal treat. Lick after lick, Chase's hips jerked toward her in search of the next tonguing.

Abi had come to his clinic claiming to be as green as the grass at Hampton Court Palace. Chase didn't, for a second, doubt that to be true, but damn, she slathered that tongue of hers around his shaft like she'd spent her life eating ice pops—

because she might have been a fucking pro, for the trembling reaction of Chase's body.

He couldn't be sure when his head lifted and rested against her inner thigh. When his breaths had deepened until they bordered on rumbling growls blowing past his lips.

He also couldn't be sure when his hips had struck up a rhythm of thrusting and grabbing any attention he could get.

What he did know for certain, though, was the exact moment her lips yielded beneath his demands and his cock sank straight into the depths of her heated wet mouth. And Chase had no fucking chance of restraining his groan at that point. Certainly no chance of holding his shit together.

The deeper he plunged into her mouth, the less he felt the feathering of her fingers across his shaft, until they brushed across his leg and both her hands moulded around the backs of his thighs.

Like she'd given him control—not that Chase even knew what that was anymore.

Like she'd surrendered her mouth to his needs.

As if she'd also surrendered to her own needs, her hips began the slow pattern of rocking he'd seen from her before. Seen from her whenever she'd sought pleasure, the answer to her desires.

Dropping down to an elbow, Chase stared at the swelling of her soft mounds against the restraining cotton. Stared at the outline of her clit and imagined it clawing its way free in search of his attention.

Would it really hurt to touch? Just once?

As he rubbed a finger lightly over the fabric of her underwear, even more juices spilled from her, and Abi released a low groan that vibrated along the length of his shaft.

Fuck. He had to clench his everything to stop himself from

leaping off her, spinning her the hell over, and fucking the holy shit out of her virginal cunt.

Except, staying where he was kept that pussy flashing up at him like damned bait, and before he could talk himself out of it, he dipped his mouth toward where she begged to be sampled. To hell with his control. To hell with holding back. Chase had done little but fantasise over Abi since the first day she'd stepped into his office, and with her finally laid out beneath him, offering a taste, he was damned well going to take it.

The moment his lips folded over the cotton of her undies, fingertips dug into his thighs and a muffled whimper carried over. His lids lowered as he ducked in for another taste, a quiet *mmm* humming up from his chest. Even with the blockage of fabric, Chase had no trouble capturing the sweetness of her essence. Had no trouble working his tongue between her folds, dipping into where cum dripped out from her. His hips still moving, his cock throbbing against the insides of her oral heat, Chase shifted back enough to pluck at her stiffened clit with his lips, smiling around the eager bud when her entire body seemed to jerk it closer toward him and the first scrape of her nails grazed his flesh.

Unable to help himself, he brushed his hand along her inner thigh. Closer. Closer to her heat, her evident pleasure. Because he needed to touch. Just one touch. Needed to *feel* how wet she was, dammit. And when her mouth clamped tight around his cock and she tried her first real suck of the session, Chase's eyes damned near rolled in his head, his lids flipping up as his groan broke out, and he decided there and then he was done with pissing about. Decided there and then that he would fucking touch Abi, even if it was the only time he ever got to do it. Even if she never stepped foot into his practice again, it would've been worth it.

He knew it would.

Plucking at the edge of her underwear, he slid a finger over the wet flesh beneath, and did a shit job of containing his next groan when more of her juices poured out and coated his skin.

Beneath the thin cotton, he guided his finger up to her clit, circled the rigid bud, slipped right back down, where he dipped just the tip of his finger into the pool of enticement.

At another suck of her mouth around his cock, his hips jerked downward. His entire body heated at the grunt she gave when he drove home against her throat.

Fuck, he loved that sound. He loved it even more when coming from Abi, and that just made him want to hear it a whole lot more.

Drawing his hips back, he poised above her as he toyed with the rim of her cunt. With the plunge of his cock deep into her mouth, he dipped his fingertip back into Abi's pussy, thrilling at the way she lifted her ass off the bed like she needed more.

Hell, she'd only to say and Chase would've given her anything she damned well wanted.

Wrapping his supporting arm around her ass, he hooked a finger around her undies and tugged them all the way aside. As he thrust down with his hips again, he lowered his face and delved his tongue into Abi's soaked pussy, fast, creating a rhythm that had them both writhing for the ultimate high and grunting out their effort. With each plunge of his hips, his cock throbbed harder. His balls cinched tighter. His supporting limbs shook that little bit more.

With each fuck of his tongue, Abi forced her hips up a little higher. Planted her heels in a little deeper. And grew wetter and fucking wetter by the second, until Chase pulled back for a half beat, his chin rolling across her overexcited clit, just so he could watch the cum pouring from her pussy.

Because it would pour. He'd make sure of it.

Teeth gritted, he sank his tongue inside her again. And

again. Curling it enough to stroke over her ever-tightening walls and fill his mouth with her nectar, a nectar he gulped down like he'd been starved for its taste without even realising.

At the same time, he rammed his cock into her wet mouth so deep, her lips hugged his balls for a brief moment before he withdrew.

Around the thickness of his girth, muffled whimpers and slow-released moans crept out, and Chase upped his pace. Both his hips and his tongue thrusting like a couple of bastards that had his whole body tense and his jaw locked wide and his teeth scraping across the soft flesh surrounding Abi's cunt as she twitched her clit across his chin like she'd found a rhythm of her own.

Her gasp blasted around his phallus on his next pull back. Her knees lifted until her toes scarcely reached the bed. Beneath him, her hips drove a manic journey of upward thrusts, her ass fidgeting all over the place, and Chase knew she was close. Knew only a couple more seconds, then she'd be his.

Driving his tongue into her, he worked a hand beneath his throat and found her clit. Gave tiny slaps against her solid bud in a way that heightened her cries and had all kinds of sparkly shit happening in his head as he continued to fuck her mouth just as fast and hard as his tongue fucked her.

As soon as the walls of her pussy began clenching, he knew he had her, but still, he kept pumping into her. Faster. Deeper. Those fingers of his working the shit out of her clit, until her moaning gasps evolved into a muffled scream and her legs railed at the air like she tried to grab hold and lock him in place.

Not giving her a chance to fall from her high, Chase shifted his fingers back and flicked over her stiffened tip, then gave gentle slaps, until her scream became a continuous vibration along his cock, and her legs all but wrapped around his shoulders, her entire body locked up tight as a fountain of cum sprayed from her pussy to fill his mouth and soak his face, spraying upward and outward like a mofo and covering just about anything it could fucking reach.

Yes! He wanted to shout it out. Fucking yes.

Instead, he just kept on at her clit between pumping his tongue back within the erratic pulsing of her cunt, while fucking her mouth with a heightened desperation that had a string of grunts bubbling through his throat.

He knew he'd be coming any second, but he'd be damned if he could do a single thing to stop it. Not anymore. It was too late.

It'd been too late since the moment Abi had first unzipped his fly.

At another wailing scream from Abi, his balls finally exploded the cum through his cock, and he held himself deep inside her mouth, something close to a bark blasting from him as he emptied himself against her throat.

Her fingers clawed at his ass, but that only had his hips bucking against her, fucking the chasing juices from his cock, until his body admitted defeat—or victory—and he just stilled. His elbow somehow continuing to support him. His hand, his face, what seemed like his everywhere dripping in Abi's cum. His body shaking like he had no control over it.

Which about summed it up perfectly, didn't it?

For how many years had Chase kidded himself that he had a grip on himself? That he could hold his shit together.

Certainly didn't fucking seem that way right then.

A muffled whimper cut through the descended quiet, and Chase slowly lifted his head.

If he'd any doubt over what he'd just done with Abi being real, that got batted right out the field with that single sound.

Because, no, he hadn't made it up.

No, it hadn't just been one of his many sick fantasies playing out inside his head.

He really had made Abi come so hard she'd turned into a fucking geyser.

He really had fucked her mouth so hard, he'd seen a bloody super nova behind his eyes.

And his cock was still in Abi's mouth. Still so deep she couldn't even speak.

What the holy fuck had he just done?

The door to the session room burst open, and Rae marched in wearing a whole new level of pissed off like it was a suit she'd had tailored to fit. "All finished in here?" she asked, and Chase had no idea how she managed to sound so fucking amenable, given her expression.

Offering what might've passed as a nod, he finally pushed himself up. His cock felt instantly cold as it slipped from Abi's mouth. His soaked face felt cold. The rest of his body felt cold, too. Like he'd fallen into an ice pond and someone had blocked all means of escape.

He didn't want to look at Abi. He didn't want to see what he'd just done to her in her face, written into grooves of distrust and disappointment.

He had to, though. He, at least, owed her that.

Rolling to the side, onto his knees, he dared glance at the woman he'd just let down beyond any of his past levels of failure, but even knowing what he'd done, how he'd fucked up, didn't quite prepare him for the wide-eyed face-full of shock staring back at him. Her chest heaved, like she sucked in much-needed air. Her hands wrapped around nothing, like they'd stiffened into position as she'd clawed at his flesh. And her mouth ... that beautiful mouth of hers stayed rounded and red and swollen as bloody hell.

Chase had done that. He'd done it *to her*. He had no bloody clue what to say, where to even start. What the hell *could* he say to put right what had just happened?

Unable to look at the ruin he'd caused any longer, he glanced toward where Rae stood watching the two of them like she had trouble reining her opinion in. An opinion that'd be warranted, no doubt.

As if she sensed his uncertainty, she jerked her head toward the door. "If you want to go and get cleaned up, Mr Walker, I'll have Samantha come in and help Ms O'Shay to the client bathroom."

Nodding as if on autopilot, Chase slid from the mattress, his knees thinking about giving up on him when he stood and made for the door. A part of him wondered why the hell he hadn't bolted out of there like his arse was on fire, but he knew why, the second he paused at the door and peered back at Abi. Because more than anything, he wanted he and Abi to be anywhere but at his clinic. He wanted Rae and Sam to disappear and it just be the two of them, so he could stroke Abi's hair, reassure it was okay, tell her how sorry he was—because it never should've been so fucking wild and out of control for her first sexual experience.

It never should've been *with him*.

He didn't do any of those things, though. At a hard, warning glare from Rae, he slunk from the room like the slimy bastard he was and trod the walk of shame toward the staff showers.

He knew she stood outside of the showers. Could sense the shifting of her shadow. Hear the quiet huff of her breaths. Ignoring her presence didn't change the fact she was there, though. Didn't change the fact she was waiting for him. Nor the fact that he'd brought enough shit into his own clinic to bury himself with.

Knocking off the shower spray, he reached for a towel, heaved in a long breath, and turned to face the wrath of Rae.

He didn't even get far enough to make eye contact, when pain blasted through his face, and he stumbled back a step, his fingers instantly reaching for the spot aside his lip where she'd hit. Not even bothering to push away from the tiles, he dared lift his gaze to hers and almost recoiled at the fury shooting at him like a heat-seeking torpedo.

"You cock-sucking, granny-fucking idiot of a wanker." She pointed at him like she could gut him with her finger alone. "You have just risked *everything*." Stepping into the shower, she shoved both her hands against his chest until his back bashed the tiles. "I hope it was worth it, you fucking *fuck*." Picking up the towel from where it'd fallen, she chucked it at his middle. "Get dressed, look smart, and get your fucking arse into your office. You better make this okay before she leaves here today. D'you hear me, Walker?"

Offering up a pathetic nod, Chase waited until she'd fired more glare missiles at him and walked away, before venturing out of the safety of the glass enclosure.

Rae was right. He had risked everything. And despite his nod to her before she'd left, he doubted he had a hope in hell of putting any of it right.

Because how could he ask Abi to forgive him, when he knew himself that what he'd done with her—to her—made him about as decent as a fucking cockroach.

Chase didn't know whether to sit, or stand, or pace the bloody room, as he waited for Sam to bring Abi in to him, so much so that, when the door clicked open, his feet almost left the floor in his spin to face them with his mouth already open.

About as far as he got. Because, he realised, he still had no blooming clue what to say.

Head tipped to the side, eyes one-hundred percent averted away—from everything, it seemed—Abi passed Sam, as she waved her forward, and stepped into his office.

As Sam squinted in his direction, her message was clear in the slight jerk of her chin she gave in Abi's direction. *Sort this out.*

Right.

He'd made the mess. It was his job to tidy it up.

Squaring his shoulders, he took a step toward Abi, but as soon as Sam closed the door on them, Abi's gaze sliced its way to his.

"I thought I was coming in here to apologise." Her words seemed to sucker punch Chase straight in the chest, as a swallow worked its way along her throat. "But now I'm in here, I'm not sure I can."

The skin around his eyes tightened as he took another step closer. "I'm not sure I follow."

She pointed somewhere over her shoulder in a half-assed motion. "For in there."

His brow creased. "Abi ...?"

"But I'm not sorry. Not really." She lifted her chin as if to enhance her own standing on that matter. "I'm not sorry I did what I did. I'm not sorry it happened ..." Releasing a heavy sigh, she crossed the room and sank down onto the chaise longue. "And I really don't know what that says about me as a person."

Her eyes shot back up to his, holding his gaze and conveying a whole lot of uncertainty and confusion, and Chase could only bring across a chair and plant his own arse down in front of her.

"Do you want to discuss today's session further?" He'd no idea how he slipped so easily back into the role of therapist, not after earlier, but it felt like the right thing to do in the moment. Like the angle Abi needed him to take.

She gave a slight shrug of her shoulders. "Isn't that how this goes?" she asked, breathing out a soft laugh. "I behave in a way I've never behaved before. You ask me if I liked it."

"Did you?" His whole body wound tight as he ducked his head a little closer, like his whole future relied on how she'd felt. Maybe it did.

"I ... I don't—" Her features seemed to flex for an instant before relaxing again, and she gave a nod so minute he almost missed it. "In there," she said, pointing off to her left, "it felt ... surreal. Like it wasn't quite happening to me, even though I was definitely experiencing it. Does that make sense?"

Chase nodded. Because it did. "And now?" he asked.

"I feel ... I feel as though I did something sordid. Or something."

She had, on an Abi level. Right then, though, the totally selfish part of Chase was more interested in how readily she'd submitted to his touch. "Would you like to focus on how you felt during your session for a moment, then? How did it feel to you, *during* the act—aside from surreal?"

"Electric," she said, her hand instantly lifting to cover her face as she averted her eyes, but she didn't quite manage to smother the smile she tried hiding.

Reaching out, Chase tugged her hand down, placed it back in her lap. "Electric is a pretty good start. You want to expand on that?"

Her chest lifted then lowered with the deep breath she took. Not quite meeting his gaze, she said, "It felt like my body was on fire. But in a good way." She seemed to stare right into his soul as she asked, "Does it always feel like that?"

That was a damned question and a half. He cleared his throat, considered where to start. "Before a person has any experience, they hear only what their friends tell them." He briefly waved a hand toward her. "Or what they've researched. But friends only tell us what they want us to hear. And research too often makes it sound like we're missing out if we're not sexually active—which is very much the case. But only if you're lucky enough to find someone you're sexually compatible with." Just as the earlier session had told him he was one-hundred percent compatible with Abi—because she'd nearly blown his fucking brains out with her touch. "And even more so if you're lucky enough to have someone you *connect* with on a deeper level." His brain chirped up that Abi fell into that category, too, but he mentally told himself to shut it. "It doesn't always work out that way, though, especially if there's a lack of mutual respect during the act. Because then one of the parties can end up feeling unfulfilled—and often disappointed enough to shy away from a reoccurrence. Which can then lead to feeling a lack of self-worth for having giving themselves up for something they didn't think was worthy of their commitment. Or doubt in themselves, uncertainty that *they* might be the reason it wasn't as great as they'd hope it would be." He wound his finger around air. "It can become a bit of a vicious circle, you know? So ... to answer your question, no. It doesn't necessarily always feel like that."

"What if I want it to?"

No wideness to her eyes. No tremble to her mouth. The question she'd asked had been done so in total seriousness, and Chase had no idea what to make of that. Hell, he didn't even know what she was asking him—not really. Because there was definitely something underlying her words, and his jaw clenched as he swallowed down her question.

Chase wanted nothing more than to ensure Abi had fantastic orgasms for the rest of her natural, but another week, or so, and that reassurance would be out of his hands. It already was, for God's sake, because no way could he offer a repeat performance of what'd gone down during her session.

"Sorry, Abi," he said, choosing his words carefully, "but I

can't guarantee your sex life once ..." ... *it's not with me* ... "you're no longer under my direction. The practice doesn't work that way."

Her gaze dropped, like he'd disappointed her somehow. He probably had. "Shall we talk about how I feel *now*?" she asked, straightening her skirt.

"How *do* you feel now?"

Again with meeting his eyes. "Dirty."

Chase had no idea if her reply was a dig at him or a come on. "Dirty, how?"

"Like ... like I just participated in something I shouldn't have." Hadn't they both? "And I'll never tell another soul about it. Like ..." She tapped a curled hand against her chest. "Like I never want to share it because it was my experience alone, and I want to keep it that way."

"Because you're ashamed to share it?" He asked it gently—he definitely didn't want to her to believe she should feel that way, but she shook her head.

"Not ashamed. More ..." Her eyes flicked upward, like she sought the answer on the ceiling above. "Privileged," she said, her gaze dropping back down.

Chase's brow lowered. "Privileged?"

He'd hoped she'd expand on that for him, but she merely added, "What happened during my session is *private*." She didn't say the word like she meant it to be nobody else's business, though. More like she considered the act an experience she, and she alone, owned. As if she thought sharing it would make it less, somehow.

Chase would've agreed wholeheartedly ... if Sam had been in the observation room. At least Rae hadn't seen the whole deal —though it probably wouldn't have gone as far as it did, if she had. Sam had been on observer duty, and by the time she'd realised how deep Chase had sunk and ran off to grab Rae, the whole shebang with Abi had pretty much already hit its explosive proportions.

Even so, he nodded to tell her he understood.

Before he could summon more of a response, she asked, "Are you setting me homework this week, Mr Walker?"

Chase just stared at her. His mouth might even have gaped a little. He wasn't sure if her sudden swerving of the convo had him off-guard, or the fact that she talked like she considered returning for more. "Homework?"

"For ... next week?" she asked. Her raised eyebrows seemed to convey as much hope as they did query.

Again with the staring. His right eye might even have twitched a little.

So, she *did* intend coming back next week. Well, *damn.* "Homework ..." he said again, giving a small nod as his brain grabbed at any coherency upstairs. "For your homework ... I want you to think about today's session." He was a sick, *sick* bastard.

"You say that like I'll be able to think about anything else." She smiled, but it wasn't quite a smile—more an expression that said *you should already know this.*

Should he? Or *had* he already known she'd be able to think of little else, and he just wanted to make sure it stayed that way? Yet again, that placed him across a boundary he'd no right to breach.

What the hell was so wrong with him that he couldn't seem to stop?

"I want you to think about it in relation to what you've learned," he said in an attempt to re-steer. "And in relation to how you could use your new skills in the future."

New skills. Like she'd learned how to read. Or ride a bike.

At least focusing on his stupid wording helped distract him from what, exactly, Abi's future held.

"Okay," she said slowly. "And next week?"

More reference to her returning—it had Chase's lungs filling up with air, like he'd been waiting for some kind of sign before he could breathe properly.

"Next week, we'll ... discuss it." At her questioning stare, he added, "We'll discuss what you've been thinking about between now and then." Seemed like the safest bet. Keep her out of the session rooms. Keep her in his office. Just talking. All clothing in place.

His cock deflated like he'd just kicked it in the teeth, but, damn, Chase needed some kind of block between him and the trouble he could land himself in where Abi was concerned.

"Next week we'll be talking?" she asked, and he nodded, despite his body's protest. "*Just* talking?"

At his second nod, all brightness seemed to dim within her eyes, turning them almost grey. Hell, even her shoulders sagged inward like he'd just pulled out a stopper that'd let all the fucking joy out of her soul.

"I'll book in for next week, then," she said, pushing up from the chaise.

Disappointment seemed to saturate his shoulders as she stared down at him for a moment before turning for the door. Halfway across the room, she paused and glanced back over her shoulder. "I thought you had more to *teach* me, Mr Walker." Her voice held a mixture of sadness and confusion, and had Chase on his feet and striding toward her.

"I do." Reaching her, he took her shoulder and spun her back to face him. "But after today ..."

"Today was good." She spoke quickly, like she held no hesitation. Or like she needed to say the words before she could lock them inside. "Today was the best session I've had here, by far."

He had to agree. But he'd got off lightly, because if he'd lost control with another client, like he had with Abi, he'd probably be looking at a lawsuit and, at the very least, a damaged reputation. Abi, though ... she'd *enjoyed* it. She'd totally fucking enjoyed it. If he hadn't figured that out already, the heat emanating from her and the high colour in her cheeks gave good confirmation.

"Today *was* the best session you've had here. I agree. But I overstepped the mark and pushed you in a way I had no right to push you."

"I'm glad you pushed me." More words gushed out. "And if I come back next week, and you push me some more, I still won't be sorry."

His head shook. "You can't know that."

"I can. I do."

His hand still gripped her shoulder, and he brought the other up to her face, her skin soft against his palm. Softening his voice, he repeated his words: "You *can't* know that, Abi. Please don't ask me to take the risk of losing more control with you than I already have."

Her fingers wrapped over his wrist, her chest making tiny flutters as she stared up at him. Stared up at him like she wanted to kiss him. Or wanted him to kiss her.

Fuck, Chase wanted nothing more than to do exactly that, but he couldn't, damn it. If Chase kissed her right then, he wouldn't stop at that. He knew he wouldn't. Not with his cock dancing a merry tune in his pants again. Not with the memory of their earlier session still burning bright in his mind.

Letting his forehead lower to hers, he rested there a moment, his eyes closing against the battle he knew he needed to face. "Abi, you're getting married in a few weeks," he said quietly. "Whatever's going on here between us, it doesn't feel professional anymore, and we need to rein it in now. Before it's too late." Letting his lips skim across her temple, he pushed back from her, released his hold. "I'll understand if you'd prefer not to come back next week." He couldn't look at her as he said the words—he'd never have gotten them out if he did.

She didn't answer him as she turned away and covered the rest of the floor to the exit. The door swung inward, and when she re-closed it, he knew she no longer stood in his office.

"Fuck," he muttered. Bringing his hands up, he gripped at his hair, tugging the strands as he raked his fingers through to the front and over his brow. "Fuck." He punched at air as he swung for the chaise and sank his butt down with a heavy plop.

His muscles ached for him to spring up and race after her. His mind begged him to tell her he was sorry and she should totally come back the next week—they'd do whatever she wanted.

Body coiled tight, his mind screaming out its disapproval, he somehow stayed put, and ten minutes later, he still hadn't moved, when the door to his office opened and heels clacked inside.

Raelyn plonked down into the chair facing him, her elbows on her knees as she leaned forward. "Congratulations. You seem to have gotten away with fucking the face of one of your clients."

Chase didn't lift his gaze to hers. He didn't feel anywhere near proud of himself.

"Whatever you said to her in here, it's done the job."

His head might've nodded. "But we've lost her as a client." *He'd* lost her. As more than a client, it felt.

"No we haven't," Rae said, and when Chase finally glanced up at her, she smiled. "She booked back in for next week."

She booked back in for next week. Such a simple sentence, but one that had his entire body and soul in fucking turmoil.

While a massive part of him felt real bloody victorious, that small, sensible part of him that didn't get a say quite so often argued how much more shit Chase could get into with *just one more session*—until Chase had no idea whether to be happy or stressed by the outcome.

As if she sensed his splitting thoughts, Rae smacked him on arm. "This is good news." Rising up from the chair, she began clopping her way back toward the door, her, "Just don't fuck it up," tossed over her shoulder on route.

"Yeah," Chase muttered. Good news. Don't fuck it up. He just needed some help making those two parts of the equation gel.

~

The unremarkable door to Roy's gym sat squashed between a car body shop and a magazine distributor. Lower half in blue-coated wood, upper half in steel-toughened glass, its description as faded and peeling as the rest of the paint job, only those who already knew of its existence tended to visit.

Pushing inside left Chase confronted by steps that could've used a good scrub and very little light by which to see the way. He made the grimy climb toward another door blocking the way past an upper landing, and shouldering his way through that took him into the gym proper.

A little less dingy than the stairway, the gym itself had windows stretching across its front and claimed the entire space over the two businesses beneath. One corner of the immediate area had been set up for weights. Another for sparring. But what Roy's was mostly about, and what really caught the eye, was the boxing ring plonked down in the centre.

A couple of guys claimed the weights, ones Chase knew by sight only, and he spared them as much attention as they did him before stepping from the shadowed doorway and into the light. As soon as he had, the couple of blokes dancing around each other in the ring quit moving and stared his way.

Chase knew them both well. Mikey, a guy who'd gone to a different school a few miles over from Chase's.

And Jones.

From the way Jones studied him, Chase knew he'd got his number. Chase only ever headed to Roy's when he needed a distraction of the non-sexual kind.

Seemed kind of ironic that Jones might be the one to knock his head into gear yet again.

Ignoring the way Jones thumped a fist against the palm of his other hand, Chase cut around the ring toward a door at the rear of the gym.

Beyond there, a glass-fronted office overlooked the gym's floor, from where Roy watched every tiny movement of his members, and a little farther long, sectioned-off completely, was the locker room and showers.

Chase never bothered to take a bag, or gear, on the odd occasions he visited the gym. He'd had the same locker since his teens—the key to which he carried around like his own personal property. Locker number twenty-three contained a gym bag that held a few pairs of sweat-shorts, a handful of vests, and two pairs of battered trainers. Above the bag, shower gel and shampoo sat on a shelf in front of a handful of towels and a pair of gloves hung beneath. He probably should've taken his gear out occasionally, maybe got it washed, but something about their teen traditions stopped him. Because he'd never bothered with laundry then. He and his mates hadn't supposed to even be there. Not a single one of them had been old enough when they'd first joined up, and every single one of them had lied about their age.

Grabbing out his bag of clothes, Chase carried it across to a bench, his gaze catching on one of the shower blocks—as it did every damn time.

Lying about his age hadn't only gotten him into the gym. And coming to the gym hadn't only introduced him to boxing.

He still remembered the day Mrs Pacton had come bustling up on him—remembered like it'd only just happened the week before.

Jones had told him afterwards how she'd barrelled through the gym and demanded to know which one of them had 'messed up' her son. When none of them had stepped forward as the culprit, she'd marched her way through to the locker room.

O ver the sound of the shower spray, heels clopped against the tiles of the locker room floor.

Heels.

Nobody wore bloody heels at Roy's.

Blinking water from his eyes, Chase stared as one pissed-off looking bird barged around the corner of the lockers, her eyes filled with fury as they razored the air and landed on Chase.

"Was it you?" She stabbed a finger his way. "You send my boy home in that mess?"

A trickle of water ran between his lips as he studied her, and he spat it out, his focus on her the whole time. "I don't even know who you're talking about."

She stopped just on the outside of the waist-high tiled wall that separated the so-called cubicle from the locker area, her obviously-dyed, golden-blonde hair pulled into a chignon at the back of her head. Hands on the hips of her tapered skirt, she jerked her chin up toward him. "My Stewie. Was it you?"

Stewie? Name didn't ring any bells. "Someone hurt him?"

"Sent him home to me covered in his own blood." Her head tipped, eyes narrowed, just those two actions somehow bouncing the flouncy bows of her blouse that hung beneath her chin. "He told me it happened down at the gym."

"Maybe. Maybe not." He shook his head free of water as it began a rapid crawl over his brow. "Either way, I doubt he meant this gym."

"What other clubs are 'round here?"

Chase shrugged and reached for his shower gel. "I dunno, lady. But Roy runs a tight ship. Nobody gets fucked up bad. And nobody leaves here without him checking they're okay." He squirted a glob of gel into his palm, rubbed it over his chest, up to his shoulder. Even as he turned into the spray a little, he sensed her still standing there. Sensed her watching him. "I dunno what else you want from me," he said, his lip movement sending a spattering of water outward.

Still, he didn't detect so much as a scrape of heel, let alone footsteps retreating the hell away. He made a slow turn toward her, more than ready to tell her to back the hell off, and her eyes skidded up to his so fast he knew they had to have been glued to his arse. Despite her being old enough to be his ma, despite the simmering fury she'd charged in there with, Chase couldn't help the slight curve of his lips at the appreciation he saw staring back at him.

He deliberately let his hands slide downward, until the tips of his fingers swept over the V of his pelvis, liking how her gaze followed the movement. "Can I help you with anything else?"

"How old are you, kid?" She didn't look up when he spoke, and the slow spread of solidity claimed his cock beneath her scrutiny.

"Old enough to not be called kid." He smoothed more shower gel southward, knowing his own touch could get him harder as easily as anyone else's.

As if refusing to take the bait, she lifted her gaze, but Chase caught the way she checked out the rest of him. The whole of him. Like she sized up a package she'd ordered to see if it matched the description. "Answer the question," she said, meeting his eyes again.

He could've told her the truth. That he'd be hitting seventeen in just under two weeks. Instead, he lied with his answer of, "Just turned nineteen. What's it to you?"

Her eyes darted down to his crotch then back up. "You know how to use that thing you're playing with?"

"Do you?" Just one side of his mouth twitched as he controlled his smile. He could tell from the way her stance had gone from confrontational to cocky that she considered his question way more than he'd expected.

Or maybe he had expected it. He'd been fucking since the night of his fifteenth birthday, when one of his auntie's friends had shown him the way to head explosions and the best kind of sweaty skin, and the only time he'd gotten no bites to his suggestive chatter since then had been the night he'd mixed vodka and scrumpy cider and created a holy mess.

Banging the shower gel down on the low wall between them, he stuck his palms down beside it and leaned over until her face stared back only inches away. "I bet you do. I reckon you know exactly what to do."

She didn't back away. Didn't even blink, as she said, "Answer my question."

He let her pin him with her eyes for almost a whole minute before smiling. "Yes. I know exactly what to do with it."

She still didn't look away as she rummaged in a bag that hung from one of her shoulders. When she pulled her hand out, she lifted it between them, and Chase's focus zoomed right in on what she held.

A johnny.

"Prove it." She didn't say it like a demand. Nor like a flirt. More a request that she knew he'd fulfil, so why bother with theatrics.

He probably could've waited a beat, made *her* wait, but his dick tapped against the tiled wall and she'd offered her cunt to him without any gooey-eyed catches attached, and Chase *wanted* to fuck her. Yeah, she might've been nearly as old his own ma, but she had decent tits and a skinny waist, and those heels made her legs look like something from *Playboy*, if *Playboy* did a section on well-dressed business women.

Pushing away from the wall, he knocked off the water spray, before turning back to the woman and holding out a hand. She smiled like she'd scored a point as she took it, and he guided her around to the opening of the shower block until she stood on the sodden tiles less than a foot away.

As soon as he reached for the bow of her blouse, she shook her head, but she still smiled, even as the, "Uhn-uhn," left her mouth.

So he couldn't undress her. She just wanted to fuck.

Lucky for her, Chase happened to like *just fucking*.

"How do you like it?" he asked, taking the condom from between her fingers.

She didn't speak, just turned her back on him, glanced at him over her shoulder, and Chase smiled. From behind suited him just fine.

It took around fifteen seconds to unwrap the rubber and roll it over the thickness of his cock's head, and by the time he'd swiped his palm over his shaft a couple of times, a solid throb had kicked up just beneath the skin.

He took a step forward until his chest met her back. Reached down for the hem of her skirt, pleased that she didn't object when he tugged it up over her hips, leaving her ass peeking out. Leaning away a little, he took a moment to check out her underwear. Black silk. And it covered an arse firmer than he'd expected from a woman her age, like she worked out, kept in shape. Chase appreciated that about her.

Hands wrapped firmly over her hips, he pushed against her. That time, she did resist, and Chase moved in close until his lips brushed her ear. "Trust me, you'll want the support."

She didn't argue a second time when he nudged her forward, but she lifted her hands as she reached the tiled wall, braced herself there.

Slipping a hand between her legs showed Chase how wet she was. For him? Or just for the fuck? He didn't really care, either way. A kick of each foot against the inside of each of her ankles spread her legs a little wider. A grip of her hip tugged her ass closer to where his cock danced around in excitement. He pushed against her shoulder, forced her to bend at the waist, the move parting the sweet rounds of her ass, bringing her pussy that little bit higher.

Reaching down between them, he yanked her undies aside and took hold of his cock, guided it toward her wet cunt. Slipped his swollen head just inside the opening. She gave a soft gasp at the invasion, and Chase thrust all the way inside, smiling to himself at her sharp cry of surprise. Gripping her in the exact position he wanted her, he pulled back out, drove his cock back in, the initial buzz of excitement humming through him when she cried out a second time. That was all it took. All it took for him to give in to his body and let his hips find their rhythm and his cock fill her cunt as deep as he could get it.

With each moan of her pleasure, he thrust into her a little harder. With each lift of her ass, his balls cinched a little tighter. Until he plunged into her so deep her face mashed against the wall and her ass bounced back at him every time he withdrew.

Reaching back, she scrabbled at his hip, but in an effort to make him go faster rather than stop him, it seemed. Her eyes, half-lidded, seemed to looked at everything and nothing. At a sharp slap to her ass cheek, her body jolted and she gave a yelp, but a second later, her mumbled, "Yes," told Chase she liked it.

She liked it a whole lot. So he did it again. And again. Whilst fucking the hell out of her and smashing her against the wall like he wanted to hurt her, all while not harming her at all.

By the time his balls had cinched into a tight knot of tension, he had his own hand braced against the wall over her shoulder, his other arm wrapped around her tight enough to hold her in place, his own grunts mixed with the higher-pitched cries of the woman. But he waited. Waited until he felt the fisting pulse of her cunt around his cock. And he fucked her hard. Harder. His cum shooting into the johnny making his body twitch all over the fucking shop.

Seconds later, they both ceased to move. His panted breaths seemed to steam the back of her blouse, while hers steamed the tiles.

Still breathing hard, she shoved against the wall, and he moved back, allowing her to straighten. Reaching behind herself, she pushed him away until his cock slipped free of her pussy, and she adjusted her underwear, tugged her skirt back down over her hips and thighs. Patting at hairs that'd broke free of her chignon, she turned to face him, her eyes still carrying the heaviness of a good orgasm.

She seemed to study him for a moment before she spoke. "You're a good looking boy."

His brow creased a little. "Thanks."

"I might have some work for you, if you play your cards right."

That time, his brow arched up. "What kind of work?"

Without answering, she weaved around him and made for the exit. She didn't look back at him as she stepped from the shower block. Nor as she paused by the benches and dropped something small down by his piled-up clothes. And she still hadn't when she reached the end of the locker row.

Frowning, he called after her. "Wait."

She paused, glancing back at him like he'd no right making demands of her.

"How am I supposed to play my cards right when I don't even know your name?"

The smile toying with her lips made her look like she'd just won a prize. Except, Chase didn't know the name of the game. And he had no idea he was the pawn. "Mrs Pacton to you, boy."

As soon as she'd left, he stepped out and crossed to the bench, picked up what she'd left behind.

A business card that carried the name she'd just given. Its reverse side held a printed phone number.

The following day, Chase had called her. A week later, Mrs P had sent him on his first escorting job. The first of hundreds.

D ragging his clothes from his gym bag, Chase tore his focus from the shower block where it'd all gone down. Seeing it always reminded him of his encounter with Mrs P. The day his life had shifted, and he'd gone from a bum begging for work, with no experience to back himself, to a sought-after escort—a role that had women paying through the nose for his company, paying even higher for his body, and showering him with gifts like they needed to make sure he returned when asked.

Chase would've returned without the gifts. Partly because he'd loved his job. Mostly because Mrs Pacton had never really given him much of a choice. As long as he worked for her, she ruled him. And Chase had never really minded that—because being beneath her thumb had earned him his dough.

At least, he hadn't minded, until Nicolette.

A couple of years into working for Mrs P, he'd gotten assigned to Nic. She'd been filthy-rich from her husband's money—a husband who was never there. And she'd been beautiful on the level of making everyone stop and stare. Long, slender body, shoulders cut like blades, high cheekbones surrounded by glossy black hair that always seemed to do exactly as she commanded.

Because Nicolette commanded everything she came into contact with. Including Chase.

Within two weeks of being her latest in a long string of escorts, he'd have been willing to get on his knees and beg for each new booking. Not that he had to. Nicolette had a tendency to like at least some consistency—kept the gossipers fuelled, she'd always said.

For some reason, she'd kept Chase around that little bit longer than most of her toys. To a kid on the cusp of leaving his teens, that'd labelled him as special. Wanted. Loved by a woman who wasn't his mother.

Nicolette had seduced him in every possible way—taken his mind, body and soul, and made them all hers. For the first time in his life, Chase had *wanted* a woman to want more from him, and for a time, he'd thought Nic did.

One evening a week had progressed to two, then three, until she'd spent as much time with Chase as she had free from her charitable organisations. Not once had she kicked him from her bed after gaining what she wanted—not like with the other escorts she'd booked. No, Chase would still be there come morning, still enveloped within her arms, her long, slender fingers combing through his hair in the best kind of therapy. And their fucking grew slower, deeper, *connected*. She'd feed him breakfast before sending him on his way for the day.

It had been the time of his life, until Chase realised she no longer felt like a job. Worse, Chase had convinced himself she felt the same way he'd grown to feel about her. It didn't matter that he still got paid for any time he spent with her. Didn't matter that he still found a wad of cash in his jacket pocket after any night she invited him to stay. She didn't love her husband, that much had been clear, but she treated Chase like she loved him. Made him feel loved.

When Chase had told her so, everything shifted. Maybe weaving in the idea of her leaving her husband for Chase had been the clincher, because she'd laughed at him—actually laughed. Even called him a 'stupid boy'. Asked Chase to explain to her why she would 'want to leave this' as she'd swept an arm toward the walls of her extravagant home ... for *him*.

That'd been the last time Chase had seen her. The last time she'd booked him. The last time Mrs P had permitted him to go —because Nic had tattled behind his back about his 'immaturity in the role he should be playing as escort'.

For far too many months, he'd pined for Nic. Pined for the way she'd looked at him, the way she'd touched him, the way she'd *looked after* him. His stupid young brain had fallen in love with every scenario they'd shared. The pampering. The compliments. The *richness* of it all.

It'd taken a whole lotta time, and a few kickings from Jones, for Chase to finally understand. He'd only truly been in love with the lifestyle.

Something banged against one of the lockers, breaking into his thoughts. Some kid Chase only knew as Tooney stuck a key into one of the doors, sending Chase something that might've been a nod as he swung open the locker.

Lowering his gaze, Chase focused back on his foot. Without even paying attention, he'd switched out work trousers for sweat-shorts, shirt for vest. He already had a set of his trainers on his feet, and he finished tying the laces that'd previously broken three times.

He probably should've replaced them—not just the laces, but the shoes themselves—but his ma had always taught him the importance of knowing his roots. Remembering that which he'd come from. Kept a man humble, she always said.

Chase had to agree.

When he'd been with Nic, he'd forgotten it all.

With his removed clobber in one hand, his gym bag in the other, he carried his gear back to his locker, and after grabbing out his gloves hanging from the shelf, he locked everything else inside and turned for the gym itself.

Out there, a couple of extras had shown up. Guy called Masters from their old neighbourhood, and his kid brother—the two often trained together. The couple of guys lifting weights had condensed the space they took up to make room for the newcomers. One of the good points about Roy's—nobody caused shit about anything.

Ignoring the slaps he could hear on a bag over in the nearest corner, Chase cut a path for the ring in the centre. Only one of the earlier two stood within its ropes. Jones. Like he knew what Chase had turned up for and he had every intention of being the one to give it. Something Chase had been counting on.

His intense eyes poured heat over Chase as he hopped up onto the platform and ducked between the ropes. Straightening took him face-to-face with Jones, and the smile he wore. Not a smile of victory. Nor one of vindication. More a *Now, what the hell has you climbing into a ring with me*, kinda smile.

Kicking out each of his legs, Chase rolled his neck side-to-side, while Jones watched his every move. He tugged one glove on, pulled it hard up over his wrist, then did the same with the other. Jones just kept up that watching of his, until Chase started feeling like a specimen about to get squashed.

Though, hadn't that been his whole purpose in going there?

Jigging his shoulders up and down to loosen them, he took a few steps closer to his friend. Slapped a fist against his palm, reversing hands to do it a second time. Finally stilling, he sniffed hard. "I'm sorry."

Jones's eyes twitched—about as close to taken aback as he ever looked.

"You were right."

"About?" Jones asked in that deep tone of his.

"The client. Abi. She's fucking me up." He banged a gloved hand against the side of his temple. "In here."

"And you think me fucking you up instead is going to help with that?"

"If anyone can thump stupid out of me, you can." Chase shrugged. "Gotta be worth a try."

Glancing away, Jones nodded toward where a mixed race kid pounded the hell out of a punch-bag. "Hey, Cam. We're gonna need a protector in here." He turned back to Chase. "Don't want to be spoiling that pretty face of yours, Walker."

Chase didn't argue. Mostly because he couldn't afford for his face to get messed up. Not in his line of work.

A couple of seconds later, a helmet flew into the ring. Jones caught it, tossed it to Chase, and he stuck it on his head, made sure the face grill was well attached.

"I'm taking you home after this," Jones told him, his voice a solid wall of *don't argue.*

Anyone else might've minced Jones's words, but Chase had been boxing with him since their mid-teens. And Jones had been battering the hell out of Chase for the entirety of that time. So Jones knew as well as Chase did: the two of them in the ring together never ended pretty—even more so for Chase. It definitely wouldn't that night, anyway. Chase wasn't sure he even had it in him to fight back.

Nodding, he jogged a couple of steps back. A couple forward. Bringing his elbows in to his sides, he lifted his forearms, beckoned to Jones.

Like the human equivalent of a battering ram, Jones swung toward him, his fist filled Chase's vision, and pain exploded through his head like the antidote he'd gone there seeking.

Staggering to the left, Chase shook his head to demist his focus. Bouncing stiffness from his limbs, he regained his stance, made the pretence of defence in the placement of his arms. Nodded to Jones.

And Jones hit him again.

And again.

Until Chase lost count of the hits. And lost the clarity of the room. And lost the use of his legs.

Not once, though, did he lose sight of that he'd gone there to boot clear.

No, Abi O'Shay clung to his brain like she'd no intention of letting go. And if not even the earthquakes of being thumped by Jones could shift her, Chase had no fucking clue what else he could do.

EPISODE EIGHT

Chase Walker showed the clients to his office door. Carl Winters and his live-in partner Janie Say.

They'd come seeking advice on how to spice up 'their bedroom time'. Chase had told them that referring to it as that was their first mistake—because believing it needed to be restricted to just one room of the house placed limitations on them, and what they could do, before they'd even begun.

It felt refreshing to him, to have a couple show up who seemed on equal footing in the decision to come see him. It felt refreshing to have a couple be openly honest about what they already had, what they felt their relationship lacked, and what they needed from him as a therapist.

"Well, thanks again," Ms Say said, as Chase opened the door to Reception.

"You're welcome." He took Mr Winters' hand as he held it out, giving a brief shake before waving them toward the curved desk, behind which sat his two partners in crime. "Raelyn and Samantha will get you booked in for your next session."

"And in the meantime, we'll do our homework," Ms Say said, barely containing her cheeky-looking grin.

Homework that boiled down to them not waiting until they got to the bedroom, like they usually did. Not waiting until bed*time*. But jumping into action at random times of the day, in *any* room of the house—because a platform for intercourse didn't need to be restricted to a damned bed.

"That's the idea." Smiling, Chase nodded toward Rae, her smoky-rimmed eyes meeting his for a second.

She'd been catching his eye for most of the day. Scrap that—she'd been catching his eye for the entire week. Chase knew why, he'd just been ignoring it. Badly. Unsuccessfully. Because what he'd been trying to ignore was too big. Bigger than him. Bigger than anything.

Abi O'Shay. What they'd done together the week before. The fact she'd be returning to his office in too short, too long a space of time. And what they *weren't* going to be doing once she got there.

As Rae released her visual hold on him and shot her impressive smile at the clients, Chase turned away, closed his door, and took a moment for himself.

Breathing in deep should've helped calm the emotions roiling through him. Sadness mixed with anticipation. Desperation toying over the edges of disappointment—a disappointment he felt at himself for having allowed his feelings for the woman get as far as they had. And bitterness. A deep bitterness at knowing she'd leave him—his practice—and walk straight into the arms of another, manned with skills Chase had taught her.

He hated that.

He didn't want to—any other client and he'd have patted himself on the back for a job well done, maybe have a sneaky brew with Rae and Sam to celebrate at end of day—but he did hate it. And there didn't seem to be a damned thing he could do to change that.

With a bottled water grabbed from his desk drawer, he crossed to the window, hoping the view would help drain some of the tightness from his shoulders. The Thames seemed pretty quiet below, though the rain could well have created the lull in water traffic. The fair weather boaters always seemed to outweigh those willing to brave the elements.

He drew in a long breath, downed a gulp of water, exhaled. He should've been writing up notes for the clients who'd just left. Despite the success of the appointment, his brain butted walls over the idea of completing paperwork, and his body seemed at odds with the idea of sitting still, even for a few minutes. Like a low wattage hummed beneath the surface of his skin, his body felt alive—which was fucking ridiculous when he'd not be stepping outside of his main office for Abi's appointment, neither of them would be removing any clothes, all they'd be doing was talking.

The only upsides to the appointment: He couldn't land himself in any shit piles by just talking, and his office didn't have cameras installed for Rae and Sam to be spying on him ....

The two positives seemed so fucking far apart in relativity, Chase couldn't help but breathe out a quiet laugh at the irony of it all. The one time he'd have a free, uninterrupted chance to do whatever he wanted with Abi, and he couldn't.

Though, why couldn't he?

Spinning away from the window, he turned back toward the room. The chaise, placed at an angle toward his desk, easily sat two people of decent size and weight, and his mind instantly conjured the image of Abi sprawled back against the fabric, her hair splayed across the single armrest, her fingers gripping his hair as she guided his face toward her cunt.

He had to shake his head to clear the image. What the fuck was he doing? When Abi arrived, the plan was to sever his connection to her—whatever that connection was—not remind himself of how she'd tasted the week before. How she'd responded when he'd tasted her. How wet she'd been—how wet *he'd* ended up as she'd sprayed her excitement all the hell over him.

Fuck his stupid cock for getting hard at the memory.

And fuck his brain for conjuring it.

Maybe he should've been writing up notes, after all, instead of mooning over a bloody client.

Ordering his body back to his desk, he sank his arse down into his chair and opened the newly-printed casefile still sitting in place. As he scanned over the intro notes Sam had already typed into their file, he swapped his water bottle for a pen and forced the thoughts in his head out of the way.

Ten minutes later, he'd jotted a grand total of twenty-four words. Ten minutes later should've been about the time Abi usually showed up for an appointment.

Tapping his pen against his teeth, he glanced toward the intercom. Toward the door. Like they'd magically perk into action by sheer will alone.

Everything in him wanted to leap up and race to the door, swing it open, just to see if she sat there. He wouldn't put it past Rae to hold Abi until the exact moment her appointment began, if only to limit the amount of time they could spend alone.

Somehow, he managed to stay in place. Even if that was the case, if Abi did sit out there patiently tapping her toes against the floor, Rae would have all the right reasons for holding her back.

Just as he'd have all the wrong ones for wanting her in there with him already.

Running his fingers through his hair, he dropped his gaze back to the paperwork beneath his chin. Where was he? Oh, yeah, Mr Winters and Ms Say lacked spontaneity in their life— possibly in all aspects of it. And they needed to do *what* to improve upon the quality of their sexual relationship? How was it *affecting* their sexual relationship? He knew the answer—he'd not long before told them the bloody answer.

Groaning, he brushed a hand over his head. Hell knew what he'd look like by the time Abi did step into his office. He felt like an addict waiting on his dealer to show up.

Except, the time ticked around to the opening of her appointment and neither the door, nor the intercom, had so much as twitched.

No longer caring about the calm he should've been adopting, he pressed the button on his desk, not even waiting for acknowledgement before asking, "Is Abi here?"

The pause on the other end filled with static that buzzed over the thoughts in his head. Maybe the girls weren't even at the desk. He'd just pushed back his seat, when the quiet click came through.

"No," Sam said quietly. "She hasn't showed."

"Could be she's just running late," Rae said, her voice slightly muffled like she spoke away from the mic.

"Okay," he said, and clicked off.

Abi running late. Abi had never once run late in all the weeks he'd been seeing her. Early, yes. Late? Never. Like promptness was a part of who she was. A habit that'd been instilled into her from a young age that she couldn't quite let go of.

Though, hadn't he, himself, encouraged her to break free of who'd she'd been forced to be all her life? Hadn't he helped her seek out her less obedient side?

Maybe her tardiness was just a result of that. Something that should be congratulated, not admonished, or scorned.

He might have considered that harder, if the clock didn't keep on ticking. And the door didn't stay shut. His intercom as silent as death.

He'd gone from being antsy as hell to fucking deflated. From needing to work off his edge to feeling unable to move. Because if he moved, he'd cross to the door, and that would only confirm what he'd already figured out.

She wasn't out there. She wasn't coming.

Despite her words of last week, despite her rebooking, he'd lived the last seven days in a world of denial. Because he hadn't gotten away with what he'd done to her the week before.

He'd gone and totally fucking blown it.

For thirty minutes, he sat there. Mentally beating himself up. Taking himself down paths of anger to cul-de-sacs of self-hatred. Probably why it took that long for either of the girls to come in to him—like they already knew he had enough with his own self-opinions to deal with, without them adding theirs into the bag.

It was Rae who came. She didn't quite enter, but stood leaning in the doorway as if judging his temperament before coming closer.

"She didn't come, did she?" He already knew the answer, but her headshake of confirmation seemed like a final blow to his defeat.

"Sorry, babe. But if it's any consolation, I don't think it's your fault. I do think she meant to come back."

"You think something has happened?" Wouldn't be implausible, considering she'd already cancelled once before because of her mother's nosiness.

"Maybe." Rae shrugged. "Maybe she just changed her mind."

He nodded, but it was barely there. A half-hearted effort, at best. "You and Sam should go on home."

"So should you."

Another attempt at a nod, though he couldn't quite meet her eyes for that one. "I will." When she made no effort to move, he glanced her way again. "What?"

"We'll go when you do." She finally pushed off the doorway. "Give us a shout when you're ready to leave."

~

I t'd taken another hour before Chase had been able to shift from his chair. Like the ever-hopeful blind-dater who couldn't quite accept they'd been stood up. Like they didn't want to do the walk of admittance past everyone, shoulders shrinking in at the thought that everyone else *knew* what the loner hadn't admitted to themselves—that their date had never planned to come in the first place.

Because that was what Chase believed. An hour of that kind of thinking was never good for the soul, after all.

The extra hour had also given the rain a chance to thicken. Fat blobs of wetness shot like bullets toward the earth. Chase didn't even bother trying to dodge them as he made his way home.

Home. It'd taken a seven-minute argument with Rae and Sam before they'd believed he did actually plan to head there. Like they expected him to head straight to the nearest bar.

Or worse—to Jones. Not that they didn't trust Jones. They more likely just didn't trust Chase in his current mood.

One of the good things about working *and* living alongside the Thames was that his route home tended to be pretty simple. As he often did when he had too much going on inside his head, he ignored the idea of a taxi and opted for the old-fashioned way of travel.

Turned out to be a good idea. Winds accompanied the rain, and with the coolness from the current dropping the temperatures by a few degrees, each tendril of air seemed to wrap around Chase's skull and freeze the thoughts in there like they knew he needed the break. Not that it helped. Not really. If he didn't deal with them, he'd only get smacked around by them once he got home. Where he'd have no distractions to lure him toward a safer passage for the night.

And he didn't even want to think about it being a Friday. Friday meant Saturday. Then Sunday. Two entire days of no work to guide his hours. Two entire days, during which he'd most likely mentally torture himself, until he found solace in a bottle, if only so he could sleep.

The evening was still early enough that a few bodies moved about alongside, or around, him. He didn't know any of them. If he had, he likely wouldn't have registered their faces, anyway. Not with the black mood spreading across his brain like a virus and the corners of his mouth sinking lower as if anchored to the depths of Hell itself. Even lifting his feet for each step became more effortful, the closer he grew to home, so much so, the journey took a good twenty minutes longer than it should have. Yet, when the stretch of wall behind which his home sat came into view, he felt far from relieved to have reached there. The sensation spreading through him only resembled a heavy dread.

A few minutes more, and the gap in the wall appeared, narrow at first, from his angle, and widening the closer he got. He ducked between the two sections of stone and down the short flight of steps.

"Mr Walker."

The voice was quiet, but it stopped him in his tracks, one foot hovering over the decking of his home. Planting his foot back onto the ground, he made a slow turn back in time to see her straightening from a crouch beside the wall he'd just rounded.

Dampness weighted her hair so it clung to her shoulders, darker than its usual pale strawberry blonde.

His brows lowered over his eyes, like they could shield them from the rain for him to more clearly see what truly stood before him. "Abi?" Even her clothes seemed saturated, clinging to her skin, like she'd been waiting there a while.

For what? For him?

"What ... what are you doing here?"

"I'm sorry, Mr Walker." The heaviness of her voice tugged his gaze back to her face. To her eyes, and the fear and desolation staring back him. "I didn't know where else to go."

He took a step toward her, but stopped at the shiver that rippled her shoulders. "Are you in trouble?" Was that why she hadn't showed at the clinic?

She frowned, seemed to be contemplating her answer, before she shook her head, sending small specks of spray diving from her hair.

If not in trouble, then, what? Her raised position placed her almost at eye level when he chanced another step closer. "Did something happen?"

She nodded, answered, "Yes." So, there had been a reason for her earlier absence—but what? Glancing away, she once again seemed to be deciding how to answer further. Whether, or not, she *should*.

Turning back to Chase, those pale eyes of hers locking onto his like she needed the connection to stay steady, she seemed unsure whether to frown, or smile—Chase had no bloody idea what her expression tried to portray. He probably should've been asking how the bloody hell she'd known where he lived, but something about her body language had him leery of saying the wrong thing, like she'd bolt any second.

"I called off the wedding."

She said it so simply, so matter-of-fact, the words didn't quite register in Chase's mind. Not right away. And when they did, they seemed to echo within there like she'd yelled them into a cavern just to see their effect.

His lips tested the unformed words for a whole three seconds before he managed, "You called off the wedding?"

She gave a rocky nod, her lips barely moving with her, "Yes."

Once again, his mouth formed the word; it took a few tries to get out, "Why?"

She merely stared at him, her eyes firmly on him, her feet planted in place. Only the small shivers that kept rolling through her seemed to threaten the resolve written in every one of her features. Shivers that deepened the longer they stood there with the rain beating down.

Against his better judgement, he held out a hand, because he was damned if he'd see her freeze any longer. "Will you come inside?"

She didn't speak, just reached out and placed her palm against his. Let him support her as she balanced back to the steps and descended to join him.

Turning from her, but totally, *totally* aware of her, he led her onto the decking. He kept hold of her hand as he worked out his keys and opened the plain-looking door to his home. And he still hadn't let go when he encouraged her up the step and into the small hallway.

Bringing her all the way in, he reached around her and closed the door on the shitty weather. The action took his soggy chest real close to her face, but she made no attempt to back away. In fact, she made no move, at all. She just stood there. Staring up at him.

Chase lifted a hand to the top button of her coat, flipped it free of its hole. "You should take this off if you want to warm up."

He expected her to take over from him, but she didn't, just held his gaze—almost as if she challenged him to continue what he started.

So he did. Freeing one button after another, until her chest broke free within the thin T-shirt she wore—at least that seemed to be dry. Sliding his hands beneath the edge of her jacket, he pushed it from her shoulders, gripping the collars as she let it glide down her arms and over her fingertips. Another action that drew him closer to her—until his cheek almost met hers, and his arms came around her. Chase let it last a good ten seconds longer than it needed to, before he lifted the coat from behind her and hung it on a peg. Shucked his own off and lined it up next to hers.

"Come on up." He took her hand again, as if the move came naturally to him. Like he couldn't imagine doing anything *but* taking her hand. Guiding her up the few steps, he led her into the living space, across to a small thermostat on the wall. "Best stick the heating on a while." Still holding onto her, he crossed from there to the sofa that faced the wall of windows. "You must be hungry. Sit here, and I'll fix something."

He tugged her rear toward the sofa like he expected her to obey without question. When she didn't sit, he allowed himself to look at her like he'd been avoiding doing so since stripping her down to a T-shirt barely thick enough to disguise the lace of her bra beneath. The wet ends of her hair brushing her shoulders didn't help, either, the way the water seeping into the fabric created two spreading patches of translucency. Not to mention she wore those damned leggings again, showing Chase every single curve of her body from hip to thigh to slender ankle, and the shallow dip toward where he knew her pussy resided.

She didn't return his scrutiny when he ordered his gaze away from the taunting V of her pelvis, but stared around his home like she'd stepped into an alien spacecraft. It reminded him of how she'd gazed around the session bathroom at the clinic. As if anything above basic living standards left her intimidated.

Chase loved how humbled that trait in her left him feeling. He thumbed toward the kitchen, despite her paying him little attention. "I'm going to grab some food. You look like you need it." He took a few steps away, but half-twisted back toward her. "Join me when you're ready. Okay?"

Her nod was a half-hearted effort, but at least she was responding, and Chase carried on around the counter, headed straight for the fridge. Inside, he found a faded ice cream tub, topped by a familiar yellow sticky-note.

'As it's Friday ...' had been jotted in his ma's handwritten. Beneath that: 'P.S. you need the red tub out the fridge, too'.

Reaching back in, he grabbed the red one and set them both on the counter. Pried the lids off them both. Enough rice to feed three Jones's in one. Yellow curry in the other.

"Your view is ..."

He twisted enough to follow Abi's gaze toward the windows. "Isn't it?"

She nodded, her gaze swinging around to where he stood.

"You eat curry?" he asked.

She smiled—only a small, barely-there smile, but he'd take it. "I'd eat pretty much anything right about now."

Her gaze darted away again, leaving Chase wondering what the bloody hell she'd meant by that. If anything. At his office, if toying with him, she usually held his eye, so maybe he read more into it than he should. Except, they weren't at his office. She'd come to his home. A place she shouldn't have even known the location of. Surely, that had to change the rules some—for her, as well as him.

First, though, he needed to know why she'd come. Because her calling off the wedding didn't answer that question. Not by a long shot.

Turning back to the food, he half-covered the rice tub with its lid and bunged it in the microwave. Hands resting atop the counter, he waited for the ping. Even with his back to Abi, he couldn't have been more aware of her presence. If she moved about, he didn't catch sound of it. So, what was she doing? Still staring about the place? Looking at him?

What the hell was she doing *there*?

The unanswered question tensed the muscles across his shoulders and had him standing as stiff as a life-art model. He felt about as scrutinised as one of those, too.

A breath rushed from him at the ding of the machine, and he switched out the rice for the curry. At least he had something to busy his hands, as he found a couple of plates in the cupboard and shared out the rice between them.

From another cupboard, he grabbed a couple of glasses and carried them across to the dining counter. Set out some cutlery for the two of them—like they dined together every day and there was absolutely nothing fucking abnormal about Abi turning up to join him for dinner.

In the fridge, he found a bottle of water and stuck that between the glasses. A bottle of wine sat in the fridge, too, but he left that right where it was. Alcohol and Abi ... totally not a good idea. He didn't trust himself around her when sober, so tossing that inhibitor into the mix definitely wouldn't end well.

Another two minutes, and he'd topped the rice with curry and carried the two plates across to the counter. "Ready to eat?" he asked, sending her a quick glance.

She didn't bother responding, but swung her legs in his direction, her hands grasped together just beneath her waistline lending her an almost coy appearance.

He pulled out a stool and motioned for her to sit, waiting until she'd done so before taking the stool next to her for himself. The placement of their bodies couldn't have been more than a foot apart. Sure, he'd been closer to Abi—only a week before when he'd lost his fucking mind—but something about the uncertainty of the current situation seemed to heighten the moment. That, or the normalcy of the situation did. Like they were a couple of actors playing house. Sitting down to dinner together like they did it every day.

"Did you cook this yourself?" Abi asked as she forked up some food.

He peeked at her out the corner of his eye, discreetly watching as she slipped the fork between her lips and sucked it clean. A simple enough act, but one that had him adjusting in his seat and having to remind himself of her question. "My ma cooks for me."

"All the time?" Her gaze skimmed toward him and caught his creepy staring, but he just nodded like he hadn't been doing anything of the sort. "You've never learned to cook?"

"I've never had to," he said with a shrug. "My ma's just always done it for me. She's always *wanted* to do it for me."

Her lips curved, and she quickly glanced away as if she tried to hide it. "That's cute."

His eyes narrowed. "What is?"

"That you call her your *ma*." She turned back to him, that smile still lingering in her features and lightening her eyes. "You don't hear that term very often this far south."

"My grandfather was a northerner."

"That explains it, then," she said.

As she stuffed another forkful of food into her mouth, Chase turned back to his own dinner with a smile. Usually, he hated questions about his family. The lines of work he'd been in since his teenage years had required him to remain guarded, had dictated a bold line be drawn between his personal and work lives.

For reasons he didn't quite understand, he liked that Abi had pried. Like the conversation had made the moment more normal, somehow. As if he could've been any guy, with any girl, having dinner together for the first time.

Except, as he reached for his next scoop of food, his arm

brushed against hers, and she glanced at him with a whole lot of uninterpretable shit in her eyes. She shot her gaze toward her plate, like she believed he wouldn't notice if only she could get it away from him fast enough. From that point on, the easy calm that'd cloaked the two of them revealed itself as the charade it was, and the awareness that prickled his skin whenever Abi invaded his space seemed to slowly creep its way back in. And, from the way her head kept twitching ever so slightly toward him, before jerking away again, he'd have sworn it affected Abi just as much as it did him. So much so, by the time they'd dropped their forks to their plates and toyed with their water glasses like they needed the distraction, Chase could've powered the lights in the place from their gravitational energy alone— because his body felt fucking wired.

Needing to create some space between them, he pushed back from the counter, grabbed up the plates and carried them across to the sink.

Stool feet scratched at the floor to his right, as he set the dinner stuff into the ivory sink. "Will you let me clean those, in exchange for such a lovely meal?"

Bracing himself, he blew out a quiet breath, and twisted his face toward Abi. She'd already half-slid from her seat like she expected no argument to the request. "Actually, I think we should talk about why you're here." The sooner they booted out the big fucking elephant standing in the way of the temporary ease they'd found, the better.

Her mouth rounded—like she mentally said 'oh', but no sound came out. As if gathering her wits, she lifted her other butt cheek up onto the stool and nodded. "Okay. If that's what you want."

It was.

It wasn't.

Hell, he didn't know what he wanted, but he definitely

needed answers before he could make any kind of decision on either.

"You said outside you had nowhere else to go." He turned to fully face her. He always felt more comfortable being the questioner than the one on the stand. "Why couldn't you stay home?" He almost winced at the way his words sounded—like he fucking berated her for coming. Like she had no right to come.

In the grander scheme of things, she didn't have a right to have shown up on his doorstep. That wasn't how a therapist-client relationship worked. He stayed out of their personal time outside of his office. And they stayed the hell out of his.

What about Abi as his client had been bloody normal, though?

"More to the point," he added. "Why did you miss your appointment today? I mean ..." He swung an arm toward the front door of his home. "How long were you even sitting out there, waiting for me?" *How did you know where to come?*

He didn't voice that last question. He'd already thrown enough at her, and the hunching of her shoulders and slow withdrawal from him showed that he'd just chucked a pile of shit at her she'd rather not have to dig her way through.

"I didn't show up today because I got into a fight with my mother," she said quietly.

"What were you fighting about?" he asked, taking a step closer.

"Everything." Sighing, she lifted her hands, dropped them back down. "Where I kept going when I snuck off alone. Who I was meeting. Why I was keeping secrets. The wedding." She scoffed out a quiet laugh. "The bloody wedding."

"This still doesn't explain why you're here. Why you thi—"

"She kicked me out. My own mother kicked me out." Her gaze met his, a glossiness brightening the blue of her eyes. "That's why I don't have anywhere to go."

"You don't have other family?" He inched closer still. "Friends?"

"Of course I do, but ..." Again with the lift of her arms. Again with the heavy sigh. Only that time, she averted her eyes before continuing, "None of them understand me like .... None of them would understand *this*, not the way you ... do."

Chase stood less than two foot away from her, like his feet had kept moving without him even giving the order. He wondered if she could hear the way his heart thudded against his sternum like it tried thumping its way out in Abi's direction. "You didn't answer my question earlier," he said quietly.

A slight frown marred her brow. "Which one?"

"Why did you call off the wedding, Abi?"

"Because I didn't want to marry him anymore."

"Why?"

"Because I realised ..."

"Realised what?"

"I realised he's not right for me."

"Why?"

She glanced away. Twisted her fingers in her lap.

"Why, Abi? Why is he no longer right for you?"

"Because of you." The words blurted from her as her gaze sliced back to his. "Because I can't stop bloody thinking about you. All the stupid time. There. Are you happ—"

His mouth slammed against hers without Chase even registering his own movement. She froze beneath the assault, but only for a second before her lips parted and softened, and when a low rumble of a moan blew from her throat to his, Chase had to grip the counter either side of her to keep from dragging her ass forward and grinding against her cunt.

He dipped in his tongue, stroked it along Abi's. As he'd expected, she tasted of innocence and fucking rainbows and, beneath those, a willingness to sin. Abi O'Shay could sin all she damned well liked, so long as she did it with him.

Her fingers snatched at the front of his shirt, bunching the fabric, sending heat through to his chest, making his cock swell to its full, hard length, and Chase pressed in on her more. Crowding her. His arms all but caging her. He just couldn't decide which of his instincts flared brightest: to control or protect.

What he did know was, if he didn't take his fucking mouth off her, she'd be getting naked on that damned barstool and Chase would be doing something he couldn't undo.

He broke away, but didn't move away. Arms still butted against her sides, breaths blowing from him like a storm brewed, he tilted his head just enough to avoid the temptation of going back in and rested his temple against hers.

"Stay." Though he barely more than whispered the word, he knew she heard him by the slight inward shift of her face. "Stay here tonight. With me."

Her entire body seemed to still. She might even have quit breathing.

Chase gave a sharp shake of his head before resting it back in place. "That didn't come out right. I didn't mean—I mean I have a room. A guest room." He dared shifting away enough to see her, and fuck, her eyes glistened with enough lust to have his cock bouncing in his pants like it'd just found its favourite toy. "You can stay here tonight, and then tomorrow, after you've gotten some rest, we can figure out what you want to do next." *We can figure out ...* Like they were somehow in it together.

Weren't they, though? Whatever *it* was.

She nodded, a tiny jerk of a movement. "Okay."

"Okay," he said, offering a nod of his own. Something resembling a smile broke free, and he pushed away from the counter, only just managing to hold the expression in place as a coolness spread over his chest where Abi's hands had been a second before. "That's settled, then."

Her gaze one-hundred percent followed him, as he slowly backed away like he had to retreat from danger with precaution and any wrong move could be perilous for all involved. Only once a few steps away did he turn his back on the flustered look of Abi, and the way her fingers still slightly reached toward him, the way her cheeks held colour from heat rather than cold, and her lips had reddened from their kiss.

Once again needing a distraction, he headed straight for the sink. The dishes. Turned on the tap.

"Do you think of me, Mr Walker?" she asked softly from her stool.

He paused in his reach of a plate, brought his hands to grip hold of the sink's lip. "Every day, Abi," he said, his voice equally as low. He twisted back toward her again, taking in the hope and desperation clouding the lust he'd just left behind. "All the damned time."

The corners of her lips quirked up. The lines of her shoulders relaxed a little. The clouding of her eyes cleared once more.

And it was like she'd just captured the fucking sun and given it to him as a gift, the way heat blossomed in his chest and spread through him like a fire of protection.

The sensation both allured and terrified him. He'd experienced a lot of unicorn shit and sparkle, but right then felt like healing hands massaging his very fucking soul and a voice whispering at his ear that everything would be all right.

Shaking off the sensation, he turned back to the dishes. It would, he suspected, be a really long bloody night.

C hase had never really understood the differing levels of silence—complete silence, dead silence, static silence … but he was pretty sure he and Abi had sat through about every single one of them at some point throughout the rest of the evening.

Sure, he'd created noise as he'd cleaned up after dinner. When he'd switched on the TV so they'd have something to focus on besides each other—he'd been an idiot to believe that would fucking work. When his cock had stiffened for around the twentieth time, like it had a shot at something Chase refused to give it aim to, and he'd jumped up from the sofa under the pretence of needing a bathroom break real quick.

Just trying to sit there like everything was normal, like Abi popped round and watched TV with him all the time, was on par with torture, considering how dark pretty much all his thoughts tended to go regarding her. He'd barely made it to ten thirty before his hands had started to twitch as much as his dick, and his eyes had refused to stay on a repeat of *The Restoration Man* when he knew a much better and more interesting view sat just a few feet to his right.

Which was why, a little over three hours since he'd found Abi on his doorstep, Chase lay in bed, all too aware of the very enticing female body lying just two rooms away.

He supposed he could've just told his conscience to back the hell off upstairs, just crossed to the sofa Abi had curled up on. Rolled her the hell over onto her back. Tore off those leggings and whatever lay beneath. And buried his face in her pussy until she screamed the screams his cock had muffled the last time he'd tasted her.

Except, his conscience seemed to be shouting louder than his perverted fantasies for a change. That Abi wasn't ready. She'd come looking for help, not a quick fuck.

She was a *virgin*.

And that was the only damned reason he'd found himself in bed. Alone. Instead of dripping sweat and panting hard and shagging the living room rug through the palm of his hand as his tongue fucked Abi's cunt. Because, just like at the clinic last week, Abi had to be the one to make the first move.

And, damn, Chase's entire fucking body ached from wanting that.

Groaning at the stupid thoughts banging at the insides of his skull, Chase rolled over in bed for the one-hundredth time. Groaning even harder when his cock ground into the bedsheets and his hips almost defied him for a few quick thrusts of pointless excitement.

The clock on his side table read two thirty-five, the numbers glowing out at him like a mocking reminder that he'd spent the last four hours coiled tight and sweating for all the wrong bloody reasons. How long would he last, he wondered, before he'd need to swap the discomfort of the sheets for that of a cold shower. Maybe an hour. At most.

Though, another hour of rolling around with his stupid hard-on, and he'd be jacking off just to try and tire himself out.

At the quiet click of a door, Chase's body locked up. He didn't move—almost like he couldn't. He didn't breathe, like his breaths might hinder him in tracking the almost hesitant pad of feet he could just about hear in the hallway.

The door to his own room stood ajar, just as he'd left it—for reasons he hadn't cared to evaluate at the time—and he knew, he just knew, the exact moment that tiny sliver of space had been shadowed.

Not daring to move, he shifted only his eyes toward the opening. Gulped down a swallow at the shadow blocking the light that should've been filtering through from the hallway porthole.

He probably should've sat up. Called out. Asked her if she was okay. Except, a bigger part of him had Chase staying exactly where he was, if only to see what Abi would do with the decisions left entirely in her hands.

A slight thump hit the outside of the door before it began a slow swing inwards. Framed by the moonlight seeping in behind her, highlighted by the glow bleeding in through the bedroom's porthole, Abi filled the doorway.

Still, Chase didn't move. Nor speak. Just watched. His entire body on alert for every tiny movement she might make.

Maybe that was why he didn't break free of his invisible self-bindings. Maybe he didn't trust himself to continue holding back.

"Mr Walker."

His name whispered through the cool room and wrapped around his mind like a fucking caress.

She seemed to sway in the doorway, as if deciding whether to stay, or go. Chase really didn't want the latter to happen, no matter how much that may have been the sensible choice.

He lifted his head a little. "Abi?"

She didn't speak for three long, torturous seconds, then, "Did I wake you?"

"No, I was awake." He pushed up onto his elbow. "Is something wrong?"

"I couldn't sleep." He didn't doubt that. "I ... I was cold." That, however, he suspected to be a lie. Considering the extra blankets he'd added to the bed for her, she'd have been as padded as a fucking Eskimo. "And ..." She heaved in a deep sigh. "And I didn't particularly want to be alone anymore."

She didn't want to be alone anymore. The way she said it made it sound like she referred to so much more than the few hours she'd been lying in bed.

"Did you want me to get up." Wincing at his wording, he added, "Out of bed. With you."

He caught her headshake. "No."

She didn't want to be alone.

She didn't want him to go upstairs.

Unless she planned on contradicting herself and heading up there on her own, that meant she wanted the same thing Chase had been beating himself up over for hours.

"You want to join me in here." He didn't ask it as a question, more a given statement. Abi preferred directness and order, after all.

That time she nodded, a quiet, "Yes," breathing from her.

His body seemed enclosed around that single word. Yes, she did want to get into his bed. Yes, she did want to lie next to him with little other than a thin T-shirt separating her chest from his. Yes, she knew exactly what she wanted, and she'd come to take it. From him.

Not wanting a chance to outtalk himself, he flipped back the bedsheets. "Before you take another step," he said, halting her as she went to do exactly that. "Be sure of your decision."

"I am sure," she said. No hesitation. She took another step. Then another. It took five in total for her to reach the side of his bed. And it took only one more lift of her foot for her knee to be pressing down on the edge of his mattress. Her palm came down next to his shoulder as she lifted the other knee onto the bed, and as she twisted onto her backside, she paused for a moment, her knees tucked high against her chest, her body unmoving. After a few short breaths, she glanced behind her as if checking for a pillow, and stretching out her legs, she slowly lowered herself down.

Until she lay on her back.

In Chase's bed.

Right the fuck next to Chase.

Ordering his stuck swallow out of the way so he could breathe, he flipped up the sheets, enclosing Abi inside. With him.

Never had he been so aware of his own body heat, as a shallow coolness slipped from Abi, wrapping itself around the narrow space separating them.

"You're cold," he said. Maybe she hadn't been lying, after all.

"Only from standing out in the hallway." Her voice in his room seemed like an echo from a dream. Unreal. *Sur*real. "The floor was cold under my feet."

As if to test her truths, he slid a foot across the sheets until he found one of Abi's, snatching it back like a mofo as soon as he had. "Jesus, you're bloody freezing, not cold." He pushed himself up until he half-sat facing Abi. "You want me to go grab more blankets for in here?"

Her fingers wrapped around his arm, the move bringing her closer to him. "I'm fine. It's ... warmer in here."

Staring down at her, he couldn't help but notice how mussed her hair was. Like she'd done nothing but toss and turn since they'd said goodnight earlier. Like thinking of the other, very warm body just along the hall had driven her almost as crazy as it had him.

No second guessing, he reached down and tucked some of the knotted strands away from her face like it was the most natural thing in the world for him to do. Just like the natural thing to do seemed to be dipping down his face, until he propped back on his elbow and his lips hovered a hairsbreadth from hers, and her eyes so fucking consumed him she could've been a damned hypnotist. Because just looking onto them had Chase at her mercy.

"All I've thought about for an entire week is how you tasted on my tongue," he said.

"How did I taste?" she asked.

371

His lips quirked at the corners. "Fucking amazing."

Her fingers tightened over his arm. "All I thought about for an entire week is how, when we were in your office and you held my face in your hands, I thought you were going to kiss me. And then you didn't. But then, tonight you did. And that kiss only told me that what I wanted to believe was true."

"And what did you want to believe?"

"That you *wanted* to kiss me last week in your office."

Lowering his face, he let his temple brush across hers. His cheek swept across hers. His lips feathered their way along her jaw until they paused at her ear. "You're right. I did want to kiss you. Just like I've wanted to kiss you since the first day you stepped into my office like the freshest blast of air I've ever inhaled." He drew back until his lips hovered over hers again, and her eyes shone back at him like they held an ocean made of stars. "Just as I really, *really* want to kiss you right now."

"Okay," she whispered.

"Okay?"

At her nod, Chase dropped through the final gap and kissed her.

Upstairs, the kiss had been a rapid-fire blast of desperation. With that first burst of frustration out of the way, Chase had the patience the take his time. To explore and discover the lines and softness of her lips. Dip in his tongue and test out the ridges of within. The way her own tongue moved in response, like it learned the steps to a new dance but was a fast learner. Just like Abi herself. Because it took only seconds from the yielding of her mouth for her to fight back and make demands in return. Her lips hardened against his. Slanted across his. Her tongue sliding alongside his and taking tastes of its own.

It took every ounce of willpower for Chase to keep his twitchy fucking fingers to himself, but then her body curved upward to fit along his, the stiffness of her nipples brushing over

Chase's chest, and she reached up and grabbed at the nape of his neck as if holding him where she needed him. And when she kissed him even deeper, the tiniest of whimpers eking from her, she about annihilated the small thread of control he clung to.

He shoved a hand beneath the covers. Snatched at the hem of the shirt she wore.

She didn't fight him when he tugged it upward, but lifted her hips to free it. Arched her back to allow it passage. Lifting her shoulders from the bed, she raised her arms.

Allowing Chase to fuck the shirt off, leaving her laying bared.

His hand sought out her hip, his thumb rubbing in small circles as he stared down at her for a moment. Her hair splayed outward. Her lips, slightly swollen, sat parted and ready, as if awaiting the return of his own. Those fingers of hers returned to clinging his arm. She'd scarcely let go since she'd climbed into his bed, like she needed the anchor. The reassurance. That he wouldn't just kiss her then fuck off.

Chase had no intention of doing that. Because one kiss with Abi would never be enough.

He already wanted more. His head wanted more. His body. His throbbing cock was all but crying tears of desperation for bloody more.

Especially when it occurred to him that his thumb was brushing over absolutely nothing.

Nudging the sheets up with his elbow, he peered down Abi's body.

Yeah, definitely nothing down there. Not a pair of cotton briefs in sight.

"You always sleep in no underwear?" Or had she just come prepared?

"Not since you've been giving me homework," she said, and

he had to smile. Because Abi couldn't have been any further from a pussy liberating stereotype.

"So, you're saying I did this to you?"

"You do a lot of things to me," she said, and Chase glanced back up into eyes that told stories of exactly that. And then she gave a small smile full of that hidden sass of hers that had his heart kicking at his ribs again. "But I'm certain I took those knickers off myself."

He barked out a low laugh. "Yes, you certainly did."

Tightening his hand over her hip, he let the sheets drop back down and sank into another kiss. One heated and fast and so fucking deep, his lips all but swallowed Abi's to accommodate his need.

He shifted to her jaw. Scraped his teeth along there. As he nibbled along the line of her neck, her fingers reached for his nape again, held him to her like he'd hit a spot she really didn't want him to move away from.

He tended there a few moments more, loving how her breaths grew shorter. Sharper. How she stretched her head to the side and allowed him more of her flesh.

Working a leg between hers, he rolled until over her, his cock swelling even harder at the easy parting of her thighs. With an arm braced each side of her, his body only inches from hers, he kissed his way over her chest. Skimmed his lips over her breast. Reaching the stiff peak, he circled its tip with his tongue, lifting his gaze long enough to see Abi staring down at him, lips parted to release her hastening breaths, eyes full and glazed enough to shine even in the dim room.

"Tell me what you like, Abi."

"Okay." A shaky whisper. Her earlier cockiness gone.

"Tell me," he repeated, sterner, and at her jerky nod, he sucked her nipple back into his mouth, his hand squeezing over her hip at the small gasp she gave. Keeping his gaze on

Abi, he flicked his tongue over its tip, watching her as she watched him.

"I like that," she whispered.

"Just here ..." He released his hold on her and swapped to her right breast. Drew in the nipple, his teeth just scraping the sides of the solid bud before he suckled again. "Or here, too?"

"That, too."

Letting his nose brush her soft skin, he dipped to the underside of her breast. Her ribcage. He kissed her there. Gently. Then harder. Like just a simple taste of her body drove him to a hunger he needed to fulfil.

Beneath him, her body pushed upward. Above him, she gave a low moan. "There, too," she murmured.

"Here?" He scraped his teeth over the dip of her waist, but she squirmed away from him, releasing a cute laugh, and he lifted his gaze until he could see hers again. "Ticklish?"

"Just there," she said, a smile lingering on her lips.

Keeping his gaze locked on hers, he moved lower still. Pressed a kiss to the top of the V leading down to her pussy. "How about here?"

That expression of concentration she wore so well stared back at him. "Yes," she said quietly.

Following the line of her leg, he let it guide the way, all too aware of her fingertips clinging to the ends of his hair. He wondered if she'd even noticed how her hand had followed him down. Maybe she felt the need to guide him.

Or maybe she just needed to be sure he wouldn't leave.

Reaching the tough ridge of her thigh tendon, he paused. Glanced back up at her again. West would take him to that pleasure pip of hers she seemed to love playing with so much. South would take him to the heart of the storm, full of pressured heat and wetness.

He went south, shouldering his way in until she'd spread

wide enough to accept his breadth. He brought his arms down and around her thighs, only his elbows supporting him. Placing his face directly in line with Abi's pussy, already glossy and shiny and offering a goodness he fully intended to taste.

"You're soaked." He met her eyes. "For me?"

Her chest trembled upward, then back down, as her head twitched in a nod.

"Do you want to be wetter?"

Another nod.

Against his arms, her legs trembled. He knew she'd feel his breaths against her cunt. Feel the heat from his face. Be aware of exactly how little a space separated his mouth from her essence.

"How?"

Her lips parted further, almost as if he'd shocked her with his question.

He blew a soft breath across her cunt, smiling to himself at the tensing of her thighs. "You know what you want. Tell me."

"I ... want you to touch me."

"Down here?"

"Yes."

"How?" He didn't once remove his gaze from hers. She didn't once look away.

"With your mouth," she whispered after a short pause.

He ducked in close enough for his lips to skim over the wetness spilling from her, made sure to strike against her flesh when he licked over the gathered flavour. "Like this?" he asked, not moving away.

"Y-yes."

"How about this?" He slid his nose along her silken folds until he'd found her clitoris, and lifting slightly, he tugged the tiny bud between his lips.

Her back arched from the bed, tilting her cunt toward him as a low moan broke free. "Yes," she breathed. Those fingers of hers tightened around the strands of his hair.

He released her clit, slipped back down along her creases. Folded his mouth over the opening of her cunt and captured a throatful of Abi as he drew back. "Fuck, you taste good," he said around her juices before swallowing. "What else?"

"I ..." Her chest shuddered with her inhalation. "I want you to do what you did before. Last week. When you ..."

"Don't worry, I totally fucking plan on it, but you should know, if I do that? It's gonna get me hard as hell, Abi, and when I'm through, I'm going to want to fuck you." It was a big ask. Of himself, as well as Abi. Because Chase hadn't been inside a woman for years. Not in that way. Not since Nic. But he had a curiosity he needed to fulfil where Abi was concerned, and he'd never be satisfied with anything less than that. He knew he wouldn't.

She didn't speak for a few seconds, just stared at him over the unsteady rise and fall of her chest.

"Are you hearing me, Abi?" He needed the response. He needed her to know the effect she had on him. "Every time you've been in my clinic, I've wanted to fuck you. Every time you've lay back on that bed in the session room, I've *wanted* to *fuck* you. Every time you touched yourself, every time you let go and orgasmed, every single time you looked at me with those fucking eyes of yours, I have wanted to fuck you. But I didn't. Because I couldn't. But here. Now. With no barriers to protect you. I am *really* going to want to fuck you when I'm through here, and I need you to understand that before I continue. Tell me you understand."

"I understand," she whispered, but her breaths had hastened like he'd just scared the shit out of her. "I understand," she repeated, and that time she sounded more certain.

Fuck, Chase almost wanted to forget pleasuring Abi, climb the hell back over her, and get inside her right there and then.

He wouldn't, though. Rewards were always sweeter when worked for.

"So, now I know what you want. And you know what I want."

He didn't wait for an answer to that before he buried his face in her cunt and drank long and deep.

From the first pull, she gasped. Arched. Chased him with her hips when he dared draw away.

At a slight tug of his hair, he let her guide him upward. Toward her clit, and he suckled it deep into his mouth. His lips massaging the tender flesh around it.

A low hum of satisfaction buzzed through him at the soft cry she gave and the bucking of her hips shoving her harder against his face.

Over his shoulders, her thighs tightened, clamping him as her pussy drove into him again. Like she rammed her heels into the mattress as she ground against his face.

A river poured from her cunt, dripped from his chin. Sliding low again, he let the liquid fill his throat, gulping before his mouth enclosed her again, milking her for more.

She pulled on his head again, gave a tiny whimper that spoke volumes of frustration. If she wanted him at her clit, she could damned well have him at her clit.

Lifting back up, Chase all but attacked her swelling bud. His lips clenched around it so tight, her body almost bounced from the bed. His tongue flicked over it so fast, she verged on scalping him. And he sucked her in so deep toward his throat, her body curled up from the bed, every muscle across her stomach taut as she fought the evident battle of trying to stay still while she had him exactly where she wanted him, and trying to thrust the fuck out of his face because she bloody well needed more, damn it.

Chase knew the look well. He just never thought he'd get to

see it on Abi. And he never, for one second, thought he'd be its cause.

She gasped, a harsh blast of air. Her head kicked back. "Oh, God."

Chase loved how the whisper sounded as desperate as his frenzied feeding. Smiling to himself, he slipped back to her cunt. Smiled broader when she let out a groan filled with annoyance. But he needed to drink her. He needed that taste. Right before a woman came was always the sweetest, and he'd be damned if he'd miss sampling that from Abi. Vising his arms about her legs, he pinned her in place as he syphoned a dose of Abi and swallowed long and deep. His hips jerked his cock against the mattress as he gulped down her arousal.

"Mr Walker …"

He let his gaze lift toward the husky whisper of his name. Her body held as much tension as it had only moments before, but her chest pumped up and down as her breaths sawed in and out of her. He shifted his gaze higher, caught the way her brows drew together. The low glint in her eyes that spoke almost of pain.

She needed to come. And she needed to come real fucking bad.

"*Please*," she whispered.

It took only one, simple word to undo him. With that one word, she had him. He would, he realised, do whatever the hell she asked of him so long as she asked him like that.

Allowing himself one final taste from her spilling cunt, he ordered himself north. Dove right back in to ravaging her clit.

She cried out as soon as his lips closed around it, and that single sound held so much relief. Holding onto her thighs as tight as he had to drink from her, he suckled and nibbled and licked, until her cunt humped against him once more, and her fingers yanked at his hair once more. Her legs braced around his shoulders with an intensity that told him she'd fight him if he tried to fucking move again.

Who would've believe Abi could be so fierce in the sack?

Who the fuck would've believed she'd know exactly what she wanted and not be afraid to take it?

The woman had been a surprise when she'd very first walked into his office, and had continued to surprise him at every meeting since. Though, never so much as she did so right then.

Fuck, he loved how she didn't hold back in expressing her pleasure. That she didn't once try to restrain the gasps and moans as she thrust at his face and took everything she needed to make her orgasm happen.

Her thighs cinched tighter still, almost circling his head. A low mewl of a sound vibrated through the room. Staying at her clit, he tongued and suckled, until she quit yanking at his hair, and her mewling became a soft series of cries, and as soon as her body arched over the bed, her cunt reduced to twitching against his face, he sank back down and drank. Drank the cum pumping from her like he hadn't had enough already. Like he'd never have enough. And he totally loved how her body gave a tiny jerk beneath each of his pulls, accompanied by her weakening whimpers, like he swallowed down her energy with every mouthful of Abi he claimed.

Only once her whimpers had quieted to long breaths did he quit feeding. Lifting from her pussy, his face covered in her cum, all he could see was the rise and fall of her beautiful tits, each nipple solid and hard and poking at the air. Just like his cock, except that poked toward the heat of Abi's cunt. That mysterious channel of hers he'd been forbidden to explore. Forbidden by rules and restrictions. Ones that no longer stood in his way—not with Abi lying naked and wet and only half as sated as he planned to get her.

He crawled back over her, his fists planted down aside her shoulders, dropping to his elbows until his chest brushed against the stiff peaks of her breasts and his face hovered only inches above Abi's.

She kept her eyes closed for five long seconds before the lids slowly fluttered upward, exposing eyes as pale as the moon outside, her small smile causing an upward curve of her lips. "Hi," she whispered.

He couldn't help himself. Chase dropped his lips to hers and claimed them like he owned them. Straight away, she opened up to him, her moan filling him as if she staked ownership on him as much as he tried to her. Her fingers scraped through the short strands of hair at his nape. Like she hadn't just climaxed, she arched right into him, her leg winding around the back of his, as if the suppleness that came postorgasm had somehow driven every one of her inhibitions aside.

He breathed hard when he released her. The way she stared up at him through half-lidded eyes, it took every ounce of himself not to dive right back in while aiming his cock for her cunt. But he couldn't. He might've wanted to. Hell, he wanted to more than he ever had with any other woman.

"What I said before," he murmured. "About fucking you."

Her lids lifted a little higher as the tiniest of frowns spread across her brow. "What about it?"

"I didn't mean it." Hadn't he, though? At the time, maybe.

"You don't want to anymore?" Her frown deepened, like he'd upset her somehow. Again.

"Abi, I want to fuck you so bad right now, my dick is crying like a baby."

She smiled, though only a little. "But?"

"But ... you're a virgin. And no matter what it sounded like, I'd never force you to do anything you don't feel ready for."

381

"I know," she said quietly. "And you wouldn't be forcing me. I want to."

"Are you sure you're ready?" he said.

"I know I am." She didn't once shift her gaze from his, but held him steady. Not so much as a flicker of hesitation entered her eyes. "I'm ready for this. For you."

He exhaled, like he'd held it in, waiting on her response, and her words had somehow given him the ability to breathe again. "Okay," he said, still watching her as he pushed away.

As soon as he had, the air of the room enveloped his body and set his skin prickling. The cool floor had his toes curling over as he set them down from the bed and padded across to his wardrobe. He sent a glance back toward Abi, loving how she hadn't moved from where he left her, and opened one of the wardrobe doors.

Inside, clothes hung from hangers across one side. Balancing them out, the other side held a stack of shelves and small drawers. Drawers meant for stuff like individual ties, or socks. Most of them did hold those things, but the one Chase slid out held a box containing his supply of condoms. A supply he usually only dipped into when heading off for a night out with the need to score.

It was the first time Chase had ever opened the drawer because he had a need in his home. In his room. His bed.

Truly the first time.

But then, Abi O'Shay seemed to have a habit of smashing down the rules Chase had in place. What was one more?

He held one up as he closed the doors and turned back. "Protection."

She didn't speak, just watched him through the wan light of the room.

He rounded the bed until he stood over her, but not so close as to crowd her. He'd be doing plenty of that just as soon as he'd packaged himself. "You sure about this, Abi?"

"Yes, I'm sure."

He loved how softly she said the words, like she hadn't an ounce of fear for what she was about to do. With the condom tucked between his teeth, he reached for the ties of his waistband, pulled them loose. As he pushed down on his lounge pants, he kept his eyes on Abi. Observing the way her gaze followed the drop of his trousers, before lifting back to where his erection throbbed like a fucking lighthouse. Hard as rock, it stuck out and up, all proud and eager, and she stayed focussed on it as he opened the condom and rolled the rubber right the way down his shaft.

"You can stop this at any time," he said, kicking his bottoms aside.

"Okay."

Okay. She seemed to love that damned word. It was definitely growing on Chase right then, too.

"It might hurt," he said, climbing back onto the bed. "At least at first." He had no bloody clue why he kept trying to talk her out of it, but, damn, he needed her to be one-hundred percent sure of her choice.

"I've heard," she said. From Rebecca, he suspected—her fountain of information.

Her legs still lay softly splayed, like she hadn't the energy to move them since he'd shifted from between them, and he nestled right back within, hooked a hand beneath her knee and drew her leg up, smiling when she matched him with her other leg. Stretching over her, he planted a hand down beside her shoulder, his chest over hers, his face above hers. With the other hand wrapped around his cock, he searched her eyes for any sign of hesitation. Of fear. He didn't see a single ounce of either.

Did she truly trust him that much? How? Wasn't like he'd earned it. Definitely wasn't deserving of it.

"Okay?" he asked her, giving her one last chance to back out.

"Okay," she whispered back.

His body nigh on trembled as he guided to tip of his cock to Abi's entrance. A quick upward swipe of his thumb checked she was still wet, and he fitted his tip to the tight opening. Swiped up some of her lingering cum and coated his shaft for that extra bit of lubrication.

Keeping his gaze totally on hers, he parted her a little, and pushed inside.

He hadn't even made it halfway when her lips popped open on a startled gasp, and he stilled. Her brows had drawn tight, creating tiny grooves over her nose.

"Talk to me," he said, though he trembled with the effort of not thrusting the rest of the way in. Because, damn, being inside Abi, even by only a few inches, felt really fucking fine.

"It stings."

"You want me to stop?" Though he asked in all earnest, he couldn't quite shut out the ugly voice in his head chanting *Please say no, please say no*.

She shook her head.

"Okay, how about we just stay here for a moment. Just like this."

"Okay." Her breath breezed over his face as she whispered the word.

He had no idea how the hell he'd keep his hips from kicking his cock deeper inside her, but he'd damned well give it a good try if it'd give her pussy time to fit around his shaft, to get used to stretch of flesh needed to achieve that. He lowered his mouth to hers, brushed over the soft plumpness there. "How about if we just do this for a moment?"

Her lips curved beneath his. "Okay."

"Okay," he murmured, and reaching for her hand, he hooked it around his neck and kissed her. Not hard, but gentle. Like he had all the time in the world.

In that moment, he almost could've believed they did.

Almost immediately, her body responded, as if it knew what it wanted the second it spotted it, and knew how to take it. Her fingers curled against his nape. Her chest pushed upward until it bumped his. And her lips parted, her tongue not even waiting for the prompt before sliding out and seeking the heat of his mouth.

It took around forty seconds longer for her hips to try joining the party. He felt the jerk of them against his own. Sensed the seizing of her muscles again at the slight shift of his cock inside her, and had to stifle his groan at the urge to drive home.

Feathering away from her mouth, he skimmed his lips across her jaw, down to that spot just below her pulse that'd had her uncurling in invitation earlier. As soon as he suckled at the sensitive flesh there, she moaned and tilted her head. Offering him more. And he took it. Attacking the skin there, he sucked and nibbled. It'd leave a mark come morning, but he didn't care. Not while her back arched up off the bed, and her fingertips dug into his skin, and those sounds—fuck, those tiny little gaspy whimpers she made had his entire body buzzing with need.

Smoothing a hand down her body, he gripped her hip and slowly drew his own back until only the tip of his cock breached the entrance of her pussy. He paused there a moment, waiting for resistance, or complaint, and when neither came, he just as slowly eased back inside her. Deeper than the last attempt, all too aware of how her breaths had lengthened, of the clutch of her other hand over his shoulder. Deeper until his shaft had sunk the entire way in and her walls hugged around every last fucking inch of him, and that groan he'd done a decent job of containing broke free.

"Okay?" he somehow managed.

"I'm okay," she said, her breath hitting his ear.

"Fuck, it feels good being inside you like this."

It'd been years since he'd taken sex that far. He'd almost forgotten how it felt to be inside a woman, and not a damned one of them that'd come before her had ever felt so fucking right. "Scratch that," he muttered. "It feels fucking amazing to be inside you like this."

"Mr Walker," she whispered, and he lifted from her throat until her eyes came into view, swimming beneath a glossy coating that made them more beautiful than ever. "Please don't stop."

"Chase." When she frowned, he added, "It's my name. Just in case you feeling like screaming it at any point."

She gave a small laugh, but he didn't wait to reciprocate before doing exactly as she'd so very nicely asked. Burying his face back into her throat and setting her stretching and nigh on purring again, he drew back his hips, long and slow, before thrusting his entire length right back into her again. As with the first time, he groaned. The sound deep and raw and, somehow, possessive. While beneath him, she gasped, a sound that spoke as much of acceptance as pain. Like the bridge between the two had begun forming, and she'd only to find the bravery to cross it to discover the pleasure on the other side.

Again, he kept his movements slow as he pulled back out until the only head of his dick clung to her entrance. Again, a deep groan left him as he drove back in.

He'd had no fucking idea just how torturous slow thrusting could be.

He'd also had no idea how fucking beautiful it could be.

Because while his entire body trembled with the urge to go

faster, harder, deeper, his mind buzzed with the prolonged pleasure of each individual plunge into her cunt. His very being seemed aware of every tiny shift of them both, every single sound they each made. So he knew the exact moment her body ceased resisting the invasion and her hips slowly eased up to greet his. Knew exactly when the underlying pain faded from her soft gasps, and only echoes of desire trailed on their tails.

Which meant he knew before it happened that she'd orgasm only a moment before himself, and as soon as she had, her walls constricted around his cock, pulsing and tugging so hard, his own climax shot through him like a fucking bullet and had him barking out a cry of sweet relief.

Heaving in much-needed breaths, he couldn't quite tell who trembled hardest. Himself, or Abi. Her thighs might've been shaking like crazy against his weight, and her hands definitely shook where they still clutched at his flesh, but damn, his own limbs scarcely held him from crushing her.

Ordering his face from its burrowed position at her neck, he somehow lifted until he peered down at her, and she up at him, and it was a like thousand words were uttered in that single moment, without a single one of them being said. Words Chase didn't understand, or didn't know the code to—he just knew they were words he wanted to hear.

"Okay?" she whispered into the shadows, and he breathed out a laugh at the switch. At her asking him what he always asked her. At the very thought that what they'd just shared had placed him at the base of vulnerability in need of an anchor.

"I'm okay," he whispered back. "Absolutely, seriously, fucking okay."

C hase couldn't stop staring. At Abi's hair, and the way the sun bleeding through his window turned it a bright gold. At her chest, the gentle rise and fall of each relaxed breast with every breath she took. Her face, and the way her eyes shifted beneath the lids, like she dreamed.

Of what, he wondered. Himself. The two of them. Together —like the night before.

Even once they'd fucked—no, not fucked. For some stupid reason, the word seemed too crude a description for what'd occurred between him and Abi beneath the cover of darkness. And it hadn't ended there. Even once they'd untangled their bodies, he'd ran Abi a much-needed bath and helped her tend to the tenderness he'd caused. *They'd* caused, he corrected. Because Abi had been as much a part of it—as much an instigator, even—as he had. Not just once, but twice, when she'd refused to settle, and he'd exhausted her all over again with his mouth at her cunt.

Her lids fluttered ever so slightly. The first sign of stirring from her in the hour he'd lay watching her. Odd thing was, he'd expected to feel panic come morning. Some kind of regret over having let her stay—not just in his home, but his bed. Instead, he felt only calm. Like the tempest that'd threatened mayhem and carnage had passed and left only blue skies and serenity in its wake.

"'Morning," he whispered, not even waiting for her to open her eyes.

She smiled, the expression slow and lazy, her lids lifting until those pale blues of hers stared back. "Hi."

He reached up, tucked hair behind her ear as it began a slow slide forward. "You okay?"

"I'm okay," she said, that smile still toying with her lips.

"Do you ..." He paused, frowning at himself, despite

knowing he'd been making plans to ask her the entire time he'd been waiting for her to wake. It was almost as if he dreaded the answer—or dreaded which way the answer would fall, at least. "You fancy hanging out today?" he asked. "Here. Or wherever. With me."

Even as he spoke, he didn't know what the fuck was wrong with him. He didn't stumble over requests, or offers, or invitations. He was Chase Walker, and he just damned well asked if he bloody wanted something, dammit. And he definitely didn't know what the fuck was up with his tightening chest as he waited for her response.

"Okay," she said, still smiling, and it felt as if someone had trepanned his lungs and let all the air out.

Hoping she didn't notice his spazzing out, he simply said, "Good."

Cupping her cheek, he leaned in closer, but barely even brushed his lips against hers before he heard a sound. A sound not made by them. Not in his bedroom. Yet, in his home.

Frowning, he lifted his head toward the door. Definitely, footsteps moved about upstairs above them. "Shit," he muttered.

"What's wrong?" Abi whispered, like she knew to be quiet.

"Someone's here." He flung back the sheets and rolled off the bed. His discarded lounge pants lay crumpled on the floor, and he scooped them up and tugged them over his legs.

"Like, a burglar, someone?" Abi asked, watching his every move.

Didn't matter who it was. If not a burglar, it could only be one of two people—because only two people had a key. And right then was a bad time for either of them to be visiting.

He sent her a quick smile. "Guess I'd better find out," he said, and turned for the hall.

Bare-footed, he padded quietly up the stairs that led to the first floor. The closer he got, the more obvious the footsteps became, alongside what sounded like opening and closing of cupboards. The moving about of stuff—his stuff.

As he neared the corner to the kitchen, the footsteps moved closer, and bracing himself, he stepped out into the open.

Right opposite his ma pulling sheets out of the laundry basket and staring at them like she'd just entered a real-life horror movie.

"Ma!" The word barked from his throat—like he just needed to get her attention off those damned sheets.

Her gaze slowly lifted, overshadowed by her heavy frown as it met Chase's. "What did you *do* to yourself?"

To myself— "What?" Quickly lifting his hands, he stepped toward her. "Ma ... it's not mine. Look." Her held out his arms. Twisted a little, side to side. "See? No blood. I'm good. It's all good."

"Then, 'oose ..." Her voice trailed off as her gaze shifted to the right, and he turned to see Abi hovering at the top of the stairs.

Hair mussed all the fuck everywhere, she stood there in only a buttoned shirt of Chase's that somehow managed to reach halfway over her thighs. Staring right back, her eyes wide and bottomless, those silky legs leading down to where her toes curled against the floor, she looked ... fucking divine.

Chase wanted nothing more than to march right over here, throw her down on the nearest counter, and see if she tasted just as good.

Damn his ma for being there right then.

Damn his ma for turning to stare at him at the exact moment he sensed his cock tenting his trousers.

He didn't dare look back, just kept his gaze on Abi and the bright spots of colour claiming her cheeks. As much as he liked the fantasies of otherwise, he really hoped she had something else on beneath that shirt. "Ma, this is Abi. Abi ..."

He aimed his hands toward his Ma as he said, "Meet my mother."

"Nice to meet you, Mrs Walker," Abi said, as polite as Chase would've expected her to be, despite the circumstances.

His ma still hadn't turned away from him. "You invited a girl to stay," she hissed beneath her breath.

He dared look at her then, and fell right under the scrutiny pouring from her inquisitive eyes. He went to shake his head, but how would that've looked—to his ma, and to Abi?

"You 'ad a girl to stay?" she said again, before he could think up a decent response. "You?"

God, why did she have to sound like she was freaking out in front of Abi? Couldn't she at least have waited until she got him alone? "It wasn't like that, Ma."

Her head slowly turned away until she stared down toward the bloodied sheet she still held. From there, she lifted her gaze toward Abi. Then to Chase, her head slightly tilted like she'd just caught him out in a lie. He knew the look well. He'd seen it a whole heck of a lot while growing up.

He reached for the sheet. "Can we just get this in the machine?"

She held tight. "You can't just wash this. It needs special treatment to get all this blood out."

"It doesn't matter, Ma. Just put it in the machine."

She still wouldn't let go of the damned thing. "I'll take it and sort it at 'ome." She tugged hard on the sheet, pulling Chase toward her with it. As soon as he got close, she whispered, "You never 'ave girls over to stay."

"Leave it, Ma," he whispered back.

"Is she a nice girl?" she whispered—like Abi wasn't standing *right there*.

"You're embarrassing me," he said, letting go of the sheet. He suspected it'd be the only way to halt her blasted whispering. As he turned away, he mouthed *Sorry* Abi's way, but despite the blotchy patches of red creeping their way down her throat, she just smiled back at him—a smile that said *what the hell have I just walked in on and how do I escape.*

"I could probably get the sheet clean, Mrs Walker," she said, sounding just the tiniest bit desperate. "You don't have to do it."

"Don't be daft, child," his mother said, as he reached beneath the sink.

Before a debate could start between the two of them, he fetched out a black bag, shook it out, and twisted back to his ma. "Neither of you should have to do it. Here." He held it open in front of her. "Put it in. I'll sort it out myself."

"I said I'd ..."

Something in his expression must've spoke volumes, because she trailed off and quit arguing and flopped the bloodied article inside the bag he held. If he thought she'd done, though, he was mistaken.

"You 'ad a girl to stay," she said, yet again, and as she turned away, some ridiculous smile on her face, he could almost hear the cogs turning in that brain of hers. Sometimes, he thanked the universe that he didn't have telepathy. "I 'ope you like sausage," she called from the fridge, and Chase had to stifle his laugh.

"Do you like sausage?" he asked Abi, as he crossed the room to her.

"Yes, thank you, Mrs Walker," she said, but her lips twitched like crazy as she said it, and he couldn't help leaning in and kissing them, just at their twitchy corner.

"I'm really sorry about this. Just take a seat and go with it," he said quietly. "It'll take me two minutes to dispose of this out of the way, and then I'll be back. Okay?"

She nodded. "I'll be okay."

"Sit yourself down, young Abi," his ma called before he'd even reached the steps down to the entrance.

"Wouldn't you like some help, Mrs Walker?"

"Are you a cook?" he heard his mother ask.

"She's a baker," he called up the stairs.

"A baker?"

He smiled at the surprise in his ma's voice. "A good one," he added. "She works in a bakery."

"You best fish out the bacon, then," she said, and Chase relaxed a little as he opened his front door and stepped out into the chilly morning air.

Hopefully, keeping them both focussed would deter his ma from asking too many questions.

The scene in his kitchen was like playing a freaky game of Happy Families. The atmosphere was easy, like the three of them always shared the breakfast bar and scoffed down a meal his ma had turned up with.

Talking of which ... "I wasn't expecting you today, Ma," he said around a gobful of beans and egg.

She shifted her attention from Abi—she'd spent most of the time they'd been eating sending her appreciative glances, like Abi pleased her, eating down the food with no complaint. "Yeah, well ..." She worked a bit of fried bread through her tomato juices. "Turned out I bought too many sausages, didn't I? Good thing, too, what with your *lady friend* bein' 'ere, an' all."

"I'm very glad you did," Abi said, while Chase rolled his eyes at his ma's inability to let up.

He should've known the second she'd set eyes on Abi, she'd have been imagining a future with Chase settled down and grandbabies on the way ....

The exact reason he'd had absolutely no intention of introducing Abi to her after a single night spent together. Hell, he didn't even know himself what was happening between them. What *had* happened between them, sure—that one was an easy answer of *something really fucking awesome*. But as for what could happen from then on out? She might up and leave before nightfall—so he'd be damned if he'd start planning anything beyond each next few hours.

"So, 'ow'd you two meet, then?"

Both he and Abi paused with food midway to their mouths. He was just running through a close-to-the truth lie, when Abi piped up with, "He tried my custard doughnuts."

Chase almost laughed at the simple explanation—mostly because his brain turned doughnuts into a euphemism for Abi's milky tits. He'd definitely sampled those. And he fully intended sampling them all over again—just as soon as they got the place back to themselves.

"That good, are they?" his ma asked, dragging him back to the moment.

He shoved in his bacon and chewed to smother his amusement, sending his ma a nod. "The best," he managed around his mouthful.

At least Abi seemed to be sticking to the same story she'd fed Jones and Ade. Would make keeping track of the porky-pies a little easier. Maybe.

"Way to a man's 'eart, through his belly," his ma muttered. "Only 'ad to feed the lad once. 'E ain't stopped eating my food ever since."

The giggle that came from Abi held a whole lotta cuteness. A whole lot. Beside her, his ma's shoulders jiggled along at her own advice. And all Chase could do was stare. At the lack of tension between devoted mother and a woman she'd found in her son's home. He'd tried imagining a few times over the past year, how his ma might respond to a woman invading the role she played in Chase's life. She'd always been protective. Always providing. Whatever he'd imagined, none of the interactions and acceptances had ever gone as smooth as the reality. Because his ma seemed to genuinely like Abi—though, what was there, really, to dislike? He guessed he just hadn't really expected such a warm reception for a woman he might've been dating a while, let alone for someone he'd spent a single night with. And as much as the relief kept his muscles loose and his stomach settled, he truly didn't really know what to make of it all.

"Thank you for the tip, Mrs Walker," Abi said, drawing him from his thoughts. "I'll have to bear that in mind."

I'll have to bear that in mind. Like she needed some kind of plan to get him to stick around. Didn't she realise she'd already pulled that off? It was he who was worried about her. She'd walked out on her parents. Possibly her church, too. She could grab her coat as soon as later that day and decide she needed to head home and rebuild the bridges she'd burned. Chase had no idea what went on in that pretty head of hers, outside of the evident lust whenever she released her shyness and embraced her horny side. Something she seemed to do more of, and with a whole lot more ease than when they'd first met.

For the next few minutes, his ma gave Abi examples that backed up her theory.

"There was this one time ..."

"At his twelfth birthday party, 'e was more interested in what food 'e was 'avin' than any party games, or presents ..."

"'Im and that Jones boy, thick as thieves they was. I often ended up feedin' the two of 'em, you know ..."

"I've met Jones," Abi said, glancing Chase's way as if checking it'd been okay to mention as such.

"That so?" His ma's eyebrows lifted a little. "'E's a special boy, that one. A good boy."

She didn't say any more on that matter, and Chase was relieved when Abi didn't probe—mostly because it meant his ma pushed away from the counter and started cleaning the dishes. Ten minutes later, and she and Abi had the kitchen looking as it had before the cooking had started, and his ma was grabbing up the big shopping bag she always carried with her.

She bustled across the kitchen to where Abi stood leaning against the units. Gripping her shoulder, as if giving her little choice but to lean in and accept it, she kissed her cheek. "It was nice meetin' you, young Abi. You take care of me boy, now, you 'ear?"

"Yes, Mrs Walker. It was lovely meeting you, too."

Spinning back toward the living space, she nodded to Chase as she hustled right on past him. "'Elp me with me coat, Son."

No arguing, he followed right on behind her, down the few steps to the hallway, and took her coat down from the hook. As he held it up, she slipped one arm into a sleeve, the other arm in, and turned to face him as she shrugged herself into it.

"You bring 'er with you for dinner tomorrow," she whispered.

"Ma, I'm not sure I'll be there for dinner tomorrow."

"Why wouldn't you be?"

"Listen, Ma. Whatever this is here, just give us a chance to figure it out on our own." He barely registered how he held his hands in front of himself as if pleading.

"Oh, Son." Lifting her arms, she waved him forward, making him stoop down until low enough for her to engulf his shoulders in a hug. "You've already figured it out," she said, drawing back far enough to see him. "You just don't know it yet."

With that, she turned for the door, letting all the cool, damp air in as she pulled it open and stepped outside.

∼

Chase had never known how happily lazy Saturdays could be. Since his ma had gone, leaving just the two of them, they'd done little beyond fucking and showering and dressing. If their refreshed clothing could even be referred to as that—because all they'd done was switch out one pair of lounge pants for another, one shirt and a spare pair of Chase's boxers for another. Sure, they'd eaten. Sure, they'd talked—about life and aspirations, and childhoods—a lot about childhoods, because Abi had loved his ma on sight, loved the evident overprotective-ness and the astute way with which she'd studied them both.

'You're lucky,' Abi had said—more than once, the words spoken beneath the weight of sadness.

The last time she'd said it, he'd placed his hands down either side of her thighs and leaned in close. 'Right now, I feel like the luckiest bastard on the planet.'

Thankfully, that'd eased the sombreness entering her mood, brought that soft smile of hers back to her face.

Having always been smothered in the level of affection he had, Chase couldn't imagine being on the far side of the fence. By Abi's descriptions, her parents had never paid her much attention beyond the achievements they'd expected of her. School achievements. Sports team achievements. Church achievements. What Chase could only fathom out to be skivvy achievements.

And the latest in a long list: marriage achievements.

Sure, his ma had dreams for him. Sure, she liked to have her say, and push and poke him into action. Not once, though, had she made any of his important life decisions. Every single one of those had been his, and his alone, and she'd supported him along every step of the way.

Giving Abi space to refresh after a dinner of coq au vin, Chase slouched onto a sofa and reached for the TV remote.

Beyond the windows, light waned, the dimness stretching through the glass to claim the living space of his home, but he didn't bother with the lights. The under-unit spotlights gently glowed over in the kitchen, providing enough illumination by which to see. He didn't need any more than that. *They* wouldn't need any more that. If he'd learned one thing about Abi over the past twenty-four hours, it was that she preferred to be caressed in the shadows, rather than the light—something he fully intended on doing.

With the TV volume down low, he listened as she moved about downstairs. A part of him insisted it felt strange having another there, sharing his personal space, making noise around him that wouldn't ordinarily be present.

A bigger part of him liked it. A lot.

Before, any rooms he didn't occupy felt like voids. Areas of nothingness surrounding the smallness of him in their centre. The river house didn't feel like that with Abi there. For the first time, he realised, his home held a warmth he hadn't even realised it was lacking.

From the bathroom, footsteps trod across to the bedroom. His bedroom. Abi had scarcely set foot in the room he'd offered her since she'd slept in his bed the night before.

A moment later, those same footsteps trotted along the lower hallway and padded up the polished steps. And he knew exactly when she'd reached the top, when she shared the same space as him, because the very air around him suddenly seemed charged with the right kind of tension. It was a tension that'd bounced back and forth between them throughout the entire day—one they'd done a decent job of defying, for the most part. If they hadn't, they'd have just spent the entire day wet and naked and breathing really fucking hard.

Maybe it was time to give in to it again.

By the time Abi had crossed the space toward him and

rounded the back of the sofa, Chase was already stiff with ideas of her supple body pressed against his. Not giving her a chance to choose the other sofa, he reached out and snagged her wrist when she went to pass him, and as he tugged her toward him, giving her little choice but to plonk her sweet ass down in front of him, she gave a small laugh.

"Maybe I'll sit here, then," she said.

"Maybe you should *lie* here," he said. Scooping an arm around her waist, he drew her back flush against his chest, as he settled against the cushions until the two of them spooned. He grabbed the remote off the arm of the seat and pointed it at the TV. "What do you fancy?" he asked, flicking through the film channels. "*Avengers Assemble ... Donnie Darko ... Fifty Shades ...*" Propped up on his elbow, he peered down at her over her shoulder. "You a Christian Grey kinda girl, Abi?"

"I don't know, I've never watched it," she said, her gaze flicking between Chase and the screen.

"I've heard it's a book, too," he said, smiling as he added, "Though, probably not the kind of book your parents would want in their house."

"From the way you said that, you're probably right."

"Yeah, well ... you're not in their house now. You're in mine. And women love this shit, so ..." He stuck the remote back down.

The film might not have been his cup of tea, but he couldn't help wondering how well Abi would accept the storyline. A part of him wanted to know what she'd make of the sex scenes. And the sick part of him wanted to know if she'd like them.

Settling in behind her, he let his hand support his head. His other hand rested on her hip, and he loved how she nestled in against him—against where his cock hardened in his trousers. A few more wriggles like that, and they'd never get to the good bits of the film.

Her hips rolled again. He couldn't tell if she did it uncon-sciously, or if she did it on purpose—because she had to feel his erection through the couple layers of clothing they wore. Either way, he didn't care. Not while it felt good.

Letting his hand slide down, he slipped it beneath the hem of the shirt she wore.

"Is that Jamie Dornan?" she asked into the quiet.

He let his gaze skim up toward the screen, at where a nervous young woman sat opposite a tidy guy in a swank office. "No idea."

"Rebecca loves Jamie Dornan."

"He's not my type." He lowered his lips to her ear. "My type is a strawberry blonde, with eyes that go deeper than forever, wearing one of my shirts."

She twisted toward him with a smile. "These eyes?"

"Those eyes," he said, dropping in to place a kiss on her lips.

She tugged at the shirt she wore, just above where the top button concealed her breasts. "A shirt like this?"

"Exactly like that."

Kissing along her jaw, he worked the bottom button of the shirt free, before moving on to the next, then the next. As he freed the top one, his knuckles brushed over her tits, their nipples already puckered tight as he released them into the air. Feathering his lips along her neck, he tugged the shirt back, until he'd exposed her shoulder. Dragged it a little more until he had her arm pinned to her side and the top of her spine exposed.

"Watch the film," he murmured against her skin. "I got this under control."

Waiting until she'd turned away from him, he tucked her hair out of the way and licked a slow line from the nape of her neck along her spine, stopping only at the restriction of the shirt. Her body curled into his, and though she didn't so much as sigh, her breaths definitely deepened, telling Chase she liked it.

Wrapping an arm about her waist, he drew her ass back even tighter against his stiffness. And when he bit down on the soft flesh between her neck and her shoulder blade, she rewarded him with a sharp gasp and an arch of her spine. Telling Chase she liked that even better.

He sank into there again, received another gasp, a backward butt of her ass against his cock. Her arm even lifted a little, like she considered reaching for him. Yeah, she liked that a whole lot. And Chase was all about giving Abi what she liked.

Letting his hand roam up her body, he sank back in again. His teeth scraping. His tongue licking. His mouth suckling in flesh until those gasps she tried taming turned into deep moans, and she grabbed hold of his head as she shrugged that sensitive spot of hers into each of his caresses. Rolling her nipple between his fingers as he sucked had her hips rocking back and forth. Almost as much as the rhythm Chase's own hips had found, and he fast gave up going for the entertainment value when he could be going for the prize.

Sliding his hand back down her body, he slipped it beneath the waist of his boxers she wore. Down over her pubis. All the way to the pits of wetness as she parted her thighs. Between that gentle exploration and the continued devouring of her flesh, she seemed unsure which to beg for the most, until her entire body sank into one fluid undulation of trying to seek out every sensation at once. Ensuring Chase's cock strained against his lounge pants and throbbed out its plea for the action.

He couldn't hold off any longer. Pushing up, he shoved at the boxers until she lifted her hips, let him force them down her legs. While she kicked them off the rest of the way, he delved into the pocket of his pants for protection. He'd taken to keeping a couple in his pockets, since there had been more than one moment throughout the day when Chase had been tempted to throw Abi down and take her in the there and then—and he'd had to quell his damn craving each time, because the bloody condoms had been all the way downstairs. After two cases of blue balls, he'd determined not to get caught out a third time.

With her pussy laid bare, and her gaze meeting his over her shoulder, he shoved his lounge pants down far enough to release his erection and worked the rubber over his girth. As soon as he had, Abi rolled toward him, but with a hand on her hip, he stopped her. Nudged her forward again until lying on her side. Gripping her flesh, he parted her legs until her thigh hooked back and over his, and shifted closer until the hand gripping his cock soaked up the juices spilling from her cunt.

"You do this like you've done it before," Abi said quietly.

"Fuck from this position?" He paused with the tip of his cock at her entrance. "Yes, many times. Fuck on my sofa? Never. You're the first."

Not waiting for her opinion on that, he pushed inside her, revelling in the immediate response of her body, the short cry she gave, holding her tight to him as he sank in the full length of his shaft and her walls hugged his throbbing flesh.

"Fuck, I hope being inside you never gets old," he murmured against her shoulder. "Because this feels fucking amazing."

With his hand wrapped over the inside her thigh, he held her spread as he drew back and thrust again. Let his breaths, his lips thrill the tiny hairs at her nape as he drove into her a third time. And within a few more plunges of his cock into her pussy, her tight passage gripping and stroking like a fucking dream, she'd reached back to grip his hair again, arched her spine like her ass was his for taking, and she moaned out at every collision of their hips.

For minutes, they remained like that, just fucking. Him giving. Her taking. The gentle rocking of her hips sending a tremble the entire length of her legs. Hitching her thigh higher, wider, he reached for her hand that gripped at the sofa's edge and guided it to her pussy.

"Show me how you like it," he ordered. "Show me how you make yourself come."

And she did. No hesitation. No questions. Hell, she didn't show even the slightest bit of embarrassment, as she let her fingers slide around the withdrawal of his cock and spread the wetness up over her clit. As Chase relocated his rhythm, Abi found hers. While he drove his cock deep inside of her, her fingers thrummed across the stiff peak of her clit, the fingers of her other hand grasping at his hair, ensuring he continued teasing her neck, her shoulder, as the slow rock of her hips demanded he keep fucking. It took only seconds for her moans, her whimpers, Chase's grunts to overthrow any other sounds in the room. The moment became about pleasure, the giving and taking of it, like they both had a mission in which they couldn't afford to fail. Because he needed to come. He needed Abi to come. And by the frantic flick of her fingers, the desperate roll of her clit between their tips, she really fucking needed that, too.

Through the moans and grunts came the slap of flesh on flesh, as Chase's groin bumped her ass with every deep thrust into her. And with every deep thrust into her, her walls clenched him a little tighter. As with every tightened clench around his cock, his balls cinched a little higher, and fire licked up toward his stomach a little hotter.

Through the effort of holding back, he gritted his teeth, until his grunts barely pushed free. The tendons stood proud through his arm, where he gripped Abi's hips, slamming her back against him with every forward thrust of her cunt.

The flicking of Abi's fingers lessened, the bucking of her hips eased, and with a few tiny twitches into where she pressed on her clit, a soft mewl spilled from her throat, her head tipped, her back arched so deep her ass shoved Chase against the sofa's rear. Pausing for just a second, he gave her that moment. Allowed her to stand on the pinnacle of climax. And as soon as she crested, her entire body folding into the freefall of orgasm, he gripped her even tighter and drove his cock deep and hard and fast into her, barking out a short cry with each fisting of her cunt, until cum spurted free of his cock and had him twitching and jerking as bad as Abi was beside him.

Sliding his hand between her thighs, he placed it over hers, moved it down until they cupped her pussy, fingers either side of his dick, both organs pulsating in post-orgasm afterglow. "You feel that?" he asked against her shoulder. "You feel what you do to me? What you do to yourself?"

She twisted until she looked at him, her lids heavy over eyes filled with the satisfaction of release.

"Any witch can cast a spell on a man," he said, his lips already curling at the corner. "But only a powerful witch can cast a spell on themselves."

"You're calling me a witch?"

Damn, he loved the lazy tone of her voice. "You must be," he said. "Because whenever you're near me, I feel like I'll go fucking crazy if I don't have you."

She somehow managed to frown and smile at the same time. "Maybe you should go to the doctor with that."

"Maybe I like this feeling crazy shit."

"Maybe I like you feeling this crazy stuff, too," she said quietly.

For a few long minutes, neither spoke. Neither looked away. Yet, it felt as though a thousand words got spoken without so much as an uttering of lips. No smile curved her lips. Only a deep seriousness stared back at Chase—one he didn't know how to decipher, he only knew he wanted to try.

Finally breaking the silence, he whispered, "Stay. Stay with me. Tonight."

"Okay," she said.

"Okay?" he asked, just to be certain, and when she nodded, he pressed a soft kiss to her shoulder before sliding the shirt back around to cover her. At the butt of his arm against her head, she lifted high enough for him to slip it beneath her, shifted just enough for him to draw her back against his chest once more. He probably should've moved his arse, cleaned himself up, but damn, he wanted to stay there so bad. Right there. If only for a little while longer. "So, what do you think of the film?" he asked, enclosing her body within his arms.

"I think it's my new favourite," she said.

Sundays had always been lazy for Chase. An occasional walk down to Tea & Toast—often bumping into Jones for a shared breakfast there. A slow stroll to his ma's for dinner after a short round in the ring at Roy's. Then back to his own place so full of food, he could only manage chilling out on his deck for the next few hours. Maybe with a book. Maybe with some music. Always alone.

For the first time in forever, he'd skipped everything he normally did. No breakfast out. No sparring with Jones. No visit to his ma's. Hell, they'd even ordered dinner in, with little inclination to head out into the real world and burst the fantastical bubble they'd done a decent job of creating.

"What's it like living here?" Abi asked, as she passed him plates for the dishwasher.

After washing her own clothing, she'd thrown on leggings after her shower that morning, but had opted for another of Chase's shirts over her thin T. With the top buttons open, Chase could just see the top of her breasts, free of the bra she'd opted not to include in her attire. Maybe she'd just figured it'd be a waste of time. Chase had to agree.

He stacked a second plate in the rack as he considered the question. "Same as living anywhere else, I guess."

She paused, glanced his way. "On a boat, I mean."

"This isn't a boat," he said, taking the bunch of cutlery she handed over. "It's a river house."

"Like a boat that people live on," she said with a smile.

He lifted a finger and wagged it. "There's a difference. A boat has an engine and the ability to travel. It's a *vehicle*. A vessel."

"And a river house?" she asked, drying her hands on a towel.

"It doesn't move. It's static."

"How, when it's sitting on a moving current?"

He jerked his chin up and held out his hand. "Come on, I'll show you."

For the first time in days, the rain had backed off, leaving only clear skies ahead and calm waters below. A soft breeze crept into the living room as Chase slid open one of the rolling doors and led Abi out onto the deck.

"Okay, over here." To the left, he took her toward the farthest corner of the balconied platform. "You see the post at the corner here?"

She nodded, as Chase drew her in front of him so she could see.

"Well, there are one of these at every corner of the house. And the house is attached to each one."

"But if it's stuck in place, wouldn't the whole place flood if the water levels rise?"

"Nope." He smiled. "Because you see the deep groove in the post?" Her nod brushed against him as he leaned over her shoulder to point. "Those are tracks. And the house is attached to the posts by runners that fit into those tracks, which means that whenever the water rises, the house rises with it."

"Clever," she said.

"Yep."

"Do you spend much time out here?" she asked, as they turned back for the doors. "It's nice. Peaceful."

"I do, actually. Mostly at the weekends." Guiding her over to the front railings, he spun her to face outwards, boxing her in from behind. "Sometimes, I come out here to relax. Sometimes, it's fun to just people watch."

"People watch—on a river?"

"Weather gets warmer, and a day like today, folks feel they have to bring their boats out before it starts raining again. It's the done thing, you know?"

Even as they watched, a few boats chugged toward them in the distance.

"Do you ever wonder what they think of you, standing up here and looking down on them from your tower?" she asked.

"My tower?" Chuckling, he slipped a hand beneath her shirt, sliding it around to rest against her stomach as he lowered his chin to her shoulder. "You only get princesses in towers. And I ain't no princess."

She breathed out a laugh. "What do you know about princesses in towers, Mr Walker?"

He grinned. "I have a ma who liked to read me fairy tales."

"Oh, that boat's nearly here," she said, sounding as young as Chase probably used to when he'd first moved to live on the water.

"Watch," he whispered against his ear. "I bet you, soon as they get close enough, they start waving."

"What are we betting for?" she asked, turning her face in toward his a little.

He nuzzled at her neck before saying, "I'll let you know." He couldn't help but smile at the small shiver that ran through her. "Now, watch. They're nearly here." He watched over her shoulder, and grinned when the first of them on board lifted a hand and waved like they were fucking royalty. "And ... they're waving."

"What do we do?" Abi asked, laughter pitching her voice.

"Wave back." Grabbing her wrist, he lifted it into the air and flapped it about. "Just wave like you're as happy to see them as they are to see you. Because we're all special people, in the special club, being out here on the river."

Abi's body bounced against his chest with her laughter. "You're an idiot."

"There you go," he said, when the boat drew alongside them and the other three people straightened and joined in the crazy waving.

"'Afternoon," a guy called from down below. "Beautiful weather."

"Answer him, then," Chase whispered against Abi's ear.

Giggling, she called down, "Stunning. Have a nice day."

"You, too," came the reply as the boat continued buzzing past.

"*Have a nice day*? What are you, American?"

"I'm being polite," she said, twisting enough to glance at him over her shoulder.

Staring back at her, Chase realised he'd had no idea. No fucking idea, at all. For months, years, he'd been wading through life. *Believing* he was happy.

Having Abi there, doing the shit with him that he often did alone?

He'd had no idea, whatsoever, just how bloody lonely he'd been. How the hell could that have escaped him? How the hell could he not have *known*?

"Want to do some more?" he asked, clearing his throat a little.

"Okay," she said, turning back to face the water.

Beneath the shirt, his hand drew small circles over her stomach, his knuckles just touching the underside of her breast with each round. Against her shoulder, his heart beat the steadiest tune it had in a long time. And it shouldn't have been—because Chase had no fucking idea what he was doing. He might as well have been chucked into deep waters with weights around his middle and drugs in his system, for as disoriented as he felt. He didn't even know it would last. How *long* it would last. Abi could pack up and leave at any second. Realise she'd made a big mistake and head back to her family, do their fucking bidding. Then he'd be left flailing all over again. And, hell, he had responsibilities, too—if she stayed, how would she feel once the bubble got burst and they no longer had their cocoon holding them in.

"Abi, I have to go back to work tomorrow," he said.

She stiffened in his arms before saying, "I know."

"I have to go in," he said, like she might not have got it the first time.

"It's okay." She nodded, her hands gripping the railing.

"What about you?" he asked.

Even with the breeze, he caught the long inhale of breath she took, the slow exhale she gave. "I can find somewhere to go."

He frowned. "What—when ...?"

"If you need me to go," she said, glancing back at him again.

"What—no, I didn't mean that." He tightened his arm around her in reassurance. "I just meant, do you have work tomorrow?"

"Oh." She leaned into the balcony railing. Another boat roamed near, the lone occupant at its wheel lifting a hand in greeting. Without Chase's prompting, Abi waved back, but the smile she offered didn't quite match her reaction to the earlier boat. As the vessel continued past, she tapped her fingers against the chromed metal of the barrier, before finally saying, "I'm not even sure I have a job anymore."

Gripping her waist, he turned her until she faced him. "Why?"

"Because the church owns the bakery, and ..."

"Your mother will have said something," he finished.

Nodding, she glanced away as if seeking something out on the water. "I'm not sure I want to go back there, anyway."

"I thought you enjoyed it there," he said, frowning.

"I do, but ..." She shrugged. "I wouldn't put it past my mother to be waiting there, to see if I turn up."

"She kicked you out."

"She did," she said, turning back to him. "But that doesn't mean she won't try getting me to behave again. She probably thinks I'll have it out of my system by tomorrow." She shrugged again. "She probably can't believe I didn't go back home two nights ago."

"Do you regret it?" He held his breath, unsure if he'd like her answer. What the hell would he do, if she said yes? His sigh eked past his lips when she shook her head.

"Not even for a second," she said, sounding as resolved as he'd ever heard from her.

"What I said before .... What you thought I meant ..." He ducked to meet her eyes. "I'm not ready for you to go. Can we just set that straight?"

"I'm not ready for that, either," she said.

"So, will you stay? Forget about work, and just stay here tonight. With me. We can figure out tomorrow, tomorrow."

"Okay," she said, her smile breaking through at last. "I'll stay."

Fuck real life. And fuck work. Chase wanted to go in about as much as he wanted to syphon out his own cum and use it to make a gravy.

He had to, though. If he didn't, the girls would make their own conclusions and assume him to be sulking over Abi not showing for her Friday appointment. Then the visits would start. Either Sam, or Rae, or both. Or, worse, Jones.

As much as he loved that they cared .... Fuck! Fuck it all.

It didn't help that Abi watched him from his bed, as he moved from drawers to wardrobe, yanking out clothes to stick on for the day.

"You sure you'll be all right here all day?" He'd already asked her twice.

She smiled a lopsided smile. A smile she tended to give when humouring him. A smile Chase decided he liked a whole bloody lot. "Yes. Again."

He let his gaze skim over her. Something he really shouldn't have done. Because her tangled hair spread over the pillow around her head like sunbursts, the soft plumpness of her breasts pushed at the sheet laying over them, and below that same sheet, her peeking pussy just about beckoned to him from between her splayed legs.

"Fuck," he muttered. Dragging his shorts up over his stiffy, he had to order his thoughts away from what'd put Abi in that position. Namely himself. With his head between her thighs. Making her scream his name like he fucking owned her—or like she owned him. All of it less than fifteen minutes earlier.

No wonder he didn't want to adult. No bloody wonder he wanted to play hooky.

Barking mental orders at himself, he somehow managed to get into his trousers, his shirt. Socks. But his tie? Damn that tie.

Standing with it draped through his hands, staring across at Abi
....

Wrapping the thing around his neck, he quickly secured it in place, then strode for the wardrobe. From four of the drawers, he dragged out more ties. Carried them across to the bed.

Her brows drew in tight. "Er ... you have to leave for work?"

"You want me gone?" he asked.

She gave a quiet laugh and shook her head against the pillow. "No."

"Good. You're right, though. I do have to leave. But ..." He reached for her arm and pulled it straight out to the side. Using one of the ties, he made a loose knot around Abi's wrist, tethered it to the frame of his bed below.

Around at her other side, he did the same with her other arm. Not once did she try arguing, or question, but just watched him with eyes full of a quiet confidence and a whole lot of curiosity.

After he'd completed the charade of securing both arms, he moved to her legs, linked her from each ankle to the lower bed corners, while Abi lifted her head and continued watching.

Once he'd finished, he stepped back. Studied his handiwork. Which did absolutely shit for quelling the throb in his pants, despite knowing her bindings were loose enough she could leave anytime. Smiling in satisfaction, he climbed onto the bed, crawling upward until over Abi, and kissed her long enough and hard enough to let her know he'd be thinking of her once he left.

"This," he said, drawing back. "This is exactly how I want to find you when I return."

And after one final kiss, he grabbed up his jacket and left.

∾

His office. He'd always loved it. What it represented. Sitting there that morning, fingers steepled atop his desk, he barely even registered the surroundings. All of it seemed so bloody mundane, knowing what he'd left behind at home.

Home. For the first time, that word felt one-hundred percent right for where he lay his head at night. For the first time, lots of things finally felt right.

With his office door open, he easily heard the girls' arrival. If not for the soft *hush* of the Reception entrance, their heels, at least, gave them away.

Not even bothering to knock, they both marched into his office, their gazes instantly landing on Chase like they sought him out.

"'Morning," he said with a smile.

"'Morning," Sam said back, while the slight twitch to Rae's eyes told Chase she hadn't been excepting anything resembling happy normality.

"I need the day's schedule, when you're ready."

Rae's eyes narrowed as she said, "Okay."

Understandable, really. Since when did Chase give a shit which clients came when? So long as he knew who was next, he never worried. Discounting his obsession with Abi's timetable, of course.

Five minutes later, the girls were at the desk out front, and Chase headed out to join them. Hands pressed to the curved desktop, he leaned in. "So, who have I got?"

After a few clicks of the mouse, Sam said, "Ms Ness," doing air-quotes around the name of the client the girls suspected to be a star in disguise. "She's first. Then—"

"We have Fawn coming in to assist with that?" he asked.

"We do," Rae said. She seemed insistent on watching him.

Any time Chase looked her way, he found her gaze already on him.

"After her?"

"Mr and Mrs Miller."

He muttered a curse beneath his breath. The couple had progressed a lot over the weeks, to the point that Mr Miller had agreed to allow his wife a third party involvement again—so long as he got to do more than just watch. To them, third party probably meant Chase. Hell, it *had* meant Chase.

"Call Mrs P," he said with a small nod. "See who she can spare at short notice."

Both Sam and Rae stared up at him. "You're hiring in?" Rae asked.

"Yes."

"For the Millers?"

"Yes. Can you make the call, or what?"

"Yeah, I can make the call," Rae muttered, reaching for the phone.

He could understand their questioning. Chase never hired in, unless it would take more than what the three of them could provide to meet a client's needs. He'd made some sharp decisions on his walk into work, though. Ones that involved him being less involved with anyone other than the ex-client waiting for him at home.

Turning back to Sam, he asked for the rest of the list. Ran through them with her. Got Rae to book someone for any appointment requiring assistance that Chase, himself, would normally supply.

By the time he headed back to his office, ready to start the day, his mind, as well as his load, felt a whole lot lighter.

Any other day, and Chase would've been happy for a gentle walk home after a day at work. Not that day. He'd called himself a cab and ordered the driver to take the quick route over the short one. However, only quiet greeted him when he closed himself in his hallway once home. Quiet, and the smell of something really fucking tasty. Kicking off his shoes, he shucked his jacket and hung it on a peg, then jogged up the few steps into the living room.

Still quiet. Still nothing. Except for a plate piled with what looked like doughnuts across on the kitchen counter. Glancing around the room, like he could somehow miss that body and hair and those bloody eyes, he strode across to where ten dough balls sat atop the plate, all perfectly round and covered in sugar. Nabbing the one from the top, he took a bite, his tongue licking out at the instant ooze of custard over his bottom lip. It was good. Possibly even better than the first one of hers he'd tried.

Normally, his first target would've been the fridge. When he'd arrived home to an empty shell, he'd had little else to do besides check on food. Little more interesting to entertain than what he might've been eating for dinner. Right then, though, meals didn't hold anywhere near enough interest to keep him stationed in the kitchen. Hell, even the rest of the doughnut could wait to be finished off. Because had far more important stuff to look into before he could even think about fuelling himself up.

Namely Abi, and where she was hiding.

Leaving the other half of his doughnut behind, he jogged down the steps in his socked feet, and rounded the corner into the downstairs hallway. Before he'd even reached his open doorway, he could see her. Abi. And reaching his room confirmed what had his lips curving into a smile.

That Abi lay in the exact position he'd left her. Arms loosely tethered. Ankles bound. With a glisten to her pussy that told him she was well and truly ready, as well as waiting.

His eyes met hers instantly, but neither of them spoke. With a kick up of his brow, he tugged at his tie, his gaze on her the whole time. Watching her, as she watched him.

With his tie lost, he worked through the buttons of his shirt, got rid of that. Tugged his socks free and tossed those. And as soon as he'd sent his trousers and boxers the same direction, he climbed onto the bed and crawled up and over her.

"A guy could get used to coming home to this," he said.

She merely smiled, her eyes full of a mischief he really fucking liked the look of.

"Speaking of," he said. "Where did you find stuff to bake?"

"Your mother."

With a quiet laugh, he shook his head. Of course his ma would've found some way to interfere, if only a little. A reason to check in that Abi hadn't left, as well as one to keep her there a little longer. Though, the fact she'd brought them round at all spoke volumes of her opinion of Abi.

But wait ... "Please tell me she didn't find you lying here like this?"

Abi's eyes widened like the idea of that hadn't even occurred to her. "No, thank goodness."

Chase laughed. "And what did she bring for dinner?" he asked.

"Pasta bake. Are you hungry?"

"Ravenous," he said. "Just not for food."

They stared at each other for a few long minutes, before he dropped a kiss to her lips. Over her jaw. Along the line of her neck. Pausing at nipples.

"Yeah, this should fill the gap, for now," he murmured, and he smiled around her nipple at her quiet laugh.

Lower still, his lips feathered her stomach, and he smiled again at her twitchiness as he passed over her ticklish spot.

Reaching the tip of her pubis, he paused again, a small frown working across his brow as he peered back up at where she watched him. "All these custard doughnuts ... they to do with what you said to Jones a few weeks back?"

Her features flinched a little, like she'd been caught out, but she didn't quite contain her smile. "Maybe."

"And ... the custard doughnut is you?"

She gave a small shrug that was in no way a negative.

"Jesus, you have no idea, do you?"

"No idea ...?" she said, her brows drawing in.

"You, Abi O'Shay, taste way fucking better than any custard."

And as if to prove his point, he dropped his mouth to her pussy, and drank in the flavour he'd been eyeing since he'd stepped into the room.

Tuesday could've been a replay of Monday. Chase had headed to work, content in the knowledge that his ties pretended to bind Abi to his bed. He'd once again run through his clients for the day, booked in an outsider for the 'extras' any of the appointments would require—though, the girls had stared at him like he'd lost the fucking plot when he'd made them run through the entire week's schedule and pre-book with Mrs P for the lot of them. And at the end of the day, he'd returned home to a Bakewell tart, one of his ma's dinners in the fridge, and a healthy dose of Abi to kick-start his evening.

Wednesday went like Tuesday, and Thursday like Wednesday. He managed to get all the way to Friday, four whole days of easy sessions at work and blissful evenings at home, before anyone tried sticking a pin in his inflated mood.

Chase had just stepped into the lift, when Rae and Sam tottered into the building foyer and made a run to join him.

"You two are keen this morning," Chase said as the lift doors closed them in.

Rae muttered something beneath her breath that sounded a lot like, "Yeah, keen for answers," but Chase ignored her, just smiled at Sam's, "Only as keen as you."

Neither of them spoke again on the ride up, but Chase felt like an alien bug—one never seen before that had spectators staring at it that little bit harder. And as he stepped from the lift, the two of them flanked him so close, he felt like he was being escorted off a premises, or to a back room where he wouldn't like what awaited.

They stayed that close as he unlocked the glass door into the clinic Reception, as he disabled the alarms and strode through Reception, and when he made his way around to the staff quarters, they trailed him through his office, going the long way around.

Although they ceased hugging him while he opened up his locker and set his phone and house keys inside, he knew they still watched him. If not outright, then definitely out the corners of their eyes. The hairs on his nape stood out like they'd aroused the buggers, and Chase had to contain his urge to shiver as the prickle worked its way over his spine.

That same sensation followed him to the fridge, from where he pulled out a couple of water bottles, and a small carton of milk he set on the counter beside the kettle. "I'll have one this morning, if you make one," he said, meaning coffee. He'd barely slept since a week earlier, since Abi had showed up—his own fault, of course. And maybe a little bit Abi's.

He flicked the fridge door shut, but he didn't even make the full turn from the counter before he recognised the wall of *don't even think about it* blocking his way.

With a sigh, he set down his water and crossed his arms—matching the stance of the two women staring him down. "Spit it out. What's going on?"

"That's what we were hoping you'd tell us," Rae said.

He frowned. "What d'you mean?" He'd turned up at the office every day, done his job every day, and hadn't fallen apart, or acted like a dick, on any of those days.

"You haven't missed a single day this week, and you're way too fucking happy," Rae said.

His eyebrow arched up. "You're cornering me for being in a good mood and showing for work? For real? I always show for work."

"She means you're in too good a mood for how upset you were last week," Sam said.

"You don't want me to be in a good mood?"

"Yes," Sam told him, as Rae said, "Not when it equates to something screwy going on."

He tilted his head, his narrowed gaze meeting Sam's before skimming left to Rae's. "Why does my being in a good mood mean something screwy's going on?" They couldn't know about Abi. Could they?

"Because we know you," Rae said.

"And we remember how upset you were the last time a woman got under your skin then fucked you off," Sam added.

"And how long you sulked for and tried burying yourself beneath the reality of life," Rae said. "So, what's going on? We *know* how much Abi O'Shay got under your skin. We *know* she got under there a whole hell of a lot deeper than that other bitch." Rae had foreveroften referred to Nic as that, ever since Chase had been a holy mess of rejection. "And we *know* how you felt when she didn't show for her appointment last Friday, because we *saw* the look on your face when you realised she wasn't coming."

"So we know *this*—" Sam waved both hands toward him like he was an object to analyse. "This isn't normal for you, babe. You're too ..."

"Happy," Rae finished. "And you shouldn't be."

"I ... shouldn't be happy?"

"Yes," Sam said.

"No." Rae stuck her hands on her hips. "Not when it doesn't fit. So, you better tell us what gives, and you better do it fast, because your first appointment's in an hour, and we ain't moving 'til you talk."

He opened his mouth, tried to summon a smart-ass answer that'd get them both climbing down off his back, but when none came, he sighed, long and deep. Better to just get it out. Get it over with. Right? Wasn't like he could closet Abi away forever. They'd have to find out sooner, or later.

"I haven't been sulking all week over Abi not showing on Friday, because I've *been with* Abi all week, since last Friday."

Nothing. At least for a few seconds. No words. No change in expressions.

Then, "What the fuck?" from Rae. "What. The. Actual. Fuck."

"Are you serious?" Sam asked, her tone much calmer than Rae's.

He nodded. "Yes, I'm perfectly serious."

"What the fuck?" Rae said again.

"How?" Sam said. "How could this even happen?"

Heaving in another sigh, he pushed past them and sank into one of the chairs. While Sam joined him, taking a second chair, Rae stood like an impatient Sonic the Hedgehog, arms crossed and foot tapping.

"It wasn't planned," Chase said. "None of it was planned." He glanced across at Sam, took in her disappointment mixed with curiosity. Glanced across at Rae, and got hit full force by her typical anger and irritation and *I really want to beat on you right now.* "Abi came to me, okay?"

"Came to you, how?" Rae asked.

"Came to my home. Came to find me." He nodded from one to the other. "She was there when I got home from the office on Friday. Waiting outside in the rain. She—"

"She was at your house?" Rae asked, and he nodded. "How the hell does she know where you live, Walker?"

It was a question he'd eventually gotten an answer to from Abi. Apparently, she'd seen him walking one night, and she'd followed him without even realising she was doing it. Maybe it'd been the night Chase had felt like someone was watching. Maybe it'd been an earlier night. Whenever it'd happened, why it'd happened, Chase didn't care. He only cared that she did know where he lived and that she'd felt able to come to him when she'd needed his ... whatever it was she'd needed.

"She figured it out," was all he told the girls. "Not hard to find out where someone lives, if you need to know."

"Okay," Rae said, but the drawn-out way she said it told Chase she didn't *quite* buy the explanation. "So, *why* was she there?"

That part was easy. "She called off the wedding."

Sam's lips popped open. Rae didn't even blink.

"And her parents kicked her out for it."

"Oh, wow," Sam said quietly.

Still, Rae didn't so much as twitch. "And she needed to come to your house specifically, because?"

"Because I'm the reason she called off the wedding," he said, meeting her hard stare head-on. "Because she couldn't stop thinking about me." He pushed to his feet. "Because she's been thinking about me as much as I've been thinking about her."

"Shit," Rae muttered, finally breaking her stare-down.

"That's ... almost romantic," Sam said. "In a fucked-up, stalk-erish kind of way."

"Match made in fucking heaven," Rae said, her gaze wholly on Chase as she said, "You do know you can't keep her? This is too much of a mess, you fooling around with a client."

"She's not a client anymore," he said, his eyes zoning in on her, and her alone. "So that's a pretty moot fucking point to make, Rae. And two," he continued, like he'd even started bullet pointing, "right now, I couldn't give a rat's ass what anyone thinks, outside of myself and Abi. Because yes, she *was* my client. And *yes,* that made her out of bounds. But not anymore. And I could not be fucking happier."

"I'll bet you can't," Rae said.

"Fuck you." He poked the air in front of her. "I couldn't give a damn what you think." He prodded toward Sam. "I couldn't give a damn what she thinks, either." He slapped his own chest. "I only give a damn what I know, and that's that I've just had the best week of my bloody life, and it's because of Abi. Because I spent it with Abi. And because of that, I plan to spend the next week with Abi, and then the week after that, and every fucking week after those, if it means I get to feel this good ..."

His chest heaved as he paused for breath. He hadn't known that morning, when he'd left for work, what tomorrow might bring for him and Abi. He hadn't had any plans for when he got home, beyond fucking and laughing and doing shit that normal couples did after a day at work, because that was what felt right. He certainly hadn't known, before blurting it at Rae, that he had any long-term plans for him and Abi, and it felt good, he realised. Felt good to have that out there, even if only for his own absorption. Felt good to *know* what he wanted, at last.

For seconds, he and Rae just stood there staring at each other. She didn't quite look pissed-off anymore, though. More resigned. Like the very outcome she'd tried protecting him from had been inevitable from the start.

"Does Jones know?" was all Rae finally said.

Chase shook his head.

"Tell him." She nodded toward his locker. "Now."

And as she marched from the room, Sam followed behind with a whispered, "You have to admit, it's quite romantic, though."

He just about caught Rae's grunt before he was left alone. Alone with the task of telling Jones he'd well and truly gone and done it, despite all of his warnings.

With Rae's *Now* still resounding through the room, he crossed to his locker and took out his phone. He had Jones on speed-dial so it took seconds to get in and press *Call*.

Jones answered on the third ring. "Walker, who told you my bed was cold and in need of your love?"

Chase took a deep breath, then, "Abi's not my client anymore."

"Okay," Jones said after a few beats of quiet. "You okay?"

"Yes."

"How long 'til she gets married?" he asked.

"She's not getting married."

"Okay," he said, suspicion beginning the slow creep into his voice. "Do you know why?"

Chase gripped the phone a little tighter. "Because she's with me."

More quiet, then, "Now?"

"Not here. At my house. Since last Friday."

"Since she didn't show for her appointment?" So, the girls had told him about that.

"Yes," Chase said.

"Okay." Just his breaths passed down the line, then, "How long is she staying for?"

"Indefinitely." He found his lips curving. It felt good to say it and know it and mean it.

"Okay," Jones said again.

"Okay?"

"Yeah, she's a nice girl."

"She's better than nice," Chase said, and a quiet laugh came through from Jones.

"Okay, so she's better than nice and she's staying."

"Are we good?" Chase asked, holding his breath as he waited.

"We're good," Jones said. "So long as you're happy, we're good."

The breath Chase held gushed out in a rush.

"So, when're you bringing her to The Club? I can't wait to get—"

"Fuck off, Jones," he said, and hung up the phone.

∾

Quiet met his ears when he returned home after work. The rest of the week, he'd grabbed a taxi, eager to get back and see if Abi waited on his bed, tethered exactly as he'd left her each morning. That day, however, he'd walked.

Spilling words to Rae and Sam, even to Jones, on how he felt about Abi's sudden existence in his life had been a lot easier than expected. For the rest of the day, he'd tried evaluating his confession, yet no matter how he looked at the situation, no matter how delicately he tried picking it apart and assessing it all, his resolve didn't budge. He didn't want Abi to leave. He wanted her to stay.

More than his own thoughts in the matter, though, he wanted her to feel the same way.

With his shoes left in their standard place beneath the coat pegs, and his jacket slung above, he stepped up into the living room. The quiet didn't bother him. He'd entered to quiet every day. What did bother him was the absent plate on the kitchen counter. The non-show of baked goods to greet him with a new taste to try.

Frowning, he padded across the living room a lot faster than he had on previous days. Practically jogged down the steps to the lower level.

She couldn't have gone. Not when he'd just figured his shit out.

The door to his room stood open, though not enough to show inside, and his feet almost skidded across the flooring as he speed-walked to push it aside. Why the hell he felt the need to rush, to have his fears confirmed, he didn't know.

With a shove of his hand, the door swung inward hard enough to hit the drawers behind it, and Chase's breath rushed out on his exhale.

On the bed, arms wrapped within two of his ties, two more around her ankles, Abi stared back at him from the bed. In the exact position he'd left her in that morning. In the same position he'd left her in every morning.

Her brow furrowed, her eyes full of concern. "What's wrong?"

"Nothing." He heaved in a sigh, shook his head. "Absolutely nothing at all. Everything's perfect."

For the first time all week, Chase broke the pattern by standing there a few minutes longer. Just watching. Taking her in. From delicate shoulders, to rounded breasts, to a pussy he knew tasted as sweet as Abi O'Shay looked, all the way down her creamy-skinned legs to the tips of her toes. And he had absolutely no idea how he'd scored so fucking high.

Once he'd got his eyeful, he reached to the back of his neck, grabbed the collar of the T-shirt he'd stuck on to walk home, and dragged the whole shirt up and over his head. "You didn't bake today," he said.

Abi smiled at just one corner of her mouth. "I ran out of flour. And if you didn't keep eating everything in one go, maybe you'd have some of the other desserts left."

"Maybe you shouldn't make stuff that tastes so bloody good, then."

She breathed out a low laugh as he unbuttoned the jeans he'd donned.

He pushed them down over his hips, kicked them off over his feet. "I've been thinking," he said.

"About what?"

"That we should go hit the shops this weekend."

"Okay," she said, in a way that suggested she hadn't been expecting him to say *that*.

Watching her, he lost his socks. His boxers. Until he stood as naked as she lay before him. "Just figured, you know ..." He knelt on the end of the bed, leaning forward to rest on his fists as he took himself closer. "If you're going to be sticking around," he said, shrugging, "you're going to need a whole lot more clothes than you currently have."

"If I'm going to be sticking around?" She almost whispered the question.

"Yes," he said, moving higher over her until his chest brushed hers and his cock sprang down like it didn't need his permission to seek out her pussy. "I did a lot of thinking today."

"It sounds like it," she said.

"I've decided you can stay." He shook his head when she frowned, uttered a curse at himself. "Ignore that, it came out wrong."

"Take a breath. Try again," she said, but she seemed on the verge of smiling as she said it, something he couldn't quite decode in her eyes.

He did as she suggested and restarted, "I don't want to ask you to stay again tonight. I don't want to get to tomorrow and have to decide what we're doing tomorrow. I don't want to figure out each day as it comes." He dropped a soft kiss on her mouth, not moving away as he continued, "I want to sit here now and ask you to stay, and if you say yes, that will be it, until you turn around and tell me you can't stand the sight of me anymore, or—"

"That's not going to happen."

"Or I'm driving you nuts, or you get bored, or ..."

"Are you asking me to stay?" she asked.

"Yes."

"As in *stay*-stay?"

"Yes."

She didn't speak. Didn't say a damned word. Just stared from her eyes that suddenly seemed too close to his face, her lips, too close to his own lips, unmoving.

He went to shake his head, went to tell her it didn't matter, it'd been a stupid idea, why the hell had he felt the need to change something that already seemed to be working for them —fuck, he was an idiot ... but she slid a hand free of his tie and grabbed his shoulder like she sensed his plan.

"If I stay ..." she said as calm as anything, like nothing even closely resembling the tornado within Chase tore around inside her mind. "If I stay," she repeated, "I get a job and pay my own way."

His head twitched. "You don't have—"

Her fingertips pressed over his lips. "If I stay, I don't want to be someone you keep. I want to be able to provide for myself. Live for myself as much as for you. Does that make sense?"

It did make sense. A lot of sense. And it earned her even more of Chase's respect than she already had. "Yes," he said against her fingertips. "But I'm still buying you some clothes this weekend."

"I can buy my own," she said.

"Fine. But you can't stop me buying you a present."

She laughed. "Okay, so we shop. I job hunt."

"And we'll decide how to share the responsibilities when the time comes?" His heart boomed inside his chest at the realisation that she seemed to be saying yes.

"I guess that sounds agreeable," she said.

"Okay, then?" he asked. He needed to be sure. He needed to know, without a shadow of doubt, that she meant what he thought she meant. That he could wake come morning and she'd still be there. That he'd leave for work, and when he returned, she'd be right where he'd left her. That no matter what, she wouldn't just vanish—at least for the foreseeable future. "You'll stay?"

"Okay," she said. "Okay, I'll stay." His breath rushed out on a quiet laugh of relief, and her body curved up toward him as she smiled. "Now, didn't you say you had more tricks you wanted to show me?"

With his lips stretching into a full out grin, Chase grabbed her hips, laughing at her yelp of surprise as he flipped her over, and did exactly that.

ACKNOWLEDGMENTS

Okay, the thanks part is important, so I better get this right. 😊

First thanks goes to my family. To Mr B for cheering when I told him I was, FINALLY, writing filth—like, fists-in-the-air cheering. To the kids for not batting an eyelid when they found out I was writing something utterly disgusting they would never *ever* be permitted to read.

To Keri Lake – you championed me doing this, and held my hand along the way, and helped me suss stuff out at the drop of a hat. I'd have been rocking in a corner on some days without your support.

To my beta readers: Wendy Eaves Seagondollar and Terri Rochenski. Your super-fast reading and feedback for each episode were a huge contribution to my writing pace for this. I couldn't have done it so smoothly without you.

To Ena and Amanda at Enchanting Journey for having great organisational skills and being super-nice to work with.

To all the bloggers who helped spread the word, with an

extra hug to those who took the time to read and review. You guys rock!

To the newly-named Book Babes. You guys have totally had my back whilst I try a change in genre, and your support and encouragement means the world. *blows kisses*

And finally to you. The reader. Because without readers, where would us writers be? Cheers for picking up my book and taking a chance on Chase Walker.

ABOUT THE AUTHOR

Best known for her Holloway Pack Stories, J.A. Belfield lives in Solihull, England, with her husband, two children, a cat and two dogs. She writes paranormal romance, with a second love for urban fantasy. And now she writes erotic romance, too. Because she can. ;)

Want to stay up to date on all things J.A. Belfield?

Want to discover what she's working on, as she's working on it?

Want to get sneak previews of her writing and covers and everything else upcoming?

Want to enter monthly giveaways exclusive to her group?

To be in the know ahead of the crowd with J.A. Belfield's writing journey, join the Book Babes today.

We'd love to have you!

Visit the Book Babes:

Or go to:

https://www.facebook.com/groups/BelfieldsBookBabes

ALSO BY J.A. BELFIELD

Holloway Pack

Beginnings

The Wolf Within

Blue Moon

Caged

Unnatural

Cornered

Hereditary

Enticed

Made in the USA
Middletown, DE
20 September 2018